MULBERRY

MULBERRY

a novel

Paulette Boudreaux

To: Brad,
It has been great working with you in these Mississippi literary endeavors. Thanks for being the Writer and missionary that you are!

CAROLINA WREN PRESS

Paulett Boudreaux
10·22·16

Cover Design by Laura Williams
Interior Design by April Leidig
Typeset in Adobe Caslon Pro by Copperline.

*The mission of Carolina Wren Press is to seek out, nurture,
and promote literary work by new and underrepresented writers,
including women and writers of color.*

We gratefully acknowledge the ongoing support of general
operations by the Durham Arts Council's United Arts Fund and a
special grant from the North Carolina Arts Council.

Library of Congress Cataloging-in-Publication Data
Boudreaux, Paulette.
Mulberry / Paulette Boudreaux.
pages cm
"Lee Smith Novel Prize winner"
ISBN 978-0-932112-87-3
1. African American families—Fiction. 2. Segregation—Fiction.
3. Alcoholic fathers—Fiction. 4. Post-traumatic stress disorder—Fiction.
5. Mississippi—Fiction. I. Title.
PS3602.O8886M85 2015
813'.6—dc23   2015027591

For Bobbie, my mother,
and Kristin, my daughter,
the elegant bookends
to the volumes that are my life

MULBERRY

CHAPTER ONE

🖤

AT THE TOP OF my mulberry tree, October wind curled around the branches, snaking through the soft yellow leaves, making them sway and hiss in the air around me. A few of the leaves released their claim and danced toward the bare dirt thirty feet below. Goose bumps rose on my face and arms and I clenched my teeth against the chill, but I wasn't ready to climb down and go inside. I was chewing my cud, as my mother would have said. In fact, I had come outdoors into the chilly air and climbed as high as I could go—to get away from her and the aggravations of my younger brothers, Earl and Roy Anthony especially.

Straddling my favorite branch with my back pressed against the strong trunk, the world seemed benign and uncomplicated. I could let my tangled thoughts and hurt feelings unravel and float away on the wind like pieces of string.

Above me the sky fanned out like pale turquoise. Below me lay my segregated Mississippi community. This enclave of dirt roads and shotgun houses was called Harvest Quarters. The neighborhood was surrounded by dense woods, but most of the houses sat in barren yards along a wide dirt road that arced off of the main street into the woods for about a mile, curving like a giant horseshoe to the place where it emptied back onto the street. A creek had etched a deep ravine that ran through the woods at the heart of the Quarters and disappeared into the rural areas beyond.

There were dirt footpaths that meandered down to the creek. In the summer I had ventured down a few of them, though Momma had told me never to follow any of those paths and to stay away from the creek.

I gazed along the road to the place where it curved into woods and disappeared into the bowels of the Quarters, and there was Daddy, emerging slowly, his eyes trained on the ground, his boots crunching quietly in the gravel. His steps were deliberate, and he was swinging his metal lunch-bucket with rhythm like he was keeping time to a song. He seemed heroic to me then as I watched him striding toward home in his gray khaki work clothes and heavy black boots. My heart opened out with relief, and I started my long climb down. Momma's mood always shifted into someplace easy and my brothers reined in their restless little-boy energy when Daddy was home and we all sat down for supper.

I had almost reached the ground when I heard Daddy's voice behind me.

"Baby Girl, what you doing up in that tree in this cold air?" Daddy asked. "You and your momma at odds again? What's it this time?"

I jumped down the final few feet and ran to where he had stopped in the road across from our house. "I didn't pass my spelling test this week," I said. "Momma called me lazy. Said I didn't put enough effort in," I added, conjuring as many of my hurt feelings as I could recall like a small storm inside my chest. Mostly my wounded emotions had fragmented and floated off on the wind at the top of my mulberry tree. It was mainly the tight pinch of indignation and shame that came forward again.

The lines on Daddy's forehead softened. He looked relieved, then he grinned at me. "Well did you?"

"Course I did. Momma even helped me study," I said.

"Your momma know you ain't lazy. Don't take too deep what she say. She ain't her natural self these days."

Even at eleven, I didn't have to think about it long to know he was right. My mother was carrying a baby inside her then, had been since before the summer started. In this, her fifth pregnancy, as in all the others, her belly had expanded selfishly around the baby. But this time the swelling hadn't stopped with her belly. It was as if the baby was filling up every part of her body. Her face and neck were heavy and swollen. Even her legs had swelled, thick and smooth like naked tree trunks.

"She hurt my feelings, Daddy," I said, kicking at the ground in front of me. I still wasn't ready to be sympathetic. I wanted Daddy to say something or do something to make me feel better. I could usually count on him for that. I didn't need much.

"Y'all's schooling important to your momma," he said. "You being the oldest she expects a lot from you."

"But—"

"Come here."

He extended his arm toward me. I went forward. He pulled me to his side and put his arm across my shoulder. "Thicken your hide a little bit more, Baby Girl. Here," he said, releasing me and pressing his scratched and dented black metal lunch box against my chest. "You need a hard shell like this pail. Maybe we can make you a tin suit."

He grinned at me again and put one wide callused palm on the top of my head. He rocked my head back and forth gently. I closed my eyes, pressing the cold metal lunch box into my chest and feeling the warmth from his hand radiate into my scalp.

"Maddy, listen. Grown folk ain't easy to figure. Sometimes we get beside ourselves. Say things we don't mean. Do things we can't account for. Your momma's outside how she normally is 'cause of her condition. She'll get back to herself after the baby comes."

I wanted to say I didn't remember her ever being so mean before, especially to me. But when I opened my eyes to look up at Daddy, he was frowning and his jaw was clenched.

"I'm late," he said, lifting his hand from my head and turning toward home. "I know your momma's been holding supper for me. Probably getting madder by the minute. Let's get on inside."

"Everything gon' be fine," he said, his eyes trained on the ground again as he went ahead of me into the yard.

Looking back to that fall day, I want to say that I noted something in the tone of his voice that wasn't especially convincing, or that I had a feeling of some kind. But all I can say with certainty is that when I walked into the house with Daddy behind me and saw the look of relief that flashed across my mother's face, and listened to the happy greetings the boys showered on Daddy, I had no idea how a world could shift on its axis in a way no one expected, making normal impossible to find.

It was my parents' whispering that woke me, summoning me from my dreams to face a drama that had begun to unfold while I slept. Their hushed, urgent tones pushed through the stagnant night air and penetrated the plank wall that separated their room from the one I shared with my younger brothers.

"Hurry up, Gene," Momma hissed. Her whisper cracked, exposing a taut, serpentine voice. "This one's different than the others. I can't tell how much time I got."

Fear rose in me. In the silvery darkness, I scanned the nooks of the room where I slept, trying to find a hiding place for my imagination. I looked into the dull shadow of the big ill-painted dresser where our clothes were kept; into the corner beside the rickety rocking chair that used to belong to our grandmother; at the foot of my bed beside the marred wooden trunk that had belonged to our great-grandmother; into the bed across the room from me where nine-year-old Roy Anthony and seven-year-old Earl slept. I listened to the adenoidal breathing of my two-year-old brother, June Bug, who slept beside me, his tiny dark head lolled in the folds of his pillow. I stared into the dark cave of his open mouth.

In the other room, Daddy mumbled something and the bed-springs on his and Momma's bed sighed with relief. Daddy's booted feet clumped across the wooden floor. The front door whined open, then shut, and Daddy was gone.

Momma moaned and began panting. It occurred to me that maybe she was about to have the baby that had been growing in her. I gazed at the ceiling and pictured her body, swollen big with the baby that had been riding low in her stomach for about a month now. "Babies move around," she had said, irritated when I pointed out that her stomach looked different. When the baby was first growing there, her belly had been high and round like a volleyball. Now it looked more like a long smooth watermelon lying on its side.

"How come babies move around?" I prodded.

"Babies ain't none of your business," she told me, and refused to say any more. This was how it often was between us, her mouth closing down around certain secrets, her eyes warning me to move on to something else.

When each of my brothers was born, I had been sleeping, or at school, or someplace else out of the way. This had been fine with me since I had never been especially interested in knowing much about the arrival of babies. What I really wanted to know was why Momma kept bringing home brothers and no sisters.

The front door hinges whined again. "The taxicab will be here directly," Daddy said, breathless. He had probably run out of the Quarters to the main street and the nearest pay telephone in front of Watkins' Grocery Store a half mile away, then back home again. I imagined him standing in the doorway, sweaty but calm, puffing and holding his chest like I did when I was winded.

"What you think?" Daddy asked.

"You may as well gone get Maddy up. She big enough now. I can tell her what to do," Momma answered.

The light from my parents' room crept across my face as the door to my and the boys' room opened. I closed my eyes and feigned sleep as Daddy tiptoed in. His shadow spread over me and June Bug. "Maddy," he whispered, his voice sounding strangely hollow as he leaned over the bed. His breath, with its sweet metallic scent, brushed my cheek. "Maddy," he said again, lifting my hand from the quilt and shaking it, as if he were introducing me to something.

I groaned and tried to turn away from him. The dry emotions I sensed in the folds of his voice and the desperate pressure of his fingers on my hand made me uneasy. I didn't want any part of whatever it was Momma thought I was *big enough* for now.

"Maddy, we need you to get up," Daddy said, squeezing my fingers more aggressively in his calloused palms. "Come on now. Get on up. Your momma needs you."

My heart beat wildly in my ears, as I sat up, crawled out of bed, and followed him into their room.

Momma sat on the edge of their bed wearing a green spaghetti-strapped summer dress with tiny yellow flowers on it. She had always warned me against wearing summer clothes after the first frost, yet here she sat on a chilly October night, dressed for summer.

Momma's coarse black hair was pulled back into a nappy ponytail at the base of her neck. The harsh glare of the bare lightbulb hanging from the ceiling made the tiny beads of sweat on her forehead sparkle like jewels against her dark skin. Her face was puffed and swollen and she was hunched forward over the baby in her belly. She looked up at me with fierce, almost angry eyes.

"Maddy, I'm fixing to go to the hospital," she said, reaching toward me.

I went to her reluctantly, afraid of the fierceness. Her cold damp hands clutched mine as I faced her. I bit the inside of my cheek when she trembled and squeezed my fingers in a crab-like grip. She shut her eyes and bent forward over her stomach again. Her cheeks quivered and she growled low in her throat then began panting, and I figured that the baby was tearing at her from inside.

My twelve-year-old friend Esther had told me that babies tore through their mothers' flesh when they were ready to be born. "The mamas scream and holler and they bleed like pigs on killing day," she had said with the air of authority. I had listened, certain it was one of her many lies. "That's why ladies have to stay in the hospital so long after they have a baby," she continued. "They have to get sewed back together. When they gets home you can see the lines on they stomachs where the skin growed back together."

Back in the middle of summer when the weather was right for Momma's spaghetti-strapped dress, Esther had extracted a promise from me. "Let's swear we ain't never going to have no babies," she demanded. We sat in the breezy shade of a weeping willow tree near the Harvest Quarters creek and went so far as to make a blood and spit pact to seal the agreement. I allowed her to prick the palm of my right hand with the hungry point of a pin. I watched the tiny crimson bubble of life rise, anxious to cover the hole the pin had made in the middle of my palm, while she pricked her own palm. Then we spit in our left palms and stared at each other, awed by the power of the ritual we had set in motion. Esther crossed her arms at the elbows and extended her hands toward me. "You too," she said. "Now gimme." I reached out, clasping her hands, my right palm to her right palm, my left palm to her left palm. "Blood to blood, water to water . . .," she intoned and closed her eyes, shutting me out of the darkness and desperation that made her so hateful toward her future.

"Are you listening to me, Maddy?" Momma's voice cut into my remembering. Her eyes were like shiny black and white marbles. "Sorry, sugar," she said, shaking my hands. "Don't look so scared. Everything is going to be fine. Daddy's about to take me to the hospital so I can deliver this new baby. You big enough to help out now and I need you to look out after the boys, 'specially tonight and tomorrow morning till your daddy gets back home. You going to need to help him and Mother Parker take care of the boys till I get back home in a week."

I glanced back at Daddy. He stood in the doorway, shoulders slumped, hands thrust deep into his pockets. He nodded.

"Every day after Daddy goes to work, you gone need to make sure the boys eat something," she continued. "Make sure Roy and Earl wash their faces and comb they heads and put on good school clothes. Take June Bug to Mother Parker's before y'all go on to school. Then come straight home like always, pick up Junie Boy and wait for your Daddy. You hear me? Take care of your brothers. Keep them out of harm's way. Promise me you'll do that, Maddy."

Momma's fingernails dug into my palms as if she and I were making a pact like Esther and I had done. Momma's eyelids narrowed and fluttered, her jaw and lips clenched, and she arched her back, making the thin fabric of her dress draw tight against her belly. It was no longer smooth like a watermelon. It was knotted and lumpy. I stared at the unmistakable shape of the curled desperate baby beneath her flesh. I was at once horrified and awestruck. The baby wasn't clawing, or scratching, or tearing its way out as Esther had said babies did to get born. Suddenly, I was aware that something frighteningly significant was happening to Momma and the baby. It went beyond Esther's dark warnings about how babies came into the world, and it went beyond any of my small fears. I relaxed into Momma's grip, wanting to enter into that place where she was—fearless, strong.

"Promise me you'll take care of your brothers," Momma said again, shaking me so I looked up to face the fierce pain in her eyes. "Promise me." Her voice was a hoarse whisper.

"I promise," I said, and to my own ears I sounded like an angry child.

Momma let go of my hands and leaned back on the bed, bracing herself with her arms. She closed her eyes, dropped her head back, and panted. I backed toward the door and bumped into Daddy. He put his hands on my shoulders and dug his fingers into my flesh. I turned to look up at him. His mouth hung open. His tongue was pressed against his bottom teeth. He had put the baby there, but he was helpless now that it wanted out. I turned back to Momma.

Her spine was curved in a graceful arch. The rounded outline of her breast and her belly rose like a lumpy mountain range at her center. Her breath was steady and shallow, moving in and out of her throat with the rhythmic precision of girls twirling a jump rope. Her image slid away from me like something seen through the wrong end of binoculars—far away and out of reach. She had become a work of art, a glass figurine that could be won as a prize at the state fair. Admiration washed over me like a warm sparkling liquid, slowing the thumping of my heart and calming my breath.

For a long moment I was suspended in a silent world with Momma where the air swirled around us like particles of light.

The moment passed, and Momma returned to herself, exhaling a long slow breath of satisfaction and relief. She lowered her head, sat up straight, looked at me, and smiled, a coconspirator's smile that pulled me into the white-hot experience of pregnant womanhood. Her eyes, dark fiery slits of charcoal and ivory, beckoned, called me to acknowledge her world—a place of exquisite pain and joy. *Did you see?* they seemed to ask.

The palms of my hands still burned with the imprint of her fingernails. Of course I had seen. I had even felt. How could I not? Her world had been slowed down and magnified for my benefit. It was still hovering around me like a foreign landscape. I was aware of everything—the muffled heartbeat of the baby; the quiet heat of the pale yellow light cast by the suspended lightbulb; the tinny tick-tick-tick of metal pieces colliding to pass time inside the clock on Momma's dresser; the slow gravity of the paint peeling in ugly patches from my parents' metal bed frame; the quick rush of blood inside my own veins; the stoic worry hidden in Daddy's heavy breath that brushed the back of my head each time he exhaled. I even felt the delicate joy of resting between the spasms of pain.

"Gene," Momma said, turning her feverish gaze away from me.

Daddy grunted, released his grip on my shoulders, and moved toward Momma. I tumbled back to a heady reality, bloated with new knowledge.

I had seen enough. I wanted to get away and come back when Momma was no longer moving in and out of pain with animal beauty and the baby was swaddled in a soft blanket, peering out at me with vacant, dim eyes, humbled by its own helplessness.

♥

The taxi came and I stood in the harsh light of the doorway and watched Momma, leaning on Daddy as they made their way along the river of light flowing from our house to the road. Daddy had one arm around her shoulders. His free hand held together the front edges of the fuzzy, dark-blue mohair sweater he had draped over her before they headed out of the house. She held a small, battered black suitcase in one hand.

Between the front porch and the taxi, another spasm overwhelmed Momma and my parents stopped in the middle of the yard. Momma dropped the suitcase and gripped Daddy's arm with both hands. I imagined her fingernails digging into his arm, initiating him into the pain of what was happening in her now that the baby wanted to come into the world. Momma stood with her knees apart and slightly bent, her spine curved and taut like an Indian's bow. "Lord Jesus, Lord Jesus, Lord Jesus . . .," she begged.

Standing like that my parents became one object, a fountain centerpiece, connected as solidly as if they were metal pieces bound by a welder's torch. Her hungry incantation was the water, blown upward from her throat and sent cascading back down, enclosing them in a world that excluded me.

I was seeing a hint of the unnamable thing that had drawn them together and compelled them to create—me, my brothers, this new baby. It surrounded them like a language only they knew.

I wanted to run forward and put myself in the middle of their little world and disrupt it. They were too much of a mystery for me in those moments—as unreachable to me as the stars winking in the dark canopy of the night sky above them. That felt unbearable to me then. I wanted to see them as I always had—simple, transparent, ordinary grown-ups—not as mystery, not as a life-giving centerpiece out of which I had been carved and set forward in the world. I wanted them back the way they were before something made Momma decide I was *big enough* to see her in labor, *big enough* for her to ask me to take care of my brothers.

Momma's pain stopped and she and Daddy retreated into their separate selves. They still moved as a unit though, leaning on each other, their steps matching, their heads bowed, into the taxi, and into an invisible world beyond the reach of our front porch light.

CHAPTER TWO

MY BABY SISTER WAS to be called Ida Bea, after my daddy's older sister who died before I was born. "Y'all Aunt Ida Bea was special to y'all's daddy when he was a little boy," Momma said. "She helped his mama take care of him."

Momma sat on the edge of the bed holding ten-day-old Baby Ida Bea so my brothers and I could get our first good look at her. Her tiny face was a smoothly swollen dark moon framed in the billowy whiteness of a baby blanket.

My imagination preened and stretched itself into the future where my baby sister would be big enough to play and be my ally in a household where I was outnumbered by three brothers. She would be the only one I would let climb my mulberry tree.

"Was I ever a baby like that?" Earl asked, staring, incredulous, at the white bundle in Momma's arms.

"You sure were," Momma answered.

"I mean little bitty like that," Earl said, leaning in to point at the baby's face.

Momma smiled and nodded.

"I never was," Roy Anthony boasted, puffing out his narrow chest and bouncing up onto his tiptoes in front of Momma.

"Every one of y'all was," Momma said and laughed. "Even I was once," she added, grinning at Roy Anthony as he shook his head and rolled his eyes in disbelief. "We all start out babies. Then somebody got to love us and feed us and take care of us till we get big enough to take care of ourselves."

Momma's smile flattened and she dropped her gaze to the floor.

Baby Ida Bea yawned at us without opening her eyes and began to squirm in Momma's arms.

"Now, now," Momma said, pulling her attention back from wherever it had wandered off to. She rocked slowly from side to side, caressing the tiny cheek. Ida Bea opened her mouth and turned her head toward Momma's hand. "I think, baby sister needs to eat," Momma said.

"What you gonna feed her?" Earl wanted to know.

"What a dumb question," Roy Anthony sang, putting the palm of his hand against his forehead and shaking his head. "Boy oh boy. Baby milk. Momma gonna give her baby milk right out from her body. You so dumb—"

"Roy," Momma said. The warning in her voice made Roy Anthony rock back on his heels and look down at the floor. "Don't call your brother names," she continued. "He younger than you."

"You ain't dumb," Momma said to Earl whose eyes were already glistening with tears. "You seven years old, too young to remember all that. Now y'all go on somewhere and play," she said, waving us all away.

June Bug pushed himself up from where he had been lying on the bed behind Momma. "Want see," he said, crawling forward to peer around Momma's shoulder.

"You can stay," she said, pulling him around so he leaned against her side as she unbuttoned her blouse to nurse Ida Bea.

Roy Anthony and Earl and I headed outside. I played with abandon, dashing about in the cool, sweet air, playing running games to keep warm. I was glad to be freed from the responsibility to make supper or corral the boys to do homework or get ready for bed.

On her fourteenth day at home, Baby Ida Bea wailed her way through the night. I fell in and out of sleep to the noise of her cries, Daddy's complaints, and Momma's futile efforts to quiet her and comfort Daddy. At daybreak, Daddy stomped off to work. Momma's heavy sighs after he left made it clear that he and Ida Bea had drained a lot out of her in the night.

I got out of bed and dressed for school, thinking Momma would be pleased when she came in at the usual time to wake me and Roy Anthony and Earl for school. I tiptoed into the kitchen and set out the bowls and spoons for our cornflakes. Then I mixed the powdered milk and water in the glass pitcher Momma always used.

"Maddy."

I went into her room and found her sitting in the big stuffed chair where Daddy always sat. She was breast-feeding Ida Bea.

"Go get Mother Parker," she said, barely above a whisper. "Tell her to come directly."

When I ran onto Ma Parker's porch in the dim morning light, she was standing in the doorway, invisible behind the rusted screen door. "What is it girl?" She sounded angry and impatient.

"Momma wants you. I think it's to do with the baby." I said, feeling grown-ups' emotions like jagged splotches of color in the air around me.

"Come see something," Momma demanded, as soon as Ma

Parker opened the door to our house. I slipped into the room behind her as she went to stand with Momma beside the bed. "What do I do for it?" Momma asked.

I crept forward to peer around the protective wall of their bodies. Ida Bea lay on her back on my parents' bed, her tiny legs and arms agitating stiffly in the air. She wasn't wearing a diaper, or the bandage that usually covered the blackening piece of umbilical cord still attached to her belly. Her cotton undershirt was flopped open exposing her tiny torso. A thin line of blood, crimson and moist, ran around the base of her cord, startlingly bright and unnatural against her dark, vulnerable skin.

"Well now." Ma Parker leaned forward and extended her hand toward Ida Bea. "Well now," she repeated, her hand still in the air above my sister. "How long has it been doing that?"

"Since last night."

Momma's mouth was drawn tight.

"In all my years of delivering I don't think I ever seen this particular ailment in a baby," Ma Parker answered.

She was the local midwife and root doctor. She spent a good deal of time handing out herbal and root cures to a loyal clientele. And even though the law said she wasn't supposed to, she still delivered babies when a black woman in the Quarters or anywhere in the nearby rural areas asked her to.

Ma Parker put her hand to her mouth. Her silence seemed false, like there was more she could have said. She had a wild, witchy look about her—her long dark dress nearly dragging the ground, a white apron with bulging pockets tied tight around her thin waist, her silvery gray hair hanging to her shoulders in stiff strands like she had just pulled a big tooth comb through it. She bent over Ida Bea and placed her palm on the upper part of Ida Bea's tiny chest. The baby's legs and arms stopped agitating. Ma

Parker turned her head as if listening to something. The furrows on her forehead and around the sides of her mouth deepened.

"I don't want to lose an—"

"Dorothy, I think you ought to wrap her up and take her on back up to that hospital and let the doctors up there tell you what to do," Ma Parker said, cutting into Momma's words. "You go on get her ready. I'll go call you a taxicab," she added, backing toward the door.

While Ma Parker walked to Watkins' Store, I hung around my mother and my sister, taking stock of the sadness and resignation that crackled in the air around Momma. She wiped the blood from my sister's stomach with a damp washrag, then dressed her, swaddling her in layers that made her look normal.

"Sit down over yonder," Momma said, indicating Daddy's chair. She placed Ida Bea on my lap and positioned my arms to support her small head in the bend of my elbow. "Hold her like that so she won't fuss," she ordered, and backed away to get on with the packing. Her hands trembled as she folded pristine cotton diapers and tiny undershirts and placed them in the ragged little suitcase.

I looked at my sister. She yawned in a meaningless way as I peered into her face. Her eyes were navy blue where they should have been black, and pale blue where they should have been white. Beyond that I could see nothing unusual, nothing that betrayed or explained why her most important commodity was oozing out of her belly.

Finally. *I have a baby sister,* I thought. When she gets bigger she will wear my cast-off clothes without complaining the way Roy Anthony does when Momma makes him wear pants that she originally made for me. Ida Bea will not mind wearing her big sister's clothes.

"I got to leave you in charge of the boys again," Momma said, sitting on the edge of the bed when she had finished packing. "Remember your promise. You gone take care of the boys till I get back?"

"Yes ma'am," I nodded, though I didn't want the job. It had taken a lot to keep order in the house when Momma was at the hospital delivering Ida Bea. Even with Daddy's best efforts, our daily lives went to pieces in small ways—shoes went missing just before we were to leave for school; June Bug cried and fought with me when I tried to dress him in the mornings; Roy Anthony picked on Earl and they got into fights; I forgot to do my homework and got into trouble with my teacher; Roy Anthony went to bed hungry a couple of times because he wouldn't hide the fact that he didn't like what Daddy cooked. Daddy simply ordered him away from the table the first time he complained. The second time Daddy smacked him across the face when he didn't move fast enough. This was a side of Daddy I hadn't seen before. It seemed that Momma's absence could bring out the worst in all of us.

"Poor baby sister," Momma said, looking at Ida Bea in my arms with an expression that made the air in the room shiver.

My brothers huddled around me on the front porch waving good-bye to Momma and Ida Bea as their taxicab disappeared out of the Quarters. As soon as the car was out of sight, Roy Anthony and Earl began flinging questions at me. "Where's Momma going? Will she be back by supper? Something wrong with the baby? When's Daddy get home? How come Momma looked like she's about to cry? What's the matter with you? How come you look mad?"

Their questions, tainted with curiosity and fear, swarmed around my head like gnats.

"Shut up. It ain't none of y'all's business," I snapped.

"I'm going to tell Momma on you," said Roy Anthony. "You ain't got no business to tell us to shut up," he thrust his chin upward and shook his head. "It ain't nice. Momma done told you so."

"Come here and I'll show you what ain't nice," I said, balling up my fist and moving toward him. He and Earl separated, leaping off the porch, one after the other, landing in the dusty yard. Roy Anthony turned and stuck his tongue out at me. Earl laughed and they disappeared around the side of the house. I hated that Momma had asked me to take care of them.

June Bug stood near the edge of the porch, crying and wringing his small hands like an old man. He stared down the road where Momma had gone. He seemed more vulnerable than the rest of us—his tiny bald head, his thin back. But his gaze was on the thing that mattered—our mother who had just vanished.

I went forward and picked him up. He wrapped his arms and legs around me like kudzu and buried his slimy face against my neck. I let the rhythm of my breath match the irregular heaving of his chest. I found small comfort in this embrace as I tried to exhale the fear that had settled in my gut.

CHAPTER THREE

THE LEAVES WERE GONE from my mulberry tree and the world was barren with the approach of winter when Roy Anthony, Earl, and I looked up from our Saturday morning play in the yard to see Momma walking up the road after nearly three weeks of being away at the hospital with Ida Bea. The boys rushed to greet her with their emotions flying. I followed as she went into the house with them bustling joyously around her. She pulled off her coat and sat on the edge of her and Daddy's unmade bed.

"Where's y'all's Daddy?"

"Gone," we all said together.

Daddy had left the house at the crack of dawn just like he did on workdays.

June Bug climbed onto Momma's lap, and Roy Anthony and Earl dropped to their knees on the floor in front of her. I sat beside her on the bed and she draped an arm across my shoulders, leaned in, and pressed her cheek against the side of my face. The subtle odors of hospital antiseptics, fatigue, and rubber bandages wafted from her clothes.

"Where's the baby at?" Earl wanted to know.

"The hospital."

"How come you didn't bring her with you?"

Momma's smile flattened. "She needs to stay where the doctors can see her."

"Look at all you nappy heads," she sang, her smile blossoming again. "You all gone get washed and clipped soon as me and Maddy clean this house."

Roy Anthony and Earl shook like puppies and jumped to their feet. "You'll never take me alive," Roy Anthony said. He posed briefly, as if he were running when someone called "red light." He opened the door and ran onto the porch. His laughter floated in as Earl disappeared after him and slammed the door.

Momma stood and lifted June Bug. The muscles in her forearms tensed, dark and sinewy as she held him in the air above her for a moment then rubbed his cheek against hers. He giggled and drew his knees up toward his chest. Momma settled him on her hip and began her survey of the rest of the house. I followed, seeing the mess through her eyes—the unmade beds, the pile of school clothes on great-grandmother's trunk and in the rocking chair, school papers scattered on the dresser-top and the floor, the mound of book-bags in the corner, toys everywhere, dust bunnies lining the baseboards, dirt trails on the linoleum from the back door to the kitchen sink, leaves huddled in little clumps around the legs of the kitchen table, food cemented to the floor in crusty patches near the stove, dirty dishes leaning against each other in the sink.

I stole a glance at Momma's face. Her disappointment and aggravation were visible in the bunched lines between her eyes and in her pursed lips.

I wanted to say it wasn't easy to keep an eye on the boys and keep the house clean at the same time. She had to know how hard it was just to get the boys up and fed and dressed and out of the house, then back home safely every day.

"You just don't seem to know how not to shame me," Momma said.

She shook her head and made that familiar sound with her

tongue like the speeded up ticking of a clock. "This house ain't got no business looking like this with a girl as big as you living in it."

June Bug pressed his head against Momma's chest, put his thumb in his mouth, and stared at me.

"Maddy, girl, you got to act more grown now. You big enough to clean a house. I showed you how. I didn't make you do as much housework as some people made they girls, but I showed you how. No excuse for this kind of mess. You got to make better use of yourself. I've told you. Ain't no room in the world for no lazy colored girl. You understand what I'm telling you?"

She was always saying things like that to me. I didn't understand exactly, but I nodded. "I'm sorry."

"What I tell you 'bout 'sorry'?"

"It don't fix nothing, and it make me sound like I'm no count and lazy."

"So why you standing here saying it to me now?"

"I'll do better next time."

"Please God, let that be the truth. Now don't just stand there like a little empty-headed sow, we need the broom, the water bucket, the mop, the wash tub . . ."

I followed her orders and we set to work cleaning the house. I helped her pull the sheets off the beds and put them to soak in a tub of scalding water laced with bleach and soap. While they were soaking, I washed dishes and helped scrub the floor of every room in our four-room house, including the little room on the back porch that housed the toilet. We took the sheets from their soak and scrubbed them on the metal scrub-board until they were pristine. Then we washed several weeks' worth of dirty clothes, including Daddy's work overalls with their stench of hay and chicken feed and droppings from his job at the poultry farm. Finally, we heated more water and the metal washtub was set in the middle of the kitchen floor and filled again with warm soapy water. One after the other, the boys and I climbed in and scrubbed away two and a half weeks of dirt.

"Is this how it is when I'm gone?" Momma had asked in a snappish voice as we ate supper without Daddy. "Go watch for him," she ordered as soon as our plates were empty.

The washing was all dry, the beds remade, supper was eaten, and it was getting dark by the time we saw Daddy coming up the road.

"Momma's home, Momma's home," Roy Anthony and Earl sang, hurrying to meet Daddy when he strode into view, lumbering slowly from inside the Quarters.

"She waiting for you," Roy Anthony said, running backward in front of Daddy. "She ain't happy neither."

On the front porch, Daddy stopped to tuck in his shirt, pull the front of his jacket together, and square his shoulders. He wiped his mud-caked shoes on the back of his pant legs, patted his kinky hair, and fixed a smile on his dark, lean face. The boys and I followed him inside.

In the kitchen Momma leaned against the sink, her arms folded across her chest, a wet dishrag dangling from one hand.

"Well, well, well, seems they was telling the truth," Daddy said with a guilty smile.

The tight expression on Momma's face didn't change. She turned her back to us all, sloshed the rag in the dishwater, wrung it out, and hung it over the side of the sink. "Y'all keep your coats on and go on back outside to play," she ordered. "Me and your Daddy need to talk." The heat of her anger fanned out, touching everything in the room.

"Junie Boy can stay," she added. "The rest of y'all go on out of here, but don't leave the yard."

Roy Anthony, Earl, and I went onto the front porch. Earl's eyes were moist. "What we gon' do now, Maddy?" he asked.

"Momma said play," Roy Anthony answered. "So let's play then. Pick a game you crybaby."

I suggested hide-and-seek. As soon as their backs were turned, I ran to the back porch, quietly opened the screen door, stepped in between the screen and the wooden door, squatted, and pressed my ear against the cold wood to eavesdrop on Momma and Daddy in the kitchen.

". . . nothing like before," Daddy was saying. "Ain't at all the same, Dot. This baby was born sick. Samuel was born healthy."

What was he talking about? Who was Samuel?

"It's 'bout me being there or not being there, Gene. I got to be there, and I got to count on you."

"I ain't going nowhere," Daddy said.

"I been hearing stories from folks coming to the hospital. Stories 'bout you at Loralee's joint."

"Don't put no credence in other folks' stories."

"I smell the whiskey on you right now."

"It's Saturday night, Dot. Don't mean I'm drinking every night."

"I'm worried 'bout these children, Gene."

"Come on home then, Dot."

"We been over this. You know there ain't no nurses up there in the ward with the colored children. Somebody's got to take care of Ida Bea, feed her, change her diapers and such."

"She dying, bleeding from her belly like that. If she don't die she likely gone be a cripple like Harold was. Dying would be better."

"You don't mean that."

"Mama ran herself to the bone taking care of Harold. Sister

did Mama's work, then died like a old woman at twenty-seven. Folks a lot older than her got flu that year. Didn't die from it though. Even with all the sacrificing, Harold ain't had what nobody could properly call a life. I used to look at him, all hunched up, slobbering on himself, grinning from ear to ear like some kind of fool, and I'd think, Lord have mercy and put this suffering fool out of his misery."

"Gene—"

The sudden silence on the other side of the door was like a quick intake of air. I waited in the darkness recalling what I knew about Daddy's family. His older sister, my Aunt Ida Bea, and his younger brother, Harold, died long before I was born. Before he even met Momma.

"We don't know what's going to happen with our Ida Bea," Momma said. "Doctors don't even know. Besides, her living or dying is God's decision."

"God loosed death in the world. Don't think he much cares one way or the other about how the dying goes. I seen a lot of bad living and hard dying in the war. Ain't seen God there for none of it."

"Maybe the dying you saw wasn't down to God. Maybe it was down to men."

"That's my point, Dot. God didn't do nothing to stop or start the dying. Whether any of us lives and dies ain't nothing to do with God. It's to do with the bad luck of sickness, or the doings of other folks."

"Just because you don't believe in God's help, don't mean I got to follow suit."

Momma continued in a smooth even voice like there were strong feelings behind it that she was trying hard to hide. "I believe God is looking down on Ida Bea. I want to be on the right side of what he sees down here. Maybe this time I won't have to lose—"

"You promised to let that go, Dot."

"I never promised my heart would stop hurting or that I would stop thinking about the loss of my first-born child."

I stiffened. Loss of her firstborn? I was her firstborn. I wasn't lost. Had there been a baby before me?

Momma's voice was hoarse and her words rolled out slowly when she spoke again. "I stopped blaming you. That's all. But he's with me all the time, Gene. Sometimes more real to me than these living ones. Sitting up there in that hospital ward, watching all kinds of sick children come and go, I can't help but think, what if I'd been there? Maybe Samuel would still be here."

"There wasn't nothing you could've done for Sam. I'm the one—"

"Gene, don't."

"What? Tell me that's not what you really thinking. You thinking you could've kept me from—"

"Stop it, Gene. No matter what you say, I won't take a chance with Ida Bea. I won't leave her to nobody else's tending. The one thing I need from you is for you to take care of these children at home. You got Maddy here to help you this time."

"I need you here, Dot. My head won't stay straight these days."

"You got control. You been controlling your head for better than twelve years. You were doing fine till you started drinking."

"I started seeing death again."

"You ain't in the army now. You ain't fighting nobody's war. Why do you keep on bringing all that back up? You can't let something from that long ago take over our lives again."

"It comes up on its own, Dot. It comes on sudden. Drink quiets it down."

"From what I can see, drink just thins out your mind so you don't see what's real."

"I'm near the edge—"

"What edge, Gene? You ain't got no edge. There's you. There's me. There's our five living children. We all twined up together. I'm doing my best to take care of our sick child. You got to take care of the well ones 'cause I got nobody else to help me. No family, nobody. Lord, Gene. You can't fail me this time. I won't stand it a second time. Won't go through it with you again."

The silence that grew in the room was soon punctuated with the heavy sound of weeping. Footsteps moved across the creaky floorboards of the kitchen.

"I ain't as strong as you think. Not like you." Daddy's voice was soaked with pain. "I can't hold on too good without you."

"You been saying things like that our whole life together. It ain't that you ain't strong. You just give up too easy. You don't get to do that this time. I can't hold up both ends of our life. With Samuel I counted on you. You let me down. That can't happen again, Gene. I don't have it in me to forgive that big again. You promised me things back then. You promised."

Silence collected inside the house.

I leaned against the door frame. My mind skittered from one bit of information to another, but it kept landing on the same piece—I have a dead brother, Samuel, and Daddy had something to do with his death.

As I stared into the darkness, I started to tremble. My stomach turned in on itself and I felt queasy.

"Olly, olly, oxen free," Roy Anthony and Earl were shouting in unison from the front yard. "Olly, olly, oxen free." They sang again. "Maddy, come out, come out wherever you are."

I was paralyzed in the flat gray air on the back porch, hearing only silence in the kitchen.

"Come on, Maddy—olly, olly, oxen free. You can come out. You safe. We don't want to play no more," Roy Anthony yelled, now from the side of the house, frustration rising high and keen in his voice. "Come on, Maddy, we don't want to play no more. I quit. Come on out."

I righted myself in the doorway and stood up. Little paisley sparks of color floated in the dark air in front of me. I grabbed the doorknob to steady myself, swallowed some air, and turned the knob.

No one stirred when I stepped inside. Momma was sitting in a chair at the table, her elbows on the watermelon-colored Formica, her face in her hands. June Bug stood on his thin legs, pressed against Momma's side with his head on her lap. Daddy was standing behind Momma, his fingers slowly kneading the muscles of her shoulders. His face was shiny with tears.

I paused in the doorway. "I need a drink of water," I said at last.

"Okay." Daddy said without looking up.

"Go find your brothers," Momma said through her hands. "It's getting time for y'all to come inside and go to bed." Her voice was wet.

When I came back in the front door with Roy Anthony and Earl in tow, Momma was sitting on the edge of her bed with June Bug curled beside her. Daddy was slouched in the stuffed chair across from the bed, leaning back with his eyes closed. He looked gray, like spent charcoal.

"I need to talk to y'all," Momma said, "'cause I'll be leaving early in the morning before y'all wake up."

"Why you have to go back?" Earl asked, dropping to his knees in front of her.

"Ida Bea needs me."

"Can't you bring her home and keep her here? You brought June Bug home. He was a little baby one time." Earl leaned forward.

"Ida Bea's got to stay where the doctors can see her. She needs the doctors."

Roy Anthony moved around the room touching things—Momma's little round alarm clock, the smooth plastic handles on the chest of drawers, the cold rounded metal of the bed frame, the smooth surface of the mirror above the dresser. He glanced at Daddy periodically. I sat cross-legged on the cold floor away from them all, trying to take it all in.

"Can't the doctors see 'bout her without you?"

Earl, in his blundering open-hearted way, kept questioning Momma.

"She needs me to see 'bout her too."

"We need you too," Earl said.

"You got your daddy and you got your big sister," Momma said. "Ida Bea's got nobody but me."

Momma looked from Daddy to me. When our eyes met, I blanched, trying to swallow whatever emotion might have been on my face. There was a free-floating mishmash of feelings that went with knowing that she and Daddy were hiding the fact of a dead child. There were no pictures of Samuel in our family photo album. There had never been a mention of his name. How could Momma and Daddy act like they always had?

My whole world was shifting. I had been removed from my place in the family. A brother had been born before me, and he had died before me. Daddy had something to do with the dying.

"I'll be home when she's all better," Momma was saying, still looking at me.

Could she read how stunned I felt? I looked at Daddy. What was he thinking about?

Back in the summer Esther and I had been drawn in to keeping a secret with him. I had followed an overgrown path shaded by longleaf pines, towering oaks, and low-lying shrubs that sloped down toward Harvest Quarters creek. Esther was close behind, letting me take the lead for once. We were headed to one of our favorite places. We went there when we wanted to avoid the other kids in the neighborhood. At the creek's edge, there were flat places where we could wade in the shallow water and catch tadpoles. We built watery corrals and let them flit around inside. Sometimes we just stood still in the water, pretending to fish with string tied on the end of a stick, feeling the cool and squishy mud between our toes and the tickling of minnows brushing against our legs. There were big rocks and moss-covered tree-stumps where we could sit and talk, or do nothing but watch dragonflies dart over the surface of the water.

We had never seen another soul in this particular spot, but that day when we spilled out of the shady path to look at the sunshine rippling on the surface of the water in front of us, there was Daddy sitting on a stump. The toes of his work-boots were submerged in the clear water. In one hand he held a mason jar, and in the other a photograph.

"Daddy?" I blurted.

His eyes were glistening when he looked up.

"Maddy? Baby Girl?"

He put the photograph in the pocket of his khaki shirt and stood. "What you doing here?"

"We kind of lost," Esther said, and looked at me quickly.

Daddy's lean dark face looked relieved. He patted his shirt pocket and stooped to retrieve something from the ground—the lid for his mason jar. Slowly, he screwed it on. For a few long moments we all stood in the music of birdsong and flowing water.

"Lost, you say?"

"Yes, sir," Esther said.

I nodded and looked down at the ground, feeling the heat rise to my face.

"You girls ain't got no business wandering around in these woods. There's some dangerous animals out here—foxes, mad raccoons, water moccasins. Maddy, you gone get your hide tanned."

"I'm sorry, Daddy," I said, though I couldn't see what was so bad about going to wade in the creek on a hot day. We'd never seen any dangerous animals except snapping turtles sunning themselves on rocks. They always slid into the water and swam away from wherever we were.

"Save your sorry for later. It's your momma you'll need to explain yourself to," Daddy said.

"It ain't Maddy's fault, Mr. Culpepper. I'm the one got us lost. We won't come this way again."

Esther was stepping from foot-to-foot and fingering the small hairs at the back of her neck.

I wanted to ask Daddy what he was doing here, and whose picture was that? But I knew better. "Bad manners to question adults. When I want you to know something, I'll tell you," he had warned before.

"Come on," Daddy said.

He led us along the creek in the opposite direction of the way we had come. I followed in his shadow, worrying about my punishment. He veered off onto an unfamiliar path among the trees. The ground was worn bare and the shrubbery had been hacked back so nothing reached out to touch my face and arms as I passed. Esther and I had never come across this path. It occurred to me that there must be hundreds of ways to move through these woods. Daddy stomped on ahead, sure-footed with his head bowed. When we came out onto the Quarters road, he stopped.

"I tell you what. I got to go take this back to the people that gave it to me."

Clear liquid sloshed inside the jar when he held it up. "You momma don't need to know either one of us was down by the creek today. It'd just worry her for no good reason. So, I'm not going to mention it. This time."

He put his hand on my shoulder. "Got that?"

He was asking me to keep a secret from Momma. What would she have a problem with—the jar, the picture, or the fact that he hadn't come straight home from work?

"Got that, Maddy?"

I nodded.

"So you and your little friend here go on home. I'll take care of what I need to and I'll be there directly, like I always am."

He tapped me under the chin with his fingers the way he used to when I was little. "Later, Baby Girl," he said, then turned and headed back into the heart of the Quarters.

"Grown-ups always got secrets," Esther said as we walked toward home in the opposite direction of Daddy.

"Maddy, are you hearing me?" Momma's voice intruded on

my memory. Her face was drawn in lines of aggravation when I looked across the room at her. I nodded. Esther's voice still echoed in my head, *"Grown-ups always got secrets."* "I'm trying to tell you that y'all's daddy's gon' start bringing y'all to visit me and Ida Bea up at the hospital. Ain't that right, Gene?" Momma moved her gaze back to Daddy.

"Uhnn huh," he grunted. Nothing on him moved except the lump of his Adam's apple, which vibrated in his throat like a hard candy he was trying to swallow.

They had both cried about their dead child. Now they were back to holding that secret with stoicism and ease.

"Now don't y'all go making me feel bad for even coming home for a little bit," Momma said.

Everybody stiffened, even Daddy, who opened his eyes and sat up straight.

"I want y'all to be good to each other while I'm away. I'll be back as soon as I can. Y'all hearing me?"

We all nodded, even Daddy.

"Now y'all go on get ready for bed. Junie Boy will sleep with me and Daddy tonight. Maddy?"

She called me back as I was leaving the room and handed me a few pieces of notebook paper. In her precise cursive handwriting she had written out simple instructions for cooking a few of the meals she usually cooked—red beans and rice with onions; spaghetti with tomato paste and ground meat; chicken backs and rice; black-eyed peas and hog jowls; chicken legs in gravy; fried pork chops; beef tails and navy beans; corn bread; biscuits.

"Put those pages some place where they won't get lost. I want you cooking supper now on. Don't know how long I'll be away this time, but y'all need good regular meals. You near grown now right?" She winked at me. "You can take care of your brothers and this old raggedy daddy of y'all's."

She grinned at Daddy. He returned her smile. For a moment they seemed like their old selves. But that idea shattered and dissolved beside my new knowledge about them.

CHAPTER FOUR

AS I LAY IN bed that night, trying to will myself into sleep, I kept thinking that my whole life had changed with the birth of Baby Ida Bea. I was resenting her and regretting the fact that I had ever wanted a sister. Looking back now, I realize that the changes had started the summer before with the arrival of wild, untamed Esther Rawlins. Since all the kids who lived near me were boys, including the three in my house, I was starved for the company of another girl. But that warm summer day in the middle of June when we met, I hated her.

"Just who do you think you are?" I was mad enough that I would have hit her if she had been standing on level ground with me. As it was, she towered about thirty feet above me in my mulberry tree, eating my mulberries and possessing the nerve to tell me I couldn't climb up and join her. Nobody had ever told me I couldn't climb a tree. Nobody. Not even my own momma. And every kid in the neighborhood asked my permission before they climbed my tree. They could climb any other tree in the neighborhood, even the other mulberries, but not this one. This one was mine. It grew in a large open field across the road from my family's house. The rough, knobby bark of its trunk was as familiar to me as the soft wrinkly skin of my knees and elbows. The slender lumpy flesh and rich sweetness of its berries were mine to savor. And mine alone, unless *I* decided to share. I'd staked my claim on this tree ages ago. Everybody understood that, and this new girl would too before the day was over.

Her cheeks bunched out in a derogatory way and she spit a mouthful of purple-red already-chewed mulberries at my feet.

"I'm Esther Denise Rawlins. That's who I am," she yelled. "I'm queen of this here mulberry tree."

"I'm Madeleine Genell Culpepper and ain't nobody climbs this tree without my say so 'cause this is my mulberry tree. And you ain't no queen. You a ugly, high-yellow cow!" These were some of my worst insults, the ones I had learned from hanging around my mama and her friends. I knew that no Negro female who liked herself even a little bit liked being called a cow. And high-yellow? Well high-yellow was something a lot of Negroes found it advantageous to be in Mississippi, but nobody liked being called high-yellow to their face.

"What'd you call me?" Mulberry juice dripped from the corners of her mouth onto her thin face, which was the color of fresh-cut pine.

"You heard me. I called you ugly, I called you high-yellow, and I called you a cow."

She stood stock still for a moment, hugging the trunk of my tree with her arm, her feet planted on my favorite branch, the one that jutted out from the trunk like a long narrow thumb. Her face turned pink under her yellowish skin. "I'm going to whip your butt when I get down out this tree."

"You and what army, you skinny, yellow, nappy-headed cow?" I had taken note of the wild mane of frizzy brown hair that framed her face like a straw hat. Hers was the first afro I'd ever seen. No self-respecting Negro female in my community wore her hair in its natural state in Mississippi in 1963. It made her look insane.

"You better not still be out here when I get down out of this tree." Her back was to me as she descended from her perch.

"I ain't scared of you, or nobody else."

I was too indignant to think about the fact that she might be bigger than me, or a better fighter than me. It turned out that she was almost a head taller than me *and* a better fighter. She fought like a cat, clawing and biting at me with manic tenacity. I don't know how long we rolled around in the dirt trying to damage each other before we were pulled apart by my mother. She walked Esther to her grandma's porch and made her go inside. Then she led me into our house and gave me a lecture that included, "Maddy, you're getting to be too close to grown to be fighting in the dirt like that. Animals act like that. You need to start acting like a lady so folks can treat you like one."

She kept me in the house with her for the rest of the day, doing housework, a round of chores that I hated. While my brothers' happy, high-pitched voices floated in through the windows, I moped in the shadowy confines of our house helping Momma clean and wash laundry. As I was pinning the clean wash to the line outside, Esther came over to apologize.

"My grandma says I need to make up to you, otherwise I'm going to be playing by myself all summer 'cause you're the only other girl around for miles. I already hate it here. Playing by myself all the time, I would hate even more. So I apologize for hitting you first."

"Accepted," I said, without even turning to look at her. I was mad about all the housework I was doing because of her. I waited for her to walk away, but she didn't. She hung around in the yard, doing I don't know what, since I refused to turn around. I kept reaching into the wash bucket and pulling out the wet clothes that I had rubbed on the washboard so hard earlier that my knuckles were scraped raw in places.

"What you doing that for?" Esther asked after a while.

"Punishment."

"I'd rather be beat."

Her words, like her hair, were insane. I turned to get a better look at a crazy person up close. What I saw was a girl a little bit taller than me with mean red welts on her wiry arms and legs.

"Who did that to you?"

"Grandma."

"Ma Parker?"

"Y'all call her that. She my grandma."

"What'd she hit you with?"

"Extension cord."

That old Ma Parker could hit someone with enough force to raise welts was unimaginable to me. Esther had picked up a plank from the ground and was swinging it like a baseball bat. She clearly had some mastery of pain that I couldn't even guess at. Watching her, I started to cry.

"Cut that out," she yelled, "or I'll never be your friend. I hate crybabies."

It was the sincerity in her voice and fear on her face that made me stop. Suddenly something in her seemed admirable. I thought again of being her friend. I wanted to keep her from harm. While I was subject to the whims and commands of the adults around me, I was sure my world was safer than hers. I could keep her safe if I brought her into mine.

During the next few weeks we became fast friends, and we were inseparable as we roamed the neighborhood, exploring the houses, the woods, and the creek. My family lived at 1 Harvest

Quarters, a three-minute walk in from the main street. Esther's grandma lived at 2 Harvest Quarters. The last house along the curved road was number 21.

Before Esther arrived, I had never set eyes on the houses from numbers 9 through 20. Occasionally, the long processional from the neighborhood to the local school included children from some of those houses, but their attendance was so irregular that I had no more than a nodding acquaintance with any of them, except one who had been in class with me since first grade, Percy Blakely. I disliked him on principle because all the other kids in my class did, and because my mother had taught my brothers and me that we were better than the other kids in the quarters and that we were not to associate with them. Momma had even forbidden me to go any farther than 5 Harvest Quarters, the last house she could see from our front porch. The only time in my eleven years that she ever hit me was when I was five and she found me building mud castles with a boy in the backyard at 7 Harvest Quarters. She dragged me home and whipped my bare legs with a thin switch she snapped from a shrub in our backyard.

"Crazy things go on deep in these Quarters, and I don't want you back there," she yelled at me when she stopped stinging my legs with the switch. She threatened to give me a worse beating if I ever went beyond house 5 again.

I had cried and sulked for hours afterward. Although the places where that switch had licked my skin did sting for a while, that wasn't the primary source of my long, drawn-out sadness. What had hurt the most was the shock of being hit by my mother and seeing an unfamiliar anger in her eyes that was directed at me. From that I surmised that what went on deep in the Quarters must be truly horrible. I imagined that fairytale monsters like goblins, trolls, and witches must live in the unseen reaches of my neighborhood. For Esther, my imagination, however vivid, wasn't enough to satisfy her curiosity.

"What your mama don't know can't hurt her," Esther teased. "Besides, you grown enough to take care of yourself. You almost as grown as me, and I don't need nobody to take care of me."

For some time I had been growing less interested in learning the kinds of things Momma wanted to teach me—how to sew, how to braid my own hair, how to properly season a pot of beans, how to iron a blouse. But my belief in her power over me remained intact. I was still afraid to lie to her. "Don't even try lying to me, 'cause you can't get nothing by me," she would say. I was sure she would spot a lie and swat it from the air and I would have hell to pay.

But that year as June wound down into July, Esther was becoming my new authority, and she was a good liar, good enough for her lies to sail right pass Momma. Sometimes she concocted elaborate stories to tell my mother about how we spent our time when we were out of her sight. Momma listened, busy with whatever housework she was doing. Sometimes she paused in the middle of one of Esther's tales and asked, "Really?"

"Yes ma'am," Esther answered, and kept on with her story. As the summer wore on, Momma stopped asking how Esther and I had spent our time.

So whenever Esther suggested it, I followed her as she meandered through the woods to come out at a different part of the Quarters. We were exploring house by house surreptitiously, seeing what we could see, hearing what we could hear. Before the summer was over we had seen nearly every house in the Quarters more than once. What we found sometimes shocked and appalled me.

We found an old woman who kept a pet monkey locked away

in her house. We saw it playing in her front window. Sometimes it got out and attacked children. It jumped on their heads and scratched their faces and necks. We even encountered kids who proudly showed their scars to prove the stories. There were several houses that I now know were bootleg whiskey joints. At the time I just thought of them as music houses. There was always loud music flowing out of those places and grinning, preoccupied grown-ups with glasses of "water" on the porches. Once, I saw my classmate Percy Blakely, shirtless and barefoot, in the yard in front of one of those houses. When he saw me, he ran onto the porch and disappeared inside.

"There goes Percy from my class," I told Esther. She went to the porch and asked an old woman sitting with a glass of clear liquid in her hand if a boy named Percy lived there.

"Child, git on 'way from here," she told Esther. "Y'all don't need to know nothing 'bout nothing or nobody up in this house."

Esther turned and grinned at me where I stood in the road. She shrugged, a magnificent gesture with her arms thrown out from her sides, palms skyward. "She say Percy don't live here."

"I ain't said nothing, but get out of my yard, you little hard-headed sow. You come round here again I'm going to take a switch to those skinny little legs of yours. Now gone."

Esther acted as if she hadn't heard. She flung her arms out and danced wildly around in the yard. I stayed where I was, looking on shyly, until the woman, mean enough to be somebody's mother, stood and moved to the top of the steps. "Y'all get on 'way from here before I tell y'all's mama."

Esther stuck her tongue out, then turned and ran away laughing.

Another time when we were exploring the Quarters, there was the old man who offered us a dollar apiece if we would come see what he had inside his pants. "It won't bite you," he assured us. "It likes little girls. You don't even have to touch it if you don't want to." It was the quick tug on my arm from Esther and the alarmed look on her face that made me turn and run. I imagined that I felt the heat of the old man's breath on the back of my legs as Esther and I ran away. We ran all the way to my mulberry tree and climbed as high as we could go and lolled about on the branches like cats until we caught our breath. Esther confided to me that she had already seen what was inside men's pants.

"I've seen my brothers' weenies," I said, confident and proud.

"It's not the same thing at all. Men's things are ten times as big, and if you touch them they get even bigger. They make babies too," she added, as a final cause for condemnation.

This explained why my mother kept swelling up big and round before she would go to the hospital and come home with a baby. It was my father who kept putting the babies there. I had asked Momma once how it happened, and she had told me, her only girl child, that it was none of my business.

Esther telling me this new information about where the baby inside my mother came from felt hateful and mean to me. But Esther wasn't even thinking of me when she said it. Her eyes had a faraway, glazed-over look she got sometimes, like she was seeing something I couldn't see. The sudden distance between us filled me with sadness, and I could smell the end of summer and see the leaves of my mulberry tree changing color.

"Last one out of the tree is a rotten egg," I shouted and started scurrying from the tree like a squirrel. I couldn't stand for her to think about things that didn't involve me, and I hated the idea of fall. That meant school, and Esther going away.

"I'm going to my mother's house," Esther said with her back to me one day as we hunted along the edge of the creek for fresh blackberries. Her grandma had promised to make us a pie if we brought back enough in the syrup buckets she gave us. Mine was half-full already.

"I thought you were staying until the end of summer." I tried to keep the panic from showing by practicing the sort of busy detachment that she was good at. I parted the weeds with the end of my stick, pretending to be absorbed in the hunt for berries.

"I am. I'm only going to her house for two nights."

"Seems silly to go home and then come back."

"I don't live with my mama, stupid." She stopped and looked at me like I was some kind of moron. "I live with my Aunt Helen up in Meridian. My mama lives right here in Blossom."

I don't know why I didn't know that, but I didn't. The idea of a girl not living with her mother had never occurred to me. I knew one girl at school, Collette Willis, who didn't live with her mother. She lived with her grandma, but her mother was dead. This was different.

"Why don't you live with your mother?"

Esther stopped her hunt for a moment and looked at me. She dragged her fingertips across her eyebrows and brought them to rest in the baby hairs at the base of her skull.

"When I was little I didn't want to," she said. "I liked my Aunt Helen better. I don't remember why. My mama loved me, but I loved my auntie."

I had watched her lie to my mother and to her grandma about all sorts of things, and I had noted her habit of fingering her eyebrows or pulling at the little hairs at the back of her neck when she was telling a lie. So I knew she was lying to me, but I couldn't challenge her. I thought I might lose something important if I shattered the image I had of her. After all, I was trying to model myself after her. I imitated her walk, pointing my toes inward toward each other to gain the feel of her slightly bowlegged, pigeon-toed gait. I let her unplait my hair when we were out of my mother's sight, so I had a dark afro to match her lighter one. I had even adopted her speech patterns, letting my voice rise high at the end of each sentence and greeting people with "hey" instead of the "good morning" and "good afternoon" that my mother had taught me. Everything about her seemed right. So I let her stay inside her lie and reassured myself that she had a good reason for it.

"Do you want to come or not, Maddy?"

"Come where?"

"My mama's, stupid."

"Can I?"

"I don't see why not. I'll just ask Grandma to ask your mama."

"Sure."

Relief spread across her face.

Esther's mama was tall and thin, an elongated version of Esther. Her skin was a deeper brown, though, and her hair was the color of mine, but she had the same angular face shape as Esther, and the same hard black eyes peering out at the world defiantly.

"Careful of my dress," she said to Esther as we slid into the backseat of the cab beside her.

Esther, sitting in the middle, pushed against me so hard that I ended up with my arm pressed against the cool, sturdy metal door handle during the long ride to a side of town that I had never visited.

Esther's mama talked to her in short little sentences. Her words, her tone, her questions all seemed unnatural for someone who was a mother. Mothers were authoritative with kids, always sure of their motherly power. They asked the right questions and were economical with the words they used on children. Economical was different from stingy, which is how Esther's mother spoke, as if each word became lost to her forever. And she behaved with a stiff discomfort that signaled fear, the kind of fear that children, like wild animals, can sense. That kind of fear usually incited wildness in us, but I sensed fear in Esther too. Her fear made me scared, because as far as I could tell, Esther wasn't scared of anything—except, it seemed, her mother.

To manage my uneasiness, I stared out the window as my shabby neighborhood was replaced by a neater one with cement sidewalks and small painted houses with screened-in porches. Some of the yards had manicured lawns and tidy flowers or hedges, unlike the bare, parched yards and ditches in the Quarters.

Esther's mama's house was white and had square hedges and yellow and purple flowers out front. Inside the house, her rooms were laid out in the same shotgun design as ours, though she had four inside rooms instead of the three that my family shared. The furniture looked new. Everything matched and was stylishly arranged like on a television show, and though it was Friday, she made a Sunday supper of pork chops and gravy, mashed potatoes, and English peas, and there was a mulberry cobbler. She even had paper napkins on the table.

Through supper and the three hours we spent in front of the small, round black and white television set, Esther used words like *please* and *thank you*. Words I had never heard cross her lips. She sat straight-backed on the sofa wearing the pink frilly dress that her grandma had insisted on, looking unnatural with her hands folded in her lap and her hair pulled back and braided into two plaits that hung heavily to her shoulders. Her scarred legs and bony elbows were shiny from the grease her grandma had rubbed onto them. I was also a model child, wearing my Sunday best and my favorite plaited hairstyle.

Esther's mama made us a pallet of blankets and quilts to sleep on the floor in one of the middle rooms. Esther and I lay whispering together in the dark until the soft sounds of her mother's snoring floated in from the other room. Esther got up and began to rummage around, striking matches from the box she had sneaked from her grandma's kitchen. She peeked in boxes and dresser drawers and looked under furniture. This was the bold, curious Esther I was used to. She wanted to see how her mother lived, she said.

"Look what I found," she whispered, coming back to the pallet with a small bottle in her hand. In the shadowy light of a match's flame, I saw that it was a bottle of pink nail polish. She turned the bottle slowly so the light glistened off the smooth glass as if it were a jewel. My mama didn't use the stuff, but I thought it was pretty on the ladies I saw wearing it. "Let's paint our nails," Esther suggested.

Little alarm bells sounded in my head. "Shouldn't we wait and ask and do it tomorrow?" It wasn't right. It was just like stealing to use the polish without permission. And besides, how would we hide it from her mama the next day?

"This is my mama's house. I can use anything I want." The irritated pitch of her voice reminded me that she had no tolerance for other people's fear. "Anyway, I'm sure she left it here for me to use," she said and smacked her tongue against the roof of her mouth making a sound that until now I had only heard grown-up women make.

I held my breath, afraid to implicate myself with even a sigh. Agreeing with her was out of the question. Something about her mother frightened me. She was not governed by the laws of other mothers. I could not tell what governed her.

"Well, go ahead, be a chicken. I'll just paint my own then," Esther hissed at me in the darkness.

And she did, carefully, methodically, while I lit one match after another and held it steady for her. When she was done, she lay back on the pallet and waved her hands in the darkness. I lay there wondering about Esther and her mama.

Esther sat up and struck another match. She held the nail polish aloft and examined the bottle from every angle. "I wonder if this stuff burns," she said quietly.

"How could it?" I answered. "It's wet. Wet things don't burn."

"I bet it does."

A new anxiety laid claim to me as I watched Esther's ghostly face wavering in the light of the match. Her eyes were dark holes in her face.

"Yeah, you're probably right." I wanted her to let go of this idea, to move on to something harmless.

"I don't think you should do this," I whispered. My anxiety was growing into a complicated fear. She turned away from me. "Esther, this is bad."

"No it ain't. Want to know something? I bet you that if we put a piece of string in this bottle it will burn just like a little bitty coal-oil lamp. Then we won't have to keep striking matches. What you want to bet me?"

"Nothing. What we need to see for? It's time to go to sleep."

But Esther was already hunting around the room for a suitable wick.

"My mama took me to a beauty parlor once and got my hair

done up like Shirley Temple's," I tried again, lying as I watched her stuff a small rag into the mouth of the bottle.

"You ever had your hair done like Shirley Temple's?"

"No," she shot back, not even glancing my way as she struck a match and held it to the end of the rag. She set the bottle down and smiled as a small yellow flame grabbed the end of the rag and moved toward the neck of the bottle. As the rag shortened, the flame sputtered and became blue. Then it disappeared into the mouth of the bottle and a pungent, sweet smell rose from the bottle in a stream of thick gray smoke with a pale bluish tint at its base.

We looked at each other in the pale gray-blue light as the smoke filled the room. It was clear that something had to be done, but neither of us knew what.

I had a sudden vision of the house smoldering silently in a pale blue flame, with the scent of burning nail polish invading the neighborhood.

"What the hell!" Esther's mama was outlined in the smoke that filled the doorway. "What the hell have you done?" She rushed into the center of the room, stepping on my arm. She pulled the chain and turned on the single lightbulb hanging from its cord in the ceiling. She gawked at the nail polish bottle smoldering in the center of the floor like a tiny volcano, then grabbed a hand-mirror and hairbrush from the dresser. She squatted beside the smoking bottle, brushed it onto the face of the mirror, stood, and rushed from the room. We heard her cursing and swearing as she slammed the back door open and, no doubt, tossed the burning bottle into the dew-dampened grass of the backyard. When she came back into the room, we were still staring at the doorway.

"Your dumb ass still ain't learned a thing." Her eyes were vicious as she looked at Esther. "You a lot bigger than you was when

I threw you out of here before, but you still just as stupid as the day is long. You just like that crazy bastard that sired you. There ain't none of me in you. But I know how to deal with you."

Two steps brought her to the pallet where we lay, immobilized. Esther let out a sharp frightened sound like a dog that has been hurt as her mama grabbed one of her plaits and pulled her to her feet. "I know exactly how to fix your smart ass," she hissed, as she led Esther out of the room by her hair.

From the other room I heard quick intakes of breath and the muted thuds and smacking sounds that my mama's fists made when she pounded dough to make bread. The noises were magnified like sounds in a bad dream that seemed to go on too long. I thought about getting up and running from the house, but I couldn't move. My heart pounded, and I prayed to Jesus for salvation as I had learned to do in Sunday School. My voice rose and fell in a frantic litany of every prayer I had ever learned. "Our father . . . the Lord is my shepherd . . . bless the little children . . . protect the meek . . ."

Esther appeared in the doorway. There was blood dripping from her nose onto her lips, and she was wavering on one leg. Her mama stood behind her with a crazed look still in her eyes. She looked at me and shoved Esther into the room with such force that Esther landed on her knees in the middle of the room where the nail polish bottle had been. "You come here," she said to me.

I got to my feet slowly, already crying and still begging for mercy from God. Esther's bloody nose and the angry red splotches on every part of her body that I could see, made it clear that her mama did not understand what it meant to be merciful. I stood before her pressing my hands together in a fisted version of praying hands.

"Put your hands down and look at me."

Her voice was no longer human. But I had been trained to obey my elders. So I lowered my arms to my sides, eyes trained on the floor, still mumbling my prayers. "Look at me," she said. What I saw when I raised my head was a matured hatred directed straight at me. Then I thought I saw a flicker of joy or forgiveness in the dark eyes that looked down into my own, so I didn't expect the hand that swung out from her side and struck me across the face, knocking me off balance. Her other hand came from the other side to deliver the real blow that sent me reeling across the room. I bumped into Esther where she was still kneeling on the floor. We ended in a tangled heap on the pallet.

"That's for not telling me what that dumb-ass bitch was up to."

As Esther and I sat up and collected ourselves, wiping tears, snot, and blood from our faces with our hands, her mama tossed two folded brown paper bags at us. "Put your shit in these bags and get out of my house. I don't want either one of you under the same roof with me for another minute."

In silence we stuffed our things into the bags and stood in the middle of the room, waiting for some miracle to take us away. Esther's mama appeared in the doorway again. "Y'all know the way to the door. Get your little asses out of my house."

With faces averted and minds burdened with guilt and pain, we walked to the door, off the porch, and into the street. The quiet night air soothed my burning skin as I turned and began marching in the direction I thought would take me home. The stinging pain in my jaw and a sharp ache in my wrist dulled as I allowed myself to think about the fact that I didn't know exactly how to get myself home. In my bruised memory the cab ride to Esther's mama's house had gone on forever.

Esther walked beside me, her shoulders slumped in a posture

I had never seen her wear. Her eyes looked at the tips of her toes. We had neglected to put on our shoes.

"Esther?" I ventured, suddenly filled with fears about rabid bats swooping down on us, or wild possums attacking as we roamed around town, forever trying to find our way home.

She looked at me with an expression so empty and bewildered that I could not form the words to ask if she knew how to get to her grandma's house. She turned her attention back to the ground, and I was content for a time to just walk beside her.

I could not imagine what it felt like to be Esther. I felt sorry that someone so powerful as her mother could hate her so much, and I was embarrassed to have seen proof of it. I stole sly glances at her face, moving there in the dark, as emotionless as something carved from stone.

After we had walked for a long time, Esther stopped under a streetlight and sat down on the ground with her back against the light pole. She set her bag on the ground beside her. Slow silent tremors began to shake her body, gently at first. Then the tremors strengthened, making her moan and shake violently. Her head dropped forward and her heavy plaits stuck out from her head like tired horns. As her shoulders heaved in her private anguish, I stood paralyzed in the street lamp's murky yellow light.

I decided to try hugging Esther as my mother did with my little brothers when they cried. Esther shrugged my hand away savagely when I touched her shoulder.

After a while she stood and wiped her face on the hem of her night shirt. I didn't realize that I had been crying until she looked at me and hissed, "I told you I hate crybabies."

"Help me untie my hair," she said suddenly, pulling roughly at one of her plaits. "These things are making my head hurt."

We unbraided her hair carefully, and she ran her fingers through it, coaxing it back to its familiar wildness until it stood out angrily, dwarfing her narrow face.

"I didn't want to stay at my mother's house no way," she said, reaching up with both hands to tug at the little hairs on the back of her neck. "She's always trying to get me to come stay with her. But even though she loves me, I just don't like to stay with her."

A voracious sense of loss clawed at my insides. It tore at my stomach until I dropped to my knees and vomited in the dirt. I didn't want to look at Esther. Something was wrong with her and her mother. I saw this as clearly as I saw the purple remnants of mulberry cobbler in the vomit on the ground in front of me. I felt weak, and I understood why she hated my kind of weakness. I didn't want to get up.

Esther simply grabbed my nightshirt and pulled me to my feet.

"It's a good thing that you ain't me," she said with disgusted pity. "Come on," she added, gentler. "Let's go find my grandma's house. She'll be glad to see us. She didn't want me to go to my mama's house no way."

I don't remember how, but we did find our way home, and neither Esther's grandmother, nor my mother was glad to see us.

"I can't believe you acted a fool in somebody else's house. I thought you had better sense than that," Momma said, clucking her tongue against the roof of her mouth and shaking her head with confused anger. "I know I *taught* you better than that."

She put her hand under my chin and tilted my head to get a better look at my bruised cheek.

"That heifer didn't have to hit you so hard. But now you know.

Don't go behaving like a fool in another woman's house. Even when I ain't around, you got to act sensible. Like you got some manners. Like I been raising you. Don't give nobody reason to think they got to hit you. Maddy. You ain't a little child anymore. You got to learn the world ain't a easy place. You my pride and joy—don't be giving me no reasons to be shamed of my own flesh and blood."

I wanted to say I was sorry—sorry for shaming her, sorry for thinking Esther was better. I wanted to tell her about the hate I had seen in Esther's mother's eyes. I wanted to ask her if it was possible, could a mother really hate her child? But my tongue was tied by shame. I watched her making poultices for me to hold against my bruised face and wrist. And for the first time that summer I noticed her swollen legs. They looked like smooth brown tree trunks planted in a pair of Daddy's old work-boots. She moved slowly, listing from side to side as she walked from the cabinet to the sink and back to the kitchen table where I sat. Her fingers, when she pressed the pungent-smelling remedy against my cheek, were like stiff little sausages.

"Hold it like this," she said, flattening the cloth on my cheek. "If you keep it still, and the pressure even, it'll stop hurting."

When I looked in her eyes I saw enough anguish and grief to swallow my whole world.

Ma Parker wouldn't let Esther and me play together for a full week. When we did try to play together like before, everything was awkward and false—our movements, our games, our speech. Neither of us ever brought up what happened the night we visited her mother's house, but I was always thinking about it whenever

I was with her. I was embarrassed for her still—the shame of her mother's violence toward her, her delusions and lies about it. I couldn't will myself back to a place or time when I didn't know that there was another side to her life.

I began to look forward to the once-dreaded end of summer. I was happy a week or so later when that blue-and-white Chevrolet pulled up in front of Esther's grandma's house. I hid in my mulberry tree when she came looking for me to say good-bye, but she knew me well enough to climb up and find me. She draped herself nearby on a sturdy branch and swung her long legs casually.

"Will you help me pick some of your mulberries to eat in my auntie's car?" she asked.

There was that familiar flinty hardness in her eyes, playing there like tiny bursts of sunlight when I looked at her.

"Ain't no more mulberries," I said sadly. "We ate all the berries a long time ago, remember?"

"Oh yeah," she said, gazing out through mulberry leaves braised by the late August sun. "Oh yeah," she repeated. "Your mulberries been gone a long, long time."

"Esther!" Ma Parker's voice soared on the hot air and found us in our green sanctuary.

"Well," Esther said. "Got to go."

She started her descent, and I climbed down after her to be gracious.

"My mama does love me, you know," she said, her wild mane of hair fanning out around her face like blackberry bramble as she got into the backseat of her Aunt Helen's boyfriend's car.

Not knowing what else to do, I nodded slowly, then stood there and watched as they drove away.

CHAPTER FIVE

"HEY KNUCKLEHEADS," DADDY SAID without looking at any of us when he came home from visiting Momma and Ida Bea at the hospital. He had gone for his weekly visit, taking a small bag of food for Momma, the kinds of things she didn't have to cook or put in an icebox—tins of sardines, boxes of saltine crackers, cans of pork and beans.

The boys and I had been waiting in the front room for his return, but he headed right past us and on through to the kitchen where he draped his jacket over the back of a kitchen chair. At the sink he washed his face and hands, splashing water onto the narrow counter around the sink.

He was losing weight despite my best efforts to cook meals as Momma had instructed during her visit home a few weeks earlier. His skin, black as wild berries, had tightened against his skull, highlighting hard angular cheekbones and a square clenched jaw. The veins in his arms and on the backs of his hands showed like small cords.

"Where my supper?" he asked, dropping into a chair as if he were in a diner.

He lit a cigarette and puffed on it quietly while I spooned up a plate of the greasy spaghetti I had made. "Thanks, Baby Girl," he said, keeping his eyes focused on the food I had set on the Formica top in front of him. He chewed with slow concentration and an expression that said his mind was on something unpleasant. While he ruminated, the boys and I practiced patience.

I stepped back into the kitchen doorway and leaned against the door frame, watching him through the smoke curling away from the cigarette on the chunky glass ashtray beside his plate.

Roy Anthony had pulled a kitchen chair up to the sink and had run more dishwater in it. Earlier I had bullied him into washing the dishes. He had cleaned everything except the pot I cooked the spaghetti in and the plate and fork Daddy was using. He didn't need to run another sink full of water for those things, but it gave him an excuse to play submarine pilot with the dishrag in the soapy dishwater. Cautious engine noises bubbled through his lips. Earl sat at the table across from Daddy, playing with a small pile of cornbread crumbs on the table. June Bug was lying on his back on the cold linoleum in the center of the room. He held one hand against his chest like a flower, his thumb pointed toward the ceiling. If Daddy weren't there, his thumb would be in his mouth, a habit he had picked up in Momma's absence. The first time Daddy saw him with his thumb in his mouth, he slapped his hand away. When June Bug puffed up to cry, Daddy had raised his hand to slap him again. "I'll give you something to cry about," he had warned. June Bug had swallowed his tears and figured out how not to suck his thumb around Daddy.

Whatever we were doing or not doing, we were all waiting for Daddy to talk to us about Momma. Thanksgiving was two weeks away, and we were hoping Momma would be home for that. Before he'd left for the hospital visit, Daddy had made us think that might be so. When his plate was empty, he sat back in his chair.

"Y'all's momma's fine," he said, fingering the dying cigarette in the ashtray. "The baby, well, she still ain't doing too good."

He fished around in his shirt pocket, pulled out his pack of cigarettes, and made a big display of lighting the new cigarette with the one from the ashtray. He took a long deep draw and kept his focus downward as he exhaled smoke slowly through his nose.

"They fixing to send her to a hospital up near Jackson. Y'all's Momma going too. It takes hours to get from here up there."

Roy Anthony's submarine splashed heavily in the dishwater and June Bug whined in a way that sounded like something was pressing against his insides too hard.

"I'm gon' get Mr. Gamet's truck Saturday to bring y'all to the hospital with me to visiting hours here. Probably gon' be the last time we'll see y'all momma for a while. I'm sorry. I'm gon' be . . ." His voice cracked and he put his hands up to cover his face.

What had he intended to say? The boys all looked at me. We all knew better than to question Daddy.

When Daddy finally uncovered his face and looked up again, his gaze met mine. I read sadness and fear in his bloodshot eyes.

Healthy children weren't allowed inside the hospital building, so we were made to "visit" outside in the chilly November brightness of the parking lot, overlooked by the red brick hospital building and the phantom baby that had stopped being real to any of us except Momma.

When Momma strolled out of the hospital on thin bare legs, she looked like an overgrown child. Her cloth coat was wrinkled and creased in the way that comes from sleeping in your clothes. Her braided hair had a frizzy, careless look. Her knees were ashy. She stopped a few feet away from us and stood, blinking back tears. My brothers were huddled around me in unfamiliar stillness.

"Well bring y'all's little nappy heads over here and give me a hug," Momma said, opening her arms in our direction. We went to her and allowed ourselves to be enfolded in a communal hug. It felt good to lean into her thin bosom. I tried to hold on to that feeling when she released us and we clumsily fell away from her.

"I been missing y'all," she said. "Lord, I wish they had nurses to look after my baby. Then I could come home more."

I walked beside her toward the back of Mr. Gamet's truck. She took June Bug onto her lap as soon as she sat down on the tailgate. I climbed up and sat beside her, my legs dangling above the hard earth. Roy Anthony and Earl played golf in the dirt, with hard clumps of dirt as balls and sticks as clubs. Daddy leaned against the back fender of the old beat-up red Ford, looking at Momma from behind narrowed eyes.

"See, these children doing fine," he said.

"Thank the Lord," Momma said.

"And me," Daddy said.

Momma glanced up to one of the second floor windows of the hospital. "Jimmie's mama is keeping an eye on Ida Bea, till I get back. She gon' signal me when the visiting hours is over," she told us.

"Early boy, sing that song you're learning in school," Daddy said suddenly. "Sing it for your momma." He winked at Momma.

Earl stood at attention and dropped his stick. He shifted his glance shyly around the barren parking lot, then began in a choppy, high pitch. "Mine eyes have seen, the gory, in the coming of the Lord, he is stumping on the village, where the great big rafts are stored . . ."

Momma chewed a corner of her mouth to hold in her laughter as Earl continued, mangling the words of the song, hesitating, searching his memory, lurching forward into verse again. He sang earnestly, his eyes rolled skyward and his hands pressed together in front of his chest. Daddy grinned and winked at me, and I was reminded of how Daddy used to make music for Momma.

I never knew what prompted his playing, but Daddy would retrieve his silver and ebony harmonica from where he kept it wrapped in a white cotton handkerchief in a small plain wooden box in the back of his top dresser drawer. He sat in his arm chair, or took a kitchen chair onto the front porch. He pressed the harmonica against his mouth as if it were a delicious piece of fruit, and the sounds that poured out were warm and happy. Sometimes he put the harmonica away from his mouth and sang in a rich, gravel-laden voice about the "hoochie coochie man" or a "mannish boy" or "mule chickens" or "mojos" and "jellyrolls."

Momma would dance, hips swaying, fingers snapping. Sometimes she grabbed the hands of whichever of us was nearest and coaxed us into her dance. The rest of us did our own versions of her dance around the room or the front yard.

Sometimes when Daddy got out the harmonica he stood, stumping out moody tap dances as he played. When I was little, he taught me how to do some dances that made Momma smile.

Other times Daddy sat on the edge of his chair in the front room, and that metal and wood instrument cried when he brought it to his lips. It bled long, sad notes that rolled out over us like molasses. At those times, Daddy seemed to forget there was anyone in the room but him. Momma would sit on their bed leaning back against the metal headboard, her legs stretched out in front of her, her eyes closed and her face hard to read.

"My muddy, moody Gene," Momma would say to Daddy looking across at him when the music stopped and he resurfaced. "Mr. Waters got nothing on you."

Once after Daddy had made his harmonica cry so deep and

so wide I felt like my insides had melted, Momma said, "Babies, y'all's Daddy got the blues in him. Ain't it beautiful? It's what he was doing the first time I set eyes on him—bringing out the blues. Everybody in the place was weeping. My love couldn't help but run to him."

Now I couldn't see how to make moments like that for me and the boys.

As Earl kept on with his song, singing way more verses than I remembered that song having, Roy Anthony circled the truck, leaving finger marks in the dusty side panels. I could see by his bunched-up expression that he was unhappy. Occasionally he stopped his circling, out of Momma and Daddy's line of vision, and stared at Earl with an older brother's resentment.

"Good job, my boy, good job," Daddy said, grabbing Earl by the neck and tickling him when he finished singing.

"My turn," Roy Anthony shouted, running back to join us. "It's my time to sing. I know a song too."

But Daddy kept tickling and wrestling with Earl who was squealing with piggish laughter. Momma was laughing too, joy, genuine joy playing on her tired face for the first time since she came outside.

After circling the truck a few more times, Roy Anthony threw himself at Earl and Daddy, kicking and swinging with his fists. His face had taken on the gnarled, tight-lipped expression of malice. He kicked and pounded on Daddy, on Earl, making noises like a small animal, grunting and straining with each blow. Daddy pushed Earl behind him and stood still. Roy Anthony kept slamming his nine-year-old fists against Daddy's legs and stomach. Finally Daddy grabbed his arms, but Roy Anthony kept swinging. Daddy pinned him in a bear hug and leaned back, lifting Roy Anthony's feet off the ground.

"What wrong with you, boy?" Daddy demanded.

"Let me go," Roy Anthony yelled, still squirming.

"Boy, you better stop. I'll take my belt off and whip your ass right here!"

Roy Anthony went stiff in Daddy's arms.

Daddy stood him on the ground. Roy Anthony's anger was still there, visible in the stiffness of his back and the belligerent angle of his neck as he looked down at his shoes.

Daddy grabbed his thin shoulders and lifted him off the ground again. He shook him. Roy Anthony's body wriggled in the air like a cloth doll.

"Gene! Gene!" Momma jumped off the tailgate and ran toward them with June Bug in one arm and her free arm outstretched.

Daddy stopped shaking Roy Anthony and let his feet meet the ground again, but he didn't take his hands or his eyes off of him. "What's got into you, boy?" There was an easy, callous anger in Daddy voice. "The only reason I'm not whipping your ass right now is because of your momma."

Roy Anthony winced as Daddy's fingers dug into his shoulders, but he didn't speak.

"Don't you ever raise your hand to me again. You hear me, boy?" Daddy shook him again. Roy Anthony's head jerked forward, then back.

"You hear me, boy?"

"Yes sir." Roy Anthony's voice was small, but still tainted with fury.

"I brought you into this world, and I can take you out. You hear me?"

"Yes sir."

"Now get out of my sight 'cause right now just looking at you makes me mad enough to want to knock your goddamned teeth down your throat. Raising your hand to me. You got to be crazy."

Roy Anthony turned and walked away, his limbs stiff, his eyes focused on the horizon.

Daddy's capacity for violence showed itself in his straight, angry back, the veins pulsing in his neck and on his forehead, his hands gripping the air like claws at his side as he watched Roy Anthony walk toward the front of the truck.

Momma's mouth was trembling, and the fine horizontal lines between her eyes twitched as she looked at Daddy. She cut her eyes to me and held my gaze for a few seconds when she found me looking at her. There was a warning there. Then she sighed and looked away.

"Don't be too hard on him, Gene," she said when Daddy's forehead had stopped throbbing and he turned to her. "He's just a boy. He's got feelings about everything and he don't know what to do with them. But he's just a child."

"Just a boy, my ass," Daddy answered, looking toward the front of the truck. "He better not ever come at me like that again."

I heard in Daddy's voice that he could have shaken Roy Anthony until his bones began to break if Momma hadn't stopped him. I had never known him to touch one of us with that kind of anger before. I swung my legs vigorously under the tailgate, making unwanted connections between the barely contained violence I had witnessed, and my older brother whose death had somehow involved Daddy.

He turned and walked away from the truck, as if headed to the hospital, or to one of the other dusty cars waiting like blind animals in the parking lot. Momma followed him. When she got close enough, she caught his arm to make him turn to face her again. I could see only her back, but I could tell she was talking to him, low and soft, like she was trying to calm a child. She let go of his arm and he started pacing back and forth in front of her. She kept talking to him as he paced, his face pointed down, his hands in his pockets. Momma looked strong, solid, a match for Daddy and his stubborn emotions.

"Momma don't love us like she love that other baby," Roy Anthony said quietly, as we rode home from the hospital, jostling along dry bumpy roads in the back of Mr. Gamet's truck with the wind whipping up chill-bumps on our faces and pressing the smell of hay and cow manure into our clothes.

"She do too," I said, hugging June Bug against my chest.

Daddy made a sharp turn around a corner. We all leaned away from the turn, slanting like blades of grass in a breeze. Daddy drove on as if he had forgotten he had children clinging to the back of the pickup.

"Why won't she come home to be with us then?" Roy Anthony shouted, looking at me with desperation and rage.

"There ain't nobody else to take care of that other baby."

"I don't believe it. She just don't love us no more."

I thumped Roy Anthony on the head with a snap of my fingers. "That's just a taste of what you'll get if you don't shut up."

His eyes showed his fury, but he kept silent.

Momma's loving us or not loving us didn't seem to matter much just then. She had left me and the boys alone with Daddy. And it was clear now that he had become, perhaps always had been, someone who could turn mean and violent, just like Esther's mother had with her.

CHAPTER SIX

❦

I REMEMBER PATCHES OF azure sky and thin white clouds outside my sixth-grade classroom windows; pale blades of late November sunlight slanting through the bank of windows and emptying into square pools of light on the gray tile floor; the itchy tightness of my kneesocks held up with rubber bands; the pleated navy-blue skirt and white chiffon blouse with navy piping my teacher, Miss Washington, wore—the compassionate and inexperienced Miss Washington, stiff and formal with ardent boredom beneath the florid lilt of her voice as she read to us from the only up-to-date history book in the classroom in that tedious space between lunch and afternoon recess.

In the middle of our history lesson and our waiting for recess came the familiar chiming of my school's public-address system bells. As the bell tones repeated, rippling across the room, Miss Washington laid the history book flat on her desk, spread her fingers over the pages, and scanned our faces. We waited for the voice of Mr. Coleman, our principal, to make some announcement or other.

Instead of Mr. Coleman's voice, crackling, scratchy radio static poured into the room like tiny airborne needles from the big cloth-covered speaker mounted high on the wall above Miss Washington's desk. My classmates and I looked at each other in confusion.

"My fellow Americans," a radio announcer began in a voice

choked with emotion. "My fellow Americans," the voice repeated. "The president of the United States of America is dead!"

For a moment we were plunged back into the stinging static-ridden silence until the announcer's voice emerged again. "Shot in the head by a murderous assassin as he rode in a presidential motorcade through Dallas, Texas, this afternoon! Ladies and gentlemen, ladies and gentlemen, regardless of your political proclivities, this is a very sad day in the history of this great nation. Indeed in the history of the world. Every red-blooded American is stunned and being plunged into grief by this horrific murder of our leader, John Fitzgerald Kennedy, the thirty-fifth president of the United States."

The radio static resumed, and somewhere in the school building a door slammed and the sounds of an adult hurrying through the hallway echoed ominously.

"Ladies and gentlemen," the announcer called again. "Here's a portion of the tape we've just received from one of our Dallas affiliates."

Through the PA speaker my classmates and I heard the radio hiss of cheering crowds and a male radio announcer reporting the progress of the presidential motorcade through the streets of a city I had never even heard of and so could barely imagine in the confines of my Mississippi classroom. Suddenly there were popping sounds in the midst of the static and formal announcing. Then there was screaming and the noises of chaos as I imagined crowds of people running in every direction. The announcer shouted, "My God! My God! Gunfire! Ladies and gentlemen gunfire! There's chaos around the president's limousine ... ladies and gentlemen, it looks like ... it looks like ... my God, the president's been hit! We can't see the president ... my God, the president's down! The first lady ... has she been hit? What's the first lady doing? My God! ...

the secret service are rushing ... the president's car is still moving ... it's picked up speed. People going every which way, running for their lives! It's pandemonium! All hell's broken loose here!"

The sounds blew forward from the PA speaker—the hissing noise of wind slapping the microphone, the clamoring of people running, shouting, screaming, of objects hitting the pavement.

"My God. My God," the announcer yelled again. Voracious radio static chewed through and overpowered his voice. The stinging sound flew through the air like a living thing, circling and swooping overhead for a while. Then the PA speaker went silent.

My classmates and I sat in shocked silence, not so much because we understood the significance of this announcement, but because our instincts told us that solemn dignity was expected of us. We watched Miss Washington and waited for her to translate what we had just heard.

Miss Washington was an outsider, new to Elm Park Elementary, in fact, new to teaching and new to Blossom, Mississippi. She told us this on our first day of school. She had talked to us about her life as if we were grown-ups, telling us that she was unmarried and had just graduated from an all-Negro college in North Carolina. "I must tell you all," she had announced, "just a few days ago I had a profound experience. I marched in Washington, DC, with half a million people, Negros and whites alike, to hear one of the greatest Negro leaders this country has ever seen, Dr. Martin Luther King, Jr. Before the year is over, I'll teach you all about him and his work for Negro equality."

Usually Miss Washington was serene and regal, like one of the ladies in Momma's issues of *Ebony* magazine—the ones who belonged to the class of American Negros who held debutante balls and wore fur stoles to charity events for the less fortunate. She looked elegant and modern with her straightened jet-black hair teased into a stylish bouffant, her pale-blue eye shadow, smooth red lipstick, and matching fingernail polish. She usually moved about inside a cloud of soft floral perfume and cheerful solicitude.

Now she sat staring over our heads at the wall behind us. The rosy blush drained from her ginger-brown skin. She shook her head and blinked rapidly before closing her eyes. Her tears came suddenly, impossibly from beneath her blue eyelids, sliding down her face and onto the pages of the book in front of her.

My classmates remained shrouded in silence, staring at Miss Washington. In a few minutes, the silence in the classroom thinned and some of my classmates started to cry, silvery tears streaked shiny brown faces and low sobbing and sniffling swept through the room. I felt a swell of emotion rising and pressing at the back of my throat, but it stayed there curled in a knot.

Miss Washington retrieved a handkerchief from her desk drawer and wiped her face. "You may not know it," she began, "but President Kennedy was the first president in over a hundred years that cared anything at all about America's Negroes. He was passing laws to make this country into a place where we could hold our heads up and walk the streets with dignity. Trying to get us an equal chance with white people."

She fell silent except for the odd snuffling sounds in her throat.

"Now they've murdered him." Her words rushed at us when she regained control. "White people truly hate the Negro. For no good reason other than our dark skin. If you didn't know it before, you sure should know it now. They'd rather kill the president, one of their own, than let you have what all white children in America have. A chance at a decent life. That shows some very deep hatred!"

She drifted back into tears. My heart beat in my ears. Anxiety mingled with shame. I was ashamed to belong to a group that had attracted the "deep hatred" of a whole country. I looked around at my classmates. Some nasty emotion hung in the room, thick and palpable like a wool cloud. I felt stripped and raw, naked in a world where everything was prickly and mean.

Until that moment, I had been insulated from the hatred of the wider world, living in my black community where our schools and even our churches were filled with faces that looked like mine. And as far as I could tell, life on my side of town was full and complete. Everywhere I went, I saw people who looked like me in all walks of life, from our Negro doctor and dentist to the principals and teachers in our schools to the preachers in our churches to the hairdressers, the funeral parlor owners, the taxicab drivers, the toothless and jobless old men playing dominoes outside the Sugar Shack Café when the weather was warm. I'd had very few occasions to interact with white people other than the handful of shopkeepers who ran businesses on our side of town—a small grocery store, a dry cleaner's, a gas station, a bait and tackle shop, a salvage clothing store—and those whites treated us the same way that black shopkeepers did, with solicitous humor and service when we had the money to pay and stern suspicion when we didn't.

Even during town-wide events, I had little chance to be in community with whites. Every year when the state fair came to the fairgrounds in the fall, there were separate days set aside for whites and blacks to attend. When Blossom held its annual Thanksgiving Parade, blacks stood in one section of downtown and whites stood in another to watch it meander by. The white and black spectators were not even visible to each other. Yes, I had gone downtown with my Brownie Scout troop to the Strand movie theater to see a double feature when I was in third grade, and we had followed the COLOREDS ONLY signs around to the back of the building, up some stairs, and into the balcony. The movies had so captured my imagination that I found nothing odd about the white folks milling about below us before the movie started. In fact, upstairs seemed like the best place to be, especially when I noted some teenage boys throwing popcorn and ice from their soda cups over the balcony railing.

I hadn't thought that those WHITES ONLY and COLOREDS ONLY signs pointed toward deep hatred. They had been to me like the signs on the bathroom doors at church, GENTS and LADIES, or the ones up the hall from my classroom marked BOYS and GIRLS. They made sense.

Momma had gone out of her way to make my brother and me believe that skin color did not define a person, in spite of the segregation in Blossom. Once Momma ventured downtown with me and Roy Anthony in tow to buy us shoes and a few clothing items for school. As we were walking along the sidewalk a white man stepped out of one of the stores and started coming toward us on the sidewalk. Before he reached us, he grimaced and stepped into the street; when he came alongside us, he turned and spit on the sidewalk in our direction.

"Damn fool," Momma said, not turning to look at him. "Just don't even study that. There are a few no-count ignorant people in the world. Don't y'all ever pay them no mind. Anybody that don't even know you and would do something like that because of the way you look? That's a fool that ain't worth the air he breathe. You much better off not knowing him and keeping clear out of his way. Thank the Lord that you don't have to deal with those kind of people every day. It ain't a person's skin color that make them better or worse than you. Somebody might someday say to you that whites is better than Negros, but don't you for a minute believe it. It's what's inside that matters. And what's inside that man that just walked by? It's so ugly it'd make God cry. You are much better than somebody like that."

She had marched us on toward Brown's Shoe Store. I noted her straight back and raised chin, her air of authority as she met eye-to-eye with the white salesclerks. Afterward, she led us through the aisles of Jones County General Dry Goods Store and through a door at the back that opened out into a small diner-style café filled with tables covered with red-and-white checkered oilcloth and populated by black folk laughing and talking over plates of fried foods. After Roy Anthony and I finished the fried fish and okra she had ordered for us, she headed us back to Woolworth, past the dining counter with its prominently displayed WHITES ONLY signs. She made us stop near the counter. She kneeled in front of us, taking her time to straighten an item of clothing on each of us, then saying quietly, "The food they serve here ain't nearly as good as what you just ate. You ain't missing nothing because of the sign over yonder. Remember that. You ain't missing a thing."

She stood suddenly. "The only thing worth eating in this place is the fudge, and you don't need to sit down for that."

She led us to the glass candy counter and bought a batch of chocolate fudge, and we headed home.

I'd never had much reason to think about the separation of blacks and whites all over America. I had always supposed a friendlier America outside in the places where slavery had not put down roots. With Miss Washington's explanation about the reason for the president's murder, the WHITES ONLY signs suddenly seemed more sinister and hateful, not just a simple fact of life in my little Mississippi town.

I thought about Momma with my baby sister in the colored

ward of the charity hospital. I remembered Momma smiling and waving to us from the hospital doorway with COLORED ONLY above it. It was clear now that "deep hatred" was the reason there weren't nurses to take care of the sick black children so Momma could come home. The kind of hatred Miss Washington had described would let black children die.

"Now," Miss Washington said, studying our expectant faces again, "as Negroes, we can't even be sure where our next meal will come from. Or even if we'll be allowed to go on living in this country!"

She lapsed into a fit of sobbing and nose-blowing.

What did the president of the United States have to do with my meals? As far as I was concerned, the president was just a picture of a smiling, pink, well-fed face in one of the current affairs magazines on the counter at the back of our classroom. He belonged to that vast unknown world outside my community. What did he have to do with me?

I looked around the room at my crying and scared classmates. The only other person besides me who wasn't in tears was Percy Blakely. He stared soberly ahead at Miss Washington, stiff-backed and defiant in some unexpected way, just like Esther had been when she proclaimed her mother's love.

Percy studied Miss Washington as if waiting for something else—some tangible thing that she had failed to give him. I looked at his profile, his small high-placed ears, thick lips like little Tootsie Rolls, his flat nose.

Percy wasn't a regular at school. It was a wonder that he got promoted every year, but he did. Momma had known enough about his circumstances to shake her head when I complained about him always borrowing school supplies. "Now there is a child to feel sorry for," she said. "Don't be mean to him, Maddy.

The boy can't help who he is." Then she fixed me with a moist-eyed look that showed me the deep sorrow I would bring to her if I turned out to be somebody lacking compassion. She set her jaw to brace against this future heartbreak, then spoke through clenched teeth. "By the grace of God, your life ain't his."

Even after Momma's warning, I still disliked Percy as much as the other kids did, and for the same reason. In second grade he was caught passing a note to Florence Simms. Our teacher that year, a stout raisin-colored woman with swollen tadpole eyes, had made him stand in front of the class and read it aloud over and over. "I love your little rubber butt . . . I love your little rubber butt . . . I love your little rubber butt," he recited, holding the crumpled piece of paper so close to his face that it touched his nose.

At first the rest of us giggled, believing ourselves removed from his obscenity and humiliation. But after he had repeated the ridiculous words enough times to tattoo them into our brains, we understood that we were all being punished. A tremble crept into Percy's voice and our giggles dried up. Those of us in the safety of our seats slyly cut our eyes at each other. I felt what I imagine all of my classmates felt without really knowing what it was, an undercurrent of shame.

Tears were streaming down Percy's cheeks, snot was collecting in the crease above his lips, and his words were no longer intelligible by the time the teacher told him to stop reading. Florence, regal and dark, sat like an offended princess with her head turned toward the windows, crying quietly.

"Whatever made you think that a young lady like Florence would want to get a message like that from a dirty little nigger like you?" the teacher asked.

Florence's daddy was the only black dentist in town. I knew this, and I understood the full weight of our teacher's insult. It had nothing to do with skin color because Florence was darker than Percy, and I had heard often enough from my mother, "Niggers come in all colors. It's the behavior that's telling."

"Tell the class you're a sorry excuse for a human being and you'll never waste anyone's time again," the teacher demanded of Percy.

He repeated with coaching from our teacher. She made him say it several times, then she gingerly slapped him on the cheeks with a wooden ruler.

"Don't ever let me catch you writing anything like that again. You don't even know what love is. You filthy little animal. Lord help me, I'm here to tame you. That goes for all of you. You're a bunch of animals. My job is to civilize you, and so help me God, I aim to succeed."

Percy became our scapegoat. We targeted him for whatever acts of cruelty we could get away with. We had made him be "it" and chase us around the playground in games of tag until he developed nosebleeds; we had teased him for not bringing a lunch, then offered him our leftovers and made fun of him when he ate them; and we challenged him to all kinds of impossible feats and berated him for his failures.

Miss Washington had been trying to change all of that. She was attentive to him in class, calling on him, praising even his small efforts. She was vigilant in the schoolyard at recess, making the other sixth-grade boys include him in their games, then stopping the games when they got too rough with him. She had even managed to get him free lunches in the cafeteria so that he no longer sat slyly eyeing the rest of us as we ate, waiting for our leftovers.

Now he was wild-eyed and alert, studying Miss Washington as she trembled and shook with emotion. No president's assassination, no teacher's grief, not even the threat of a hungry future full of hatred had touched him.

At last came the chiming of the school's public-address system, bleeding into the room again. This time the voice of our principal came on to offer a prayer for the "continued stability of our great nation" and to announce that Elm Park Elementary would close early for the day.

As I headed out of the schoolyard toward home with my brothers trailing behind me, Percy was a few paces in front of us. He walked slowly, as he always did, his gaze trained on the ground. I strode quickly to catch up with him.

"What do you think about them killing the president?" I ventured.

He cast a sideways glance in my direction and shrugged.

"Don't you care about it?"

This time he looked directly at me. His question, *Why are you talking to me?*, was readable in his eyes. This was probably the first time in all of our years of sitting near each other in the same classrooms and walking the same way home that I had started a conversation with him that wasn't required of me by a teacher.

He kept walking as he stared at my face. I tried to keep my expression steady.

"Don't mean nothing to me," he said finally.

"You heard what Miss Washington said. About our next meals."

"I don't see how that could be so. President don't live here."

"The president decides things for everybody."

"It's the white folks and the grown-ups in our town decides things for us."

"What you mean?"

"They decide where we can go to and not go to. White folks put those signs up, and our grown folks make us pay attention to them."

"But the president tells the white folks what to do?"

"Maybe, but I don't think so. Miss Washington said he was telling the white folks to treat us better. He was making new laws, but nothing was getting better here."

"So see, Miss Washington's right. They killed him so they wouldn't have to listen."

He stopped walking and turned to face me. "How come she didn't just say it like that?"

It was my turn to shrug.

"You been knowing me a long time," Percy said. "I don't see my life changing because of no president. My life's going to go like it's been. The president got nothing to do with what I eat, except maybe the school lunches. I lived without that before. I'll do okay if they take that away again. The only thing that's gon' change my life is when I get grown and I can do everything for myself."

I had been wrong. Percy wasn't like Esther. Nothing stopped him from saying the truth, even when it was something I could use to make fun of him later. As we stood there on the edge of road, building a flimsy bridge that might have led to friendship, a woman came out onto her front porch. She wiped her hands on her apron as she hollered across her barren yard to us.

"Y'all children go on home and go indoors. It ain't a good day for y'all to be hanging about in the road. They killed President Kennedy. No telling what these people might do next. Y'all need to be indoors. So go on home. Bad things liable to happen around here today."

CHAPTER SEVEN

"YOU OLD ENOUGH to know there ain't no Santa Claus."

Daddy's words were like a dodgeball to the belly. I tightened my guts against this assault. Of course I didn't already *know* there wasn't a Santa Claus.

"Your brothers, well," Daddy mumbled, fingering the frayed fabric on the arm of the overstuffed chair where he sat.

He had called me into his and Momma's room, away from my sleeping brothers. I didn't know what to expect, but whatever I expected, this wasn't it.

He cleared his throat. "Your brothers they still little kids—still need to believe things like Santa Claus. You big now, Maddy. I need you to help me get stuff for them. We'll get you something too, and say Santa brought it. Whatever you want."

What I wanted was the same Christmas I'd always had.

Every year as far back as my memory reached, my brothers and I had gone downtown with Momma and some other black families from my neighborhood to watch the Thanksgiving Parade and talk to Santa Claus. We stood in the crystalline November sunshine on the part of the parade route designated for black folks. I stretched my attention past the high school marching bands, the floats covered with tissue-paper roses, the Knights of Columbus in their convertibles and funny-looking hats, the clowns flinging candy into the crowd. I was waiting for Santa Claus, who always brought up the rear. His cheerful pink face smiling and waving from his "sled," a different one every year—a small white airplane with a red nose and red wings one year; a school bus painted like a peppermint stick another year; a brilliant red fire engine decorated with a big green ribbon and bow.

When the parade reached its destination, a shopping center anchored by a Sears and Roebuck department store on one end and A&P supermarket on the other, the kids lined up to go for rides with Santa, black kids near the A&P, white kids near Sears. We went, in segregated groups of five or six, onto Santa's sled, which churned around the outskirts of the shopping center and through the downtown streets decked in their holiday glitz.

During the ride, each of us got to sit on Santa's lap. I would sit for my allotted minutes in Santa's fuzzy red-and-white embrace and lean in as close to his ear as I dared to confide my wish list. On Christmas morning I found at least one of the things from my list—a pair of white Dale Evans cowgirl boots and a set of pearl-handled cap guns, or a hard-plastic brown-skinned doll that stood almost as tall as me.

This year, with Momma still away at the hospital with Ida Bea, we did not go to see the parade or Santa. But I had written my wish list and dropped it in the big red-and-white striped box Principal Coleman had fixed to look like an old-fashioned mailbox and placed in the hallway outside his office. The sign attached to it read THE NORTH POLE. At the top of my list was for Momma and Ida Bea to come home.

Daddy had just destroyed my hope. I may well have been old enough to know, and maybe I should have known, and maybe on some level I did know. But that night it felt unfair.

Tears stung my eyes and my throat constricted. Why was Daddy so bent on making me unhappy?

His mouth was set with a pursed-lip plea. The rest of his face was drawn and tired. His long legs were stretched out in front of him as he kept picking at the threadbare chair arm. He looked like a big version of Roy Anthony, helpless.

"Can you help me with this, Maddy Girl? I got no idea what to get everybody. It's y'all momma who kept track of that. Even though she all the way in Jackson and y'all ain't gon' get to see her, I still want y'all to have a good Christmas."

He wasn't thinking about me or the boys. He was thinking about Momma, trying to do what she would've done. I felt sorry for him, but I also felt slow-growing anger. The feeling curled inside, whipping around like a lizard's tail.

"I wish I was—," Daddy started. "Your brothers so little they need—"

He drew his legs in, leaned forward, and put his elbows on his knees. "I just wish—goddammit. I don't want y'all suffering 'cause of me."

My anger fell in on itself and burned quietly. He was right about the boys. They were too little to be dropped into this grown-up world where he was in charge of us. I promised Momma I'd take care of them. Wasn't giving them a happy Christmas part of taking care of them? It's what Momma always did. I resented that Daddy couldn't give us that. "Bikes," I told him. "They want bikes." That had been Roy Anthony's wish. I had no idea what Earl or June Bug wanted.

I wanted Momma to come home.

I awoke from a dream where I had been handed a piece of ham on a small green plate. I sat up in bed, shivering with the cramping pains in my empty stomach. Two weeks had passed since

Daddy told me about Santa and talked about wanting us to have a good Christmas without Momma. But he hadn't said a word to me about Christmas since. Not only was it looking like we would have a bad Christmas, it seemed possible that Daddy had abandoned us. We hadn't seen him in three days. He usually came home on his payday, Friday, with bags of groceries for the week, but this time he didn't show. By Saturday afternoon we had eaten the last can of pork and beans from the cabinet. By Sunday night even the ketchup bottle and the mayonnaise jar in the icebox were empty. We had eaten their contents by the spoonful.

We couldn't even go next door to Ma Parker for food. She was up in Meridian, visiting Esther and her Aunt Helen. She wouldn't be back until after Christmas, she'd said. I didn't feel right asking to "borrow" food from any of the other folks farther in the Quarters. So we had gone to bed hungry. We were piled in Momma and Daddy's bed. The boys were sleeping fitfully, but they were sleeping.

I crawled out of bed and went to check the kitchen again. The cabinet doors hung open revealing the same inedible kitchen flotsam that had been there earlier—dishes, a box of plastic straws, a bottle of vinegar, a box of matches, and a box of salt. I tried the vinegar. The pain in my belly intensified. Frustration and anger welled up more grinding than the hunger. I slumped onto the kitchen floor with my back against the counter and cried angry tears that seemed to scald my throat and my cheeks.

My brothers and I could starve to death and no one would know for a long time. I pictured us posed serenely in our beds as if asleep. It would serve Momma and Daddy right to find us dead. But the gurgling and tearing pain in my stomach told me there would be nothing peaceful about starving to death.

What was wrong with Daddy? Why couldn't he do what he

was supposed to? Fathers were supposed to feed their children. It was love that made them do it. "Love takes care of its own," Momma had said when I asked her about love. "Your Daddy works a job he don't like to put food on the table and a roof over our heads," she had said. But she and Daddy weren't taking care of their own anymore. Was Roy Anthony right—had they stopped loving us? What had we done to turn them both away?

Rage was billowing out in me like a sheet in the wind. It wasn't us, it was them. I had the sudden urge to ransack the kitchen—turn over the table, throw dishes against the walls, put my fists through the glass windows. I wanted to be an evil creature with angry scaly limbs, a dragon with fire rushing from its nose. I would tear everything to pieces and what I couldn't tear, I would burn, reduce it all to hard, black charcoal. That story grew in me until I could feel the fire burning in my throat and I was choking on the smoke. The size and shape of my fury stopped my tears. I sat in silence for a while, my knees drawn up to my chin, staring at the floor.

Then I had an idea that sparkled like a star. I would go look for Daddy.

I would start with the bootleg whiskey joints in the Quarters. I imagined the joints, hulking dark shapes in the barren landscape of winter, their insides alive with laughing adults with their endless supply of "water" and the loud, happy music Esther and I had coveted in the heat of summer. Daddy would be in one of those houses. I would find him and bring him home, or, at the very least, get money for food. He must have lost track of the days. I would remind him. There are children you got to feed.

I put on my coat and crept out the back door into the cold December night. There were boogeymen and wild animals in the night. I remembered this as I went down the steps and into the moonlit night. Evil would be waiting for a girl like me who was made stupid and careless by hunger and rage. I stopped in the middle of the road in the safety of my mulberry tree's moon-shadow to listen for signs of wildness and danger.

The lacy black silhouette of the bare mulberry tree lay against the smooth surface of the night sky, seductive and mysterious in the still cold air. My breath floated before me in silent, wispy clouds. Hanging above my tree was the polished-silver moon, and beyond that, tiny points of light winked at me from the dark night sky.

My breathing and the light scuffle of my shoes on the gravel road were the only sounds as I turned toward the heart of the Quarters. Ma Parker's house was dark and quiet as I passed by, wishing for the hundredth time this weekend that she were home. It would have been so easy to knock on her door and ask for food.

The houses were like big sleeping animals, the shiny glass of their front windows like closed eyelids. The woods on the other side of the road loomed like a dense gray wall. Anything could be in there. I kept to the middle of the road listening, reminding myself why I had come out here. As I walked through the silvery shadow of house number 5, I looked back and I could no longer see my house. Would the boys be okay? The sharp edge was fading from my anger, and my resolve was thinning as I thought about the distance between me and the safety of home. I had no idea how far I would have to walk to find the first whiskey joint. Esther and I never followed the road. We always meandered through the woods to come out at different places. I couldn't even remember the numbers on the whiskey houses, though I was sure I would recognize them easily. They would be booming with music and light.

The noise of rustling shrubbery reached me from the woods,

and I stopped. The sound continued like something was moving steadily through undergrowth. Before I could decide what to do, an animal trotted onto the road about fifteen feet in front of me. It froze and turned a small pointed face in my direction. Its eyes flashed gray in the moonlight, and it lifted its long, bushy tail slightly. My heart quickened. Was it the pet monkey Esther and I had seen in the summer? Monkeys walked on two legs like people, didn't they? This animal was on all fours, though it wasn't a dog. It angled its whole body toward me, and I could see more clearly the thinness of its legs and a swath of white around its mouth. Fox, I thought, and tried to remember what I was supposed to do—run, don't run. It took a step in my direction. I started backing up, afraid to take my eyes off of it. It tilted its head, first to one side, then to the other. What would I do if it ran toward me? It turned and sprinted across the road in the direction it had been heading, then disappeared into a field of tall dried weeds between two houses. I turned toward home and ran.

I wasn't as brave as I thought.

I was crying by the time I got to my mulberry tree. I climbed up, soothed by the familiar notches and bumps of the bark in my cold hands as I made my way to the first branch where I could sit. When I caught my breath the world seemed cautiously peaceful. Leaning back, my legs straddling the heavy branch and my head resting against the trunk, I studied the sky. Everything up there was still so orderly, even beautiful, while my empty stomach ached and my brothers were no doubt having hunger dreams. Why was it like this? The dark sky gave no answers, but it beckoned, pulling my attention away from my stomach. Something was out there, between the stars, in the calm of the empty space, a power that was soothing, sweet, and satisfying. I looked from one edge of the starry horizon to the other, and the stars sparkled through the tears caught in my eyelashes. One star winked more brilliantly than the others. Staring at it, I thought of the Star of Bethlehem and the story of the baby Jesus being born in the place where the animals slept. Children aren't supposed to be hungry. I squinted at the stars, waiting. The sense of sweetness and peace remained in the air. I looked at the neighborhood below. The houses along my stretch of the Quarters squatted like dormant animals. It was down there among those stark shapes that I had to figure out how to survive.

I was about to climb down when I heard boots scuffling along the dry gravel and dirt of the road. I watched as a large, oddly shaped figure shuffled along from the interior of the Quarters. The boogeyman I had feared. The figure wavered, stumbled backward, then lurched forward, staggering from one side of the road to the other. It was making grunting sounds that followed some sort of rhythm. As it got closer I could see that it was carrying something over its shoulders, and the grunting noises were separating themselves out into words. It was singing "Jingle Bells." The elation of embarrassed joy crowded out the hunger in the pit of my stomach. It was Daddy.

I wanted to run to him and hug him, but I also wanted to pelt him with rocks. I stayed still as he passed under my tree. He stomped onto the porch, and the singing stopped. He groped around in the darkness for the door handle.

I climbed down from the tree and ran to the back of the house. I came into the kitchen just as he came into our bedroom. He had not noticed the sleeping boys in his and momma's bed when he walked through the front room.

He stood in the middle of our room swaying back and forth, his hand on the light string. Dried mud covered the tops of his shoes and was smeared along the front of his pants legs and the hem of his unbuttoned coat. His shirt was open at the neck and only partially tucked into his pants. Blood was caked in one corner of his mouth. Some had dripped and left dark stains on the collar of his shirt. He reeked of urine, cigarette smoke, and whiskey. Behind him, in the front room, the boys were stirring. He turned and went back into the front room. I followed him.

"Oh, there y'all is. What you doing up in here?" He looked at the boys with his dull bloodshot eyes. They were stretching and squirming and wiping their faces, startled and blurry with sleep.

"Come see what I got y'all." He grinned at us.

Roy Anthony and Earl crawled out of bed. June Bug started to cry, and I went and picked him up. "Is it Christmas?" Earl asked, bewildered as he looked at me. Daddy had gone out onto the front porch and was backing into the house, pulling something through the doorway.

"Not yet," I answered.

"Well now, looky here," Daddy said, turning to face us as he pulled a lopsided tree upright and leaned it against the wall in the corner behind the door.

We all stared with disappointment at the scraggly, drying pine.

"Ain't it just about the most beautiful tree y'all ever seen?"

In previous years, Daddy used to borrow a truck a few weeks before Christmas and take us kids out into the country. He would park along some dusty stretch of road and we would all pile out and trudge over orange and gray dirt, through the chilly underbrush with dried pine needles and other decaying vegetation crunching underfoot. We roamed the woods, chasing after Daddy who had a long-handled axe slung over his shoulder. With glee and giddiness we examined and rejected baby pines, lopsided pines, scraggly pines, until we found just the right one. Daddy would chop it down and we would haul it back into town. When we got home, Mama would have the box of decorations out. We would decorate the tree and sing Christmas carols. It was official then. Santa would have to come. We had a tree.

Now, in the harsh cold air of my first Christmas without Momma or Santa Claus, it was impossible to be grateful for this tree that Daddy had dragged in by himself.

"Maddy, you know where your momma keeps the decorations?"

Roy Anthony and Earl looked at me. They had been sleeping in their clothes and they were wrinkled and disheveled. The crustiness of sleep stuck in the corners of their eyes and mouths. June Bug clung to me, his face buried against my neck, his breathing slow and rhythmic. He had drifted back to sleep. I looked at the clock on Momma's dresser. I wound it meticulously every day, its ticking like Momma's heartbeat.

It was after 2 a.m.

"Did you bring us some food?" Roy Anthony asked.

Daddy's jaw slackened, his eyes glazed over.

"We hungry," Earl said.

"I brought food the other day," Daddy answered, frustration creeping into his voice. "Don't tell me y'all done ate it all?"

The boys all turned and looked at me. I looked at the floor.

"This time I brought a tree." Daddy hollered. "Let's decorate it."

A hungry groan seeped out of Earl and he started to cry.

"Daddy it's kind of late. Can we do it tomorrow?" I ventured.

"It ain't too late." His voice had that dangerous whiskey-sharpened edge. "Y'all been sleeping . . . y'all ought to be rested. I'm the one that should be tired. I done gone through all the trouble to drag this damned tree up in here. Every Tom, Dick and Harry was fussing at me 'bout my children and Christmas. So I found a tree and I brung it here. Now show a little 'preciation."

He went to the tree and tilted it away from the wall. "See how pretty it is? Roy go git me a bucket so I can set it up. Maddy, go find them decorations."

Inertia had set in for me and I could see confusion on Roy Anthony's face. He didn't function well hungry and sleepy, none of us did. He stared at Daddy with his mouth hanging open.

"What's the matter with y'all? Standing round looking at me like a bunch of little wild animals. Do I need to knock you upside your heads? Maddy, put that boy down, he's big enough to stand up by hisself. And go git the goddamned decorations. Roy git your ass out there on the porch and bring me a bucket. Now!"

"Go git a bucket," I hissed at Roy Anthony after I put June Bug on the bed. June Bug whined but curled himself into a ball to drift back into sleep. Roy Anthony just stared at me, tears welling in his eyes.

"What bucket?" he whined.

"Just go," I ordered, pushing his shoulder.

"Where the bucket at?" Roy Anthony cried, lifting his bare feet up and down like he was trying to figure out how to use them. "I don't know where no bucket at," he cried.

If the bucket had been in his hands he wouldn't have known where it was. I felt sorry for him, and scared. Daddy grabbed his shoulders and twirled him around. "The bucket better be out yonder. On the back porch. And you better git on out there and git it."

He hit Roy Anthony on the back with his open hand. Roy Anthony stumbled a few steps and pitched forward onto his stomach. There was a moment of stunned silence as if the wind had been knocked out of him. Then he let out a shrill cry that made June Bug sit up on the bed. Daddy stood over Roy Anthony looking surprised but remorseless. "I ain't got time for your games, boy. Git up off that floor before I hit you again." Anger played across his face. Roy Anthony curled into a fetal position and locked his hands behind his head, whimpering.

When Daddy started to move closer to Roy Anthony, I ran between them. Daddy's whiskey-tainted breath grazed the back of my head and his anger radiated hotly, making me aware that nothing stood between me and the violence I had seen in him in the hospital parking lot. I felt a confused tingle along my spine as I stayed the impulse to turn around and face him. I couldn't believe that he would hit both of us. I squatted beside Roy Anthony and tried to pull him to his feet, but he stiffened and held himself tighter. "Get up, I'll show you where the bucket is," I whispered frantically. Still he wouldn't move, so I pulled him, sliding him along the splintery floor, afraid to look up at Daddy. My knees began to shake and my fingers felt like they would give way. Roy Anthony kept still at first and let me drag him along, then in his confusion he started struggling against me.

"What's the matter with the little motherfucker?" Daddy asked.

"Nothing," I mumbled, my own furious tears flowing now as I dragged Roy Anthony into the other room, through the kitchen, and onto the back porch.

"Why do you have to do stuff to make him mad?" I demanded once we were outside.

Roy Anthony got up and pushed me so hard I stumbled backward and almost fell off the porch. "Leave me alone," he moaned. Tears and snot ran in slimy rivers onto his chin and down his neck.

I grabbed his shirt. I was still at least a head taller than him. "Why can't you for once act like you got sense?" I wanted to pummel him with my fists, to beat some sense into him. Why couldn't he see where the real danger was?

He stood before me in the silvery darkness with his arms held stiffly at his side. "I don't know . . ."

"You better wise up."

Grabbing his skinny shoulders, I tried to shake him for emphasis, but he wrenched himself free from my grasp. "Do you hear me? You a damn fool. Daddy's going to hurt you if you keep it up. He going to beat the living shit out of you. Don't you get it? He don't love us neither. Nobody loves us!"

Roy Anthony looked at me with big startled eyes. "You said it first," I hissed. "You said it first and now it's the truth."

"I didn't do it," he whined back. "Leave me alone."

"Well Daddy's going to beat the shit out of you if you don't do what he tells you."

I was surprised at myself, my cussing and my anger at Roy Anthony.

"I don't care," Roy Anthony said. "I ain't done nothing."

He folded his arms over his chest. At first he looked defiant, then he simply looked lost, the way I felt.

In the end, Roy Anthony, Earl, and I solemnly hung decorations on the tree while Daddy sat on the edge of his bed watching us, his shoulders hunched and his neck arched like a predator. He flopped back onto the bed and began snoring loudly before we were even finished.

After we had all gone to our own beds and the boys had somehow managed to drift back into sleep, I sneaked back into Daddy's room. He lay on his back, still wearing all of his clothes and his muddy shoes. His face looked peaceful, his mouth slack and open like one of his sleeping sons. I sat in the stuffed chair and watched him for a long time, afraid to do what I had decided to do, but the rumbling in my empty stomach had become a vulgar voice telling me to do what needed to be done.

I sat carefully on the edge of the bed and waited, my heart beating wildly. Even if I were caught, I told myself, the punishment couldn't be any worse than this weakness and pain I was already enduring. I reached into one of Daddy's pockets and pulled out the contents. I rummaged through cigarette papers and tobacco crumbs. I examined another pocket—pocket knife, old silver lighter, small plastic comb, crumpled receipts, and dirty lint. I nudged him until he rolled onto his side so I could slide my fingers into his back pockets. From one pocket I pulled out folded receipts, a claim ticket for dry cleaning, and four one-dollar bills, a ten, and a five. I took the ten and two of the ones and went and hid them at the bottom of the dirty clothes box in the bathroom on the back porch.

Then I went back to my bed and lay staring out the window, praying and waiting for sunlight. I hoped that when he woke up he wouldn't remember how much money he'd had. For once I wanted him gone. I wanted him to take his brutality and his lack of love for us and return to his haunts so I would not have to worry about anybody's safety, and I could go to the grocery store.

CHAPTER EIGHT

♥

THE SOUND OF DADDY's unmistakable clamor on the front porch signaled the arrival of Christmas day. Moody daylight hung pale and unpromising outside the window. I was sprawled in the stuffed chair in my parents' room. I had stationed myself there, keeping vigil, waiting for Daddy to bring the toys home on Christmas Eve as he had promised. I glanced at the desolate corner of the room where the tree had been standing for more than a week. Rust-colored pine-needles were the only things on the floor beneath it.

Daddy pushed through the front door and stopped, looking boyish and embarrassed when he saw me in the chair.

"Where the toys at, Daddy?"

"Well, we need to go git them."

"But the boys will be woke soon."

"That's okay 'cause they need to come with us to get them."

"Daddy?" I wanted to say *Can't you even get a simple thing right?*

"I found out about a place where we can go and they'll feed us a big Christmas meal and they have toys for all the children," he said, looking at me like I had the power to say no to this idea. Surprisingly, he was sober.

"Daddy . . ."

"I'm doing the best I can for y'all. I brought you a dress."

He threw one of the brown paper bags he was carrying on

the floor at my feet. "I got some clothes for the boys too. I didn't know y'all's sizes so I don't know if this stuff will fit y'all or not."

From the bag he had given me, I pulled a short-sleeved pink cotton dress that had a narrow bodice and a gathered skirt. The dress had a pink-and-white striped sash that tied in back. The cloth was worn, frayed at the hem like it had been washed many times on a scrub-board. Still it was pretty, the sort of thing I would have been proud to wear at Easter. Daddy was grinning from ear to ear when I looked up.

"I knew you would like it," he said. "The white lady, Mrs. Dereemer, out at the chicken farm was throwing it away. Used to belong to her girl who's all grown up now. Asked me if I knew anybody could fit it. 'Sure do,' I told her. And I snatched it right up. She said she's got more stuff and she'll give it to me next week."

I caressed the pink wash-softened fabric of the dress with my palms, thinking to feel something of that other world where it had come from—a place with a mother and father and food and Santa Clause and toys.

"Well, what you got to say?" Daddy asked.

"Thank you, Daddy," I said.

He took some more clothes from the other bag—three pairs of pants that I could tell would be too big for all of the boys and three small long-sleeved shirts, all white. "The Dereemers had a boy too, though he's all grown too now, just like the girl. He lives up in Jackson now. And the girl's married and living up in Jackson too. Mrs. Dereemer hunted among they old clothes in the attic and found these when I told her I had some boys too."

He laid the clothes on the bed as if they were breakable treasures. "I hope you appreciate what I do for y'all."

When he looked at me, I could see fear in his eyes. But he winked and turned away. "Now, let's get this show on the road," he said.

He went to the kitchen to get the ironing board and Momma's heavy electric iron. "Wake up, sleepy heads," he called at the boys as he passed back through the middle room.

The boys got up and followed him into the front room, all bleary eyes and expectations. They looked at our childishly decorated tree and the empty space beneath it, then turned to me with disbelief and disappointment that was as solid as the frozen mud in the bottom of the drainage ditch outside.

"Santa didn't come yet," I said, my voice small with deceit. "He left our stuff somewhere else and we got to go get it."

"What y'all looking so sad for? There'll be toys enough for everybody," Daddy said, coming back from the kitchen. "We just need to get cleaned up and go get them."

There was a hint of shame in my father's voice.

"Hand me them clothes, Maddy, so I can iron them. And y'all better put on some happy faces or Santa's going to take all his toys back to the North Pole."

We piled out of the taxi in front of a one-story white clapboard building with a high pitched roof. The letters v.f.w. were painted in hard black letters inside a bronze circle with two American flags angled above the door. The building sat in the middle of a denuded patch of frozen countryside. A number of ragged, dusty cars sat in a parking area that fanned out to one side of the building. Beyond the building, loblolly pines and other evergreens huddled in the still, cold, blue air. Sleet had fallen in recent hours, or perhaps it had rained lightly and had frozen before the winter soil could drink it, because there was a thin, white film of ice on the ground in the shade of some of the trees.

My brothers stared squinty-eyed and gaping at the seal above the doorway. "What V. F. W. stand for?" Roy Anthony wanted to know.

"Veterans of Foreign Wars," Daddy answered.

"What is a veteran?" Earl asked.

"A man who use to be a soldier."

"What does foreign war mean?" Roy Anthony wanted to know.

"Veterans of foreign wars is soldiers who fought in wars overseas."

Daddy stood with his hands on his hips, his heavy gray flannel suit jacket pulled back at the waist.

"How come *we* going in here, Daddy?" Roy Anthony pressed.

"'Cause I'm a veteran of a foreign war, boy—damned if I ain't a veteran of a foreign war." Daddy's voice had an edge of disbelief. "The government tells Santa to leave toys here for children like y'all. And they make sure there's a Christmas meal for all veterans that wants to come and bring they families."

"Why we never come here before, Daddy?" Roy Anthony asked.

"Ain't never needed to."

"Why we need to now?"

"Boy, quit asking so many question and let's just go on inside," Daddy said, and turned toward the building.

I studied the boys and Daddy, trying to find cause for pride, or shame, as they moved ahead of me toward the building. Daddy had fluid, unexpected grace, his back straight, his chin high, striding forward in the dark gray dress slacks that he had ironed creases into, his dark gray flannel suit jacket, a starched white shirt, a narrow black tie, and his black felt hat. The boys tried to imitate Daddy, but neither their clothes nor their boyish bodies quite allowed it. Roy Anthony in his gray dress slacks, white shirt, and green corduroy jacket came closest to the arrogant ease of Daddy's stride. Earl's pants were too big, so the legs had been rolled and pressed by Daddy. But he looked too often at the ground, hunting thoughtfully for the best places to set his feet with each step. For June Bug we had cut the legs in one of the pairs of pants and had folded them under and pressed the hems into place. Already the ragged edge with the scissor marks had slipped down and was visible in the back of one pant leg. He looked like an old man, stumbling over the hard ground behind Daddy. I couldn't stop my teeth from chattering as I made my way across the yard wearing a coat that was too small for me and a festive spring dress in the icy cold of a Mississippi winter.

When we entered the warm busy air of the building, tinny Christmas carols were playing on a jukebox in one corner of the enormous meeting-hall-style room. The building had unnaturally bright lights mounted in the high, angled ceiling. The languid scent of warm pine hung in the air from the decorated tree that scraped the ceiling near the jukebox. The pine mingled with the smells of roasted turkey and ham, fresh cornbread, baked sweet potatoes, and hair-grease baking under the hot lights.

The place was full of noisy activity—an assortment of women and small children seated around tables eating and chatting on one side of the room; fathers, husbands huddled together on folding chairs on the opposite side of the room, laughing and talking in low rumbling tones, swigging from paper cups under a subtle cloud of cigarette smoke; boys of different sizes and ages in starched white shirts and dark dress pants, playing with toy trucks and cars and army figures on the floor in the center of the room; young girls with dolls, plastic tea sets, and miniature makeup kits on the floor near the boys; a group of older boys playing some type of board game at a table away from the women; and a few teenage girls in clean, pressed dresses with their grease-shined legs and arms and hot-combed hair, milling around with the women at the tables.

All of these Veterans of Foreign War families looked like the dressed-up poor. They had put on their best clothes and their best manners to come here, just like we had.

Daddy stood rigid with one hand resting heavily on my shoulder and the other on Roy Anthony's. His mouth was set in a hard, tight line as his eyes swept the room. He grinned and nodded at the men, and his fingers tightened and relaxed on my shoulder.

"And who have we here?"

A stout high-brown woman with a big, broadly smiling face had stepped in front of us. Tied about her well-fed body was a white apron decorated with red and green candy canes. She clasped her hands, extended them in front of her, and leaned forward. Her eyes darted across my brothers' faces and mine. June Bug backed away and disappeared behind Daddy's legs.

"The Culpeppers, ma'am," Daddy said, quickly removing his hat and fingering it in his hands. He looked into the woman's light-brown eyes. "The Culpeppers," he repeated.

"Well, welcome, Mr. Culpepper. Where's Mrs. Culpepper? We had it on our list that you all are a family of seven."

"My wife is up at the hospital near Jackson with our baby girl who's very sick."

"Well, I'm sorry to hear that," the lady responded, drawing her clasped hands to her chest as if in prayer. "What a terrible time to have a child in the hospital. Glad you came out to our little party and we hope you can have some joy this Christmas Day." She extended her hands toward us again. "Why don't you bring your young ones over to the tree and let's see what gifts Santa left them. Were you good little children this year?" she asked, brushing her gaze across our faces again.

"Yes ma'am," I answered for my suddenly mute brothers.

"Good," she said and winked at me, then turned and led us to the tree.

EARL CULPEPPER said the label on the first gift-wrapped box that she handed out from under the tree. "Which one of you is Junior?" she asked, looking from June Bug to Roy Anthony as she picked up the next box. I pointed to June Bug who was still mostly concealed behind Daddy's legs. The next one she handed out was for me, MADELINE CULPEPPER. They had spelled my name wrong.

Roy Anthony pranced from foot to foot until he was handed a wrapped box.

"Why don't you all go and find a table and sit down. You can see what Santa left you. Myself and the other ladies in the kitchen will bring your plates over."

Daddy led us toward an empty table. The metal folding chairs were still pushed neatly against the red paper tablecloth.

"Let's see what Santy Claus brung you," he said, with a smile that only touched his mouth.

June Bug opened his gift first, and retrieved a pale blue and silver metal dump truck. He watched indulgently as Daddy rolled the truck back and forth on the table, making motor noises with his mouth and tilting the truck bed up and down. Earl found a bright red fire truck with several little plastic firemen, removable ladders, and a tiny black fire hose in his box. Roy Anthony got an olive green truck and a jeep with U.S. ARMY stenciled on the doors. Inside the back of the truck was a troop of metal soldiers squatting, standing, running, all with tiny rifles poised for war.

"You were like these soldiers, Daddy?" Roy Anthony held up a couple of the tiny men. "Did you get to have a gun too?"

Daddy's jaw clenched as he stretched his lips back into another false smile and nodded. "Yep. Just like that."

"Did you get to shoot anybody, Daddy?"

In the long silence that Daddy let follow that question, Roy Anthony faced off a couple of his metal soldiers and made shooting sounds with his mouth. Daddy watched, the lines deepening between his eyes.

"Yes siree, me and all the men over yonder were soldiers that got to carry guns," he said after a while, frowning at the rest of the metal soldiers still piled in the back of the truck.

"Hot dog. Hope I can be a soldier!" Roy Anthony exclaimed. Daddy looked away.

In my box I found a soft-bodied, pink-cheeked baby doll with tiny cloth diapers, a small baby bottle with orange juice that disappeared when you held the bottle upside down, a similar bottle with milk that did the same trick, and a plastic comb and brush for her chalk-white hair. This doll was bigger than Ida Bea had been when Momma took her back to the hospital.

"Now, isn't this better than sitting at the house missing y'all's Momma?" Daddy asked after a group of charity ladies, dressed just like the one who had greeted us at the door, brought us plates laden with turkey and dressing, ham, sweet potatoes, green beans, and cornbread and set them regally in front of us.

As we ate, Daddy kept glancing at the side of the room where the men were. Once I followed his glance in time to see a man raise a paper cup in Daddy's direction and nod tersely.

"Y'all finish eating and play with your toys," Daddy said, standing up from his half-empty plate. "I'm going over yonder to say my heys to the other men."

When he stopped in front of the men, one of them looked around toward the charity ladies in the kitchen before handing him a paper cup. He sipped and nodded, his back still to me. Uneasiness began to grow in me.

"Hey, Madeleine Culpepper. That's your daddy, ain't it? Me and my mama knows him." Percy Blakely from school stood beside our table, dressed in his Sunday best, including a blue-plaid bow tie and a starched white shirt. He was hugging his toys—a green army truck and jeep, and a fishnet bag full of metal soldiers—against his chest. He blinked watery eyes at me, grinned, and looked down at his shoes when I didn't answer right away.

"Yeah, that's my daddy," I said. "Where your daddy at?"

"He ain't here. He used to be here every time. But then he up and stopped coming home one day. Me and Mama still come here without him. Mama say we entitled. She over yonder." He pointed in the direction of one of the tables of women.

"Hey, I got the same thing," Roy Anthony said, standing and pulling his Christmas gift across the table toward Percy.

"Hot dog," Percy said and went to Roy Anthony's side. "Come on, let's see."

They found a spot on the floor. Exclaiming and comparing, they spread their things out and disappeared into little-boy land.

Earl joined them on the floor with his fire truck, leaving me and June Bug at our table, sitting watch over their half-eaten food. I looked at one of the nearby tables to see a mother's finger pointed in my direction. "See how grown up that girl is acting? Why can't you behave and sit pretty like that?" she said in an audible, shaming hiss to her daughter who was standing in front of her, lips poked out, arms folded across her skinny chest. The girl stuck out her tongue at me and stomped over to the group of girls playing on the floor near the boys.

Daddy was laughing and having too good a time in the men's corner. His head went back with a sudden burst of laughter, and he seemed on the verge of tipping his chair over. But he went on swilling from his cup. He winked at me across the room when he caught my gaze on him.

The boys had left turkey and ham on their plates, along with turkey dressing, mushy cooked green beans, big chunks of cornbread, and some candied sweet potatoes. I glanced around the room while I unfolded a paper napkin on the table beside me. When I was sure that none of the grown-ups were looking, I took pieces of turkey, ham, and cornbread from the plates and put it in the napkin, closed it and stuffed it into the pocket of my coat hanging over the back of my chair. June Bug had watched me with his hooded, old man eyes. With wobbly little-boy fingers, he started wrapping some of his food in a napkin. One of the women at a nearby table was watching him too. I told him to stop. "No," he stammered and snatched away from me. "No, no, no!" he yelled. I smiled and shrugged at the staring lady and left him alone. I was glad he was taking food.

The day dragged on in the sticky suffocating air of the room. All the people, the noise, the smells had begun to blunt my senses. Across the room Daddy was slouching in his chair now, still sipping from his cup. Amid boasting and encouraging laughter, Daddy and one of the other men got up and, leaning on each other, began doing a sloppy and careless tap dance while some of the other men sang a song about "jelly rolls" and "big-legged women" that made the women look away.

One of the charity ladies from the kitchen went over and said something to the men, who became abruptly quiet. The dancers sat down like scolded boys. But when the lady went back into the kitchen, Daddy got to his feet again and began mumbling a song and dancing across the floor. The men ducked their heads and hid their laughter behind their hands. After a while Daddy collapsed back into his chair, laughing.

"Come dance with your Daddy," he called across the room to me the next time he stood up. Several faces turned and looked at me. I pressed my back into the metal chair.

When I was small, Daddy had taught me to do a few of the tap steps he knew. He used to tease, "my little colored Shirley Temple." Now he waved his arms for me to join him on the other side of the room. "Come on, Maddy," he yelled across at me. "Show these jokers what my girl can do."

The men behind Daddy were grinning dumbly. The pity on some of the women's faces told me they were experienced enough to know that humiliation was likely to follow this invitation from my daddy.

"Come on, Maddy," Daddy hollered again.

I stood and slouched across the room, intricate fear creeping along beside me.

The scent of whiskey and cigarettes on Daddy's breath made my stomach churn in the hot air of the room when he leaned toward me to suggest we do the "Milk the Cow" dance. He started singing, "Don't you worry 'bout the cow goin' po', just drank that milk and ask for mo' . . ." I started doing the steps he had taught me, counting them off in my head, looking down at my feet. Tap two three four, tap two three four, tap two three four, shuffle together slide. Daddy was doing the steps beside me.

He sang on in a gravelly, liquor-soaked baritone. I began to feel the joy and the simple pleasure I used to feel at home, seeing the smile on Momma's face when Daddy and I danced for her.

We finished one dance, and the whole hall erupted in applause and calls for more.

"All right," Daddy said. "One more. Remember 'Twilight Blues?'" Daddy asked. I did. It was one of my favorites.

"Where has the time gone," Daddy sang. He did his opening steps, tapping easily, holding the lapels of his jacket and affecting a sad face to fit the song about a man wasting time. I counted off the rhythm and began my steps beside him.

Suddenly Daddy lost his balance and stumbled backward into the chairs where the men sat behind us. Back, back he went, as if he had been shoved. Chairs tipped over as he went. Some men ended up with their feet in the air. When the banging and clanging of chairs and falling men was over, most of the children were laughing as "Joy to the World" wound thinly around the room from the jukebox.

When Daddy extracted himself from the pile of chairs and the other drunk men, he looked at the man nearest him. "Why'd you trip me, you son of a bitch?" he yelled.

"Man, ain't nobody tripped you," one of the men said.

"You tripped over you own clumsy-ass feet."

"One of you sons-of-bitches tripped me," Daddy said, straightening his pants and pulling his tie back to the center.

"Ain't nobody came near you, Culpepper."

"You calling me a liar?"

"Ain't no need to get bent out of shape, man."

"Ain't going to stand here in front of my little girl and let you make no fool out me."

"Culpepper, ain't nobody making no fool out of you, man."

"Yeah," someone else said, "you ain't needing no help with that."

"What that you say?" Daddy whirled about.

"Culpepper, maybe you ought to go on home 'fore somebody have to whip your ass."

"Whip my ass? Ain't none of you son of bitches got what it take to whip my ass."

One of the ladies from the kitchen came up behind Daddy.

"Mr. Culpepper, maybe it's time for you to go on home. I'll call a taxicab for you and your children."

"I don't need no goddamned taxicab. I just want to see one of these niggers try to whip my ass."

"Mr. Culpepper," the lady resumed, "there's no need to fight. It's Christmas."

Daddy turned and swung at the lady, who backed up just in time.

"Come on, Eugene, man, you don't need to be swinging at no lady," one of the men said. "Why don't you go on home with your drunk ass like she suggests."

"Why don't you make me go home."

Daddy stepped back and put his fists in front of his face like a boxer. "You ain't nothing but a big pile of chicken shit. That's why. Everyone of y'all is chicken shit."

Three of the men separated themselves from the others and surrounded Daddy. He turned inside their circle, swinging randomly. One of the men swung. There was a dull fleshy cracking sound and Daddy's head snapped backward. For one crazed moment there was a look of astonishment in his eyes, then he dropped to his knees and slumped face forward onto the floor.

"You killed him," I yelled and rushed forward.

"May-dee, May-dee," June Bug cried, running toward me from across the room.

"He ain't dead," the man said, the one who had hit him. "I ain't never killed a man with my bare hands. See?" The man kneeled on the floor beside Daddy and turned him over roughly. Blood trickled from Daddy's nose, but as I watched, his chest rose slowly in a long protracted breath, then collapsed, then up, then down.

"He's just in the land of the dead for a little while." The man boasted, and a little puddle of pride gathered around him as he chuckled.

The ladies of charity stood beside Daddy and the man kneeling over him. They looked unprepared, but not surprised, by the violence.

"Culpepper sure do gets mean when he drinks," one of the men said.

"Sure 'nough," another one answered.

"My pop was like that," one of the women said suddenly. "Got his self killed in a knife fight that way. Uh-huh. Sho' did." She looked at me, then turned away still nodding.

"Well, that don't make no never mind. This one ain't dead. He's just kind of sleep," someone else said.

"Well, he can't just stay here until he wakes up. Y'all got to get him up," one of the Christmas aprons said. "He's ruining our little celebration."

Earl and Roy Anthony were kneeling beside Daddy, shaking him. "Wake up, Daddy," they repeated as if they were singing rounds. Tears were streaming down Earl's face, but Roy Anthony looked angry.

"You couldn't wake him up with a bucket of water and a team of mules," one of the men said. "When Buck puts them out, they out for a while."

"Sorry, little lady," Buck said, grinning up at me from the floor by Daddy. "He was getting a little too big for his britches. Just had to knock him back down to size."

"Put him out of his misery for a while," another male voice said.

"Dumb bastard," another said.

"Watch your mouth, man, there's ladies and babies present," one of the other men said.

"Buck, you got your car here, why don't you take him and these kids on home."

"I reckon I can do that," Buck said. "Y'all come on and help me get him to the car."

A few of the men shuffled forward with swaggering manly purpose and intent. The women stood around now, talking in low voices to each other and looking embarrassed.

Two men were on either side of Daddy at his shoulders and his feet. They lifted him stiffly. His head dropped back and hung there, mouth open, eyes closed. Daddy snorted softly like he sometimes did in sleep. As they moved toward the door, the crowd parted, suddenly reverent. I herded my brothers together, got our coats, and shepherded them across the room behind Daddy's procession.

"Madeleine." Percy came running toward us with the boys' Christmas toys bundled in his arms. While Earl and Roy Anthony gathered everything from Percy, I looked over my shoulder.

The younger children were already reenacting what they had seen—stumbling, laughing, crumpling to the floor.

Outside the day had gotten colder. Pale gray sky touched everything, and a breeze had come up. We walked slowly over the frozen ground, the wind pressing our clothes against our backsides. The men carrying Daddy looked shame-filled and burdened, as if the wind had blown the humor and pride out of them. My brothers and I waited while they wedged Daddy into the backseat of an old green Buick with rounded fenders and rust-flecked bumpers. We only needed to be told once to get into the front seat with Buck. We pressed in beside him, Roy Anthony and Earl in the middle, me at the window with June Bug on my lap.

The ride home was silent except for Roy Anthony humming Christmas carols. His muffled voice rumbled stubbornly through his nose, flowing haphazardly from one song to another. There was something derogatory and spiteful in his humming, some underlying emotion that had nothing to do with joy. His barely hidden emotion made me want to lash out. But I didn't move or say a word. Something that felt like a knot of puke was stuck in my throat, and I was afraid that if I opened my mouth it would fly out. Behind it would be a flood of tears that I wouldn't be able to stop. The only thing that would have been worse than the shame blocked inside me would have been drawing attention to it. I would have shattered like frozen glass in the heat of such attention.

In the backseat, Daddy groaned and began snoring like he always did when he fell asleep drunk. I knew that he was going to be fine. Everything would go on as it had been going with Momma away at the hospital and me taking her place with the boys and Daddy getting drunk every chance he got.

I watched the wasted landscape slide by the car—fields of hay-colored grass and weeds; patches of thin clear ice; low-lying bushes, dry and brittle in the cold; bare trees with branches like bony fingers reaching into the sky; and the dull green shades of lonely evergreens wrapped at their bases with spidery tufts of frost. I calmed my emotions and fastened them away. I would be strong for my brothers.

CHAPTER NINE

ONE FRIDAY IN EARLY January as the approaching darkness was draining the color from everything and the cold was making it too hard to be outside, I herded the boys inside. When I pulled the light cord in the front room, no light issued from the bulb. I went through the house pulling all the cords with the same result.

"What's the matter, Maddy?" Earl asked when he found me standing in the middle of the kitchen dumbfounded.

"The lights are out."

June Bug, who had followed me through the house, was whining now and pulling on the hem of my skirt. "Quit it," I said. "Go play or something."

"Light," June Bug said, still holding on to my skirt.

"It's gonna be all right," I said. "Now let go."

"Maybe something is the matter with the light-box outside," Earl suggested.

He and June Bug followed me out the back door and around to the side of the house. I learned nothing from looking at the metal wheels and dials enclosed in the small glass dome of the electric meter, but staring at it for a few minutes delayed the full-on assault by my fears. June Bug wasn't the only one bothered by the thought of spending the night without lights.

"What y'all doing?" Roy Anthony asked, coming up behind us.

"The lights are out."

"Go tell Ma Parker," he said. "She know more than you," he said with scorn in his voice.

Since the Christmas party, a certain kind of little-boy meanness was settling onto him like a fine layer of dust. He ran ahead of me and Earl, turning from time to time to walk backward so he could stick out his tongue at us and roll his eyes as he went.

"I don't know nothing 'bout electricity meters," Ma Parker said.

But she did have a small coal-oil lamp she could let us use until Daddy got the lights back on.

"Don't leave it burning when you go to sleep," she warned as she showed me how to take the glass globe off of the metal base and place a lighted match near the wick to ignite a tiny dancing flame. "Might burn the house down. This here is where the coal oil is put in," she said, pointing to a metal cap protruding from one side of the base of the lamp. "It's full of oil so you don't need to fiddle with that at all. Boys, don't y'all mess with this lamp. Let your sister take care of it. You hear me?"

They all nodded, even June Bug, who had stumbled along after us to her house. He stood now, sucking his thumb and pulling his ear.

We walked back to our house with the glass-enclosed flame banishing the darkness in front of us.

When Daddy finally came home carrying bags of groceries, he found us huddled around Ma Parker's little lamp in the front room.

"Goddamned electric company," he said. "How could they leave children in the dark? I'll set those sons-of-bitches straight first thing Monday."

He picked up the lamp from the circle where we sat on the floor and headed for the kitchen. We followed and stood around watching as he busied himself, washing off what he called "my chicken-shit job."

He unbuttoned the top of his grimy gray khaki overalls and peeled down to his waist, exposing his narrow, dark chest. He splashed ice-cold water from the sink under his arms and onto his chest and face, then blotted himself with a dish towel. He whipped up lather in his sand-colored shaving mug and smeared the white foam on his cheeks and square jawline with the bent bristles of his shaving brush. After scraping the hairs from his face with the glinting blade of his straight-edged razor, he slapped sharply scented aftershave on his face. He turned with a big grin and patted a little from the scented bottle onto the giggling faces of Earl and Roy Anthony.

"One day you little knuckleheads will sprout hairs on your faces and have to shave them off to please the lady-folk," he said.

"No sir," said Earl, "that shaver knife too scary. I'm going to keep my face hairs."

"Then you won't never get no beautiful lady like your momma. If I'd kept hairs on my face she never would've looked at me and you little folk wouldn't even be here."

Earl and Roy Anthony looked at each other trying to work out what Daddy meant. "Just you wait and see," Daddy said. "Come here, little man."

Daddy gestured for June Bug who had climbed onto one of the kitchen chairs. When June Bug went forward, Daddy squatted in front of him and rubbed a little shaving foam from the cup onto his face. "Now hold still," Daddy said. He cupped his hand over the top of June Bug's head and tilted it back. He lifted the razor and ran it along the side of June Bug's face. My stomach sucked itself in.

"Nothing to it. Right, little man?" Daddy asked when all of the foam was gone from June Bug's face.

June Bug rubbed his small hand on his cheek, incredulous.

"Mo', mo', mo'," he said, giggling into Daddy's face. Daddy lifted him into his arms and stood.

"The finishing touch," Daddy said, and splashed aftershave on June Bug.

Earl and Roy Anthony, who had been watching in stunned silence, whooped and jumped toward Daddy. "Me now. Me now," they sang in unison.

"Well, tonight I ain't got time. I got somewhere to go. I'll show the rest of y'all next time. I'll teach all my boys how to take off face hairs. Show you how to be a man."

Still holding June Bug, he rinsed his shaving cup, wiped off the razor blade, and put it and the cup on the high shelf above the sink where he kept them.

The rest of us followed him back to his bedroom, our shadows dancing along grotesquely in the lamplight. We huddled in the doorway, watching as he set the lamp on Momma's dresser and set June Bug on the bed and stood in the middle of the room.

Daddy unbuttoned his overalls the rest of the way and stepped out of them. His legs, lumpy muscle on straight unyielding bones, looked fragile sticking out of the wide legs of his boxer shorts in the dim light.

"Where you going, Daddy?"

Earl was the only one of us brave enough to ask. Even in Daddy's good mood, we couldn't be sure how he would take to being quizzed by one of us.

"Gon' hear some fellows I used to play with. These cats playing big now. Traveling all over the place. Decided to stop and give us a little show."

He turned sideways to look at himself in Momma's mirror as he put on the starched-white shirt and stepped into the dark gray pants that he had brought home from the cleaner's. "I wish y'all's momma was here," he said. "She used to love hearing me and the fellows, back then—in Hattiesburg."

"Play us some music 'fore you go, Daddy?" Earl asked.

Daddy looked surprised, but he went to the dresser and fished around in the back of the top drawer. He pulled the wooden box out and removed the white cloth. He unwrapped the harmonica slowly and stood rolling it between his fingers. The lamplight flashed off the shiny silver and made Daddy's shadow dance on the wall behind him. He brought the instrument toward his mouth but stopped midway, then retrieved the handkerchief from the dresser, rewrapped it around the harmonica, and stowed it back in the wooden box.

"Don't have the time," he said, pulling on his crumpled winter jacket. He shoved the box into his jacket pocket. "Maybe the fellows will let me play with them tonight."

His sounded a little bit sad, and for a moment I felt sorry for him. He grabbed the doorknob, and, turning back to me and the boys, he stared at us the way he had looked at the harmonica.

"Y'all don't need me here. Ain't scared of a little dark is you?"

The sadness was still there in the edges of his voice.

We shook our heads.

"Everything's going to be all right. Daylight'll be here before you know it."

I was happy to open my eyes the next morning to the pale blue light of day outside our windows. I went into Daddy's room. Of course he hadn't come back home. He seldom slept at home on weekend nights anymore. At least he had brought us food this time.

I had no problem with Earl and Roy Anthony's request to go outside. June Bug didn't want to come out, so we left him inside. The three of us spent the morning chasing each other in high-strung running games like tag and "T-Lock." This was one of the good things about having absent parents. We could play outside from sunup to sundown, even though the air was cold enough to make our noses run and our teeth chatter when we stood still. Only our grumbling stomachs drew us back inside.

When I hurried into the kitchen, June Bug was lying in the middle of the kitchen floor amid the collection of battered pots and baby-dolls I had put out for his play. His legs were drawn up to one side, and he was lying on one of his arms, his other arm stuck out in front of him at an unnatural angle. He looked like a doll that had been dropped. My heart quickened.

"Junie Boy," I called from the doorway and went quickly toward him. "Junie Boy." His eyes were half open and they gleamed pearly, iridescent white.

"He's just playing," Roy Anthony said and went to the cabinet to get food.

When I dropped to my knees beside June Bug, the pungent smell of coal oil rose to me from his open mouth. Ma Parker's lamp lay on its side among the pots. "June Bug, wake up." I pushed him, gently at first, then angrily. He was limp.

"Get out of my way," I yelled, knocking past Roy Anthony who had come up behind me.

"He's just playing," Roy Anthony repeated.

Ma Parker grabbed an old carpet bag and went quickly into her kitchen when I told her I thought June Bug had drunk coal oil from the lamp.

"I think he's dead," Roy Anthony said when Ma Parker rushed into our house. She looked at him with a fierce expression that made him drop his gaze.

June Bug was still where I had left him on the kitchen floor. Earl was on his knees by his head, stroking his brow murmuring, "It's going to be all right."

These were words he had heard from Momma often enough. Earl was accident prone, Momma said, always falling, or slamming his fingers in drawers, or scraping his knees, or stepping on broken glass outside. "You are one more clumsy child," she would say with frustration when he brought in some injury for repair.

"You boys go on out of here," Ma Parker said, squatting beside June Bug's still body. There was a hardness in her voice that made her sound angry, but her expression was calm and remote. She bent forward and put her ear close to June Bug's mouth. She peeled his eyelid back, revealing more whiteness.

"Is he dead?" I asked.

"Course not," she said.

I started a litany of prayers asking God to keep it that way.

Ma Parker sat on the floor, stretched her legs straight in front of her, flattened her faded red apron over her lap, and pulled June Bug onto it. She held him there with one arm. With her free hand she took two sealed mason jars from her carpet bag and set them on the floor. "Here, put my bag over yonder out the way," she said, pushing her bag toward me. "Get me some water."

I set her bag on the table and hurried to get water. It sloshed onto my shaking hands as I offered it to her.

"I'm gone need a whole lot more than that," she said, looking up at me as if I wasn't very bright.

I ran to the cabinet to find more glasses, then went back and forth filling the glasses at the sink, then lining them up on the floor beside her. As I did this, she mixed small amounts of the dusty brown contents from one of her mason jars into some of the glasses of water.

When I could find no more glasses, I stood beside her and June Bug. My heart was pounding unevenly and my legs shook as my mind skittered around like a chipmunk. It would be my fault if June Bug died. Why didn't I think about him messing with the lamp? Why did we need to be outside? I should have stayed in the house with him. Momma will be so disappointed in me.

Ma Parker propped June Bug up against her chest and pried his mouth open with her fingers. She poured some of the murky water into his open mouth, then rubbed his throat until the muscles there moved up and down and he swallowed.

"Put some more of this in the other glasses," she said motioning toward the jar of dusty powder.

I made more of the murky potion that had a tight tinny smell while she forced June Bug to swallow glass after glass of it.

"Open that jar," she ordered after a while, pointing to her other mason jar on the floor near her feet.

I opened the jar and held it out to her. She took something from it that looked like tree bark and stuck it in her mouth. She chewed casually, then took the wet, fleshy bark from her own mouth and placed it on June Bug's tongue. She probed and prodded, moving the bark around in his mouth with her fingers until I heard the unmistakable, loathsome sound of June Bug gagging.

She kept prodding until he vomited, spewing a stream of oily brown liquid with the heavy nauseating stench of coal oil and stomach acid. It flowed down his front and splashed onto her apron and the hem of her dress and the floor.

I looked on in horror.

June Bug kept throwing up until he seemed empty. Then he began to whine and flail his arms feebly. Ma Parker pinned them against her chest and forced his mouth open for more of the brown water. He twisted his small head from side to side. But she succeeded in getting more of the liquid into him. After a few minutes he vomited again, retching like a perverse little fountain. She stared into the murky mess that he had expelled, then fed him more of the liquid until he vomited again. After a few more rounds of this, she rocked him in her arms while he squirmed and cried, his eyes shut tight, tears squeezing free at the corners like silver honey.

"Maddy, get my other medicine jar from my bag and mix two teaspoons of what's in there in a glass full of water and hold it up there in the window light for a minute."

I did as I was told and stood holding the glass, an old jelly jar, aloft in the sunlight. Crumbled brown leaves floated on the water until it gradually turned pale gold. Then the leaves began to drift down and settle at the bottom of the jar. I watched this transformation as my arms began to tingle from the effort of holding the jar up.

A slow lazy strength surged through me, rumbling like a hungry stomach, only instead of spreading pain, it spread warmth that filled me up and seemed to spill out of the top of my head and cover me like liquid sunshine. My fears about June Bug dying because of me were draining away into that jar of golden liquid.

"Hand it here now," Ma Parker said.

She took the elixir and gently coaxed June Bug to drink it. She fed it to him slowly, and he did not gag when it was finished. He leaned against her flabby, old lady bosom and put his thumb in his mouth. For a moment he peered at me serenely through his familiar dark, old-man eyes. Then he closed them softly and nestled into Ma Parker's arms.

"Junior's going to be all right," she said. "Thank the Lord you had the good sense to come get me when you did. Your mama's lucky to have a girl as sensible as you to look out for these boys. Lord knows y'all daddy ain't of much use."

CHAPTER TEN

"MADELEINE, I NEED TO see you after school." Miss Washington looked up from an open folder on her desk as my classmates and I were scribbling our responses to the last reading assignments for the day.

My heartbeat quickened, and I could feel my classmates' eyes on me when I mumbled, "Yes ma'am."

It was hard for me to go back to concentrating on the words I needed to pencil into my workbook. I poured back through the events of the day to see where I might have done something wrong. Maybe it wasn't me. Perhaps it was about one of my brothers. Roy Anthony's fourth-grade teacher had the humiliating habit of requesting my presence in her classroom to point out Roy Anthony's various failings in front of his whole class. Three times in recent months this had happened. Once when he showed up without his homework; another time when he fell asleep at his desk; and a third time when he kicked one of his classmates. He said the girl had called him Harvest Quarters trash when he refused to let her play in a game he had organized during recess. He refused to apologize. I had to stand in front of his classmates and listen to his teacher's recounting of his offense, while he sat in a corner facing a wall. Then I had to escort him to Principal Coleman's office where I watched him get paddled twice on the butt. "I still ain't sorry," he said as we walked home later.

By the time the release bell sounded and my classmates had

emptied out of the room, my stomach was cramping like I hadn't eaten in a couple of days.

"I didn't know your family had fallen on hard times," Miss Washington said when we were alone.

"Ma'am?"

"I have a letter from Principal Coleman's office indicating that you and your brothers are eligible for free lunches and government commodities." She opened a folder and took out several pages. Skimming one of them she added, "Apparently, the Daughters of Saint Paul Charity applied on your family's behalf."

I felt my face get hot as an image of the ladies who had served us food at the Christmas party floated into my memory. What had they written in the papers Miss Washington now had?

"Your file at the start of the school year said your father was gainfully employed. Clearly something has changed. Do you want to talk about what's happened at home?"

"No ma'am."

So they hadn't written about Daddy's drunkenness, and there was no way I was going to tell her. It was a source of shame that my mother wasn't home taking care of us and my father was becoming a drunk.

"There's no shame in needing help," Miss Washington said.

I figured she was wrong about that. One of the reasons my classmates and I were so hard on Percy Blakely was because he needed help. Somewhere along the way we had all gotten the message that it was due to some sort of personal fault if you were poor enough to need handouts. It meant your family was weak; you were weak.

"Are you worried about your classmates knowing?" Miss Washington offered into the silence. "No one but you and I and Mr.

Coleman's office will know who's paying for your lunches. Your names will simply go on the list of pupils entitled to a full lunch every day, just like the names of the children whose parents send lunch money at the beginning of each month."

Tears sprang to my eyes. We did need the food.

"What is it, Madeleine? What's happened?"

My tears slid down and dripped onto the backs of my hands on my desk. I raised my head enough to see that she had come from behind her desk and was offering me a lacy white handkerchief.

"The letter says your family is also entitled to commodities. Do you know what commodities are?"

I shook my head and wiped my face with the handkerchief that smelled of the floral perfume that always hovered in the air around Miss Washington.

"The county gives out free food from the government once a month, peanut butter, cheese, canned meat, items like that, depending on the number of people in your family. They just need the signature of one of your parents on this letter and someone will have to go pick the food up."

My heart made a little leap—free food at home too. Then it occurred to me that Daddy would have to sign the paper *and* pick up the food. The government food would be as unreliable as the food we waited for Daddy to bring home now.

"Madeleine, you need to talk to me so I can help you."

"My daddy—my daddy—," I tried. "He won't—we can't—"

"Your mother can sign and pick up the food."

I shook my head. "She ain't at home." I covered my face with the frilly handkerchief.

"Your mother *isn't* at home, Madeleine. Remember your English. Now tell me, do you and your brothers need food?"

I nodded.

"You don't think your daddy will sign for it and go get it?"

I shook my head.

"Well for heaven's sakes, why not?" Miss Washington's voice was pitched with frustration.

In the silence that followed, I finally uncovered my face and looked at her. She was squinting and her mouth was moving like she was chewing the inside of her lips. She turned away from me, facing out the window toward the straggling clumps of kids flowing out of the school yard.

"Maybe we can work it out so *you* can get the food and bring it home. Would that be possible? Could you manage that?"

"Yes ma'am."

A few days later, Roy Anthony and I left Earl and June Bug with Ma Parker and headed out of the Quarters, pulling Earl's red Radio Flyer wagon toward downtown Blossom, following a map Miss Washington drew on notebook paper. "Lord, Lord," was all Ma Parker said when I showed her the papers.

I had never gone downtown without Momma. This adventure was not altogether unpleasant. I was riding high on the knowledge that I was doing something to take care of myself and the boys. It made me hopeful as we walked through some of the shabbier parts of our community, on through to the better maintained areas that had paved roads, cement sidewalks, and painted houses with winter-bare hedges. As we got closer to downtown the streetlights became more numerous and the houses were larger and set farther from the street. Some of the yards even had big magnolias and oaks out front. The black families here were prosperous enough to afford brick houses and the occasional shiny car pulled alongside in a paved driveway.

I knew from Momma that most of the black teachers and a couple of Blossom's black professionals—our one black dentist, one of the two lawyers, and the one black doctor—lived here. Some of my classmates lived here—like Naomi James, whose daddy was a bricklayer and whose mama was a beautician; Harold Thomas, whose daddy did some kind of work in one of the banks downtown; and Faye Mangrove, whose daddy ran a dry-cleaning business. But I didn't want to see any of my classmates. I didn't know what I would say, so I hurried us along.

At last Roy Anthony and I came to Koon's General Hardware Store, a block-long glass-fronted building with a sun-weakened green awning, which marked the official beginning of downtown. When we stepped in the green shade of the awning, my stomach tightened and my breathing sped up.

A row of bright-green wheelbarrows with yellow handles and some black hand-push lawnmowers hogged much of the sidewalk in front of the hardware store, so we had to maneuver our wagon around them. Through the windows we saw white people, mostly men, shopping inside. My uneasiness grew.

A block farther up the road we turned onto a road that skirted downtown. It bore a latticework of railroad tracks pushing through blistered and buckling strips of dusty blacktop like bones showing through torn skin. Cavernous brick buildings with high cement steps and raised platforms lined both sides of the road. It was above the door to one of these buildings that we saw the small square sign with red lettering—JONES COUNTY FEDERAL RELIEF CENTER. We left the wagon at the bottom of the chipped concrete steps, climbed in cowed silence to the platform above, and went inside.

A white lady with startlingly bright reddish-brown hair sat behind a desk on the far side of a large room filled with sunlight pouring in through high windows. The room was empty except for the woman's desk and a row of file cabinets lining the wall behind her. She watched us with a pinched expression as we came toward her—me with bold calmness, Roy Anthony with sullen pride.

I handed her Miss Washington's note and the paper she had signed.

"We ain't supposed to give food to *children.*" The woman looked at me with deep-brown eyes made large and sly by blue cat's-eye glasses with rhinestone edges. It was unclear whether the gaunt distaste on her red lips was there all the time or just for Roy Anthony and me. She leaned across her desk, offering Miss Washington's letter back to me.

Prickly sweat surfaced in my armpits and the palms of my hands as I stared tongue-tied at the tiny hairs at the corners of the woman's mouth and the spidery blue lines visible through the papery skin of her cheeks.

Did she mean that children couldn't eat the commodities?

"Did y'all *hear* what I *said*?" she asked. Her eyebrows arched above the glistening rhinestones of her eyeglasses.

I nodded but couldn't keep tears from blurring my vision. Nor could I will my hand to reach out and take back the letter. We needed the food. I had come this far.

She leaned back in her chair and stood up. "Y'all wait *here*," she said, frustration edging her voice.

Holding Miss Washington's letter like a lantern, she disappeared through a door near the row of file cabinets.

Roy Anthony trembled stiffly. "What you gon' do, Maddy?"

I shrugged, wiped my eyes with my hands, and wiped my hands on my dress. "We just gon' wait."

The cat's-eyes returned with a chubby crew-cut man in tow. He was holding Miss Washington's letter. A crimson tie and matching suspenders lay against his white shirt like bloody stripes tracing the shape of his Santa Claus belly. He looked at Roy Anthony and me like he was considering hiring us. I looked at the floor.

"Where y'all mama at?" he asked.

"The hospital, sir."

"How long she been there?"

"Since before Halloween, sir."

"What y'all been doing for food all that time?"

"My daddy was bringing some home."

"What's happened to y'all's daddy?"

"Sometime he gets home real late, sir."

"What hospital your mama in?"

"I don't know its name, sir. Daddy says it's up past Jackson."

"I see," he exhaled slowly.

I glanced up to see him reading Miss Washington's letter. The rhinestone-rimmed cat's-eyes watched us as he read.

"Please sir, we need the food," I ventured.

"What's 'at you say? Speak up, girl."

"Please sir, we need the food."

I raised my head enough to stare at his tie. I heard an affronted exhalation, a "see-what-I-told-you" kind of a sigh from the lady.

"Pitiful. These nigras don't seem to know how to take care of they own children. Hell, give 'em the food," he said, handing the letter back to the woman. "Certainly looks like they needs it."

"This going to be a lot of food to carry," the woman said when the man was gone and she was back behind her desk. "How y'all planning to get it back on y'all's side of town?"

"We brought a wagon, ma'am."

"How many of y'all is there?"

"My three brothers and me, my momma, my daddy, and my baby sister."

She flipped through several pages on a clipboard, pulled out one page and pressed a button on her desk. A buzzer sounded faintly somewhere in the back of the building where the man had gone.

"They got a wagon out front," the woman said, handing the page from the clipboard to the black man who had appeared in the doorway.

Big sweat stains made half-moons in the armpits of his khaki shirt, and his dark pants were stained and dusty at the knees. He wiped sweat from his forehead with a dingy blue rag and nodded at the woman.

"Yes ma'am," he said, grinning in the direction of the cat's-eyes. He winked at Roy Anthony and me before he disappeared through the door again.

"*Y'all* can wait outside," the woman said.

I led Roy Anthony out, glad to get away.

"How you little nappy heads doin'? Where y'all people at?" the black man asked, grinning over the box he was bringing toward Roy Anthony and me as we stood beside our wagon.

"Sir?"

"Just playing with y'all. No need to be looking like I said I was gon' kill your dog."

"We ain't got no dog," Roy Anthony said.

The man grinned slowly. "Well, that's good I suppose, 'cause he might've eat up all this food I'm 'bout to give you."

"If we had a dog, I'd punch him in the nose if he tried to eat my food," Roy Anthony said. He made a fist and punched the air.

"Ouch," the man said, and staggered.

He set the box in the wagon and tied it in place with pieces of rope from the warehouse.

"Y'all got a lot of food in there," the man said, and counted off on his fingers, "jars of peanut butter, cans of potted meat, cans of powdered eggs, canned vegetables, bags of navy beans, flour, rice, powdered milk, cornmeal, cheese, and grits. Government thinks it's enough to feed y'all for a month. You want to make that so. No wasting."

"Yes sir," I said, picking up the wagon handle to turn it toward home.

"Let me," Roy Anthony said. He grabbed my hand and tried to peel it off the handle.

"Hold on now," the man said. "Y'all here by y'all self. Means your grown-ups slipping up somehow. Y'all got to look out for each other. Work together. Little Man," he said, reaching toward Roy Anthony, "can we shake on that?"

Roy Anthony folded his arms across his chest and bunched his lips.

"Come on, Little Man. Ain't you the biggest brother in the family?"

Roy Anthony nodded.

"Well now, Big Brother. You got to help Big Sis. Don't fight with her. Be like y'all a team. Big Brother, let's shake on it, man-to-man."

Roy Anthony grinned and put his small hand in the man's hand. "Yes sir. Man-to-man."

"Now roll that wagon-train on home," the man said.

Roy Anthony's grin expanded with pride. I stepped back and let him take the wagon handle. It hadn't occurred to me before to think of him as anything but a responsibility.

CHAPTER ELEVEN

WE CAME HOME FROM school one afternoon near the end of January to find all of our stuff in the front yard. Rusted metal bedsprings leaned against each other; mattresses slanted against the porch for passersby to see the pale-brown amoeba-shaped pee stains; dressers with their drawers partially open faced each other; boxes of clothes squatted haphazardly like gutted animals; dishes rose in untidy piles from the dirt; grandma's rocking chair perched upside down near the road; Momma's sewing machine rested on its side; our commodity food in plain brown cardboard boxes and bare cans huddled in the middle of the kitchen table near the porch steps; toys scattered around the yard with Momma's books as if they had been thrown from the doorway. It looked like the town dump.

The lead-gray padlock that we used to lock the door when we weren't home lay twisted on the porch. In its place hung a shiny new lock, glistening arrogantly. A bold white sign pasted to the front door read:

QUIT ORDER
BY ORDER OF THE JONES COUNTY COURT AND
THE JONES COUNTY SHERIFF'S DEPARTMENT
THE CURRENT OCCUPANT OF PROPERTY AT
1 HARVEST QUARTERS, SAID <u>EUGENE CULPEPPER,</u>
IS HEREBY ORDERED TO QUIT PREMISES UNDER PAIN OF LAW.

Even if I hadn't understood the notice, there was no misunderstanding the deliberate sprawl of our furniture in the winter-hard dirt or the hunched snickering of the other schoolchildren walking past into the Quarters.

Complicated physical shame rose in me then, making my skin tight and itchy. It oozed out around me, covering everything in sticky layers of anger.

"What happened?" Roy Anthony asked. "What's that paper say? Why's our stuff in the yard?"

"How we gone git in the house?" Earl wanted to know. "You got the new key?"

"Shut up! Shut up!" I whirled around, prepared to charge at them, fists flailing. They stared at me through eyes dark with confusion, their mouths open with surprise.

"Come on," I said, and led them next door to Ma Parker's house.

I banged on her screen door until I opened it to see that there was a padlock on her door.

"Where's Ma Parker?"

"What you gonna do now, Maddy?"

"Where we supposed to go?"

I moved away from their questions and sat down on Ma Parker's porch steps. "Leave me alone. I got to think." Ma Parker would have to be home soon. She had June Bug. Then I could leave all of the boys with her and go look for Daddy. He had to come fix this.

I hugged myself, leaning forward over my knees, staring ahead through my anger and fear until the world blurred and my eyelids felt like tight bands of leather.

"Maddy, are we gonna stay out here forever?" Earl asked.

"No. We just gonna wait for Ma Parker. Y'all gonna stay with her and I'm gonna look for Daddy."

Roy Anthony sat on the edge of the porch, swinging his legs

and making grotesquely cheerful spit bubbles. Periodically he glanced at me slyly, cautiously, out of the corners of his eyes. Suddenly he turned to me. "How you know we ain't just been throwed away?"

"Don't mess with me right now, Roy Anthony."

"I think we been throwed away," he said.

Earl, sitting farther back on the porch, started crying, whimpering and sniffling softly. I wanted to punch Roy Anthony in the face.

"You big crybaby," Roy Anthony said menacingly to Earl. "Crybaby, crybaby, suck your Mama's titty," he sang and jumped to the ground. He skipped back and forth in front of the porch. "Earl is a crybaby . . . crybaby, crybaby, suck your Mama's titty."

"Quit it. Leave me 'lone," Earl whined.

"Crybaby, crybaby . . ."

"Let him alone, Roy. Remember, you supposed to be helping."

"I can't help no crybaby. He needs a big titty. Crybaby . . . crybaby . . ."

Earl jumped off the porch and charged at Roy Anthony. They ran across Ma Parker's yard to our yard, dodging in and out between the pieces of our lives.

The sun was setting when a dusty green pickup truck stopped in front of Ma Parker's house and she got out carrying June Bug.

"Well Lord have mercy. What's happened here?" she asked, looking from our raggedy possessions in the yard to the three of us huddled on her porch with the boxes and cans of our commodity food lined up beside us.

"I knowed this might happen," she said, shaking her head and digging around in her apron pocket for her key. "When I saw that white man over there last week. He don't come around less somebody's real far behind in the rent. What's got into y'all's daddy? Anybody would think there wasn't nobody in the world but him. Your mama up there in the hospital with a sick baby. You kids here half starving to death, and there he goes, burning what little bit he makes in them juke joints, drinking hisself stupid. Getting to be so he ain't worth the piss it would take to wet his clothes."

This was that brutal side of Ma Parker, the side that had beaten Esther with an extension cord until raw welts rose on her legs. She stomped onto the porch still spewing words like poison arrows in the direction of my daddy's image. Her charges against him made me want to defend him. But I kept my mouth shut and followed her into her house.

"Y'all hungry?" she asked.

The boys looked at me. "No, ma'am, we ate," I answered. "Our food was in the yard."

"What'd you eat?" Ma Parker demanded.

"Cheese and bread."

"And y'all ain't hungry for nothing else?"

"No ma'am."

Earl and Roy Anthony looked at me as if they wanted to contradict me, but neither said a word. They sat on the edge of Ma Parker's sofa with their hands in their laps, afraid of the fierceness still in her voice.

"Must've given y'all quite a scare to come home and find your things out in the yard, and me and your baby brother gone. Sheriff's men hadn't showed up when I left this morning to tend to one of my mothers in Soso. I thought sure we'd be back 'fore school let out. You never do know. Babies come in they own time."

Ma Parker pulled back the curtain at her side window and

looked out into our yard. "Sneaky bastards, those sheriff's deputies. Not that I could've done a thing, even if I'd been here when they come round. Money's the only thing they'd paid attention to. I ain't had none of that to give no how. When's the last time y'all seen y'all daddy?"

I shrugged. She knew as well as I did when he was last home. In the middle of the night he had staggered down the road singing his favorite blues songs as loud as he could. "Don't worry about the cow going po', just drank that milk and ask for mo'"—he kept repeating it, pausing from time to time to do a soft-shoe shuffle. Looking out the front window I had seen Ma Parker's light go on and her door open a crack. Daddy had left the next morning to go to work, and we hadn't seen him since. That was two nights ago.

"Now you home, will you keep the boys? I'm gonna go find my daddy so he can come fix things," I said.

"No you ain't." Ma Parker's voice cut the air sharply.

"Child, you ain't got no business in the kind of places where y'all's sorry-ass daddy likely to be. I'll find him tomorrow. I got a few ideas 'bout where he might be. You and your brothers can sleep here for the time being. I'll make pallets on the floor."

Grown-ups had boundaries, lines and sharp edges it didn't pay to cross. Ma Parker was clear about hers. Our first night in her house she had gone into the kitchen and called us to the doorway.

"Touch anything in this room," she said, "and I'll have your fingers for supper."

There was not a hint of humor in her voice.

There were hundreds of things in her kitchen—canning jars and big glass jugs on counters, in doorless cabinets, on top of the cabinets. The jars and jugs were filled with dark things floating in murky liquid, pale things in clear liquid, powders, animal fur, leaves, twigs, bark, dried flower petals and buds, plant roots, even something that looked like bunched-up spider webs. Cloth bags and cardboard boxes huddled in one corner of the kitchen. Drying plants swayed from clotheslines strung high across one side of her kitchen.

I kept a close eye on my brothers for any signs of disrespect or behavior that might lose them fingers. We all stayed out of her way, except June Bug. She tolerated him following her around, leaning against her legs to study whatever she was doing.

When we were under our own roof, she never came to check on us. Never asked questions when I kept June Bug home with me on the few occasions when I couldn't face my classmates, my teacher. Sometimes Ma Parker offered us food. "I made too much supper, y'all want some?" she would say, and always when I asked to borrow food—a few pieces of bread, a cup of rice, some eggs, a cup of beans—she was obliging. With us in her house she stepped into a short-tempered grandmotherly role as if we had become part of her collection of jars and jugs of things that needed tending. She made meals for us, made us do our schoolwork, made us keep regular sleep times.

Going to school, I got accustomed to walking pass the ghostly mound of our possessions. Ma Parker had let us bring into her house the things she thought people might try to take in the night like food, clothes, and Momma's sewing machine. The furniture and other big items she helped us pile together in the side yard and throw blankets and big pieces of plastic over that first night our things were in the yard. She said Daddy better show up soon or the landlord was likely to have our stuff hauled to the dump. "He ain't gon' let it sit there forever."

On the third day when the sun had already set, Daddy came by just as we finished supper.

"Y'all git your things and let's go," he said, looking irritated.

"You found a house?" Ma Parker wanted to know.

"I got someplace I can take 'em."

"Well, I told you, it ain't no bother for me to have 'em here til you git yourself set up proper."

"They've imposed on you quite enough. We ain't needing no more charity."

I didn't trust him because of the way his eyes slid around the room as he spoke, and because of the way he said, "they've imposed on you" as if it were some failure of ours that had landed us on the floor of Ma Parker's front room.

Even though I didn't trust Daddy, I had to follow him away from Ma Parker's and away from the nearby house where I had spent my first eleven years. I couldn't send the boys out in the world with only him to look after their needs. There was no telling what would happen to them, and I had promised Momma I would take care of them.

Daddy plunged ahead in front of Earl, Roy Anthony, and me. He carried June Bug, moving like a man wading through deep water. June Bug clung to him and peered over his shoulder at me, his small head bobbing up and down to the rhythm of Daddy's steps. He kept his wide-opened eyes trained on my face. His worry flowed to me in Daddy's wake as Daddy led us deeper into the Quarters.

Roy Anthony and Earl zigzagged along the road between me and Daddy, oblivious to any possibilities of danger.

"It ain't too far," Daddy said, after we left the Quarters main road and turned onto a footpath that led toward a dark clump of woods. The narrow dirt trail meandered through scraggly pines and dense hickory-nut trees. The only sounds of life were us stomping along and the whisper of flowing water. The bubbling hiss had grown to a low drone by the time we came to a narrow footbridge—two logs laid side by side—across a gaping hole in the countryside. The water was at the bottom of that gap. In the gathering darkness it was impossible to see just how far down the water was, but this gap in the world was wide enough to swallow Mr. Gamet's pickup truck.

"Step lively," Daddy said as he set foot onto the logs without looking back.

I watched as Roy Anthony and Earl approached the bridge and then hesitated. They turned startled faces to me. I shrugged and made silent "go ahead" gestures toward the bridge feigning annoyance and fearlessness. Roy Anthony stepped onto the logs first, one foot on each log, arms splayed at right angles from his sides like a tightrope walker. Earl followed.

Before I stepped onto the logs, I looked into the crevice. All I could see was dark gray air. Something tugged at me like an invisible cord fastened at my gut. The air around me shifted subtly, as it must under the wings of a bird. It was a seductive softness that seemed like it might sustain me, float me above the world where Daddy and Earl and Roy were hurrying along. I could leap into the open mouth of this gap in the world and become airborne, then soar quietly away. The insanity of that idea struck me suddenly. I was aware again of my wingless body, swaying earthbound at the edge of a deep gully with water dribbling through it. Panic pierced me like a thin, supple arrow. Daddy and Roy Anthony were already on the other side, continuing along on solid ground.

Earl was still on the logs, his arms wide open, looking for all the world like a fledgling. I concentrated, as if my thoughts would help get him safely to the other side.

When he did step onto solid ground, I steadied myself and stepped onto the bridge as my father had, glancing at the logs in front of my feet and into the empty space that spread out on both sides of me like a smooth gray sheet.

My fear was not of falling. My fear was of jumping. Of allowing myself to yield to the subtle invitation offered by the sweet, soft air—the promise of flight. But keeping my eyes on the logs in front of me, I put one foot in front of the other.

I stopped in the middle of the little bridge and looked up ahead of me at my brothers, now running along after Daddy. Roy Anthony turned back toward me.

"Come on, Maddy. Quit slowpoking around," he yelled. "You gon' lose us if you don't hurry up. It won't be my fault," he said in his exasperated whine. "Daddy is way up yonder." He gestured ahead toward another clump of trees.

It took a surprising effort to move slowly, deliberately along the rest of the bridge until there was dirt beneath my feet. When I looked up, I saw another well-worn footpath that wound into the trees. I followed it and found myself stepping out into a small clearing. There stood Daddy and the boys, waiting for me.

"We here," Daddy said, and pointed across the clearing. "There's where we gon' be staying for a while."

The house loomed, a silvery gray hulk isolated in a field of grassy stubble. It had a wide front porch and several windows on either side of the front door. The windows glowed red as if they were painted that color. A buzzing sound flowed out from the house like the noise of a wasp's nest. "Come on," Daddy said, heading toward it.

As we got closer, the noise grew and stretched out into the sound of Daddy's favorite music—the blues—music that always rose and fell to the same rhythm, with words groaning and growling to the whining complaints of guitar and harmonica. In this mix, I could hear a piano too. Riding on top of the music was the steady rumble of grown-up voices talking and laughing.

"What is this, Daddy?" Earl asked. "Where are we?"

The alarm in his voice matched what I was feeling.

"We home, my boy. We home."

CHAPTER TWELVE

WHEN WE STEPPED INSIDE and Daddy closed the door behind us, the rumble of voices, the squeal of a blues guitar, and the noise of an upright piano mingled with dense cigarette smoke rushed at us and closed in overhead like creek water swallowing stones. Grown-ups huddled around several card tables in the middle of the room drinking and chatting. Red-shaded lamps in the middle of each table tinted the hovering smoke and made teeth and the moist corners of people's eyes flash like rosy sparks in otherwise dark faces. Other grown-ups lounged on sofas backed up against one wall. Couples, arms and legs entwined, swayed to the music in a small dance area in one corner. This place made me think of hell as I had imagined it when Momma used to take us to church and I would sit listening to the preacher yell about the "fiery pits of hell" that awaited sinners. I wouldn't have been surprised to see the devil—glowing red with horns, barbed tail, and pitchfork—grinning at me from some shadowy part of the room.

My stomach lurched, my skin tingled, and my thoughts spiraled toward the ceiling. I wanted to turn and run. Ma Parker was right; children had no business here. How could Daddy bring us here? I wanted him to say that he had been joking, that we were just stopping here on the way to our new home. But we were lost to him as he slowly surveyed the adult faces in the room.

The boys looked around silently from where we stood, bunched around Daddy with our backs to the door. Daddy's attention went to a thin knock-kneed woman who stepped, like an apparition, from behind limp curtains draped across a doorway. She had one hand on her thin hips while the other held a tray of jelly jars half-full of clear liquid. She looked around and fixed a lopsided smile on her face. She headed to the people on one of the sofas and bent from the hips like a plastic doll to offer them the jars on her tray. When she straightened up and saw us, her smile disappeared and she marched our way.

"Eugene, what these kids doing up in here?" she asked.

"These my kids, Loralee." He winked at her. "You said they could stay here a while."

"I don't remember saying no such thing. I must of been under some kind of spell."

She flashed a smile and her face tightened again into that lopsided grin. When she relaxed the grin and turned her gaze on me and the boys, I saw the cause. There was a wide, smooth scar that looked like a snake moving from the hairline near her left temple across her cheek to her nose, down the side of her nose, over the corner of her mouth, and on down under her chin. As grotesque as the serpentine scar made her smile, she was still what most people would consider pretty—when she wasn't smiling. She had a heart-shaped face and large dark eyes angled seductively above high cheeks. Her wide nose had a majestic, purposeful shape, and her lips were generous and full. Heavy dark hair framed her mahogany face and hung in crinkled waves down her back.

"I didn't know you had so many," she was saying to Daddy.

"They ain't going to be no trouble," Daddy was saying. "You can put them in one of the back rooms."

"I can't be responsible for no kids and run a club at the same time."

"I'll take care of them."

"Like hell you will. You can't even take care of yourself. How old are you, girl?" she asked, bending forward and bringing her scar closer to my face. She smelled like cigarettes, hot sauce, and musky perfume. Her open mouth, waiting for my answer, showed an empty space where a front tooth was missing in the bottom of her mouth.

"Eleven, ma'am."

"You know how to take care of your brothers?"

"Yes ma'am."

"Alright then, that's your job. Take care of 'em, and keep 'em out of the way."

"Yes ma'am."

"They can stay," she said, still looking at me.

"Your heart's like gold, woman. I'll pay you a little something."

Daddy winked at her. Something startling, like the sudden sizzle of a wet finger touching a hot stove, flashed between them when she returned the wink.

"Can they go in the back now?" Daddy asked, still grinning at her.

"In a little bit. They can have Earlene's room. She's 'bout done for the night. Just let me straighten it up a bit."

"Loralee, can you get me a glass of water while we waiting?" Daddy asked.

"Yeah. Why don't you come on in the kitchen and get it while I go see 'bout the room for your kids."

"Y'all wait right over there now." Daddy pointed at an empty sofa and handed June Bug to me before he followed Loralee through the curtains. I pushed Roy Anthony and Earl in front of me toward the sofa. They sat down quietly, still staring gape-mouthed around the room. After a while Daddy joined us on the sofa. He eyed the other people in the room as he sipped his strong-smelling water.

Finally, Loralee appeared from behind the curtains again and motioned to Daddy. "Go on with her," Daddy commanded. I was glad to leave the noisy chaos that was agitating me and making my belly knot itself up with uneasiness.

The room where Loralee led us was at the end of a long narrow hallway with doors along both sides. It was big and empty except for a wide metal-framed bed pushed up against one wall and a rickety little table beside it holding an oil lamp. The one window was open. A cold breeze swept through, but even that did not chase away the musty scent of sweat, coal-oil smoke, and whiskey.

"I just remade the bed," she said. "It's big enough to hold all of y'all. Go to sleep anytime you like. Just don't burn out all the coal oil in the lamp, and don't any of y'all come back out in the front room, or go in any of the other rooms, you hear me?"

There was nothing to do once Loralee left, so we all piled into the big creaky bed. I listened as the boys gave in to the allure of sleep. At some point I must have fallen asleep too because suddenly I was jarred awake. Someone was leaning over the bed.

A whiskey-scented voice whispered close to my face. "I've got something to give you."

Moist eyes and pale teeth glistened in a dark unfamiliar face, glowing in moonlight seeping in the open window.

"Can I lay down with you?"

"No," I said, shaking my head.

"I swear I won't hurt you. I won't do anything you don't want me to."

"No," I repeated.

"I just need a little bit of room," the man said and sat down on the edge of the bed.

I pulled my knees up against my chest and pushed against him with my feet and hands.

"Come on. Just want to make you feel good." His hand snaked between my knees. "I just want to make you feel good," he said again. "Don't that feel good?"

He moved his hand roughly. I felt nothing but wild panic.

With his free hand he pushed me toward June Bug who was sleeping closest to me. I kicked and swung my fists at the man, pounding his arms and chest. He grabbed at my arms and legs. I heard the noise of my breath rushing in and out of my throat as I flailed like a wild animal, clawing, scratching, kicking, and biting at any of his flesh I could reach. But he stayed on the bed, trying to pin me against the mattress.

In the midst of my blighted desperation, when I felt close to some kind of irreversible devastation, a furious cry rose high and shrill in the moonlight. It pierced the wrestling noises of me struggling with the man. He froze, holding on to one of my legs. I kept kicking and flailing.

"See what you did!" he hissed. "You woke up that boy. He gonna git us in trouble."

On the mattress beside me, June Bug sucked in air, creating a sudden angry silence before he let out another wail. The man let go of me and stood up, backing away from the bed.

Roy Anthony turned over but didn't wake from his sleep.

"Goddamned baby—shut him up," the man said. "He gonna wake everybody."

I stared in stunned silence at the thing, like a stubby cucumber protruding from his pants. "Just wanted to make you feel good," he repeated and ran toward the door, the thing flopping in front of him, he stopped and turned back and ran toward the window. He quickly zipped his pants, then pressed his palms onto the sill, swung his legs through the gaping window, and disappeared.

June Bug was now in full wailing mode, hollering like his world was coming to an end. Earl sat up at the foot of the bed, looking toward the window. "Who's that?" he asked. "Why Buggie screaming?"

"What on earth is the matter with that boy?" Loralee was standing in the doorway, wearing an under-slip.

"Where's my daddy at?" I demanded.

"What you want him for?"

"To—to shut the window," I said, pointing furiously.

"Ain't you got sense enough to get up and shut it yourself?" Loralee asked.

Standing in the moonlight, wearing only a pale slip, feet wide apart, her fists planted on her hips, her dark hair hanging free like a loosened veil over her thin shoulders, she looked like a dark witch from a fairytale. I thought everything that had just happened had something to do with her.

We stared at each other.

"You must be seven different kinds of stupid," she said finally. "Young'uns. That's why I thank God I ain't got none!"

She stomped across the room and slammed the window down. The glass rattled in its frame.

"Y'all damn lucky that glass didn't break," she said in my direction.

"Where our daddy at?" I asked again.

"He's sleep and he ain't gon' be none too happy if that boy wakes him up. Better keep him quiet and go on back to sleep. If that boy cries again, I might just wake your daddy myself and send him up in here with a belt."

She slammed the door as she left.

I sat up on the edge of the bed and held June Bug, rocking him, my breath coming in short painful gasps, my toes barely touching the cold splintery floor. He curled comfortably on my lap, his thumb in his mouth. I don't know how long I sat there with my mind scurrying around like a mouse caught in a box trap. There was no way that I would try to sleep again in Loralee's house. I decided that in spite of her warning I would find Daddy and ask him to get us out of there.

Carrying June Bug, I crept into the hallway. I looked at all the closed doors along the long narrow hall. None of them showed any life now, except one where light was gleaming beneath the closed door. I stopped in front of it and weighed the possible consequences of opening it. Nothing could be worse than what had already happened. I turned the knob slowly and pushed.

Loralee and a man were in bed together, naked except for a sheet thrown over the lower half of their bodies. The man was on top of her, pumping up and down, grunting with each downward movement. His face was turned away from the door. But Loralee was facing it. Her eyes were closed, serenely. The scar lay placidly across her expressionless face like a gaudy decoration. She ran her fingers, along the man's back. "Do it to me, baby," she said suddenly, digging into the flesh of the man's back with her fingernails. She thrust her body upward a few times to match his grunting. Then she opened her eyes and looked at me where I stood in the doorway, hugging June Bug to my chest with one hand, clasping the doorknob with the other. For a few seconds there was the shock of surprise in her eyes, then it faded.

"It feels so good, baby. Don't stop," Loralee said, still looking at me. She brought her finger up to her mouth in a gesture of silence. Out of the corner of my eye I saw something familiar, and I turned to face what I must have known was there all along, Daddy's clothes, his pants, his shirt, his jacket, thrown over the back of a chair, his shoes sitting at muddy attention beside the chair.

"Oh baby, that's the way," Loralee moaned, and her fingers slithered along his back leaving white ashy marks in his dark skin with her fingernails. She kept looking at me with a passive glint in her eyes as Daddy grunted into her.

An image of the man's blunt penis sticking out of his pants as he ran toward the window rose in my mind. I staggered backward into the hall, pulling the door shut.

I leaned against the wall in the hallway, choking back vomit. June Bug clung to me as if I were a confusing part of his body. I could feel his puzzled gaze on my face.

The acrid taste of vomit irritated the top of my throat. There wasn't enough air in the hallway. I couldn't fill my lungs. Then there was too much air rushing in and out of my nose and mouth, making tiny red and purple paisley shapes do a dizzying dance inside my eyes. I leaned there, staring blindly into the dark hallway until my vision and my breathing returned to normal.

I went back to the room where we had been sleeping and shook Roy Anthony and Earl awake. I threatened to whip their asses if they didn't do as I said. I directed them, still half-asleep, into their shoes and jackets and ordered them to come with me. Obediently, they followed, bleary-eyed and confused, as I led them down the hall and through the cavernous front room with its now mute piano, deserted tables, lumpy sofas, and shielded windows. The door opened easily, and we filed onto the porch and out into the yard.

The night was sharp and transparent. The moon hung pearly and solemn in one corner of a silent expanse of silvery midnight sky. It cast a quicksilver halo over the woods. I faced the woods and the moon and led the boys across the clearing and back toward the footpath we had followed to get to Loralee's. I shut my mind to everything that had happened in Loralee's house, letting the cold, free night air rush easily into my lungs as I followed the path into the peace of the woods.

When we came to the log-bridge over the gap in the earth, I stopped. I had forgotten about it. In the moonlight, the emptiness of the gully touched the bottom of the narrow bridge and fanned out on either side of it like calm, still water.

"I can't," Roy Anthony whined. "Maddy, I'll fall."

He started to cry.

Earl stared mutely at the bridge, his face a mask of terror so tightly woven there was no avenue for tears.

"We got to cross," I said, submerging my own fear. "Ain't nobody gonna fall. We did it before."

"But Daddy was here." Roy Anthony whined.

"We got to cross, and we got to cross now."

The thought that we couldn't go any way but forward welled up in me like anger. Their weakness was a liability, opening a road to failure. I would not tolerate it.

"Well, I'm going, and if you don't come, wild animals or the boogie-man or something else bad will get both of you. Don't expect me to care," I hissed, and stepped forward onto the logs with June Bug in my arms.

"Wait, Maddy. Hold my hand and I'll go." Earl reached toward me, his eyes wide.

I shifted June Bug's weight to one hip and held onto him with one arm, offering my other hand behind me toward Earl. "Come on."

His desperate fingers curled around mine.

I glanced back at Roy Anthony, who stood safely away from the gully's edge, stepping from foot to foot and swinging his arms stiffly. "I can't, I can't—," he whined.

I hoped seeing the rest of us crossing would urge him forward, if for no reason other than not wanting to be left out. But when we got to the other side, he was still where we had left him, crying and wringing his hands.

"Y'all please don't leave me here," he wailed suddenly. I watched him, still hoping that some instinct, some need to survive would make him get on the bridge.

"Please don't leave me here," he pleaded and his voice rose and fell on the air, dropping into the gash in the earth that may as well have been as vast as the night sky.

"Maddy, please, please—"

Roy Anthony fell to his knees in the dirt and let his head fall forward. "I'm sorry I made you mad. I'm too scared—"

June Bug laid his head against my neck and sighed, a long wizened breath that rose into the air like a tiny sad cloud. Earl, who had not let go of my hand yet, squeezed my fingers tighter. But neither said anything. I watched Roy Anthony's heaving, shaking body on his knees on the other side of the gully, and still all I could feel was fury at him for being so weak.

"Don't leave him, Maddy."

Softly Earl started to cry, pinching my fingers tighter. "Don't let the boogie-man get Roy Anthony," he said.

Of course I couldn't leave him, but how was I supposed to make him cross?

I shook Earl's fingers free of mine and stood June Bug on the ground. "Both of you sit down here. I got to go make Roy come on across."

"Can't we stand?" Earl looked around. "May be snakes on the ground."

I was afraid to leave them standing alone so close to the gully's edge. "You got to sit," I said. "There ain't nothing on the ground gonna bother you. All the bad things on the ground already asleep."

They sat down.

Crossing back to Roy Anthony was slow and deliberate, with a pretense of ease that I did not feel. None of my brothers could ever know the fear that this open hole in the ground caused in me.

"Get up, Roy, and let's go," I said when I got to the other side. "We ain't got all night to be here. I'll hold your hand."

Roy Anthony looked up at me like he thought I would hit him. Some part of me wanted to. My fury had not subsided.

"I'm sorry," he whimpered. "There's something bad off in that hole. It's gonna make me fall 'cause I'm bad too."

"Roy, we got to go across."

He started a new round of sobbing, and a keen collection of angry frustrated feelings curled around me. As I struggled to bury them, it occurred to me that maybe I could carry him across.

"I'll take you across," I said and squatted down in front of him. "Get on my back!"

I felt the tentative weight of his thin body along my spine, and then he wrapped his arms around my neck and his legs around my waist. I stood and we stumbled around on solid ground while I tried to steady myself and get used to the weight of him. He was much heavier than June Bug, and heavier than he used to be when we were younger and I would give him piggyback rides. I had liked the high excited sound of his laughter in my ear when I jumped and twirled in circles. That was when I still liked him.

These days he was too mean for me to like him. But something in me still wanted him to survive.

I grabbed onto his legs and shifted his weight until holding onto him and crossing the logs seemed possible. "Now when we get on them logs don't you move. Don't you even breathe!" I growled. "If you do, we'll drop into that hole and die."

"I don't want to die, Maddy."

Under our weight, the logs seemed to sag slightly and the distance we had to cross seemed to have doubled. I had the impulse to run, but instinct told me that was foolish, you have less control about where you end up when you run. So I walked, lifting and planting my feet cautiously with each step, feeling for movement beneath me.

Roy Anthony clamped his arms more tightly against my throat with each step I took. After a few steps his arms were pressing so tight on my windpipe that my throat hurt. I was afraid to say anything until desperation forced words out of me. "You're choking me," I whispered. He loosened his hold.

My legs began to shake, and still the dull stumpy shadows that were Earl and June Bug seemed far away. Sharp pains were shooting through the middle of my back, and my sides where Roy Anthony's legs touched me felt like they might cave in and I would fold up like an empty can, crumpling and dropping us both into the bottom of the dark pit below us.

One foot touched solid ground. Then the other. I staggered, hanging on to Roy Anthony's legs, before I collapsed on the ground in front of June Bug and Earl. Roy Anthony released his grip and rolled away from me. Spasms of relief shivered through my legs and back as I lay there in the dirt feeling like I needed to cry. But I couldn't indulge the dark emotions that had gathered in me. I sucked in my feelings and got on my feet again.

❦

"What's the matter?" Ma Parker demanded when she opened her door to find us gathered in the moonlight on the porch.

"We can't stay where Daddy took us," I said.

"Lord have mercy, girl why'd you drag these children out here in this cold at this hour of the night? Your daddy took y'all where he wanted y'all to be."

"*Please*, let us stay here. *Please*."

"What on earth happened?"

"I just can't stay where Daddy took us."

"Child, where'd he take y'all?"

"To a lady name Miss Loralee's."

"Lord have mercy."

Anger blazed suddenly in Ma Parker's voice. "He took you up in that whorehouse? Did somebody hurt you?"

She grabbed my shoulders and shook me. "I'll kill the son of a—"

"No ma'am. Tried to—didn't get to—don't make me go back."

Even in the moonlight I could see the fury dancing in her eyes and tightening the lines around her trembling mouth.

"Y'all daddy ain't worth a damn," she said. "Least he can do is keep his own girl away from filth. You tell him what happened?"

"No ma'am."

"Child, why not? It's his job to keep you safe."

"He was somewhere else."

"I just can't believe your daddy didn't know better than bringing you up in that place. You done the right thing getting everybody away from Loralee's. I'll deal with your daddy."

Once again the boys and I were sleeping on the floor of her

front room. The boys drifted back to sleep, but every time I drifted into sleep, I kept startling myself awake. My mind kept running to thoughts of Daddy and Loralee and the man trying to get into bed with me. Why had he come in there? What had I done wrong?

Daddy showed up in the middle of the afternoon the next day.

"What the hell y'all doing over here?" he asked. Roy Anthony and I were in the front yard of our old house. Ma Parker had sent us to ferret out more of our school clothes from the dresser drawers. We froze, struck dumb like field mice caught out in the open. We hadn't expected him to show up so soon.

"Y'all hear me?"

"Daddy, I can't be at Miss Loralee's," I said.

"Why is that?" It was more an accusation than a question.

I stared at the ground in front of him. I couldn't tell him about the man. I was sure he would blame me for it.

"I just don't want to go back, sir."

"What'd you say girl?"

"I don't want to go back to Miss Loralee's."

"This ain't about what *you* want and don't want."

I could feel the heat rising in his voice. My stomach was beginning to knot up.

"You'll go where I tell you."

"Yes sir."

"So go get y'all things and let's get away from here."

Flashes of the man's grasping hands and whiskey-scented breath mingled with images of the slyness in Loralee's eyes as Daddy humped on top of her. That was all waiting for me at

Loralee's. Nausea tugged at my stomach. My knees began to shake and my hands trembled. I couldn't do as Daddy wanted.

"No sir, I can't."

"No sir, what?"

I picked each foot up and set it down again, trying to steady myself. "We ain't going to Miss Loralee's."

"This got to do with me and Loralee?"

"No sir."

"Don't lie to me girl. Loralee told me about you spying last night. What I do ain't your business. I'm your father and what I say still goes."

I looked up at him. His teeth were clenched and his face was set in hard lines, but he didn't say anything more. He just watched me through bloodshot angry eyes. Anger stirred in me—anger about all the ways he was failing us in Momma's absence. Just a few feet beyond where we were standing most of our belongings were still sitting in the dirt under old raggedy blankets and plastic tarps. He didn't have the right to call himself a father. He wasn't doing any of the things a father was supposed to do. My anger swirled, filling me up like hot air. I wanted to fly at Daddy kicking and scratching.

"I ain't got no father no more," I yelled. "You just some old stupid drunk!"

I put my hands over my mouth as the look on his face went from surprise to fury.

"You done got a little big for your breeches," he said through clenched teeth. "Boy, your sister gonna get a whipping."

I glanced behind me at Roy Anthony standing in the yard.

"Run, Maddy, run!" Roy Anthony yelled.

Roy Anthony's voice skidded on the air behind me as he ducked and disappeared around the side of the house. Before I could act, Daddy grabbed my arm and yanked me toward him. He had unfastened his belt and was pulling it from the belt-loops.

The insanity of my anger flew away when I realized the danger I was in. "I'm sorry, Daddy," I said. "I didn't mean it—please don't hit me—I didn't mean it." I pleaded as he raised the belt into the air above my head.

"Ain't such a smart-ass now, are you?"

His jaw clenched tight around his words and his eyes hardened.

When the belt touched my legs it felt like fire. The world shattered into pieces like glass. Splotches of blue sky, Daddy's dark face, his brown wool jacket, his dark-gray pant-legs danced like colored fragments in a kaleidoscope as each lick of the belt sparked new fires on my legs, my arms, my back, my shoulder. I ran to and fro, but Daddy's hand gripped my arm like a vise. I stumbled over my own feet and fell. My breath rushed out. Stunned, I looked up. Daddy's face was distorted by rage as he leaned forward over me. The belt dangled like a lazy snake in the air above his head. The dark hatred in his eyes was old. It didn't seem to have anything to do with me. It was as if he was looking at a stranger.

"Daddy," I said. "Please. Don't hit me no more."

Nothing changed in the lines and folds of skin around his narrowed eyes. He bared his teeth in a way that I had never seen him do before. I drew my knees in toward my chest as the belt came down, catching me across the face. The air flashed black around me. "Please, God, please make it stop," I mumbled, scrambling to get to my feet.

"Eugene, let her go, or so help me God I'll crack your skull."

Ma Parker stood behind Daddy holding a thick wooden plank as if it were a baseball bat.

"I mean it. You got no right to whip her. You shouldn't have taken her up in no whore house where some no-count child-raper could mess with her. She was right to run away. Now let her go, or I'm gonna do my best to lay you in the ground."

Somebody was wailing. I looked around to see where the boys were. People from a couple of nearby houses had come outside. I saw them like shadows in the distance. June Bug and Earl stood together on Ma Parker's porch. It was June Bug who was screaming.

"You hear me, Eugene?" Ma Parker hissed. "Somebody tried to rape that girl while you were off doing God knows what. We wouldn't be standing here now if that son-of-a-bitch had succeeded. You understand what I'm saying?"

Daddy lowered the belt and let go of my arm. I pushed away from him, scooting and sliding in the dirt. Ma Parker lowered the plank. When Daddy looked at me again, the sparkle of rage was gone and his eyes were glazed with disbelief. He slumped forward and dropped the belt on the ground as if someone had hit him.

"Did you completely lose your mind?" Ma Parker's voice was laced with her own brand of rage. "What possessed you to take your children to Loralee's juke joint?"

"I thought—"

"You didn't think. Not about your children. If you'd thought for a second about their welfare you'd have never taken them up in there. You know what kind of men go up in that place."

"Maddy—," Daddy said in my direction.

Ma Parker spat on the ground. "By God you are one poor excuse for a father. Why Dorothy trusting you can take care of these children, I don't know. I know y'all ain't got no family 'round here. I been trying to help 'cause I sure don't want to see no colored children taken away by white people. No sensible colored person do. Our children ain't the business of white folks. Only the sorriest, worst kind of colored folk lets county white folks take they children. But I'm about ready to count you among the sorriest and set the sheriff on you so the county can take these children. I sent your boy to have Mr. Watkins get the sheriff."

Daddy straightened up suddenly and put his hands out in front of his chest. "Hold on now, wasn't no need of you doing that. You don't need to get white folks involved here. I ain't done nothing that bad. Just one wrong decision. I can fix that."

"It ain't just one thing, Eugene. You been leaving these children by they self an awful lot. I used to find them hungry. You let the lights get cut off. You quit paying your rent—lost the roof over they heads. You just ain't taking care of them right."

"I swear I'll do better. You know it'd kill Dorothy if these kids went to the county. She already lost—I got to be a stand-up man for her this time. Just give me a chance to make this right."

"I'm tired of watching these kids suffer behind your drinking."

"I'll quit drinking. I swear. I'll get another house. Just don't turn my kids over to no law. You said yourself it ain't right for colored kids to get into the hands of white folk. I'm begging you. Let me fix this."

He and Ma Parker faced off, drawing the world into silence around them. Fear rushed into that terrifyingly quiet space, and I felt like I might drown in it. We could be taken from Daddy by the sheriff? The same people who had thrown our furniture into the yard? What would they do with us? Send us to live with strangers? Split us up? My ears were ringing, and my emotions bounced from corner to corner in my mind.

In that moment, Ma Parker's gaze found mine.

"No sheriff," I mumbled, shaking my head.

The lines of Ma Parker's face softened as I kept shaking my head.

"One last chance, Eugene," she said, turning back to Daddy. "But you got to quit your drinking, and you got to swear you'll never raise a hand to one of these children again."

"Yes ma'am, I swear. I won't drink no more, and I won't hit my children."

"You know I can make your life more miserable than it is, and I ain't talking about no law neither."

"Yes ma'am, I believe that," Daddy said, ducking his head.

"Now get away from here before the sheriff's deputy shows up. Don't come back till you got a decent place for these children."

"Maddy," Daddy said again. "I—"

My mind and my body had become one big flame. There was nothing he could say that would fix that.

"Go, Eugene," Ma Parker said.

Daddy turned and took a few steps, then suddenly he was running toward the heart of the Quarters.

Awareness broke in on the dull gray world of my sleep, and I awoke to a hazy feeling of loss. Ma Parker had given me something that made me drowsy as soon as she got me inside and cleaned my wounds with some kind of mineral waters. The gathered darkness let me know that I had slept the rest of the day away, lying on a pallet in her front room. Still, I resisted my mind's effort to come fully into the present where my whole world was in shambles. I wanted to slide back into that quiet dreamless sleep. But images of what had happened crowded around me like angered wasps. The arm that Daddy had gripped so tightly throbbed. Pain streaked out from my fingertips when I touched my face to find that my right eye was swollen shut. My legs burned, and efforts to move them sent startling jolts of pain into my feet.

June Bug stirred on the pallet beside me. His small hand reached out and touched the side of my face. "Hurt?" he asked.

"Okay," I whispered. Even my teeth hurt.

"Hurt." He repeated, and made me hurt even more as he crawled around me, stood up, and left the room. He came back with Ma Parker. She stood in the doorway with a small coal-oil lamp.

"You awake, Maddy?"

"Yes ma'am."

"How you feeling?"

"My daddy hurt me," I said when she kneeled and brought the light close to my face.

"You need to go on back to sleep," she said. "This'll help."

She offered me a metal cup. The warm bitter liquid went down easily, and the world receded again.

The swelling on my face went down in about a week, and we found I could still see out of my right eye although it had a discolored brown spot like a vague smudge on the white. Scabs covered what had been bloody welts on my legs and arms and I could bend my sprained elbow again.

"You were lucky," Ma Parker said. "It could've been a whole lot worse. You gonna patch up just fine. Good as new."

I was sure that I would never again be "good as new." There was a big bundle of grief and rage inside me that hadn't been there before, and none of her ointments and talk was even coming close to touching it, let alone healing it. But she wasn't giving up, even if I wanted to. She wouldn't let me wallow in grief or anger. She put salves on my outward wounds and fed me healing potions and talked to me, at times harsh and impatient, about survival.

"No point in sitting around looking all sad and feeling sorry for yourself. Ain't gonna get you nowhere in this world. Come on, girl, find your spite. You can't let one beating make you roll over and die. Got to toughen up or the world gonna eat you alive. It takes strong colored people to make it in this god-forsaken place. Even the Lord Jesus didn't find this world easy."

Neither the brutality nor the practicality of her words were lost on me, but my most compelling reason to heal, to "toughen up," was my brothers.

"What's gon' happen to us, Maddy?" Earl asked me at least once a day. Even Roy Anthony did everything I asked him without back talk or teasing. He understood now what the man at the commodities office had told us—we had to be a team because our grown-ups had slipped up.

"I'm sorry this all happened. You got to forgive me," Daddy begged. He sat on the edge of Ma Parker's doily-draped armchair. "May God strike me down dead if I ever do something like that again."

There was sincerity in his voice, but I refused to let my feelings attach themselves to his words. I sat as far from him as possible on Ma Parker's sofa, looking out the window at the boys playing in the yard. Anger boiled up in me when I gazed at him directly.

"I want to make this up to y'all, Maddy. But I need your forgiving."

When Momma used to take us to church, more than once I

had heard Reverend Hallowday preach about forgiving and turning the other cheek. He told us about Jesus asking God to forgive
the people who had hung him on the cross. Did God forgive
people for killing Jesus? If he did, why does he still let bad things
happen? And if God couldn't forgive, how was I supposed to do
it? People always said forgive and forget. Did forgiving mean forgetting? I couldn't see ever forgetting or going back to how I used
to think and feel about Daddy. My whole inside world gave way
to darkness when I tried to think about it.

Daddy came back a few days later with store-bought clothes—a
red corduroy dress for me, blue jeans for each of the boys—a big
block of fudge, and the news that he had found a new house.
"Not in the Quarters either," he boasted. "In a better part of town.
Nothing but the best for my family."

We had to go with him, Ma Parker told me, as I stood in her
front room looking out the window across the yard at Daddy and
Buck loading the rest of our stuff from the yard into the back of
a borrowed truck.

"He's your daddy," Ma Parker said. "He still got legal rights to
take you wherever he wants. I don't want y'all to go to the county
home 'cause nothing good ever comes of that. Your daddy's your
only other choice. You got to put up with him a while longer.
I ain't smelled whiskey on him recently. He swears not to start
again. I can't tell you for sure he'll stick to that. He like a lot
of men I've seen that was overseas in the war. They ain't none
of them real normal like. They came back with trouble inside.
Some worse off than your daddy—doing much worser things.
Your momma kept your daddy all of one piece. Pray to God she'll

be home soon. While she still gone, it's up to you to keep yourself and your brothers safe.

"When your daddy mad or full of drink, don't try to stand up to him. Keep a handle on your feelings. Do what he say. If you can't do what he say, act like you going to, then get away like you did from Loralee's. Get the boys and go somewhere safe till he comes back to himself. 'Cause you ain't never gonna be no match for him and the crazy things inside his head."

What she was telling me I had already figured out. Regardless of the promises Daddy made, I knew I was the only one the boys could count on. That meant I could no longer afford to behave like a foolish child, and by now I knew it was pure foolishness to try to stand up to Daddy. I would have to find ways around him.

CHAPTER THIRTEEN

THAT HOUSE ON DORSEY Street haunts my memory, crouching on stubby brick legs in the middle of a stark gray yard. It's flat-faced with dingy white paint peeling in flaky strips. Screenless front windows gape like blank eyes. When I let myself think about it, a barren place opens inside me and a blighted sense of loss threatens to drown me.

The house was bigger than our house in Harvest Quarters had been. It had five rooms laid out in a square and an inside bathroom—a small room with a toilet and a face bowl just off the back of the kitchen. Under different circumstances this new house could have been cause for celebration, but even after Daddy had put all of our familiar things inside, it still didn't feel like home.

Momma was nowhere to be found in that house. There were no memories of her sitting on the bed, or walking from one room to another, or standing over the stove cooking meals there. Her commands hadn't leapt around, bouncing off walls and furniture urging us toward civilized habits—"Pick your clothes off the floor . . . wipe the mud off your shoes before you come in . . . don't talk with your mouth full . . . take a comb to that head before you go out the door . . . treat your brothers like you care about them . . ."

I was sure she would never come back to us in that place because I couldn't picture her there.

"My Ma'dear wants to know if she can borrow a cup of sugar."

When I peered out through the screen door, the three boys from the house next door stood on the porch, grinning.

The day we moved in, they had sat on their own porch watching as Daddy and Buck hauled our things inside. They laughed a lot, like they were watching a funny show. Seeing them up close, I saw that the biggest one was a little taller than me, with a dark round face and ears that angled away from his face like small wings. The other two were scaled-down versions of him, with hungry bubbly lips and the wide-set dewy eyes of baby cows. Their faces were ashy with the crustiness of sleep lingering in the corners of their eyes and around their mouths. Their uncombed hair looked like black BBs. They leaned and stretched like feral cats, trying to look past me into our house.

"We ain't got no sugar," I answered.

"I didn't think so," the biggest one said. "Y'all looked like poor niggers to me." He smiled smooth and slow, and the other two ducked their heads and laughed.

"Takes one to know one," I said and slammed the door.

The next day when we got home from school there was a pile of human feces on the front porch.

"Now how you know they did that?" Daddy said when I told him about it later. "Did you see them boys put it there?"

"No sir."

Daddy was standing at the stove making supper. He turned toward me, steam and smoke rising from the skillet in which he was frying chicken livers and onions. He lifted the skillet out of the reach of the pale blue flames as he spoke. "Well then, how you know they did it? Maybe a dog come on the porch. You can't go around saying things like that about people. You got to give people a chance if you want to make friends."

It'd been two weeks since the move and Daddy was still cling-ing to his promised sobriety. He was a bit irritable but more like his old self—the Daddy he was before Momma and Ida Bea left home. On the first school-day after the move, he had walked me, Roy Anthony, and Earl to school to show us the route. Somehow he found a lady a few blocks over to look after June Bug while the rest of us were at school. He was still coming home at the end of each day, even on weekends, and he insisted on cooking. But he was wrong about the porch.

There was a difference between human waste and animal waste. It seemed to me something very basic. I couldn't have told him what it was, but there was a difference. If Daddy didn't know it, it meant he couldn't sense the danger in it being on our porch. Momma would have. She could find the danger in the simplest gesture or carelessly dropped word. "Stay away from dogs you don't know. They may have rabies . . . Don't play near the railroad tracks, a strong wind could come up and blow you on the tracks in front of a train . . . That boy's got a dirty mouth. It's gon' land him in deep trouble one day. Steer clear or he'll pull you down with him . . . Bad things go on deep in the Quarters. Bad things will happen to you too if you go in there."

To prove what nice boys our new neighbors were, Daddy went next door that evening and invited them over. He didn't seem to care that their clothes were dirty and raggedy, and that one of them kept wiping his snotty nose on the sleeve of his shirt, and that the oldest one kept putting his hands in his pants.

Daddy made us get out toys and play with them. They mimicked and made fun of my brothers and me behind Daddy's back. June Bug was the only one of us who got to avoid them. He let out a shrill, piercing scream whenever one of them got near him or the dump truck he had gotten for Christmas. I was ready to tear the world to pieces when they were finally leaving and Daddy gave them each a nickel for playing with us.

A few days later when we were on our way home from school after picking up June Bug, those boys met us in the road a block from our house.

"Ignore them," I told Roy Anthony and Earl as I pulled June Bug along by the arm.

"Y'all can't go this way 'less you pay me a nickel," the oldest one said. He and his brothers grabbed hands, spread their arms, and stretched out across the road as far as they could. When we meandered around them they fell in behind us.

"Why y'all go to school?" one of the younger boys asked.

"'Cause we want to," I answered. In truth we went because I knew Momma wanted us to, because we had nothing better to do, and because we got free lunches.

"They go to school 'cause they stupid little niggers, and they think school's gonna' fix they stupidness," the oldest boy said.

I hurried us along, checking my impulse to run. "Never run from a dog," Momma said. "They smell fear. If you run, they'll chase you, and you can't outrun a dog. Just act like you ain't scared."

When we reached our yard, I sent my brothers in front of me across the plank over the drainage ditch. The oldest boy grabbed me from behind, wrapped his thin arms around my waist and humped against me. His brothers' laughing voices rose on the air like the noise of cackling hyenas as they egged him on. I scratched and pawed at his arms. Roy Anthony ran back across the ditch, and I caught glimpses of him tussling with the younger boys.

"Albert, leave that girl alone."

The boy released me. A fat soot-colored woman was on the porch where he lived. She stood with her fists pressed onto her wide hips, her bosom vibrating in a shapeless housedress made of pink flowery fabric. Her furrowed forehead sloped elegantly away from the edge of a head-rag made of the same material as her dress. Angry lips protruded in a mix of bloated cheeks and a wide flat nose. The startling ugliness of the woman's face and brightly colored clothes was like something I might have conjured in a nightmare.

"You leave her alone right this minute," she bellowed. "Come here directly!"

"Raymond, Robert, y'all get over here too," she said.

When the oldest boy reached the porch, she hit him on the back of the head with the heel of her hand. "Is your mind that small? What'd I tell you?"

She hit him again with both hands.

"I'm sorry, Ma'dear," he said, trying to duck away.

She followed his movements and kept slapping at his head. "Don't sorry me. I don't want your sorry. I want you to do like I tell you. You suppose to be showing your brothers how to be. Here you is out here acting like a animal. I ain't raising no animals—Lord knows I try with you, but you keep on finding ways to shame me and make me look like a fool in front of the whole world."

She grabbed his arm and pulled him into the house, still hitting him as they went. The two younger boys crept along onto their porch and followed her inside.

I hurried my brothers onto our porch. With trembling hands and a heart beating way too fast, I opened the padlock on our door, pushed everyone inside, and wedged into place the wooden two-by-four we used as a night latch across the door.

"Was that his mama?" Earl asked.

"Dog, she sure is ugly," Roy Anthony said.

"Was she ugly, Maddy?" Earl wanted to know.

"She looks like the boogie-man," I said.

"Is she the boogie-man?"

"Could be."

A few days later those boys lay in a ditch and threw rocks at us as we walked home from school. A few mornings after that when we were on our way to school, one of them ran up behind us and pummeled Roy Anthony in the back, then ran away. They kept up these kinds of tactics as the weeks wore on, though they were careful not to pick on us in sight of their house and their Ma'dear, or when Daddy was home. When he was around, they came into our yard full of grinning politeness, tossing "yes sir" and "no sir" to any of his questions. The younger boys seemed to genuinely enjoy playing with Roy Anthony and Earl, but the older one had a sharp mocking edge, even to his politeness.

I told Daddy they picked on us when he wasn't around. He told me I must have just misunderstood something. "I'm sure they were trying to play with y'all," he said. "I don't know why y'all don't like those boys. They seem nice enough to me."

I stopped trying to convince him otherwise, and my brothers and I developed our own ways to deal with them.

One day I was out in the backyard hanging up clothes I had

just washed by hand. Roy Anthony's fourth-grade teacher had called me into her classroom during recess earlier that day to say that he smelled like pee. "Give your mama this note when you get home."

I tore the note up and spread it on the side of the road as we walked home. But I set about washing our school clothes. As I pinned the clothes to the line, Earl, my lookout, yelled, "Run Maddy, run." I headed toward the house, but the neighbor boys got between me and our back steps.

"We got you now," one of them said as they rushed forward. In the struggling that followed I was knocked to the ground. The two smaller boys pinned my arms to the ground and the larger one kneeled beside me.

"No use in you yelling nothing 'cause Ma'dear ain't home," one of them warned.

The oldest boy unzipped his pants and pulled out his fleshy hot-dog-sized penis. When he leaned near me, I kicked at him. Suddenly, Roy Anthony was there swinging the broom. The bristle end caught one of the boys holding my arms. He fell backward, scrambled to his feet, and ran away crying. I heard the dull clunk of metal hitting flesh-cushioned bone, and the oldest boy collapsed onto his face in the dirt. Earl was standing over him with a small pot.

The boy got to his knees, his hands pressed against the back of his head. "You hurt me," he said, sounding surprised. Roy Anthony swung the broom and slammed it against his shoulder.

"You've done it now. I'll git you little niggers," he threatened as he got to his feet and ran into his own yard.

"We beat their butts," Roy Anthony said, once we were all inside with the doors locked and the windows closed. "That'll teach them to quit messing with us."

But it didn't. Later that day, they pulled our wet clothes from the line and dragged them in the dirt.

We came home from school one day to find that a window was broken in the back of the house. Some food was missing, mainly commodities—cheese, jars of peanut butter, cans of meat. Flour and rice had been spread over the kitchen floor. Some of Momma's things—her hot curling iron and straightening comb—were missing. Our photo album was gone from its spot in Momma's dresser drawer. Some toys were missing.

Daddy wouldn't believe that the boys next door had broken in and taken our things. Though he did go next door to ask their mother if she had seen anyone in our yard. She said no, and of course her sons denied seeing anything or knowing anything about it either.

A week after the break-in, we came home one day to find pieces of photographs scattered over the backyard like confetti. Even then, I understood that I had lost something vital. I knew there would never be another session with me and my brothers crowded around Momma as she sat in Daddy's stuffed chair with the photo album open on her lap. Her stories had always been the same, her words careful and slow. "This is my daddy," she said, pointing to a picture of an unsmiling man with hard, dark eyes and a square angry jawline beneath a flat topped military hat that matched the dark uniform he wore. Momma said his granddaddy had worn it to fight in the Civil War. "He was a slave that ran off and joined the Union Army. They were fighting to free the slaves," she said proudly. "Y'all's great-great-granddaddy helped free our people. My daddy was real pleased to have that uniform passed down. Don't know what happened to it, but we got it here in the picture. My daddy left this world four years before you were even born, Maddy," she added before pointing to the sepia-tinted portrait on the next page. "Now this here is your grandmomma," she said. With her fingertip, she carefully traced the chin of the sullen and serious face her mother had turned toward the camera. "She never saw you neither. She died of the TB when I was still in high school, and you didn't come along till five years later. And this," she said turning the page, "is your daddy and me when we was first married."

There they were, Momma smiling broadly into the camera. A wide-brimmed white hat with a spray of flowers framed her face. Her tailored white jacket was cinched at the waist with a wide black belt. Her white pleated skirt stopped just below her knees and her shiny white high heels looked like they were patent leather. Daddy stood at her side, his body angled to face her so the camera caught him all in profile. He wore a pale-colored suit and black shoes. Their outfits were clearly chosen to match. Daddy's arms were wrapped around Momma's waist, and he was laughing, chin tilted up, mouth open. They looked like they had just shared a private joke.

That was all gone. Proof of my family's history had disappeared piece by piece, and there was nothing I could do to get it back.

I didn't tell Daddy about the photograph confetti. For a few days I moped around feeling sad. Then anger, more profound than sadness, surfaced. I figured I needed to make those boys leave us alone once and for all. I looked through our kitchen knives and chose a butcher knife with a smooth wooden handle and a blade a little longer than my hand. I wrapped it in a dishrag and tucked it in my book-bag.

Those boys came at us on our way home from school. We were taking a shortcut through an alley behind a block of stores—a dry cleaner's, a barber shop, a small grocery store. I had led my brothers this way several days in a row, thinking myself clever for realizing this route let us avoid the neighbor boys' favorite ambush spot. But they had figured out the changed route, and there they were, holding hands, stretching the width of the alley.

I pulled the dishrag from my book-bag and dropped my bag in the dirt, motioning for my brothers to get behind me. I unwrapped the knife and gripped it in front of me with both hands.

"You ain't gonna cut nobody with no knife. You too chicken," the oldest boy said.

"Try me," I said.

"You too chicken," he repeated.

"I'm sick of you messing with us," I said.

The younger boys looked at each other with something akin to fear. They snatched their hands away from their older brother and backed away from the blade pointed in their direction.

"She ain't gon' cut nobody," the oldest boy said and stepped closer, his grinning mouth looming bigger, his eyes shining with arrogance.

A flush of heat warmed my chest and face.

"I double-dare you, pussy girl with no mama," he said.

His words hit me like darts, causing sharp little pains. My anger blossomed. I felt the wooden handle of the knife smooth and sturdy against my palms.

His smile broadened. "You heard me, pussy girl. Where your

mama at? She ditched your ugly butt," he taunted, moving closer. "Even your own mama don't like you."

I swung the knife. He threw his hands up to shield his face. Red appeared where the tip of the blade grazed the back of his fingers. He backed away from me and looked at the little spots of blood.

"You cut me," he said with disbelief. "Why you do that?"

I couldn't believe what I had done either, but angry emotions were squeezing my heart so tight I could hear it pounding in my ears. "Come closer and I'll cut out your goddamned guts," I said, as if I had been cussing and swinging a knife all my life. "I'll cut your face off. Your *Ma'dear* won't even know you."

The quality of light in his eyes shifted, and I watched his disbelief turn to something dark.

"Don't say stuff about my Ma'dear," he said. "She ain't done nothing to you."

"Go suck her big titties," I said.

"You nigger trash. Your own mama don't want you. That's why she ran away."

Spiting in his face was a reflex.

He charged at me. I swung the knife again. He ducked and stumbled backward. The blade slid across the inside seam of his pant leg near his knee. He grabbed the place where the blade had almost found his flesh again and glared at me. I crouched forward with the knife pressed in my fisted hands. I wanted to see something go to pieces.

"You crazy," he said.

"Like a mad dog 'cause of you."

He backed farther away. "Crazy little bitch."

I took a step toward him. "Come on, pick on me some more. Yellow-belly chicken-shit coward."

"Somebody ought to put you in the ah-sane asylum," he said. "I ain't even studying you no more." He turned and walked slowly away. I watched him till he turned out of the alley.

"You should've just kept on cutting him till there wasn't nothing left," Roy Anthony said behind me. He sliced the air with an imaginary blade.

Earl and June Bug stood back, staring at me and the knife in my hands with quiet bewilderment.

"What if they tell their momma?" Earl asked.

"I ain't scared of their *Ma'dear*," I answered, still riding the crest of insanity.

"Maddy can just cut them all up," Roy Anthony said, grinning and still brandishing his invisible knife. "Chop chop chop, into a thousand little bitty pieces. Then bye-bye. They ain't nowhere no more. They all gone."

I looked at the knife in my hands. My anger receded at the sight of the red smudge on the tip of the blade. I started to shake. What had I done? I had hurt someone. I didn't know I had it in me to swing a knife at another person. What would have happened if that boy hadn't gotten out of the way? The knife had been a bluff. I just wanted to scare them away from us, but my anger had surged beyond my control. Was I becoming like Daddy? A danger to everybody?

I was afraid to look at my brothers—scared of what they must be thinking of me.

I picked up the dish-rag and wrapped it around the knife.

"It's okay, Maddy," Earl said. "You didn't cut him bad."

Earl's jaw was clinched and his lips pressed tightly together when I looked at him. He seemed much older than his seven years. "From now on he ain't gonna bother us. He think you crazy now 'cause you cut him. You gone crazy, Maddy?"

I shook my head.

"Crazy like a fox," Roy Anthony said, looking at me carefully. "Right, Maddy?"

"Just had to act like it," I said, but I wasn't sure about that. "Let's go on home."

I was still shaking when I retrieved my book-bag from the ground and reached for June Bug. At first his touch was hesitant, then he curled his fingers around mine and held on for dear life the rest of the way home.

CHAPTER FOURTEEN

BY THE TIME FEBRUARY pushed into March, we had been free from harassment by those boys long enough for me to start to feel easy about our life.

Then Daddy started drinking again. We found him asleep on the porch one Saturday morning, still smelling of whiskey. Roy Anthony and I poked and prodded him until he was awake. His own embarrassment hurried him into the house before any of the neighbors were up and about. Once he fell off the wagon, he stayed off, and we were back to the familiar rhythm of him being gone more often than he was home, especially on the weekends. But this time I wasn't worried about food. I had found another way to add to the commodities that Roy Anthony and I still picked up every month.

One day while waiting at the counter in the small grocery store we passed on our way to and from school, I overhead the grocer telling his teenaged worker to toss a couple of loaves of bread out back. The loaves were mashed up inside the bags as if someone had walked on them. Later, when the store had closed, Roy Anthony and I went down the same alley where I had confronted the neighbor boys with a knife. A row of battered metal trash cans leaned against a brick wall at the back of the store. We looked in the cans and there, near the top of one, were the mashed loaves of bread that the young clerk had been ordered to throw out. Hunting through those cans became a regular practice. Sometimes under the cover of darkness I locked Earl and June Bug in the house, and Roy Anthony and I sneaked to the alley and searched blindly through the garbage cans, ignoring the scent of bad meat and overripe fruit and vegetables to haul home any items we thought might be edible. What we found varied from week to week—bread with patches of pale, fuzzy mold inside cellophane bags; limp, discolored vegetables; crushed boxes of macaroni noodles or breakfast cereal. But there was always something we could keep when we examined our find in the brightness of our kitchen.

Even with the added food source and the end of our daily harassment by the neighbor boys, I was sometimes overcome by fears about our survival, especially when Daddy wasn't in the house and my brothers were sleeping. I lay awake imagining bad things that might happen to us—Daddy deciding never to come home, being set out in the street again, those neighbor boys climbing through the window while we slept, the house caving in on us. Sometimes to stave off these waking nightmares, I put off bedtime by gathering my brothers on the sofa to read to them from the Andersen and Grimm fairytale collection Momma had gotten for us years earlier through some book club or other that she belonged to.

One restless night when I was getting ready to read to my brothers, June Bug was nowhere to be found. I hurried through the house calling his name. A new fear—that the boys next door had taken him—taking root in me. Maybe they had just been pretending to quit messing with us while they hatched a plan to take June Bug. But when I opened the bathroom door, June Bug was sitting on top of the box where we kept our dirty clothes. He looked up at me with guilty fear. In his clumsy three-year-old hands was the box of kitchen matches. Several spent matches lay on the dirty linoleum near the toilet.

"Bad boy," I yelled at him, and snatched the box from his fingers. "What are you doing with these matches? Haven't I told you never to touch these?"

I pulled him up roughly and whacked him on the behind to the rhythm of my words. "Don't ever let me catch you messing with these matches again."

He whimpered and started to cry.

"I mean it, you little numskull. You want to burn the house down and kill everybody?" I hit him again and pushed him out of the bathroom and into the kitchen. He ran crying across the kitchen toward the front room where his brothers were. I closed the bathroom door and set myself down on the closed toilet, feeling sorry for myself. I hated having to be on guard all the time to keep everybody safe. I didn't want to be June Bug's trainer. It wasn't supposed to be my job to teach him right from wrong. That was Momma's job. That was Daddy's job. It wasn't fair that I was stuck doing it.

"Come on, Maddy," Roy Anthony yelled, pounding on the bathroom door. "You gon' read us a story or not?"

Bristling with resentment, I tucked my feelings inside and went and sat with the boys on the couch. I chose "The Snow Queen." I read absentmindedly, envying Kay, the frozen boy with no laughter and a heart turned to ice. I wished I could be free of my feeling like he was. I was tired of feeling sad and scared. I was tired of holding everything in to keep my brothers from knowing just how scared and sad I was all the time. If I were carried away to the ice palace, I wouldn't want anyone to find me. I would want to be left alone. My feelings flowed forward in me like a stinging tide. I paused to let them recede, but they clogged my throat.

"Keep reading, Maddy," Earl urged.

I handed the book to Roy Anthony and headed to the bathroom to cry in peace. A crackling hissing noise met me when I headed through the kitchen to get to the bathroom. I looked up to see brilliant orange and yellow flames reaching from the bathroom doorway across the kitchen ceiling.

"The house is on fire," I yelled, running back to the front room.

Roy Anthony flung himself off the sofa and headed toward the kitchen. I grabbed the back of his shirt.

"Out the front door, you stupid moron."

He twisted and squirmed trying to break my hold. We stumbled together and I landed on top of him on the floor. I was on my feet before him. He turned over onto his back and looked up at me, his face contorted with little-boy rage.

"Roy, I ain't joking. Get outside!"

"Don't call me Roy. I hate it. I want to see the fire."

"You can't! We got to get out of here!"

Earl was already at the front door on his tip-toes, pushing up on the night latch. The two-by-four moved a few inches but not enough to clear the top of the brackets that held it in place.

I pulled Roy Anthony to his feet and pushed him toward the front door.

"Help Earl."

I reached for June Bug who was still on the sofa, drooling with his mouth open. His head bobbed as his confused gaze shifted from his brothers struggling at the door to me. He looked through the living room doorway toward the kitchen and suddenly scrambled up into my arms. I ran to the door and bumped Roy Anthony and Earl out of the way. When I pushed up on the wooden bar, it flew up out of the brackets, landing on the floor nearby. Earl was whining like a wind-up toy. He pulled on the doorknob with both hands. Roy Anthony pulled at the door frame, grunting frantically. We could all hear the fire roaring softly in the kitchen now.

The door swung open and Earl and Roy Anthony tumbled onto the porch. I couldn't resist the temptation to look back. Smoke was wafting through the doorway into the front room. June Bug's fingernails dug into my shoulders and he screamed in my ear. I hurried onto the porch and followed Roy Anthony and Earl across the yard and into the street.

The world was silent as we huddled together in the street. We watched as the windows in the front of the house began to glow orange. The voice of the blaze grew as fire pushed through the roof at the back of the house and waved skyward. A window in the side of the house exploded, spewing glass into the yard. Fingers of flame poked through the square hole, waving toward the house next door. Earl ducked his head and started crying. More glass shattered and a warm wind brushed my face as the fire reached out through the front windows.

This was the thing secretly wished for, called forth quietly and fervently in my dreams—destruction, quick and dramatic. I had always known that this was possible. My fury had escaped the boundaries of my mind and taken on a life of its own—the fire-breathing dragon I had wanted to become. I stared, shocked by the speed of the destruction and pleased that the hateful house was being devoured.

The neighbor boys' Ma'dear came onto her front porch. "Lord have mercy," she yelled above the noise of the fire and ran back inside. She came hurrying out a few minutes later with her sons in tow. They came into the road, groggy and ill-tempered. They quieted their complaints when they noted the flames from our house stretching and yawning in the wind toward their own.

Other neighbors along the street were coming out of their houses. Somewhere there was wailing, a steady undulating sound, and when I saw the red flashing lights round the corner onto Dorsey Street, I realized it was the fire truck sirens.

"Is your daddy in there?" someone asked, stepping in front of me.

I stared into the woman's face, her bulging eyes, her open mouth, the panic in her voice more menacing than the fire.

"Your daddy in there?" she persisted.

I stared beyond her, watching our possessions transformed to fire and smoke and spiraling toward the stars.

"Your daddy—"

I shook my head to get her out of my way.

"Thank the Lord," the woman said, and moved away.

The fire department's hoses, straining engines, flashing lights, and rushing firemen added more excitement and organized chaos to my drama.

"It's a shame," someone said nearby.

"They ain't had much no way," someone else answered.

"They lucky none of them children didn't burn up. They all out, ain't they?"

"How many of them was there?"

"There's four of them over there."

"That's all of them, ain't it?"

"I'm pretty sure."

"Wonder what happened?"

"I heard they mama run off and left them years ago."

"You know the daddy's a drunk. Saw him passed out on the front porch a few weeks back."

"I heard the momma's sick in the hospital."

"They daddy's a drunk, that much I know."

"My William sees him in the Quarters joints all the time."

"Your William taken to reading the Good Book in the joints?"

"Don't be trying to say nothing bad 'bout my husband. He goes from time to time, and they ain't no harm in it."

On and on the bits and pieces of conversations went around us while I felt alternately elation, sadness, and shame. There was something glorious yet pitiful about being singled out by fire.

I looked around at the spectators' gloomy excitement. Shadows danced on their faces and along the fronts of their clothes as they feasted on my family's tragedy.

When the fire was finally out, the house hadn't burned to the ground after all. Jagged shards of glass stood smoky and brittle in the front windows. Long black shadows of soot scarred the walls and the window frames and the gaping mouth of the open front door. Firemen came out like big red ants, carrying smoldering wet items, which they tossed into the yard.

"Who lives here?" one of the firemen wanted to know. The neighbors parted away from my brothers and me like a receding wave, exposing us like minnows washed ashore. "They're the ones roused you white folks and brought you into our neighborhood in the middle of the night," our neighbors' silent shrugs and pursed-lip expressions seemed to say.

"Where's your mama, or daddy?" He leaned toward me a little, his grimy fingers clutching a pencil above the clipboard he held.

I stared into the man's pale eyes, tongue tied. I held onto June Bug, thinking about my feet, which were suddenly itchy with cold.

"She deaf and dumb?" the fireman asked, turning to someone near me.

People shrugged and shook their heads.

A woman stepped forward out of the crowd. "Their mama's in the hospital and their daddy's at work," she said.

The fireman turned to her, relieved to find someone communicative.

"Well, it looks like the fire started at the back of house."

His attention turned to me again, and I retreated inward, shaking my head when he asked if anyone had been cooking or using matches.

"You sure about that?"

I shook my head again. I wasn't about to admit to this white stranger that June Bug had been playing with matches earlier. What would he do to June Bug? What would he do to me since it was supposed to be my job to keep everybody out of trouble?

"Well, it's all out now," the man said. "But the house ain't fit to stay in. Whole back end is gone," he added. "You know how to reach their daddy?" he asked the woman.

"I'm Mrs. Keyes, a friend of the family. I'll take the children to my home until I can get word to their father."

Who was this stranger claiming to be a family friend and offering to take us in? I studied her face carefully as she listened to instructions from the fireman. She had a shiny ebony face with a wide nose that lay flat and dignified between pious, near-sighted eyes framed in thin black cat-eyed glasses. Her thinning hair was swept up in graying old-fashioned waves that lay against her head like a swim cap. Her face was friendly, but I was sure I had never seen her before.

"Santa Lady," June Bug said quietly.

Suddenly I recognized her as one of the charity ladies who had come running from the kitchen when Daddy was knocked unconscious at the Christmas party. She had been the one to suggest that someone give us a ride home that day. What was she doing here?

"Alright then," the fireman was saying, "just don't let them stay in that house tonight. Can't guarantee nothing when you got a fire like that. They can take a few items of clothing, if they can find anything ain't burnt or wet. Just don't touch nothing in that back part of the house." The fireman touched his black helmet and backed away.

When the firemen had pulled their large serpentine hoses out of our house and recoiled them in their lairs and rolled their trucks away, Mrs. Keyes beckoned for us to follow her into the house.

"The man said we can get a few things," Mrs. Keyes said.

Roy Anthony and Earl shook their heads. "We gon' wait," Roy Anthony said, and neither of them moved from their spot on the side of the road. I could see that they were trembling from cold and fear. So I went with Mrs. Keyes.

Going back into our house was like stepping into a melted photograph. Everything was swathed in shades of gray and black. The heavy, pungent odor of charred wood and burnt fabric hung everywhere. The hairs on the back of my neck tingled, and my nostrils burned from the acrid smell of the burnt walls and my family's possessions as we walked through the front room.

The sofa where we had sat a short while earlier had exploded, puking up guts of wet, dingy clumps of cotton and straw. The ceiling in the front room was burned away, revealing the charred beams that held the roof. The paint on the walls was blistered and blackened; the firefighters' muddy, sticky boot prints danced across the floor; in the kitchen stars were visible through a gaping hole in the roof; the back wall and the bathroom were gone. The bedrooms had fared better, but not much. The ceilings were intact, but the wood was blistered and singed. The chairs and dressers were covered with soot, and the beds were soaking wet.

"Get the things you all are going to need over the next few days," Mrs. Keyes commanded.

I stood in the middle of our bedroom. June Bug felt like a doll in my arms. My dragon was still alive, and I was certain that at any moment, the house could burst back into flames. I lifted my chin and started screaming, long shrill wails of grief and fear pouring out from my mouth. Mrs. Keyes simply stared at me, and I realized that I was not making a sound. Only in my mind was my distress so clear. The only noise coming from me was the thin rasp of my hurried breathing. Inside my head I was hearing again the high roar of the flames, the crackling of burning wood, the terse shattering of glass.

"Snap out of it, child, and help me gather some things for you all." Mrs. Keyes went to work, opening drawers, pulling out clothes and wrapping them in a wet blanket.

As I watched, orange-yellow flames were snaking through all of my thoughts, lurking in every shadow in the house, waiting to be released again. I didn't want to touch anything. I didn't want to bring anything from that house with us, wherever we were going.

"Go see if you need to get anything from your parents' room," Mrs. Keyes suggested.

In Daddy's bedroom, part of the ceiling was blistered and smoky and there were puddles of water on the floor, but otherwise the room seemed untouched. I opened Momma's dresser and looked at her clothes—blouses, skirts, underwear—folded neatly. She had taken her best clothes with her to the hospital, and I couldn't imagine what to take now. In the corner of her top drawer was a tube of bright red lipstick and a small, round mirrored compact with pressed face-powder. I grabbed those things. I don't know why since I had only vague memories of Momma ever putting on lipstick, and I had never seen her apply face-powder.

When I looked in Daddy's dresser, there were his dress shirts starched and pressed from the dry cleaner's. His harmonica box was pushed into the back of the top drawer. An image of him playing and Momma smiling swept through my memory. So I took the box. Those were the only items I was holding when Mrs. Keyes looked in and asked if I was ready to go.

"For my momma," I said when I noticed her staring at the objects in my hand.

"What about your school books?" she asked.

Back in my and the boys' bedroom, I found our book-bags in their usual place, in our grandmother's rocking chair in the corner. The weather-treated cloth fabric was smoke-scented but untouched by fire or water. I grabbed the three of them. I moved my books aside and stuffed Daddy's harmonica and Momma's lipstick and compact into the bottom of my book-bag and piled my books and paper on top, then followed Mrs. Keyes outside.

The fear melted away from Roy Anthony's and Earl's faces when June Bug and I were again standing with them on the side of the road. As we walked toward where Mrs. Keyes said her car was parked, I glanced one last time at the house. At least for the moment, my dragon was quiet.

CHAPTER FIFTEEN

A PALE-GRAY DAY WAS already peeping in around the edges of heavy green velvet curtains when I sat up in bed. For the first time in my life, I had slept in a bed by myself. I smiled.

My roll-away bed and the other two where my brothers slept were lined up within arm's reach of each other in the center of a large room that had the sharp smell of cinnamon, roses, nutmeg, and a scent that reminded me of Daddy's aftershave. Along one wall in the dark-green room stood a tall wardrobe and a large bureau with drawers made of shiny pecan-colored wood. Both pieces had gold handles shaped like seashells. An oval mirror was perched high atop the bureau. A big bed with a headboard and footboard that matched the bureau and the wardrobe was against another wall. A white chenille bedspread draped the bed, crisp and formal. I had never been in a room like this, and it was one of several such rooms in Mrs. Keyes' house.

"Welcome to my family home," she had said the night before, after we piled out of the backseat of her car and she shepherded us inside her house. She had stood smiling at us in the middle of her living room. She was dressed in white, smudged here and there with soot from our house, but still sparkling as she stood amid the elegant clutter of her home. "Welcome," she said again.

My brothers and I gaped at the voluptuous gray velvet sofa with starched white doilies draped over its camel-hump back and plump arms. Matching armchairs were angled toward each other and the sofa, making a circle around a dark polished-wood coffee table. Small tables on either end of the sofa had the same kind of frail bowed legs as the coffee table. A gleaming mahogany whatnot cabinet with curved glass doors stood against a wall near windows draped with heavy gold fabric tied closed with tasseled ropes made of the same gray velvet as the sofa and chairs.

On the walls were ornate framed pictures of dignified black people dressed in the clothing of an earlier time when women wore high-necked, heavy-skirted dresses that swept the floor and kept their hair pulled away from their faces to form tight knots at the tops or backs of their heads. The men were dressed in long suit jackets that hung near their knees, like my great-great-grandfather's Union Army jacket, only these men were not wearing uniforms. These black folk looked just like the images of white people in our history books. It had never occurred to me that there were such wealthy black people that far back in history.

"These were my family members, God rest their souls," Mrs. Keyes said waving toward the images on her walls. "This has been my family home for several generations."

"Ma'am?"

"Before slavery was ended, child," she added smiling. "The Keyes have been here since before the emancipation."

This house revealed a history of black wealth and black privilege, a kind of privilege that reached a long way back and beyond even the reach of my more well-to-do classmates like Florence Simms whose daddy was a dentist and Harold Thomas whose daddy wore suits to work in a bank. Their houses were small compared to Mrs. Keyes' house, and not nearly as old.

My brothers and I didn't belong in this refined space. They

huddled around me shivering, I think as much from the shock of our new surroundings as from cold.

"You children need to rest," Mrs. Keyes said and led us down a carpeted hall to this elegant green room. She wheeled in the roll-away beds and unfolded them as if she had been expecting us. The boys had climbed into their beds and fallen asleep easily. Apparently, I had also.

Now here I was, on the first morning after the fire. Visions of the hungry flames flashed through my memory, and I was scared all over again. Would I always be able to get us to safety?

One by one my brothers came noisily out of sleep. I quieted them, pressing my finger to my lips and shrugging when they tried to question me. Earl was content to sit quietly on the edge of the roll-away bed he had shared with June Bug, who lay sucking his thumb and staring at the ceiling.

Roy Anthony climbed out of his bed and crept around the room, running his hands along the surfaces of the furniture, his smile blooming extravagantly with each surface he touched. His skin was almost the same pecan color as the furniture so that when he touched a piece his fingers seemed to melt into the surface and he appeared to become just a boy-shaped handle. When he saw me watching him, he tiptoed over to my cot and leaned in to whisper, "Can we stay here forever?"

"Children, you all may as well come on out now," Mrs. Keyes called from the other side of the doors. They were double doors made of small glass windows covered by a lace curtain. Mrs. Keyes' outline was visible through the glass and lace.

"I know you're up," she said when we didn't respond. "It's okay now. There's nothing more to be afraid of."

We sat on chairs with carved backs and cushioned seats at a large polished-wood dining table in the center of the dining room. Mrs. Keyes fed us a breakfast of pancakes and scrambled eggs on glass plates with gold edges and flowers painted in the center. She had cooked the food and announced that it was the first time in years that she had made a meal for anyone but herself. "I'm out of the habit of cooking, but you all seem to be enjoying it," she said.

When we had eaten our fill, Roy Anthony and I washed the dishes while she ushered Earl and June Bug down the hall to a real bathroom to get clean. Eventually we each bathed in the white porcelain tub that had hot and cold running water and stood on carved animal feet in a room by itself. The toilet and a tall pedestal sink were in a small room next door.

Later, she bundled us up in the smoke-scented remnants she had salvaged from the fire and some of her old sweaters and drove us to the Salvation Army Donation Center where we spent hours hunting through boxes of free second-hand clothes and shoes. When we headed back to her house, the trunk of her car was filled with several large bags of old clothes that were new to us.

When she finished with us we sat in her living room and waited—the boys like frightened polite animals on the velvet sofa, me in one of the armchairs—while Mrs. Keyes made phone calls on a heavy black telephone I had noticed on a high wooden desk in the room next to the living room. The occasional words that drifted from the other room made it clear that the calls were about us, ". . . all together four . . . hospital neighbors said . . . Culpepper . . ."

The fire lingered in my imagination as I strained to hear her conversation. I wondered what Daddy would do when he came home to find us gone and the house burned. How would he find us? What if he couldn't find us? What would become of us? Where would we go? We had no home to go back to. If I had to, I was sure I could find Ma Parker's again. Maybe Mrs. Keyes knew her and could drive us to her. I was sure she would let us stay there as long as we needed to. Not knowing what was to come next made me feel a little jumpy. I wondered if I should take the boys and sneak out while Mrs. Keyes was on the phone. I could try to find Ma Parker's on my own.

"Looks like you all get to stay with me for a little while," Mrs. Keyes said when she came back into the living room. "Would you all like that?"

"Yes ma'am," Roy Anthony answered, looking at me and nodding.

The first couple of days we were in Mrs. Keyes' house we sat straight-backed and rigid before her, startling like birds when she left the room and came back. In the beginning she kept us home from school.

"You all need to rest away from the harshness of what has happened. The world won't stop if you miss a few days school," she said. I was fine with that. I watched the boys, following them around quietly when they left her front room. She was patient with us, especially Earl when he started acting out his nightmares in bouts of sleepwalking and she had to run into the yard in the middle of the night wearing only a flannel nightie and a hairnet to retrieve him. She was patient with me too when I woke one morning to find a huge yellowish stain fanned out around me on the sheet and soaked into the mattress of my cot. In spite of her quick old-lady smile and her saying, "Accidents do happen, Madeleine Genell," I sank into a cloud of humiliation and self-pity. I had never wet the bed before.

She prayed over us every night. Once we were all bathed and lying in bed, she stood, palms clasped, eyes closed. "Thank you, Lord, for giving these children a second chance. Lift them up and let them know that you have not forsaken them. Remind them of your love, Lord. Thank you, Great Redeemer, for choosing me to help them. Give me the strength to be worthy of this task."

I didn't know whether to be grateful or ashamed that we were the subject of such fervent prayer.

She took us to church too. On Sunday we piled into her car and rode across town to sit in the cushioned pews of St. Paul's Baptist Church with some of Blossom's other well-to-do black folks, though none of them were as well-to-do as Mrs. Keyes. Everyone dipped their heads in respect when they talked with her after the service.

Church was not foreign territory to us. Momma used to take us to church, though we hadn't been in a long time. Our little church, Sweet Hope Baptist, with its simple A-frame wooden building, plank steps, scrubbed wood floor, bare pews, plain glass windows, and rowdy optimism, was nothing like St. Paul's, which had a cement sidewalk leading to the front of the building, brick steps, shiny brass door handles, carpeted aisles, cushioned pews, stained-glass windows, and a sober quiet air that smelled of privilege and certainty.

The first Sunday we attended St. Paul's, Reverend Bruckner preached about "the wages of sin" and the "young innocents caught in the falling beams of their parents' sins." He even mentioned "houses of ill-repute in Harvest Quarters" and "the less fortunate little children" who needed the prayers and "Christian helping hands of the St. Paul congregation."

I sat, hot with shame, staring into space, afraid to look at anyone, thinking maybe the fire had been not my secret wish, but God's judgment.

Some of my classmates were there—Faye Mangrove, Harold Thomas, Naomi James, Florence Simms. They sat as they did in school, wrapped in lives untouched by tragedy or shame. I envied their calm untroubled faces and well-fitting clothes.

My knees shook on the church steps when Reverend Bruckner grabbed my hand and bent forward to grin into my face as Mrs. Keyes introduced my brothers and me as "the young ones I spoke about."

"Welcome to our church, little sister." He smiled with his mouth opened, revealing gold teeth in the back. He looked into my eyes, his face settled in a gentle expression of kindness. When he turned his attention to my brothers, I hurried down the steps and into the parking lot at the side of the church. I waited beside Mrs. Keyes's car, turning my face from the pitying smiles of parishioners as they walked by.

"Hey, Madeleine Culpepper," Faye and Naomi said, almost in unison. They stood in front of me. "Is Sister Keyes your Grandmomma?" Naomi asked.

I glanced at Mrs. Keyes where she stood, still on the church steps with my brothers and Reverend Bruckner, encircled by others from the church. "Yes," I mumbled and looked at the ground.

"How come you've never come here with her before?" Naomi asked. Faye stood by demurely, holding a small black patent leather bag in her white-gloved hands. Mostly they ignored me at school, but they were never mean. I wished they would ignore me here too.

"We go to our own church," I lied, pulling myself up straight and grinning. The heat was rising in my face, and I had the feeling that I was piling heavy weights on top of myself. A lie was a lie. "We're just visiting with her for a while, because our momma's away with my sick sister and our daddy's out of town," I added.

The world didn't open up to swallow me, and no bolts of lightning materialized out of the overcast March skies.

For three weeks I went to school wearing starched and ironed clothes that I didn't have to wash. Mrs. Keyes had someone come in once a week to wash and iron and take care of some of the cleaning. I had been surprised to learn that a black person might hire another black person as a maid. I thought that was something only white people did.

"I'm a lucky so-and-so to be working for a colored lady as generous as Mrs. Keyes. She a much kinder boss lady than the white ladies I work for," the woman said when Roy Anthony, Earl, and I returned from school one day to find her there.

Mrs. Keyes had left a note for me. She was off somewhere "doing the Lord's work," her note had said. "Please behave for Mable as you would for me," the rest of note had read.

"Y'all some lucky little children too," Mable said. "That this big-hearted lady would bring y'all into her home. She didn't have to you know. Y'all situation would've been very different if she didn't live by her belief in Jesus."

"Ma'am?"

"It ain't my place to talk to you about that. It would be kind of like gossiping. Ask her 'bout it sometime. Just don't do nothing to make her regret taking y'all in."

When I came home I didn't have to think about food, or bad neighbor boys, or taking care of my brothers. I was liking life in Mrs. Keyes' house. I started praying for Daddy to stay away.

So I was more than a little disappointed when I looked up one day on the way from school to see him walking toward us in the road. I couldn't bring myself to smile when he stopped in front of us and said in a sober, pacifying voice, "Y'all know the county court said I had to leave you with they appointed guardian till I dried out?"

I didn't know that, but learning it didn't soften my heart toward him. If he had been a different kind of person he would have seen my disappointment when he bent forward and cupped his hand under my chin to make me look up at him. But probably all he saw were the tears welling up to blur my vision of his haggard face.

I snatched away from him and ran the rest of the way to Mrs. Keyes' house.

"Madeleine, keep your brothers inside. I'm going to step outside and talk to your father for a minute," Mrs. Keyes ordered when Daddy came into the yard.

I made the boys sit on the sofa, and I went to eavesdrop by the door that I left open just enough for me to lean into the opening and listen to the conversation outside.

"Could have you thrown in jail right now," Mrs. Keyes said. "You were supposed to go through the agency before you contacted these children directly. Do you have papers saying you met the court requirement for getting sober? What about work? New housing?"

I couldn't see, but Daddy must have shaken his head.

"You're lucky these children aren't gone from you for good," Mrs. Keyes said. "Do you know why it's against the law to leave children under the age of twelve on their own?"

"Yes ma'am. I understand. I never meant to leave them that long. I don't know what they told you, but I only went out to get cigarettes. When I came back the house was burned and they was gone."

"Mr. Culpepper, I'm not as dumb as I must look to you. I know where the sheriff's deputies found you the day after the fire. I know what they threatened to do with these children. The county child welfare office located your wife up at the state hospital. She's the main reason I agreed to step in and foster these children for a time."

"I don't know what she's been telling you either. But I takes care of my family."

"Well, you weren't doing such a good job to see the state they were in when I found them, skinny as unfed chickens, their clothes dirty and stinking, that girl's hair all knotted up."

"I do the best I can. My children ain't nobody else's business."

"Mr. Culpepper, I don't want to fight with you. But I want you to know that if something doesn't change, the county will take these children. Now they've records and files opened on your family circumstances."

"You can't—"

"It won't be my doing. It will be your doing, and yours alone."

"I love my children, but things is hard. Nobody understands what I go through."

"Save your excuses, Mr. Culpepper. Have you thought about what your wife is going through up there at the state hospital with your sick baby? I spoke to her on the telephone, and she told me that some days she eats nothing but a candy bar for dinner because she has no money for anything else. She's relying on the local charity organizations to bring her food most of the time, and she's worrying herself sick about you and the four here at home."

"You don't understand how hard it is to come home day after day—"

"Life is not a cake walk for anybody. You need to start acting like a man, Mr. Culpepper."

"I am a man."

"Right now your eleven-year-old daughter is acting like more of a man than you are. If it wasn't for her, those children inside my house would be dead right now."

"You ain't got no right to talk to me like this. I came here to get my children. My twenty-one days is up. I ain't had a drink in all that time."

"I'm not giving you those children until you bring me papers from the courts telling me to release them to you. And I know they will need to see proof that you've rented a house to take them to, and a letter from your boss proving you've still got a job. If you can't do that, you'll have to explain to your wife why the county has her children."

There was silence in the yard. Daddy didn't say anything more, and I imagined him trying to stare Mrs. Keyes down. She must have held her ground, because after a while I heard him trudging up the road.

Mrs. Keyes came inside and smiled a depleted shaky grimace. Her eyes were moist behind her black cat's-eye glasses and her hands trembled as she locked the door.

"Your daddy said he will come back to see you all later," she said when she turned her back to the door. She leaned against it and stared at us. Then she started crying. Exhausted flat tears rolled down her face. She pulled a handkerchief from a pocket and dabbed at her eyes and cheeks like she was wiping away dust and not sadness.

"I'm sorry," she said finally and headed down the carpeted hallway to her bedroom at the back of the house.

My brothers looked at me, I shrugged and dropped down into an armchair. I was alarmed by the knowledge that we were once again in danger of being taken by white strangers. Would Mrs.

Keyes really hand us over to the county or was she bluffing? Certainly she would not go on caring for someone else's children forever. That had been my fantasy. But I knew that reality lay some place in that cloudy adult world that I still wasn't old enough to enter.

My emotions simmered as I examined the idea that my brothers and I could vanish into a world run by pale-eyed people whose veins showed like spidery lines beneath skin too thin to really understand us. No, I couldn't let that happen. I decided that if Daddy didn't come back in time, I would take the boys and run away. I wagered I could find Ma Parker's house somehow. Maybe I could even figure out how to get to where Momma was. If she saw just how bad things were, maybe she would come home.

But as the days went by I grew too nervous to eat, because when it came right down to it, I didn't know how long to wait for Daddy, and each time I thought of leaving Mrs. Keyes or not returning there at the end of a school day, I was terrified to the point of nausea and dizziness. So I began to pray and wait for Daddy's return. Being loose in the world with Daddy was better than being scattered among strangers.

CHAPTER SIXTEEN

♥

DADDY CAME THROUGH. HE found us a house, another three-room shotgun with the toilet in a little room on the back porch. He had salvaged what little furniture of ours had survived the fire—the beds and dressers mainly. He put my and the boys' beds in the middle room and his and Momma's bed in the front room. All of our kitchen stuff was destroyed, but he had found a second-hand wooden table.

It was important to me that we appear like normal, cared-for children. Without asking Daddy's help, I had followed a group of kids one morning to figure out how to get to school from our new location. Roy Anthony and I alternated in our attendance because one of us needed to stay home each day with June Bug. Although my teacher Miss Washington must have wondered at the changes in my appearance and the lapses in my attendance, she never said anything to me. Eventually, Daddy announced that he had found a woman near our school to keep June Bug.

The people in our new neighborhood showed no interest in us, and the children steered clear, probably because their parents told them to. That was fine with me. After our experience on Dorsey Street, I no longer automatically assumed that other children would be kindreds. I looked for signs of malice in everyone and stayed ready to defend myself and my brothers from all comers.

Mrs. Keyes came to visit us a few days after we moved. She brought two bags of groceries, some dishes, old battered and scuffed pots and hard plastic plates (no doubt from the Salvation Army like the clothes she had gotten for us), and a few toiletries—soap, toothpaste, and a handful of toothbrushes. I told her that we were doing well, though I could see her looking around the rooms, summing up our situation as she passed through to the kitchen.

"I'm mighty glad to hear that," she said, with old-lady intonations that meant she wanted to believe me but knew better. She could see for herself how things stood with us.

"Where's your daddy now?" she wanted to know.

"He don't come home from work until late."

She nodded at me as she took the food from the bags she had brought. She stacked most of it, cans of soup and vegetables and potted meat, in the cabinet and then set about making a meal for us. While we were eating, she heated water on the stove and set the metal washtub in the middle of the kitchen and filled it with the water.

"Bathing is important," she said to me when it was my turn in the tub. "Especially when somebody wets the bed. You don't want your schoolmates to know."

Although I hadn't wet the bed since that one time at her house, I was sharing a bed with June Bug again, and he wet the bed nearly every night. He was refusing to wear diapers anymore. He wanted to wear undershorts like his brothers. During the day he did all right, dragging someone along to the back porch with him. We would help him on to the commode. He would hold one of our arms as a railing while he sat, sometimes grunting and straining to do his business, his tiny feet dangling above the floor. He was resolute, and I felt a bittersweet appreciation for him as he pushed himself, trying to train his body to follow a predictable schedule. But in the middle of the night I could not get him up for that trip to the back porch, so some mornings I awoke to the cold dampness of pee-soaked sheets. I wiped with a damp cloth those parts of myself that it occurred to me might smell like my little brother's pee. But judging from the polite teacherly tone in Mrs. Keyes' voice as she scrubbed my back in the tub, there were some places that I had missed.

Mrs. Keyes was about to leave when we heard the unmistakable sound of Daddy's boots on the porch. The boys and I knew from the slurred singsong of his cussing as he fumbled with the door latch—he was drunk. He had fallen off the wagon as he would have said it. I was sure Daddy would not be happy to see Mrs. Keyes.

"Go out the back door Mrs. Keyes," I pleaded, while Daddy pulled at the front door.

She looked at me blankly, ignorant of the meanness my daddy drank from the bottle.

When Daddy finally flung open the door, Mrs. Keyes stood in the middle of the room, a vulnerable old lady with her brown cloth coat buttoned up to her chin and her black patent-leather pocketbook pressed against her chest like a shield.

"Good evening, Mr. Culpepper," she said.

Daddy blinked awkwardly, then grimaced with anger as recognition descended into that drunken no-man's-land where he was.

"What you doing in my house, old woman?"

"I came to look in on the children."

Her voice, steady and calm, conjured up generations of well-meaning, long-suffering women who had put up with much to keep children alive.

"I don't want you in my house bothering me and my kids. Keep your dried up old ass away from kids."

"There's no need to be rude. I was just looking in."

"Daddy," I said, as he took a menacing step toward Mrs. Keyes.

"She was just going, Daddy," Roy Anthony said, coming up close to me.

"We told her we fine, now she going," I added.

"Shut up. This ain't none of y'all business," Daddy warned. "Don't come near my kids again, old woman. You hear me? We don't need your charity."

Daddy had taken another step toward Mrs. Keyes and stood glaring down at her. He clenched and unclenched his fists at his sides.

"I was just leaving," she said.

Her voice trembled.

"You damned straight," Daddy said. He grabbed Mrs. Keyes' elbow and yanked her toward the door.

Roy Anthony and I rushed forward and fastened on to Daddy's arms.

"No, Daddy, don't. She been nice to us."

"Oh no, oh no, oh no," Earl said, pacing circles around us.

June Bug stood back, wide-eyed but quiet.

"You and Buggie gone!" I yelled at Earl. "Git!"

"Let go of me, you little sons-of-bitches," Daddy yelled at me and Roy Anthony.

He lifted his arms and shrugged, trying to shake us loose. There were moments of chaos with Daddy holding on to Mrs. Keyes and me and Roy Anthony holding on to him—the four of us heaving back and forth in the doorway like we were doing some kind of crazy dance steps. Daddy shoved Mrs. Keyes onto the porch and pushed her toward the edge. She grabbed onto a porch post and wrapped her arms around it and held on—her cheek pressed against the dry wood, the rims of her glasses crammed into the skin of her temples. Daddy pulled and pushed at her.

Roy Anthony and I pulled on him from behind. He let go of Mrs. Keyes and spun around, swinging his fists at Roy Anthony and me. We ducked away from him.

"Wait till I get my belt," he yelled, clutching at the top of his beltless pants. "Just wait—"

He stumbled back into the house, momentarily forgetting about Mrs. Keyes. She let go of the post. Her breath came in shallow gasps. Her hands shook as she straightened her glasses and patted her clothes in front of me and Roy Anthony as if we were a mirror. She nodded tersely, then turned and hurried down the steps. We watched her scuttling along toward where she had parked in the pale light of the only street lamp on our block.

Roy Anthony and I looked at each other, our hearts thumping, aware that the danger was not past. The sounds of Daddy's rage rumbled inside the house—the noise of small objects being thrown around. He was cussing the whole time. The back door slammed open. I jumped off the porch and ran to the backyard with Roy Anthony following. Earl and June Bug were at the bottom of back porch steps. I grabbed June Bug in my arms, and we all ran back to the front yard. I looked up and down the road, but Mrs. Keyes' car was gone. Now what? We had to get away from Daddy.

"Come on," Roy Anthony said. He dropped to his knees and crawled under the porch. The rest of us followed him.

"Everybody quiet," I said as we crouched in the darkness. Earl pressed his face into my shoulder to keep himself from crying. I could barely hear the other two breathing. The front door burst open, and Daddy's heavy footsteps stormed across the porch above our heads.

"We don't need no motherfucking charity," he grumbled, and

some of the food Mrs. Keyes had brought flew into the yard in an angry shower. Canned goods hit the ground and rolled, the loaf of Sunbeam bread slapped the ground in a crunch of cellophane noise. Daddy repeated this scene several times, stomping through the house and back onto the porch to fling our food into the yard.

"Where y'all hiding? I'm gonna whip everybody's ass when I find you," he ranted inside the house. "Ungrateful little sons-of-bitches. You may as well come on out. Everyone of y'all gonna get a whipping. Telling that old biddy I ain't feeding y'all."

He clumped through the house again and came onto the porch. For a long time there was silence, then the sound of water. The warm acrid scent of urine filled the air at the edge of the porch and splashed toward us. After a while, Daddy went back inside.

It seemed that hours had ticked by in the cold dark air under the porch as we waited for Daddy's angry boot-steps to stop pounding the floor above us. When it had been quiet for a while, I made the boys stay put, and I crept out from under the house and tried to look through the front window.

"He may be sleeping," I whispered to Roy Anthony from the edge of the porch.

"I'll go see," Roy Anthony said.

"Not the front way," I said.

We went quietly around to the back door and Roy Anthony went inside. My heart pounded waiting for him to come back. When he did, he said Daddy was passed out on his face in the bed.

"What do we do now?" Roy Anthony wanted to know.

"Let's get our food."

We went back to the front yard and gathered whatever food we could find in the dark and brought it to the back porch.

"I'm cold," Roy Anthony said.

Earl whined softly. "I don't want to go inside. I'm scared," he said.

"Daddy never wake up when he been drunk," Roy Anthony said.

"He might this time."

"But I'm cold, Maddy," Roy Anthony said.

"You such a baby sometime," I hissed.

"I ain't no baby, I'm cold."

"Come on, we can go in the toilet room."

That night we all slept—at least they slept, I dozed in and out—huddled beside the commode with its stench of human excrement and urine. When the night sky began to fade toward daylight, I figured the whiskey was all out of Daddy. I woke the boys and led them into the house to lie down on our beds.

They had all escaped back into sleep, and I pretended to be asleep when Daddy came stumbling through our room to go to the toilet.

I heard him bringing in the food from the porch. I wondered if he remembered what he did the night before. Did he feel guilt or shame as he knocked around in the kitchen toasting warped slices of bread in a skillet and boiling a pot of grits for our breakfast?

When he came to wake me before he left for work, he sat on the edge of the bed. "I made y'all breakfast," he said, looking at the blanket beside me.

I stared at the planks of the ceiling, stained and dingy from other people's smoke.

"Maddy, I'm sorry," he said after a long silence. "I'm real sorry. I never meant to hurt nobody. You the oldest, I want you to understand that. I'm sorry if I hurt anybody last night."

I looked at him. His eyelids drooped halfway over his blood-shot eyes. A single wet line was running down each cheek, collecting in the creases around his mouth and disappearing under his chin. Sadness rose in me like some kind of black tide. I stared back at him, but this time I didn't feel sorry for him. I felt sorry for myself and angry at him.

"You almost threw Mrs. Keyes off the porch, Daddy."

Embarrassment played in his eyes. "I'm real sorry," he said again. "I wish there was something I could do."

"You could stop drinking, Daddy," I said.

I hadn't planned to say those words. But there they were, hanging in the air between us. Daddy's eyebrows went up. His mouth opened and closed, but no words came out. I sat up in bed and leaned my back against the wall, bracing for whatever might follow.

As I watched his expression change and his focus go inward, I had time to think about what to say next. It was already too late to save myself if I was going to be punished for talking out of my place. I swallowed, then let my words fall out and flow along whatever grooves they wanted to follow.

"I don't understand why you don't love us enough to stop drinking and stay quit."

"It ain't that I don't love y'all," Daddy said suddenly, keeping his eyes on mine. "What I feel about y'all got nothing to do with my drinking."

"One time Momma told me love takes care of its own. She said that when you brought food and did stuff like that for us, it meant you loved us. You don't hardly do that now. You don't care what happens to us. You use to. I don't know what we did to make you stop."

Daddy's gaze slide away from mine. He looked across the room at the gray morning outside the window. He wiped his cheeks with his hands and ran his fingers across his forehead. "You too young to understand," he said. "I do love y'all."

"If that's how you love somebody, Daddy, I don't want your love. You suppose to be taking care of us. But you just making everything harder. You won't even let nobody else help. Ma Parker tried to help us. Mrs. Keyes tried to help us. But you was just mean. It's like you want us to all just die. I'm scared you gonna hurt somebody bad when you come here drunk. I just want to take the boys and run away from you."

Daddy picked at tiny balls of lint on the blanket. He looked slowly around the room, at Roy Anthony and Earl sprawled on the bed across the room, at June Bug curled into a fetal position in the bed beside me. When his eyes met mine again, I could read nothing in them.

"Well, I—," he said and cleared his throat. "Got to go to work," he said finally.

He pushed himself to standing and hesitated, looking down at me. His face contorted for a moment like he was going to say something else. When he turned and headed out of the room, there was shame hovering over his slumped shoulders.

My brothers were still sleeping when I got out of bed and began gathering our school things from where Daddy had scattered them during his rampage the night before. Clothes, books, papers, toys were all over the room. My book-bag was upside-down against the wall. When I lifted it, everything spilled onto the floor. There on top of the papers and books were Momma's lipstick and compact and Daddy's harmonica box. I had forgotten I put these things there after the fire. They had gotten covered up by my books and school papers.

Kneeling over the pile, I picked up the box with Daddy's harmonica, trying to draw together the image of the daddy who played music that made us all dance and laugh and the image of the man who had tossed our food into the yard and peed off the front porch.

I opened the box. The sight of the harmonica wrapped in its white cloth conjured up memories of Daddy gliding along the floor in a soft-shoe tap and Momma clapping her hands rhythmically as I fell in step beside Daddy, imitating his movements. Did Daddy even think about his harmonica anymore? He hadn't played it for us since before Momma left home with Baby Ida Bea. The last time I saw it in his hands we were still in our old house in Harvest Quarters.

I fingered the harmonica through the white cloth, then lifted it from the box. It felt heavier and more substantial than I had expected. I almost dropped it when I noticed a photograph in the bottom of the box. I carried the picture to the window and stood in the light. It looked like it had been taken at the state fair. The background was a fake window with lace curtains. In front of the window was a long low table. Daddy was sitting on the table top as though it was a chair, and he was smiling into the camera. Standing beside him on the table was a child, a boy about June Bug's age dressed in a white sailor suit with a big floppy collar and a dark ribbon tied at the neck. The child's body was turned toward Daddy, and the palms of his small hands were pressed against one side of Daddy's face. The boy's face was turned toward the camera, caught in the middle of an open-mouthed giggle. I couldn't recognize the face of either of my brothers in this laughing boy. My heart sped up. Was this Samuel? It had to be him.

I kept the boys home from school, letting them sleep as long as they wanted. When they woke up, I fed them the grits and toast Daddy had made and made them stay in the house all day. When I could, I would steal a few minutes in the toilet room to stare at the photograph—Daddy's easy smile, Samuel's happy round face. When Momma and Daddy were arguing in the kitchen all those months ago, Momma had said she thought about Samuel every day. "Sometimes he's more real to me than these others," she had said. Daddy hadn't said anything, but now I imagined him sneaking away to look at this photograph. I remembered that he'd had a photograph in his hand when Esther and I found him at the creek last summer. So Samuel was real to him too. Why didn't he want Momma to know that?

What had happened to Samuel? Had Daddy been drinking? Did he get mad the way he does with us now and do something to Samuel—something that made him die?

I sat in the grayness of the unlighted toilet room and let my memory run as far back as it could. The sweet metallic smell of whiskey on Daddy's breath breezed calmly through every part of my childhood that I could recall. But I had no images of him being sloppy drunk—as Ma Parker called it—when Momma was living at home. Maybe that was what Ma Parker meant when she said that Momma had been able to keep him "all of one piece." She kept him from going too far. But she wasn't there when Samuel died. She thought she could have kept death away if she had been there. *That's why she's away from us now, trying to keep death away from Ida Bea*, I thought. *She thinks I'm big enough to keep death away from my brothers.* "You big enough ... promise me you'll take care of your brothers," she had said. So far she had been right. But I needed her to come home soon.

I stared at the black-and-white photograph in my hand and tried to imagine how Momma must feel when she thought about Samuel's dying. Was there a way for her to get over that feeling and come home?

CHAPTER SEVENTEEN

THE BOYS AND I were headed home from school after a day of
spring rainstorms that had confined us in our classrooms. The
downpour had turned the school playgrounds into muddy fields,
but with the sun peeking through clouds, it felt good to be out
in the fresh warm air. Sparkling raindrops had collected on the
lime-green leaf buds on hedges I passed. I put my hand out and
let my fingers brush the branches. Emotions sputtered to life as
the water droplets flew into the air around me, sprinkling my face
and dripping onto the sleeve of my jacket. I dropped to my knees
to retrieve a big tiger-striped marble half-buried in the dirt at the
edge of the sidewalk.

I rolled the perfect orb in my palm, admiring the yellow and
orange bands of color captured in the center of the clear glass.
This marble would have made me a winner when I played with
my brothers and some of the neighbor kids in Harvest Quarters.
I imagined being on my hands and knees in the dirt, poised to
snap this tiger-shooter across the circle and claim the marbles I
had knocked out of play. When was the last time I played? Too
long ago to remember.

"What you doing, Maddy?" Roy Anthony asked.

He and Earl had been running ahead of me, playing some version of tag. They were studying me now.

"Nothing," I said, dropping the marble into my book-bag. I
heard a soft plunk as it hit the wood of Daddy's harmonica box at

the bottom of my bag. I was still carrying it around with Momma's cosmetics.

"Giddy up, cowboy," June Bug said behind me. He was bouncing up and down as if he were running in place. "Hi-oh, Silver," he added, giggling.

"Let's go." I started walking again.

June Bug galloped around me to catch up with his brothers. He was learning cowboy talk and cowboy ways from the television set at his new babysitter's house. In the no-nonsense way that Daddy had when he was sober, he had gone door-to-door in the neighborhood around our school and found Mrs. Caroline, a woman who kept the preschool children of other working parents with no nearby relatives to watch them. Every afternoon when Roy Anthony and Earl and I stopped on our way home to get June Bug, he and the other children were parked on blankets on the floor in front of a small black-and-white television perched on top of an old floor-model wooden radio. "I'm the Lone Ranger, Maddy," June Bug said one afternoon.

In the few weeks we had been taking him to this new sitter, his speech had gone from one- and two-word demands to full-strung sentences. Most of them questions, "Why your skin black, my skin brown? Why dogs don't walk on two legs? Do elephants fly? Can we get a elephant? Why not? Can we get a dog? If I climb that tree and jump can I fly?"

"What's that up there?" he asked one night, pointing to the curved sliver of moon in the night sky. We were on our way to the back-porch toilet so he could pee one last time before going to bed.

"The moon," I said.

He went to the edge of the porch and stared, his head swiveling from side to side. "Can't be the moon," he announced finally. "The moon a big white ball. That like Daddy's face when he happy. Big dark face. Big white smile. How come Daddy don't wobble no more when he come home?"

I shrugged, though I thought it possible that my boldness in telling Daddy what I thought of his drinking might be part of the reason he wasn't staggering home to us drunk anymore. There were still weekend nights he didn't come home, and some nights when he did come home he had the smell of whiskey on his breath. But he hadn't come home sloppy drunk since that night he tried to push Mrs. Keyes off the porch.

"Why you don't know, Maddy?"

I shrugged again. I didn't want to jinx anything by talking about it. I was just grateful for this small change in Daddy.

June Bug turned and went into the toilet room. "Don't need no help," he called from the darkness of the little room.

I heard the rustling of fabric, and the thin sprinkling of his pee hitting the water in the commode.

In Momma's absence, June Bug had gone from clingy toddler, waddling around in diapers sagging under the weight of whatever his body deposited there, to boy, full blown and solid on his feet. He was another miniature version of Daddy, but unlike Roy Anthony with his sharp edges and easy aggression, or Earl with his timid, fearful ways and easy tears, June Bug was always smiling just like he was now as I hurried us along from school. For the first time in a long time, I was enjoying feeling like a kid who could play marbles if I wanted to.

As we turned the corner a couple of blocks from the house and I saw the dusty shape of Mr. Gamet's truck parked in front of our house, my heart stirred. Was Momma home, or was he going to take us to see her?

When we stopped in front of the house beside the truck, disappointment settled about me like the dust in the road. In the truck bed were our mattresses and bed-frames and dressers, the kitchen table, and other odds and ends from the house.

"We moving," Daddy announced, coming onto the front porch with another box in his arms. "I found us a better house. It's closer to y'all's school."

He grinned, his mouth stretching bashfully, his eyes wandering away from contact with mine. Roy Anthony and Earl grabbed each other's hands and began jumping around in a circle. June Bug clapped his hands and ran in circles around his brothers.

"We moving, we moving, we moving," they all sang. Watching their wild, strange joy, I was nervous. I didn't mind this house. I had gotten used to it, and who knew where Daddy might be taking us.

When the truck stopped in front of our new home, an unpainted wooden structure bleached slick and silver by the sun, a woman with thick legs and a bulging baby-filled belly was going up the front steps with a wicker basket overflowing with clothes. She turned and stared with eyes that slanted elegantly above high cheekbones and a slack, open mouth. A smile spread across her angular face, revealing large perfect teeth and a deep dimple in each cheek.

"Well, I'll be," she said, looking at Daddy. "Eugene Culpepper, it's you rented the place next door?"

"Good afternoon, Glenda." Daddy winked at me before opening his door to get out of the truck. "We your new neighbors," he said and gestured toward his forehead as if he were touching the brim of a hat. "These is my children. Y'all come on out here and meet Miss Glenda."

As we poured out of the truck and into the road, other children wrapped in more silence than my brothers and me, came out of a door on Miss Glenda's side of the house. I noted that the house had two front doors separated by a plank partition that ran to the edge of the sagging porch.

"And these my children," Miss Glenda said, inclining her head in the direction of her brood, now gaping at us. "They was having a snack."

I counted the children on the porch, six.

"This here is my oldest, Maddy," Daddy said, suddenly pushing me forward. When Miss Glenda introduced her lot including three girls—her oldest Rita and a set of twins, Babs and D.D., about Earl's age—each looked shyly at their feet. These children would be easy playmates. They had none of the sly vulgarity of the Dorsey Street boys.

The house was another story.

Our new home was bordered in front by an open drainage ditch that ran along the edge of the road. On one side of the house hedges as tall as trees shielded our house from the neighboring one. On the other side a wide flat yard was bordered with a high wooden fence that concealed the neighbors' yard on that side. Near the road, at the front side of the fence, grew a tree that had the gnarled knobby branches and pale blossoms of a mulberry tree. The house faced the back side of a block-long building with high, corrugated metal walls and tiny blind windows set way up near the roof. It was the Masonite plant, I learned later. During the day, especially in summer, it filled the air with the shrill metallic grind of mill saws and the primitive smell of earth, piney wood, and sawdust.

When we went inside the house, it took away any joy I might have felt about moving next door to girls. It was obvious that the shabby little house, now changed to accommodate two families, had once been a single-family dwelling of four rooms. There was a boarded-up doorway in the front room that would have led right into Miss Glenda's part of the house. A pot-bellied wood-burning stove stood in one corner, its cast-iron sides blanched from previous fires. The room had two large windows, one on each outside wall. In the second room the floorboards were rotted through in one corner, and damp black and green mold was visible on the ground beneath the hole. There was no sink or faucet, but an enameled metal washbasin stood on a rusted metal stand against the wall. Sheets of thick translucent plastic covered the two windows in the room, permitting only a filmy light.

I felt Daddy watching me as I stood with my back to him, quietly taking in every splintering board. He cleared his throat a few times, swallowing explanations for why he had moved us here. He owed rent at the other place was my guess, or he was trying to make it hard for Mrs. Keyes to find us. It surely wasn't because this was a good place to live. I didn't turn to face him. Finally he left me standing in the middle of the room and went to work unloading the truck. Miss Glenda's two older boys and Rita helped Daddy and Roy Anthony and Earl, setting all of our boxes in the middle of the back room as Daddy talked aloud to himself about where to put the beds. As far as I could tell, it didn't matter.

When I went back to the front porch, Miss Glenda had brought a chair from inside her house and now sat, smiling her dimpled smile each time Daddy looked her way as he went back and forth from the truck to the house. I remembered, with an inward shrinking, the image of Daddy and Loralee, and I thought about the possibilities being unleashed by whatever was passing between Miss Glenda and Daddy.

Rita came and stood behind her mother's chair and put her hand on her mother's shoulder.

"You and my Rita about the same age. How old are you?" Miss Glenda asked, turning her dimples in my direction. Rita smiled too, showing a young version of her mother's dimples.

"Eleven," I said.

"Rita here is ten. What grade you in?"

"Sixth."

"Rita's in fourth. Course she should be in fifth. She stayed back a year in first grade. Poor baby was having some troubles learning her ABCs. More important that she learn what she need to know—reading and writing and adding her numbers. We don't care 'bout how long it takes. Right, sweetheart?"

Miss Glenda patted her daughter's hand. "Took her two years to get them ABCs right. She knows it all now, don't you, sweetheart?"

"I likes it where I is," Rita answered.

There was a sincerity in her voice and something in the way she half closed her eyes and bowed her head that revealed a mental slowness. She reminded me of Nadine Cox, a girl who had joined our class in the sixth grade. She looked old enough to be in high school. We all knew she was mentally retarded. But she smiled sweetly and looked at us with wide friendly eyes when we tried to talk to her, though she never spoke. She kept to herself, so no one ever had any cause to bother her.

"Daddy, where the toilet at?" Roy Anthony ran from the house onto the porch and squinted up at Daddy, who was standing in the back of the truck.

"It's out back."

"I looked and I didn't see it." Roy Anthony pranced from foot to foot. "I really got to go pee."

Daddy flashed a quick embarrassed smile at Miss Glenda. "You just didn't look in the right place. Come on, I'll show you."

He bounded down from the truck onto the porch and marched past Roy Anthony, into the house, and on through the back room with all of us following. He didn't stop at the back porch, which was really no more than a small plank platform at the top of the six rickety wooden steps. He went down the steps and strode about ten yards to a little wooden shack in the middle of a patch of knee-high weeds. The shack had two doors just like the house. Rusty springs protested with a metallic whine when Daddy opened one of the doors. The nauseating odor of human waste radiated from the open door. "This is the toilet," he said, with a slick, challenging edge to his voice and a grin. "Git in there and do your business, boy."

Roy Anthony bowed his head and walked past him into the foul-smelling little shack. Daddy let go of the door and it shut behind Roy Anthony with an angry slap.

"What everybody gawking at? I know y'all seen a outhouse before," Daddy said, the challenge still glinting on the edge of his voice when he turned and saw Earl and June Bug standing on the back porch and me at the bottom of the steps.

"Yes sir," we sang in unison. The boys hurried back inside, and I walked slowly around the side of the house, noticing for the first time a faucet, which rose from the ground like a gray metal cobra close to the house. A little bit better than a pump, I thought. Still someone would need to bring a bucket from inside and fill it with water for drinking, cooking, washing. Most likely it would always be me.

It had never occurred to me that such places existed in town, or that I would ever live in a place where I would have to face the extravagant humiliation of spider crickets hopping around my feet, blowflies buzzing around my head, and the stench of human feces every time I needed to relieve myself. I wanted to cry.

I sat on the ground with my back pressed against the roughness of my new mulberry tree. I was scratching in the dirt with a stick and resenting everything and everyone, my brothers and even Rita, who were content to play wild running games in the freshness of spring. They screeched back and forth to each other on the pale green air, their games like scrimmages in a war. In the month that we had lived here, the space near this new mulberry tree had become my station for thinking, or brooding, as my mother would have said. The tree itself was only barely taller than our awful little house and didn't provide the kind of perspective and view of the neighborhood as the one I used to have in the Quarters.

"Hey girl. What you doing?"

The woman who lived in the house on the other side of the high fence stood a few yards away. I had seen her before, driving slowly by our house in a shiny tan-colored Chrysler, her high-yellow face studying the road in front of her car like someone conscious of being watched. She stood over me now, her thick, well-fed body like a cotton bale on legs, pressing against the seams of her brown-and-white-checked wool dress. She looked like a school teacher, but she was grinning at me like someone who needed a favor.

"Nothing."

I hoped she wanted me to run to the store for her. She was the kind of person who might give me a dime for such an errand.

She kept grinning down at me and shifting her weight from foot to foot. "I'm Mrs. Hazel Garfield." She paused indulgently, as if the name carried a message. "Can you go to the store for me?"

"Yes ma'am."

"I wrote down what I want and the money's at my house."

I followed her. Even though her house was only a few yards from mine behind the high wooden fence, it was bigger than ours and it looked well-cared-for and happy with a coat of white paint and a screened-in front porch.

Mrs. Garfield's living room had a deep green sofa and an armchair that matched. In fact, everything in her house matched. There were end tables and a coffee table of the same brown wood and identical brown lamps perched on the end tables. An old-fashioned radio as tall as me stood against one wall, and a console television stared blindly from the corner. Paintings of children and animals with abnormally large, sad eyes hung on the walls. As I followed her into the kitchen, I noted that hers was a four-room house that had not been subdivided and had been kept up better than ours. The walls were even painted, soothing pale shades like spearmint green in the living room and pale lemon in the kitchen. Mrs. Garfield's dinette set, a sunflower-yellow Formica-top table with matching marbled plastic chairs, sat in the middle of the large bright room like the center of a flower. She had a modern gas stove and a sink with faucets.

She handed me a five-dollar bill from the table and a piece of paper. In a sprawling, looping handwriting that used circles to dot the *I*'s, she had written 5 LB. SELF-RISING FLOUR, 5 LB. WHITE SUGAR, 1 DOZ. EGGS, 2 CANS CARNATION MILK, 1 BOTTLE KETCHUP, SOMETHING SWEET FOR YOURSELF. She was watching my face as I read the note, and I knew she expected a smile because of the last item. I obliged her.

"You're a very smart girl. You know how to read cursive. What grade are you in?"

I smiled bashfully.

I hurried to the store after telling the boys where I was going. Miss Glenda was home in the dim quietness of her house. She could be counted on if a need arose. We counted on her to keep June Bug now on school days.

In the store, I eyed the Pepperidge Farm layered cakes in the freezer as I waited for the grocer to gather the items on Mrs. Garfield's list. The cakes were $1.10. I didn't know if that would be an acceptable sweet for myself. Maybe she had simply meant a nickel candy bar. So I chose a Baby Ruth. When I set the bag on Mrs. Garfield's table and handed her the change, two dollar bills and some coins, she told me to keep the coins.

"I got something else for you. I just baked this big ole chocolate cake, and you know I don't need it with my big butt."

She patted her behind. The gesture was too girlish, or too grown-up. Either way it was unusual for an adult to share with a child. Maybe she wasn't thinking of me like a child.

"I don't know many folks around here," she said, taking the lid off a metal cake dish in the center of the yellow Formica. "I only moved here a few weeks before y'all did," she said as she sliced the cake. She put a generous piece on a saucer and pushed the slice toward me. "Have a seat."

"Thank you, Mrs. Garfield." I sat down in one of the table chairs as she handed me a fork.

"Don't call me Mrs. Garfield. That feels intolerable to me at the moment. Call me Hazel." She sat down across from me and cut a piece of cake for herself.

"Yes ma'am."

But I couldn't call her Hazel. It would have been like calling my mother by her first name. The closest I could come was to call her Mrs. Hazel.

"I bet there are some interesting people live around here," she said without looking at me. "The folks where I used to live were some kind of interesting," she continued. "The preacher's wife, for instance, used to dress up in men's clothes, every day but Sunday. On Sunday there she'd be, sitting up in the front pew, wearing the most frilly dresses you ever seen. But them other six days, there she was, strolling around as big as you please in men's shoes and britches, and button-down shirts. She even wore ties sometimes."

I smiled, but I was more intent on my cake than on gossip about people I didn't know.

"Would you like more cake? How about some Kool-Aid to wash it down?"

"Well, no ma'am," I stammered. It seemed the polite response.

"Aw, come on."

I looked away as she cut me another slice.

"My old community in Hattiesburg was really something," she resumed as she set the second big slice of cake in front of me. "I didn't even want to leave to come here. My husband's work brought us here. Course he's from here anyway. He's a bricklayer, what they call a skilled worker. His work sent him down to Hattiesburg in the first place, and it kept sending him back up here with all the building going on. So I agreed to move here too. But I ain't finding this to be such a friendly place. Seems interesting enough, just none too friendly. But you seem like such a smart girl. You spent your whole life in this town, right? You must know everything and everybody."

I started to feel a bit giddy, swinging my legs with abandon under the table, eating cake, drinking Kool-Aid with a grown-up talking to me like I was grown.

"Tell me, you must know quite a bit about Glenda," Mrs. Hazel suggested. "She lives right next door to y'all. She's got an awful lot of children, and they all look different."

" 'Cause they all have different daddies," I offered.

Rita had told me her mother's business as if it were something to be proud of. "I got a different daddy from all the others," she said once when we were digging in the spring-softened soil, getting ready to make mud and mulberry blossom pies. "My own daddy was name Jimmy. William Ray's daddy name Chester, Addly's daddy name Donald Earl, of course the twins got the same daddy, even though they don't look alike, and Stanley he got a whole 'nother daddy."

I told Mrs. Hazel this.

"Which one is the baby boy?"

That was Stanley, sweet and dewy-eyed. He preferred to play alone in his mother's shadow. When Rita and I tried to get him to play games, even patty-cake or peek-a-boo, he would smile weakly up into our faces with vacant simple joy, but he held his arms stiffly at his sides, and any attempt to lift them into the game brought terror, sudden and feral, into his eyes. I had never heard him speak. Rita said he was two, almost three. But his understanding seemed too simple, his movements too clumsy for a boy almost the same age as June Bug.

"What's the names of the twins' and that baby boy's daddies?" Mrs. Hazel wanted to know.

That I didn't know. Rita hadn't said, but she had told me about the time her mother sent the twins to the house of their daddy to get money. "We had fallen on hard times," Rita said, and I could hear those words coming out of her mother's mouth as she packed them off with a note for their father. "Their daddy's wife whipped their little butts and sent them back to us crying." Rita had told me that with an air of confusion. "But they daddy did come by and give my mama some money the next day," she had added.

"Silly cow," Mrs. Hazel said. "Sounds like that happened a while ago. She done anything interesting lately?"

"Miss Glenda ain't done nothing. But a man my daddy called Curtis came by our house one evening, and Stanley was sitting on our porch and the man gave him a silver dollar. He ain't gave nobody else nothing."

"Well, I see." Mrs. Hazel's piney face was suddenly tinged with a coppery redness.

"Ma'am?"

"Nothing, child."

I ate my cake slowly and waited. Mrs. Hazel picked at her slice with her fork. We sat for a few minutes in silence before she said, "Well, you better run on along and see about your brothers. You like to watch television?" she asked as I stood to leave.

"Yes ma'am," I answered, although I had only watched television once, during that visit to Esther's mother's house.

"There are some good shows on tomorrow evening. Why don't you come on over and watch. You can bring your brothers too."

My brothers and I were mesmerized by the flickering silvery blue light pouring into the darkened room from the big wooden box with its small screen.

June Bug lay on the woven-rag rug in front of the television, sucking his thumb in the cozy darkness. Roy Anthony, Earl, and I sat on the sofa. I glanced around the room occasionally to make sure that every part of this experience was real—the television set, the solid walls, the sofa, the plate of cookies that had been set on the coffee table in front of us, the glasses of purple Kool-Aid, the chubby motherly woman sitting in the armchair staring blindly at the television screen.

"Who these kids?" Mr. Garfield wanted to know when he came in and found us there in the dark with his wife.

"These Gene Culpepper's kids," Mrs. Hazel answered.

She didn't stir from her chair but folded her arms over the heavy bulk of her breasts. Her face was alive with the television's light shimmering across it. Mr. Garfield was standing between me and the television. The screen glowed behind him, turning his body into a fuzzy silhouette. I thought of the *Outer Limits* show we had watched earlier in which an unseen creature had terrorized a group of astronauts who crash-landed on an alien planet. There *was* something alien, even a bit dangerous, in the air around Mr. Garfield. My fingers tensed like cat claws on the arm of the sofa. I wanted to bolt from the room.

"Time to send them home, ain't it?"

He set a metal lunch-bucket on the end table nearest Mrs. Hazel. She picked it up and held it against her chest as if it were a treasure.

"They were just keeping me company till you got here, Curtis. You always working late. I get lonesome."

"Well, now I'm here, they can go."

"The show's about to end. Let them see the ending," Mrs. Hazel said, looking beyond Mr. Garfield to the screen. Though it didn't seem that she was really paying attention to the television before he arrived.

He glanced in the direction of the television. "Alright," he said, but did not move from where he stood.

In the last few minutes of the show, which I could not see because of Mr. Garfield's silhouette between me and the tiny screen, I was struck by the strangeness of the whole scene—Mr. Garfield standing in the middle of the room, Mrs. Garfield hugging a cold metal lunch-box against her bosom, my brothers and me facing the television like stuffed animals. It seemed that the only life in the room was in the tiny humans inside the television. Between the Garfields there was an empty space where there should have been feelings flowing, or pooling and waiting to flow like when Momma and Daddy were in a room together, and as much as I didn't like to think about it, there was even some kind of feeling that flowed between Daddy and Loralee and Daddy and Miss Glenda. There always seemed to be something, something alive in the spaces between grown-up men and women. But there was nothing between the Garfields, not even anger. My uneasiness grew and spread out like the anxiety I had felt for the astronauts on the television show.

I was glad when Roy Anthony, Earl, June Bug, and I stepped out into the night air and Mrs. Hazel closed her door behind us.

"Last one home is a rotten egg," I called out and started sprinting when my feet touched the ground at the bottom of the Garfields' steps. The boys were all ahead of me, and they started running, but I could outrun them with ease. When I started to pass Roy Anthony, he grabbed my arm and started laughing. Earl caught the back of my dress. I pretended to be held back by their grasping. We struggled together, lurching forward haphazardly, me feigning determination to win, them laughing and pulling on me until finally June Bug ran past us.

"I win, I win." he yelled, jumping up and down on the porch. "I'm not a rotten egg."

Earl seized the moment, let go of me, and ran to the porch. When Roy Anthony tried the same thing, I held onto his arm and we played push-me-pull-you all the way to our steps.

"Ha ha, you both stink," Earl said, pointing at us.

"Here let me rub some of my stink on you," Roy Anthony said, thrusting his arms out in front of him and rushing up onto the porch.

We tumbled through the door of our sad, raggedy house in a happy, carefree knot, free of whatever it was that seemed to hold Mrs. Hazel and her husband like flies in a spiderweb.

For a few weeks that April, I spent chunks of time sitting in Mrs. Hazel's kitchen after school, feeding her what gossip I stumbled across and eating whatever goodies she had to offer. Or I sat with her in her living room watching afternoon soap operas and re-peats of programs like the *Donna Reed Show*, *Leave It to Beaver*, and *Father Knows Best*.

In the evenings, before Mr. Garfield got home, my brothers and I sat in the surreal bliss of the Garfields' living room watching the black-and-white images on their television screen, soaking up a white American culture that was foreign and intoxicating. We watched the easy humor in the lives of families on shows like *My Favorite Martian*, the *Andy Griffith Show*, *Mr. Ed*, and the clean, manageable drama on shows like *Lassie*, *Rawhide*, and *Bonanza*. We laughed at the slapstick jokes on the *Red Skelton Show* and the *Carol Burnett Show*.

We were all absorbed into worlds so unlike our own, though Mrs. Hazel's life seemed to come close to those white television families', except she had no children of her own. I thought that might be why she kept inviting me and the boys over, so she could feel like she had children. I didn't mind being her stand-in family. In those moments we were all happy—Mrs. Hazel, my brothers, and I. The hopeful world we saw on the tiny screen was full of possibilities, and always had a happy ending.

CHAPTER EIGHTEEN

JUNE BUG COULD BARELY see over the chrome edge of the yellow Formica-topped table, but he was content to reach up and grab the coconut cake with his fingers and push it politely into his mouth. I glanced at him furtively and worried about the crumbs he was dropping onto the polished linoleum. But Mrs. Hazel didn't even seem to notice that he was there. She had just gotten back from spending a week in Hattiesburg, visiting her own momma and daddy, she said. Now she wanted to know what had been going on while she was away.

"Stanley was up in your house," I said, gleefully, eating my cake with a fork.

"Who's Stanley?"

"Miss Glenda's baby boy."

Rita had told me that Mr. Garfield came and got Stanley and brought him to his house. "Rita said her mamma didn't want him to come here. She and Mr. Garfield argued about it. But in the end, he brought Stanley here and kept him all night."

"Did Glenda come too?"

"No ma'am, she didn't. Rita say her mamma told Mr. Garfield she wouldn't set foot in this house unless she was dead."

"Be kind of hard for her to come up in here dead, but maybe I will find her up in here someday, and dead is how she'd be if I caught her here."

I looked up from my cake, surprised by the anger in Mrs. Hazel's voice. Her mouth was lopsided and childlike as she pushed pieces of coconut off the edge of her plate onto the tabletop. She grinned when she saw me watching her, and color rose in her face.

"You see that it's funny, don't you?" she asked. "She say she won't set foot in here unless she dead, but when something is dead, it can't set foot nowhere except the grave. Ain't that funny, that she don't know any better than to say something stupid like that?"

"Yes ma'am, I guess it is sort of funny."

Mrs. Hazel put a piece of cake in her mouth. "Anything else going on with Glenda and her brood while I been gone?" Pieces of coconut dropped onto the plate in front of her as she spoke.

"Well, no ma'am."

"Nothing? That don't sound like Glenda. She always up to *something*."

Then I remembered Miss Glenda whispering through the fence, but that had happened since Mrs. Hazel's return. "Night before last, I heard Miss Glenda whispering and laughing with somebody at the back fence," I offered. "Don't know who she was talking to."

"Did it sound like a man?"

"Yes ma'am, I think so."

Mrs. Hazel got up and went to the sink. She stood with her back to me, staring out the open window. The high clear voices of children outdoors floated in through the window. Roy Anthony and Earl and some of Miss Glenda's kids were undoubtedly playing their usual wild running games in our yard. Suddenly, I felt restless being indoors with Mrs. Hazel.

She said something, but the words disappeared out the window.

"Ma'am?"

"I ain't feeling all that well. I'm getting a terrible headache. I think I'm going to take a couple of aspirins and have a lie-down. You and your brother ought to go home now. Y'all can come back this evening and watch the television again if you want to. But I don't want any more company right now."

The softly moist heat of early May swept back and forth over the yard, jiggling the new leaves on the hedges and the pale blossoms that would soon become mulberries on my new mulberry tree. Miss Glenda sat in the shade on her side of the porch, braiding Rita's hair into neat little rows. She had offered to braid mine too. So I was sitting on the edge of the porch, swinging my legs and dragging my toes in the dirt, waiting my turn. It would be nice to have a grown-up comb my hair for a change.

Stanley and June Bug kneeled on the floor nearby, making a fort out of kitchen pots and some empty cans for a collection of little metal soldiers. Before he and Earl ran off to play with some bigger kids up the street, Roy Anthony had entrusted his collection of soldiers to June Bug. It was a ploy to keep June Bug from trying to follow him into his big kid games.

I looked up from the porch to see Mrs. Hazel marching toward our house. It had been two days since she abruptly sent me away from her kitchen. I smiled in her direction, anticipating an invitation to join her in her kitchen or for an evening of television. It was Sunday, the night for the *Ed Sullivan Show*—one of my favorites.

But it wasn't me she looked at when she stopped in front of our porch. Her face was splotchy with emotion I did not recognize. She held a plank as long as my arm idly at her side.

June Bug and Stanley stopped playing, alerted to danger by some childish instinct.

"Glenda, come off the porch. I'm here to whip your ass."

Miss Glenda looked up from Rita's head. For a few seconds she stared into Mrs. Hazel's eyes, her hands poised in her daughter's hair. Then she rolled her eyes skyward, exhaled a loud dismissing snort. "Go home, Hazel," she said, and her fingers went back to braiding Rita's hair.

"You've laid up with my husband for the last time, you whoring bitch."

Mrs. Hazel leaned forward over the plank as if it were a walking stick. I drew my legs onto the porch and scooted back toward June Bug and Stanley.

"Curtis can't seem to make up his mind between you and me," Mrs. Hazel continued. "He thinks he can have us both. Well he can't. So I aim to make up his mind for him. I'm going to beat you right out of our lives, or die trying. So bring it on out here in the yard and fight like the she-bitch you are."

"I don't know what you talking about."

"I'm talking about you and my husband, humping like dogs every time my back is turned."

"Woman, take your filthy mouth on back up in your house before somebody has to wash it out with soap."

"I know you was in my house while I was gone to Hattiesburg last week."

She was repeating something I had said. But she had it wrong.

"Miss Glenda wasn't—," I started.

Mrs. Hazel's eyes were hard with anger when she looked at me. "Shut up, girl," she said. "This ain't your business. This between me and this bitch over here."

"I ain't no bitch, and I wasn't in your house," Miss Glenda said. "Nobody couldn't drag me in there by my hair. You ain't got nothing I want in there."

"I know that little bastard sitting right there belongs to Curtis." She pointed her plank at Stanley.

I covered my mouth with my hands. The truth of that was easy to see in the light of Mrs. Garfield's words. Why hadn't I put it together before? No wonder Mrs. Hazel was always asking about Miss Glenda and her children. Stanley was a miniature of Mr. Garfield—the same soft brown skin, curly black hair, large forehead, and pointy jaw. Miss Glenda was sooty black with kinky hair, a round face, and dimples, which were faintly visible even now in her tight-lipped anger.

"My child's daddy ain't none of your business," she said.

"It's my business when the daddy is my husband. I'm tired of you making a fool out of me."

"*You* making a fool out of yourself, standing here saying stuff better kept inside your head. I wouldn't blame Curtis for a wandering eye. You done let yourself go, and seems to me you a little touched in the head."

"You with your litter of dim-witted little bastards. You the crazy she-bitch. Grabbing at other people's men. Sleeping with every man that looks your way."

Miss Glenda stood suddenly and Rita scrambled sideways. "Shut your mouth about my children. They ain't none of your business."

Mrs. Hazel stared, gape mouthed at Miss Glenda's bulging pregnant stomach. In all of my gossiping, I hadn't mentioned this current pregnancy. It hadn't occurred to me that it was worth saying anything about.

"Another bastard for my husband?" Mrs. Hazel asked.

"Somebody's got to make babies for him since you sure can't, you barren, dried-up cow. Look at you, fat windbag. Go home before I tell Curtis you been acting a fool in public." Miss Glenda stood with her hands on her hips, belly thrust forward.

"Maybe I'll just bust open this little bastard's head first." Mrs. Hazel looked at Stanley. "You and Curtis can just make more."

She raised the plank like a baseball bat and swung at Stanley with one smooth stroke.

"Mrs. Hazel," I yelled, pushing myself to my feet. Miss Glenda bumped me aside as she heaved her body between the plank and her child. The plank struck her in the thigh and she stumbled. Mrs. Hazel swung again, catching her in the side this time. Miss Glenda pitched forward toward the edge of the porch, grabbing at the plank and kicking at Mrs. Hazel who just kept swinging.

Rita was on the floor behind me with her back against the wall, she seemed to be chewing her lips as tears streamed down her face. June Bug ran to me and wrapped his arms around my legs. Stanley crawled toward his mother screaming, "Ma'da, Ma'da." I caught him by one leg and pulled him backward, hobbling toward the screen door with June Bug.

"Help me get him inside," I yelled to Rita. It was clear to me that Mrs. Hazel had lost her mind enough that she would just as soon hit Stanley as hit Miss Glenda. I couldn't let that happen.

Rita looked at me, and for one crazy moment there was no recognition in her face, just terror. Then she scurried on all fours to the screen door and flung it open. Stanley was flailing and trying to get away from my touch, but I held on, pulling him to the open door and finally pushing him inside with Rita. I peeled June Bug's arms away from my legs and pushed him in too, then slammed the screen door shut and plastered my body against the frame so none of them could come back out, and I was out of harm's way.

Miss Glenda's face was distorted with panic when she turned around to see where her children were. The next blow from Mrs. Hazel landed on her butt, and when Mrs. Hazel swung again she grabbed the end of the plank and the two women tugged back and forth.

Stanley shrieked in high long bursts behind the screen door, summoning the rest of the neighbors who hadn't already started to gather in their front yards. Miss Glenda and Mrs. Hazel tussled with the plank like kids playing tug of war until Miss Glenda slid off the porch and landed in the dirt on her knees, losing her grip on the plank. She threw her arms up, and the sound of wood hitting bone rang out as the plank slammed her across her shoulder. She managed to get on her feet, wrestle the wood from Mrs. Hazel, and throw it onto the porch behind her. They rushed at each other, scuffling and swinging with open palms. They locked arms, whirling, grunting, and kicking, dust and dirt flying up around them. Suddenly, like a wind-blown tree, the women toppled over. When they hit the ground, there was a loud huff of breath as if the wind was knocked out of both of them, but they didn't separate. The grunting became the growls of wild dogs as they rolled in the dirt. They slipped, still entangled, into the muddy drainage ditch. The blunt sounds of flesh pummeling flesh rose from the ditch, fanning out on the spring air. Some of the spectators moved forward to see more easily into the shallow ditch. A sharp scream pierced the air and some people recoiled, hunching their shoulders, but none of them moved away from the edge of the ditch.

A man pushed through the hunched crowd.

"What the—," he yelled.

It was Daddy. He hopped in the ditch and grabbed at the women, their clothes, their arms, their legs. But they refused to be coaxed apart, and at first Daddy looked like he had joined the fight, scrambling in the mix of flailing legs and arms. Finally, he got a handful of Miss Glenda's thickly braided hair and yanked upward. Then he wound the fingers of his other hand into Mrs. Hazel's curly brown mane and pulled. He pulled until the women stopped swinging at each other to claw at his hands. He kept pulling until the women were on their knees and you could see space between them.

"Joe!" Daddy yelled.

Another man pushed forward through the crowd, jumped in the ditch, and wrapped his arms around Mrs. Hazel from behind. He dragged her away from Daddy and Miss Glenda.

Dirt, twigs, leaves, scummy moss, and all kinds of other yard debris clung to the fighters in a muddy collage. Mrs. Hazel had blood on her chin and her dress was ripped down the front so that her bra and part of one breast were exposed. Four angry red slashes ran across her cheek, down her neck, and onto the top of her bared breast. Miss Glenda's dress was hiked up around her belly showing mud-stained panties. Blood dripped in a steady stream down one side of her face. Both women's hair stuck out haphazardly. They panted. But even gasping for air, they managed to glare at each other and growl.

"Knock it off," Daddy said, standing between the two women with his back to Miss Glenda. "Hazel, git on home and clean yourself up 'fore Curtis gits in," Daddy said, looking at Mrs. Hazel. "He slave so you can have stuff like a white lady. Why you shaming him? Glenda can't take your man. Only one thing she got he want. That's gone get old. No need to lower yourself like this."

Mrs. Hazel's body went soft. She looked down and pulled at her torn dress, but her breath was still coming in hungry gasps. She struggled to her feet with the help of the man Daddy had called Joe. He stepped out of the ditch and offered her his hand. She looked only at him and at the ground as he half-lifted, half-pulled her up into the yard.

"Now Glenda," Daddy began when Mrs. Hazel was a few feet away.

"Go to hell, Eugene," Miss Glenda said. "She the one started it."

"Glenda, what you 'spect was gon' happen? You know you been doing the woman wrong. Carrying on with her husband right up under her nose. Bad enough you got that boy by Curtis. Rubbing her face in it every day. Nobody need to tell you that ain't right."

"I was here first. Curtis the one moved her up here. 'I got it under control,' he said. Men always think they got everything under control. Control, my ass. Not a single one of you know shit about control."

Daddy stared down at Miss Glenda kneeling in the muddy ditch. I could see the anger rising in his stiffening back. She was lucky he wasn't drunk.

"As your friend, I'm telling you it ain't right for you to be screwing Curtis then fighting with his wife like a dog."

Daddy had squeezed his words out through locked teeth.

Miss Glenda glared at him like an angry child. "*She* came in *my* yard. I didn't start nothing with her. She ain't got no business messing with me. I ain't married to her. Curtis is. If she want to whip somebody's ass, it should be Curtis' ass. He the one married to her. He spilling his seed outside the marriage. Ain't my fault the devil dried up her womb."

"Git up and go on in your house, Glenda. You leaning up against my limit now."

"Eugene, don't you be judging me. The ground you standing on ain't all that high."

"I been your friend for a long time, Glenda, from before you moved down here. And right now I'm probably your only friend." Daddy glanced in the direction of all the watching faces. "I'm telling you, be quiet and go on in your house. Don't make yourself look no worse."

Miss Glenda followed Daddy's glance, slowly taking in all the staring eyes. Some of them met her gaze with bold disgust. Some stared with pity. Some looked away.

Miss Glenda got to her feet and straightened her dress. She brushed herself vaguely and patted her hair. Then put her hands on her hips and looked into the crowd again.

"I ain't never gone after nobody's man. Man end up in my bed 'cause *he* come after *me*. You high and mighty married women think y'all special. Y'all know I'm telling the truth. He marry you. Then first chance he gets, he sniffing after somebody else. That's a man for you. Ain't a damned thing you can do about it. So don't come trying to blame me for they straying. I ain't *stealing* nobody's nothing. I just accept what's offered. I'm trying to live just like the rest of y'all."

Miss Glenda pointed at a couple of faces in the crowd. "Albert, Smiley, don't be standing there looking down your noses at me in the daylight. I ain't never asked neither one of y'all to come sneaking up to my back door when the sun goes down. Keep y'all's own damn marriage vows if they mean something to you. That goes for Curtis Garfield too. He the one disrespecting his vows. Hazel can't put that on me. Y'all should be judging her for attacking a child and a woman in my condition."

Miss Glenda pressed her pregnant belly forward.

"Don't matter whose baby this is besides mine, it ain't right for her to be trying to hit me with no stick. I ain't never gon' stand by and let nobody hurt me or one of my babies when I can help it. Y'all can all just go straight to hell."

Some of the men put their hands in their pockets and turned and shuffled away. Murmuring rose from some of the women I imagined to be wives. Some made indignant grunting noises through closed mouths and pinched faces, but all turned away and headed toward their homes, mumbling as they went. Only the children stayed.

Miss Glenda cupped one hand to her bleeding ear.

"Come on," Daddy said, extending his hand to help her up and out of the ditch.

She stretched herself slowly, and rested her weight on Daddy as he led her across the yard and onto her porch steps. Her children skulked out of the clumped groups of children and followed her inside.

From our side of the front porch I watched Mrs. Hazel's body shaking as she walked toward her house, leaning against Daddy's friend, Joe.

"Stop blubbering," Daddy said, coming around to our side of the porch. "Women fighting like animals ain't got nothing to do with you. Both of 'em halfway decent women too. Neither of 'em need to be carrying on like that. No wonder colored folks ain't amounting to nothing. When our women can't even stay upright and act like they got some sense. It's a damned shame, but it ain't got nothing to do with you."

I looked at him and I wiped tears and snot from my face with the back of my hands. I felt small and stupid. He was wrong. It had everything to do with me.

"Git on in the house," he said. "Call your brothers on in too. I'm gon' go see about Glenda. Looks like Hazel may've bit off a piece of her ear."

When I ventured outside again, the yard was deserted and the sun had dripped to one corner of the sky, laying long, lazy shadows across everything. I could still see the crazy haphazard patterns left in the dirt by Mrs. Hazel and Miss Glenda. I peered in the ditch at the mashed leaves, the weeds pressed flat and muddy, the slick green moss, the black dirt. I slid down the side of the ditch and looked around. I picked up a swatch of cloth from Mrs. Hazel's dress, and a few clumps of hair. A dark fleshy lump lay on a small dark mound that looked like dried blood. It could have been the piece of Miss Glenda's ear. I didn't touch it. Red ants were already swarming over it and marching away in uniform lines. They had the right idea, dismantle and haul away any traces of the horrible thing that had happened.

Clutching my mementos, I climbed out of the ditch and sat under the mulberry tree. Daddy was wrong. I felt bruised and wounded because it was me that fed Mrs. Hazel gossip about Miss Glenda and her children. It had made her mad enough to want to hurt Miss Glenda, and Stanley. I had liked thinking I was grown as I sat in Mrs. Hazel's house running my mouth about things that I knew very little about. It had made me feel special to be singled out by a grown woman who treated me like *I* was grown. It fit how I felt after all of the months of taking care of my brothers—too grown to play outside with the other kids. I thought I had earned a place with the grown women. But I didn't realize that my words could cause pain for Mrs. Hazel, or make her want to pick a fight with Miss Glenda. A real grown-up would have. No matter how grown I thought I had become in Momma's absence, I wasn't grown enough.

As I watched the sky fade from pale blue to steely gray, I wondered for the first time what it would really feel like to be a grown woman. How would it feel to be able to make my own decisions about where I could go and where I could live? Would I understand myself and my life any better than I understood the grown-ups around me now? What kind of woman would I be? Certainly, I didn't want to be like Mrs. Hazel, nor Miss Glenda, clawing and scratching and biting each other in the dirt because of a man. I didn't even want to be like my own momma who went away to look after one of her children while the others had to fend for themselves. Would I have a choice? If I could choose, maybe I could be like Mrs. Keyes or my teacher, Miss Washington.

"Come on back in this house, Maddy."

Daddy was standing on the porch steps, his timing bad as usual.

"In a minute," I called, realizing after the words were out that they would sound like back talk.

"That's all you got."

I watched him go back inside, surprised that he hadn't balked at my refusal to come in immediately.

Before I came outside, I had helped him clean and dab Mercurochrome on the scratches Mrs. Hazel and Miss Glenda made on his arms when he was breaking up their fight. He had watched me soberly without saying a word, even when I set the bottle down and walked outside. It felt, for a moment, like the whole world had turned inside out.

A few days after the fight, Mr. Garfield came to talk to Daddy and asked him to make sure the boys and I stayed away from their house. I heard them talking on the porch that night, their voices muffled and comradely. There was even some manly chuckling that went on. Daddy never said anything to me about what was said. He simply announced, "Y'all ain't to be visiting with Hazel no more."

Two weeks later, when May was running its course, Mr. Garfield drove their tan Chrysler by our house with Mrs. Hazel in the passenger seat. She looked neither left nor right as they drove by, though she must have known I was standing there watching. Was her good sense still blunted by the rage that made her act out the kind of violence found mostly in children and wild animals? Or was she returned to the motherly woman who served chocolate cake and grape Kool-Aid on yellow Formica?

The next day, a truck with high-slatted sides, like the ones the farmers drove to town in summer to hawk watermelons, stopped in front of the Garfields' house. Two pitch-dark men loaded up Mrs. Hazel's furniture—the green living room set, the TV console, the shiny Formica and chrome dinette set, mattresses, bedframes, wall hangings, everything—and drove away.

Mr. Garfield I saw once more late in the summer, after Miss Glenda had baby number seven. Rita said they had named the new baby girl Ebony. She was barely home from the hospital when Mr. Garfield's car stopped in the road in front of the house. A woman who looked like a short stout version of him got out of the car with him and went into Miss Glenda's. Rita and all of the children, except Stanley and the new baby, were sent outside. They sat on the porch looking gloomy and confused until the woman emerged carrying baby Ebony bundled in her arms. She sat in the passenger seat without acknowledging anyone in the small crowd of curious children gathered in the yard.

Mr. Garfield came out later, with a bag of clothes in one hand and Stanley in the other.

"Ma'da,' Ma'da,'" Stanley yelled, squirming as Mr. Garfield headed down the steps with him. He reached his thin arms around his father's torso toward his mother who stood inside the closed screen door.

She opened it to wave at the ravaged face of her youngest son as his father strapped him into the backseat of his car. By this time Stanley's crying had become a hoarse visceral scream that flowed out across the yards, striking chords of pain in all the children within hearing.

"God, take care of my babies," Miss Glenda said quietly when the car had disappeared from sight.

I lay awake that night, listening to Miss Glenda crying on the other side of the wall. It occurred to me that however bad she was feeling, Stanley was probably feeling even worse, as upset as he always got when he was out of sight of his mother. Now he was away from everybody and everything he knew. How could Miss Glenda let that happen?

I fell into a fitful sleep thinking about the unfairness of a world where children were always paying for their parents' mistakes.

CHAPTER NINETEEN

IT WAS MY BIRTHDAY. All day at school I had held on to the hope that my teacher, Miss Washington, would pause the lessons and announce, "Okay class, Madeleine turns twelve today. Let's sing her the birthday song." But school was over—we were on our way home—and nothing had happened. I remembered with a tiny stab of pain that the birthday girl or boy usually brought some kind of sweets, mostly baked goods, to share with the whole class on their day. Momma used to send me to school with a batch of freshly baked molasses cookies, my favorite. Maybe Miss Washington had ignored my birthday because she didn't want to embarrass me by drawing everybody's attention to the fact that I didn't have a mother at home to bake cookies for the class. That would have ignited questions from some of my classmates and whispering from others. I cringed with shame at the thought.

Roy Anthony and Earl were running ahead of me as usual, trying to get me to race with them. On another day I might have, because I was still faster than both of them. But I was in no mood to play. Even the silly faces they were making to bait me weren't pulling me away from brooding.

I stopped in front of an old, rambling clapboard house that sat high off the ground on wide brick legs in a corner lot. The house was big compared to the others nearby. It had a sharply angled roof, and some of the white paint on the sides of the house was flaking away, exposing patches of silvery gray wood. The subtle blossoms of a wisteria vine draped the front of the house. The feathery green leaves and the lavender flowers formed a lacey curtain from the ground to the roof, shading most of the front porch. A bay laurel tree, its trunk like a rough dark hand with splayed fingers flung heavenward, stood near the road, creating a spotty canopy of pale-green shade over the yard. I had told Roy Anthony and Earl that this was a witch's house the first day we walked past it. I said it because I was aggravated with Roy Anthony about something, and I had wanted a way to humble him a little, to make him scared. He had decided to deal with the possible threat by challenging me and Earl to race by this house every day. "The witch won't never catch me," he had announced. "On your mark, get set . . ." He always took off before he said "go."

Today the house and the yard looked peaceful, but there was a girl playing in the side yard with a stick and a hard red ball. She bounced the ball on the bare ground, then hit it with the stick. The ball banged against the house and flew back in her direction. She let it bounce before she hit it again. She ran back and forth with her stick, smacking the ball deftly with smooth easy strokes. There was something soothing in the rhythmic "thunck . . . thunck" of the ball hitting the house. I stood in the road, first struck by the cleverness of the girl's solitary game, then struck by some vague familiarity in the girl. I studied her hair, skin color, long thin limbs, movement. With a jolt, I realized it was Esther.

I watched her for a while, my heart pounding, my hands sweating. I wanted her to turn and see me. I was afraid to call out a greeting. It would have been like saying a birthday wish out loud, jinxing the vision for sure.

Finally, she stopped her game and turned in my direction. Rubber ball in one hand, stick in the other, she put her fists against her hips. "What you looking at?" she asked, chin up, head tilted back.

"It's me, Maddy."

"So?"

Needles pricked my guts. "We met in the summer. Remember when you visited your grandma?"

"I visit her lots of times. Fact I'm visiting her right now."

"Ma Parker lives here now?"

"Yes, my grandma's last name is Parker."

"I lived next door to y'all when she lived in the Quarters."

"What Quarters?"

Suspicion played like a wind-blown veil on her face. She walked across the yard and stood at the edge of the road, peering into my face.

"Harvest Quarters. Where I use to live . . ." My words died in the harshness of her stare.

"You trying to tell me you know me?"

I nodded. There wasn't even a hint of recognition in her narrowed eyes. Her hair was braided, tight and obedient, in two thick plaits that hung below her shoulders. A single red rubber band graced the end of each plait. She had a new, pale, shiny scar running thinly along one cheek. Her face was wider and there were more freckles on her pine-colored skin than I remembered. But her eyes still had their old flinty hardness as she glared at me.

"What's my whole name?" she asked. "I always tell people my whole name first time I meet them."

"Esther Denise Rawlins."

Fear flickered in her eyes. But she grinned. "I remember you," she said. "I was just jiving you. I remember you."

But I could tell that she did not. I could see by the flush of pinkness on her cheeks that I was the only one who had not let anything from our summer go. Only I had kept the memory of our expeditions into the bowels of the Quarters. Only I had enshrined the pungent scent of burning nail polish, the passionate hatred and violence of her mother, the tears of despair because her own mother had thrown her out into the darkness.

It hurt my feelings a little bit that I had been forgotten, but in those moments as I stared into her familiar face, I remembered climbing my mulberry tree in Harvest Quarters to pick berries for Ma Parker or Momma to make into cobblers; my memory flashed to dragonflies hovering in the sunlight over the Quarters' creek. A spark of joy rose in me as I thought about my family all together before Momma went away and I became weighed down with the burden of taking care of my brothers. It didn't matter that the past summer didn't open out in front of Esther like a road leading somewhere safe. She had brought with her a whiff of the good part of my past. I was glad she was back.

In the mornings when Roy Anthony, Earl, and I passed the wisteria-covered porch on our way to school, Esther was never anywhere to be seen. Some days on the way home from school she was waiting on the porch and would invite my brothers and me into her yard. Sometimes Ma Parker would come to the door and offer us some kind of treat: tea cakes, dried fruit, biscuits and gravy. Her shoulders were more stooped than I had remembered and there was softness around her eyes and beneath her chin that had not been there before. I wondered why she had moved from Harvest Quarters, but I didn't dare ask her. It was an impossible question coming from a child. I would have seemed rude and too nosy. But there were questions I could ask Esther.

"How come you don't go to school?" I asked. We were eating tea cakes behind the blooming wisteria, leaning back in metal yard chairs whose rusted backs fanned out behind us like half shells. Mason jars filled with sassafras tea sat on the floor at our feet.

"'Cause," she answered, "I been sick and I needed to get well. Besides, I just got back here and Grandma says there ain't no need for me to go now 'cause there's only a little piece of a school year left. Y'all just got a few more weeks, right? I already missed a whole bunch of school before I came here. She says I got to repeat seventh grade, no matter what, so I may as well wait till next year and start fresh."

"What were you sick from?"

She looked at the soft green leaves enclosing us. She opened and closed her mouth several times, stretching the thin scar on her cheek. She got up and walked to the edge of the porch. Parting the wisteria leaves and blossoms with one hand, she leaned her face forward as if looking through blinds. There was nothing beyond the leaves but the bare yard, the bay laurel, the empty road. Roy Anthony and Earl had taken their snack to the back-yard to play in the shade of some pecan trees there.

"Maybe I'll tell you some other time," Esther said, her voice drifting back emotionless. She sat down again and pressed her tea cake against her mouth without opening her lips. Little pieces dropped onto her lap.

She was changed from the girl I had known in the summer. She didn't seem especially interested in the outside world any-more. This new Esther would never have gone deep into the Quarters just to see what was there. She wouldn't have set fire to her mother's nail polish just to see if it would burn. Most days when I stopped by, she was content to sit on the front steps or hide behind the wisteria and question me into telling stories that kept me from questioning her. She would ask me to tell her about what she and I did in the Quarters. I did, with brazen exaggeration, after I realized that she didn't remember any of the details of the summer. Our experiences grew into adventurous tales about two girls as disconnected from Esther and me as the girls with yellow hair and tragic blue eyes in the Grimm brothers' stories.

Sometimes she asked about school, and there was no shortage of school stories. As spring pushed toward summer and the close of the school year, some restlessness was growing in my schoolmates, especially the sixth-grade boys who had become tornadoes of rude behavior. On the playgrounds, they initiated wild running games, they teased and bullied the kids from the lower grades, making them huddle in cliques for safety at free-play recess. Most of the time a yard monitor, some unlucky teacher, marched around the yard maintaining a loose semblance of order. She would quickly stop the wild games and the bullying. But one day when the yard monitor had disappeared to the other side of the building on some errand, several of the sixth-grade boys held Percy Blakely down and pulled his pants off. No one was surprised that he wasn't wearing underpants. Children converged on the place of Percy's humiliation to laugh and point at his dangling genitals as he ran around the gaggle of boys, trying to get his pants back. They were being passed between the giggling boys like a rock in a game of hot potato.

Miss Washington, who must have seen this through our classroom windows, came running across the yard waving a yardstick at the knot of spectators gathered around Percy and the older boys. The boys scattered, dropping Percy's pants as they went, and everyone else ducked back into ordinary play.

I had watched this from a distant part of the yard because I had Earl with me, as I usually did at recess. Roy Anthony didn't need my protection at school. After a few playground brawls Roy Anthony had gained a reputation as a mean kid who would fight boys twice his size, so no one bothered him. In fact, he had created his own little gang of fourth-grade boys and refused to let Earl join them. "Early's such a crybaby makes *me* want to beat him up," he protested when I tried to get him to take care of Earl at recess. It was true. Earl was timid and had a habit of crying at the least little thing, which made him a target just like Percy. I felt sorry for Percy though, and angry at him too. Since talking to him the day the president was assassinated and seeing the sympathy on his face at the Christmas dinner, I felt a vague kinship with him, but not enough to invite him to join me and Earl at recess. In the same way that I wanted my brothers to be strong enough to take care of themselves, I wanted Percy to figure out how to keep himself out of harm's way. I admitted none of this to Esther as I recounted the story of his humiliation on the playground.

In fact, I had avoided looking at her as I spoke. When I turned to face her, I was surprised to see tears on her face. She stood and went to the wisteria, turning her back to me and peering into the yard.

"People can do terrible things to other people," she said, sending her words out into the shade of the bay laurel in the yard. "Something really bad happened to me, Maddy. My life was never really good from as far back as I can remember. I just pretended all the time. When that real bad thing happened, I got tired of pretending. I started thinking life is just one bad thing after another, and I didn't want it no more."

A fragile silence settled in a pool between us. Was the bad thing that happened to her any worse than all the things that had happened to me since last summer?

"Bad things happened to me too," I ventured.

"Not like what happened to me. You still too—"

"Still too what, Esther? What happened to you?"

She turned to look at me. Her eyes were dark with pain.

"My uncle—." Her mouth closed around the rest of her thoughts and we stared at each other.

Something kicked itself alive in my memory—the shadowy image of the man sitting on the edge of my bed at Loralee's. My stomach pitched forward, squeezed again by the panic I had felt as I wrestled with that man. That fear rushed out and hung in the air between Esther and me like white-hot light. Esther's face wavered before me as if I were seeing her through ripples of summer heat rising from blacktop.

"I just can't talk about it," Esther said, dropping her gaze to the floor. "I need to forget," she added.

The world became solid again. She went to the porch steps like she might run down into the yard to get away from what I had made her remember, but she stopped and stood still.

"Do you believe there is a God, Maddy?" she asked, still facing away from me. "Not a mean God like the preacher be yelling about in church. A God that knows everything and loves everybody?"

I shrugged, trying to chase away the emotions still tugging at me.

"Do you believe there is a God that is good?" she asked again.

When she turned toward me, her face glowed with emotion, and I could tell she wanted a real answer from me.

Her question was one I didn't have an answer to. I had never really thought about my belief in God. Momma believed in God. She had taught me that there was a God responsible for the world, just as she had taught me that I had to say "thank you" when someone showed me a kindness. "If you're good, God will be good to you," she had said. Thoughts rattled in my head about the bad things that had happened in the months since Momma left home—even Momma leaving home was a bad thing. Did the bad things that had happened mean that my brothers and I were bad? Or were there worse things that God kept from happening? Or was it Momma and Daddy's bad that we were all paying for?

My voice sounded small when I said, "Yes, I believe there is a God."

"I tried to die," Esther said. "I stopped eating. My Aunt Helen couldn't make me change my mind. When I felt like I was very close to going over the edge of life, something strange happened."

Esther stopped suddenly and frowned at me. "Now don't laugh or make fun of me, Maddy. I ain't talked to nobody about this before. Didn't figure nobody would believe me, or understand. You don't get to tell nobody neither."

There was fire in her eyes and her voice. This was the summer Esther, the fiery, confident Esther.

"God talked to me," she said. "Right in that dark place where I was trying to die. He told me it ain't my fault that there were so many bad things happening. It ain't my fault my momma don't know how to love me. It ain't my fault that somebody—"

Fear flitted across her face, and for a moment she recoiled inward. "It was a really bad thing that happened to me," she said finally. "God told me that even with all the bad things, there's good in the world and I can find it. Said he'd be with me all the time. I just said, 'Okay God.' When I did that, my bad feelings went away. Esther Denise Rawlins went away too. I didn't need to pretend I wasn't scared anymore. I turned into a new girl, just plain old Esther Rawlins. By that time, Aunt Helen had sent for Grandma to come fix me. And I let her."

She had been staring directly into my eyes as she spoke, and I had been unable to break the line that seemed to be holding us.

"I see you looking like you don't believe me," she said suddenly.

"No that ain't it," I said. And it wasn't. I believed her. Believed something had made her change. But I still hadn't thought enough about God to know what to say about that. What she saw on my face was me wondering if I would change, become a new Madeleine Genell Culpepper. I was wondering what it would take for that to happen.

"It's okay if you don't believe me 'cause I'm telling you the truth. God really talked to me and showed me some things too—picture of the world like I'd never seen it before. It was really pretty—all green and blue and brown and white like a big snake-eye marble spinning in the sky. The world is pretty, even though there's still people that do ugly in it. Just now when you were telling me about how people treat that boy Percy, I started thinking about the bad things that people do and how they don't care if they hurt somebody else, 'specially children. We be counting on our grown-ups, and some of them just don't care. I bet Percy's grown people don't treat him good. And I bet you bad things happen to him all the time. That's how it is when your grown-ups don't take care of you. We can't do nothing about it till we grown enough to take care of ourself. Before that real bad thing happened to me, I thought I was grown enough to take care of myself. Now I'm here with my grandma waiting to really be grown. Grandma knows a lot, though she was wrong about my auntie. She thought Aunt Helen would take care of me. But she didn't do no better than my own momma.

"I want to find what's good in the world. Don't you, Maddy?" she asked. "Otherwise there is just no point to anything. Right?"

She came and sat down in the chair beside me. "Why don't

you tell me another story from the summertime," she said. "Tell me a story about my momma. I don't care if it's a bad story. My momma is one of the bad people. Now that I stopped pretending, I know that."

I told her the story about the nail polish fire, but I left out details like Esther crying under the streetlight, and I added a few details to make us more heroic than we were that night. In my story, it was *our* choice to leave her mother's house. We fought her mother when she tried to stop us—punching and kicking her when she tried to whip us. Then we ran out into the street to get away from her.

"Mother Parker wasn't around . . . ," Miss Glenda was saying to someone when I started up the porch steps to her house. I stopped in front of the screen door. I had been on my way to tell her that I was back from Esther and Ma Parker's house and she could send June Bug home whenever she wanted. I turned to head back down the steps.

"What you want, child?" An unfamiliar woman's voice asked from inside Miss Glenda's.

"I'll come back," I said.

"Just come on in here, child," the woman added. "I ain't gonna bite you."

When I opened the screen door, the woman, a more round version of Miss Glenda, sat in a rocking chair facing me. She leaned forward in the rocker and grinned at me with her mouth open.

"Maddy, this is my cousin Sofi from Meridian. Visiting for a few days." Miss Glenda was sitting cross-legged on the end of her bed.

"Your daddy's the one with the missing wife," Sofi said, still grinning at me.

"His wife ain't missing, Sofi. She up at the state hospital north of Jackson with one of they sick babies," Miss Glenda said.

"Where your daddy, girl?"

"Sofi, leave that child alone," Miss Glenda answered. There was laughter in her voice and her dimples were showing. "Her daddy's got a wife, and you ain't his type no way."

Sofi laughed and rocked back and forth. "Honey child, where me and available men is concerned I can be anybody's type," she said.

"You do think highly of yourself, Sofi. Tell me why you still ain't got yourself no man of your own?"

"Hush Glenda, can't you see me and this child is having a conversation? Tell me, Miss Maddy, is your daddy a good-looking man?"

"Leave that child alone. Maddy, don't pay no mind to Sofi. She trying to make some kind of joke. Child, your daddy wouldn't want her, even if he didn't have your mama. Sofi know that well as I do. Go on back outside, child. Rita's round back with the other kids."

I left the women's company happily. I didn't like Sofi's way of joking. Remembering Loralee, I didn't know what Daddy's type was.

"You were saying something about Mother Parker, before the child came in," Sofi said as I went down the steps.

I wasn't interested in playing with Rita, or my brothers. Instead of going to the backyard, I went to my side of the porch where I couldn't be seen from Miss Glenda's doorway. I sat down with my back against the wall to eavesdrop.

"... gone from here for quite a while I know," Miss Glenda was saying. "I sent for some medicine after my little run-in with that heifer Curtis married. Rita come back and said her house in the Quarters was all boarded up."

"She was up in Meridian for a couple of months, I'm thinking," Sofi said. "She left to come back down here a month or so ago with her grandbaby, Bell's little girl. Mother Parker's gon' finish raising her like she should of gone ahead and done in the first place when Bell turned out to be such a mean heifer herself."

"I heard the child was raped. They catch the bastard that did it?"

"Honey, it was her Aunt Helen's boyfriend."

"Girl, hush!" There was sudden anger in Miss Glenda's voice.

"The child got sick behind the whole thing, nearly died in fact," Sofi continued. "Helen called Mother Parker up to Meridian to come see about the child. Ain't told her what made the girl sick, maybe she truly ain't had no idea herself. But if you living with a man that has a taste for children, how could you not know? Girl, do you know that man was stupid enough to still be living up in the house with Helen and that child when Mother Parker arrived?"

"My Lord. There's no accounting for the sheer arrogance of some men. Think they can get away with anything," Miss Glenda said.

I felt the slow beat of my heart in my throat. I had been right in guessing about the bad thing that Esther couldn't bring herself to talk about. It might've happened to me if I hadn't fought and June Bug hadn't started crying when he did.

"Mother Parker figured it all out, though," Sofi said. She nearly killed that man for it. Heard she beat him with a baseball bat when he was sleeping in Helen's bed one night. Helen got a few lumps too, even though Helen denied knowing anything about that man messing with that child."

"Mother Parker get jail time for trying to kill him?" Miss Glenda words floated over from the other side of the wall.

"A little bit. But they had to let her go 'cause they say there wasn't enough evidence to prove nothing. Somehow or other the police couldn't find the bat, or whatever she used to beat him with, and there wasn't nobody would testify against her. Course nobody had seen what happened but Helen and the girl, and neither one of them was going to talk against Mother Parker. Apparently the man can't talk no more. He got some kind of brain damage. Eventually they had to send him up to the state hospital."

"Serves him right. I ain't got no kind of understanding for no man that will lay up with a child. If one ever tried it with one of my girls, I'd try to kill his ass too."

I thought of Miss Glenda wrestling in the ditch with Mrs. Hazel. Yes, I believed that she was capable of killing to defend one of her children.

"I feel sorry for the poor child," Sofi added. She got bad blood from her mama and the devil's luck. But with that evil heifer Bell for a mother how could her life go anyway but bad."

"She's only twelve or so. She'll get over it."

"Yes, children bounces back from all kinds of stuff, thank the Lord."

It was difficult for me to be around Esther after I learned that rape was the bad thing that happened to her. I couldn't bring myself to tell her that I knew, yet I couldn't stop thinking about it every time I saw her. The knowledge tainted my vision of her. I would look at her, slouched in her chair on Ma Parker's porch, eating a tea cake in the air scented with bay leaves and wisteria, and the world would pause. A man had actually lain on top of her and she hadn't been able to fight him off. The man's blunt, cucumber-like penis in the bedroom at Loralee's would materialize in my memory, and I would remember Daddy grunting like an animal on top of Loralee. I could think only of the degradation, the humiliation, the helplessness of being a child at the bottom of that. No wonder she had wanted to die.

How did you keep going after something like that? Yet Esther did, and that made her admirable to me, so I hung on to the friendship. Could I hold on to hope like hers? Would I find the good in life, even without Momma?

"So tell me a story about them Harvest Quarters girls." Esther's familiar call always pulled me back into the present and shattered the fragile glass wall between my bunched-up sad feelings and the sunlit world of Ma Parker's porch.

Esther lay a wisteria blossom on her lap and watched my face while I hunted around in my imagination for a tale about heroic girls in the Mississippi wilds.

CHAPTER TWENTY

♥

THE GENTLE HEAT OF a late June morning warmed my face as I stood in the middle of the road in front of our house, driving my imaginary car. I was heading out of Blossom, Mississippi, escaping into another part of the world to find some of that goodness and beauty that Esther talked about. I was pretty sure I wasn't going to find it in Blossom. As I looked down the road beyond the Masonite plant and the other sad-looking little neighboring houses on my block, stretching my imagination into the future, there was Momma.

She was far enough away to be just a dark outline in the distance, but I knew it was her. The certainty of it had come to me as easily as a growl in my stomach comes to let me know I'm hungry. So I went and sat down on the edge of the porch to wait, listening to the thump of my heart and feeling the swirl of emotions in my belly.

"Hello, Maddy," Momma said, when she stopped in the road in front of me. A thin smile spread across her face. "I'm finally home."

I didn't know what to make of the tremble at the corners of her mouth as it closed around those last words, or the new lines of gray in her frizzy hair, or the faded corduroy jumper she wore, or the battered little suitcase she held in front of her with both hands, or her shadow lying on the ground behind her. I had wanted this, but now as she stood before me, all I could feel was confusion so dense it churned the air around me.

"Come here, Maddy," Momma said, bending to set the little suitcase in the dirt. Standing there with her arms outstretched and her eyes sparking in the sunlight, she didn't look like somebody who had stopped loving me.

My body felt heavy as I stood and willed one foot in front of the other to move reluctantly toward Momma, feeling the distance between us like a wide, flat field. When I reached her, I let her wrap me in her arms, and I buried my face against her flabby chest. I breathed in the familiar, earthy smell of concentrated motherhood laced with the sterile smells of hospital corridors. That's when I knew that my sister was dead.

My mother's body began to shake and the grief trapped inside her chest rumbled in my ears like distant thunder. As I trembled and shook to the rhythm of my mother's sobbing, my emotions broke free from their hiding places and I was flooded with sadness so wide and deep that I thought it was bottomless. My chest ached as I wept into the stiff cloth of Momma's threadbare corduroy jumper and felt all the pains and losses from my childhood flowing through my mind in one dark stream.

The sadness wasn't really bottomless. Beneath it was a pool of anger that roiled and rocked like boiling water. It made me want to push away from Momma's embrace and pound the bones that were all too easy to feel beneath her skin. I flailed and squirmed, the voice of my rage pushing through me in a high, angry whine, matching the mechanical grinding of the plant machinery across the road and making my throat raw. But no matter how much I tried to break free, I couldn't separate myself from Momma. She kept me close in her thin, wiry arms.

When I ran out of tears and anger, I felt hollowed out and light-headed. A small breeze of relief washed through me, and I softened into Momma's embrace. She was no longer crying. She was holding me in quiet stillness with her chin resting on the top of my head. She sighed and relaxed her hold on me, and I moved away from her, wiping my face on my hands.

We stood side by side in the road, and I watched Momma staring at our house, the crumbling chimney, the sloping porch, the plank partition down the middle of the porch separating our side of the house from Miss Glenda's, the four plank steps leading to the porch. "My Lord," she said softly, and she wasn't even seeing the worst of it—the two shabby rooms, the holes in the kitchen floor, the outhouse in the backyard. I wanted to say something, but I had no words to soften what she was seeing. Yes, we had fallen backward in her absence.

"I'm so sorry," she said, draping her arm across my shoulder. "I wish I could've done it all different, but there wasn't any other way."

I leaned against her. She had been right in earlier times when she told me that it was useless to say *I'm sorry*. The words didn't fix anything. She would have to do the fixing now that she was home.

"I'm home now," she said. "And I ain't going away again. Everything'll get sorted. Where your brothers?"

I was glad to shift away from thinking about her regret and our raggedy house. "Everybody's fine," I said. "June Bug at our neighbor Miss Glenda's playing with her littlest boy. Roy Anthony and Earl out picking dewberries with Miss Glenda's biggest kids up by the school. They'll be back soon."

Joy flickered across her face for a moment, but her smile flattened out again and she asked about Daddy. He was at work, at least that was where he was headed when he left in the morning. Most days now he kept a pretty regular schedule of coming and going during the week.

"Let's go get June Bug. He'll be happy you home," I said, grabbing her hand and leaning us in the direction of Miss Glenda's side of the house. I didn't want her to ask me any more questions about Daddy, or anything else that might draw up more sadness for either one of us. I wanted to hold on to what felt good—she was finally home. Everything else could wait.

CHAPTER TWENTY-ONE

♥

I LEANED MY HEAD out the window of Mr. Gamet's truck. The Mississippi countryside streaked by with its shades of green in the trees, bushes, and vines and its multicolored patches of wildflowers huddled together in open fields. Azure sky spread out over orange clay hills freckled with pine, live oak, sassafras, sweet gum, and cedar. Even as a twelve-year-old, I appreciated the beauty and peace of that scenery.

Inside the truck, Daddy was intent on the road, his fingers curled tensely around the steering wheel and an unlit cigarette dangling from a corner of his mouth. Momma sat between us, staring ahead, her thoughts probably hovering around some image of my baby sister, Ida Bea. Momma turned to me as if sensing my gaze. The corners of her mouth lifted in a faint smile. She patted my knee, then turned her attention back to the emptiness in front of her. I felt strangely afloat, like a dust mote drifting on a current of air.

We were on our way to bury Ida Bea. She was to be put in the ground in the graveyard in Tate County, where Daddy's family was from. "They're all there," Daddy had explained the day before. "Your Grandma Inez, your Grandpa Sugar Pie, your Aunt Ida, your Uncle Harold, and a whole slew of other relatives that I won't name right now. Now we'll be adding your baby sister."

Three nights earlier while Momma slept on a cot beside Ida Bea's metal hospital crib, Ida Bea had died after more than eight months of attention from doctors and Momma. "She just up and died," I overheard Momma say to Miss Glenda, making it sound like it was some sort of decision that my sister had made.

The hospital staff had taken up a collection to buy a Greyhound bus ticket for Momma to come home. She and Daddy had argued about that the first night she was home. My brothers were deep in their dreams, but I was lying there with my eyes closed trying to will myself to sleep.

"You've got to wire money tomorrow to the hospital so they can have the funeral home pick up Ida Bea and take her on up for the burial," Momma said quietly. "Send enough to cover my bus ticket."

"That ticket was they charity to you, Dot. They ain't expecting to be paid back."

"You just don't get it," Momma said, her voice shaking with emotions. "How humiliating it was, week after week, sitting up there leaning on other people's charity when you didn't come through. I know how charity was taking care of these children back here. Paying a little bit of something back is the least you can do without arguing with me about it."

"Dot, it's not—"

"Eugene, I can't do this with you right now. Just send the money."

The next morning Daddy, contrite and more than a little unhappy, had talked to me about the funeral. He didn't realize that I knew Momma was mad at him. I'd heard Momma tell Daddy, "I don't want no comforting from you just now. Go on and leave me alone."

She had carried June Bug next door to Miss Glenda's and left Daddy sitting on the edge of their bed. I followed her, but she shooed me away. "Go on, play with the other kids," she had said.

She didn't know that I had long since lost interest in playing with my brothers and Rita and her siblings. I wanted to be around her now that she was home. But I had come outside obediently and sat on the porch listening to her with Miss Glenda, talking and crying because my baby sister was dead.

Daddy had come and sat down beside me on the edge of the porch.

"You have to go with us to the funeral, Maddy," he said, staring at the Masonite building across the road. "Your momma's gon' need you there. The boys is all too young for a funeral, but you big enough now to come along and be a comfort to your momma. It's a tough thing she gone have to get through. Besides, you'll get to meet some of your kinfolk you ain't met before. Won't that be good?" He grinned.

A day later we left my brothers in Miss Glenda's care and set out on the five-hour drive north to Daddy's homeland. Now we were rumbling along in the silence of Mr. Gamet's truck that Daddy had washed and scrubbed until its red paint was almost shiny. He had even swept the bits of hay and cow feed from the truck bed and washed it to ease the farm smells.

I kept stealing glances at Momma's face, and each time my heart would do a little flip. It was good to have her nearby again, even silent and grieving.

As Daddy turned Mr. Gamet's pickup into the dusty front yard of an old yellow two-story farmhouse, chickens scattered, screeching and clucking. Daddy brought the truck to a halt under a towering pecan tree. I opened my door and tumbled out into the yard, grateful for freedom after so many hours cooped up in the truck with my silent parents. Daddy got out and came around to help Momma climb down. I stared out across the road where a rusty barbed-wire fence enclosed a lumpy green pasture with brown and white cows grazing casually in the bright sun. We were going to be here for a few days Daddy had told me. Ida Bea's burial would not be tomorrow, but the next day. Then we would stay one more day and go home.

"Lord, y'all here, I wasn't expecting you till closer to evening."

I turned to see a wiry dark woman hurrying toward us. She was wiping her hands on a blue gingham apron tied over a sleeveless yellow summer dress.

"Johnnie Mae, it's been a minute," Daddy called, going toward her with open arms.

When Daddy released Johnnie Mae from his hug, she reached for Momma who fell into her arms and buried her face against her shoulder. The two women swayed, and Daddy dropped his gaze as a look of pain spread across his face. Momma was crying again.

From the woods that fanned out along the horizon a few yards behind the house came the high, happy noises of children playing.

"Don't tell me this is Madeleine," Johnnie Mae said, when she and my mother stepped apart.

Daddy looked at Momma who was absorbed in the search for a handkerchief in her pocketbook. "We call her Maddy now," he said, grinning at me with a splash of joy on his face that I hadn't seen in a very long time.

"Last time I seen this child she was still in diapers. You sure is big, girl. Come over here and give me a hug. Child you look more like your daddy than your momma," she said, holding me at arm's length after the hug. "Your daddy ain't the best looking of your parents. But God prettied up the face a little more on you than on your daddy."

"Johnnie Mae knows all about not being the best looking one in any crowd," Daddy said with a wide grin. "Back when we was all in school she could win first prize in the ugly contest even when Mr. Ugly himself was in the crowd. Hope your children fortunate enough to look more like they daddy than they momma."

Daddy's laughter floated skyward on this country air. When I looked at him he winked. This was a side of him I had never seen. I noted the clear whites of his eyes as he laughed with this cousin under a pecan tree in the countryside where he grew up. The tension had drained from his jaws, and the lines between his eyebrows had softened.

"Don't listen to him, child," Johnnie Mae was saying. "He don't know nothing 'bout good-looks. Best looking thing about your daddy is you and your momma."

Cousin Johnnie Mae's laughter was warm and fluid. "Where y'all other children?" she asked.

"They too young for this kind of trip," Daddy answered. "Left them with a friend."

"That's good I guess, though I was looking forward to meeting them. I ain't never even seen pictures."

A clan of kids burst around the side of the house, whooping and hollering and grabbing at each other in some game. They stopped when they saw us.

"Come meet y'all cousins from Blossom," Johnnie Mae called, waving them over.

They shuffled forward, cutting their eyes at each other and looking everywhere but at me and my parents. They were four girls, all long skinny legs and arms like their mother. Their colored short-sets in pink, blue, green, and yellow were full of early summer heat, like the wildflowers we passed on the road. They clumped around their mother. The biggest one was Roy Anthony's size, and the smallest one was a little bigger than June Bug. The little one wrapped her arms around her mother's legs and buried her face in her apron when Johnnie Mae told us her name, Raven. The oldest girl was Robin, and she grinned and reached out for my father to shake her hand. The middle girls were Chickie and Blue Jay, and I couldn't tell them apart. "Twins," Johnnie Mae said.

They ran back toward the house when Johnnie Mae ushered us onto the porch to get in out of the sun and have something cool to drink. Momma turned and walked slowly to the edge of the road and stared in the direction of the woods beyond the pasture and the cows.

Johnnie Mae looked at Daddy. "She said anything about—"

"Nope," Daddy cut in and shook his head. "Not a word."

"Must be the worst thing in the world for her. Back here again to bury a baby."

"Don't know how it's gon' go this time," Daddy said, shrugging.

"This wasn't your fault. Neither was before really. You couldn't—"

"Why don't you go on up on the porch with the other girls," Daddy said, suddenly turning to me.

As I walked away, Daddy and Johnnie Mae went back to talking in hushed careful voices. I was turning over Johnnie Mae's words, "back here again to bury a baby." I imagined she was referring to Samuel. That meant that he was buried here too.

A few hours after we arrived at Cousin Johnnie Mae's, other people started dropping by. Mostly they were Daddy's relatives with a few friends mingled in, but none of them stayed very long. Their expressions were mild and their conversation polite, and behind all of their words I sensed something else, like a question they wanted an answer to but weren't going to ask.

Each new arrival offered a hand for Daddy to shake. Some told stories that conjured up images from Daddy's childhood and young adulthood. Some of the womenfolk tried to talk to Momma, offering her reassuring or comforting words. But Momma still wasn't saying much to anybody, just turning up the corners of her mouth with the same vague smile she had been using since we left Blossom. She sat in a wingback chair in one corner of Johnnie Mae's living room, drinking glass after glass of iced tea and smiling at Daddy's well-meaning country cousins and the men who said they had gone to school with my father.

I couldn't imagine my father in school. I couldn't imagine him carrying schoolbooks or sitting at a desk. What kind of a boy had he been? Had he been like Roy Anthony or Earl or June Bug? They were all so different.

No one came to Johnnie Mae's to spin stories of Momma's childhood. No one here had known Momma as a girl because she wasn't from here. She had spent her girlhood many miles southeast in another part of Mississippi. All I knew about Momma's childhood was that both of her parents had died before she was out of high school. Her mother's mother had moved in to finish raising her, and when she died, that was the last of Momma's blood relatives. I had overheard her tell Ma Parker this a few years ago. "It was the most terrible time of my life the year she died," Momma told Ma Parker. "I lost everything precious to me that year, Mother Parker. My whole world ground to a stop. Gene was all I had left."

Slumped quietly on a wooden stool beside my mother in Johnnie Mae's living room, I wondered if that "most terrible time" was connected to Samuel's death. In my presence Momma and Daddy were still keeping silent about the fact that they had another child that died. Momma had not even said to me that Ida Bea had died. Daddy had talked about burying my sister but had said nothing about her dying. So I was not old enough for them to talk to me about death, but I was old enough for them to make me face it. I looked at Momma's vacant profile and her hands wrapped tightly around the sweating glass of iced tea she held on her lap, and I knew that she was thinking about Ida Bea's death and Samuel's death and her grandmother's death and her parents' deaths. I could feel the pain in the air around my mother like a net thrown over her. I looked at Daddy and wondered what he was thinking. He was across the room chatting with his old school friends and Johnnie Mae's husband, Frank.

My parents seemed to be purposefully staying away from each other. Daddy had made no conciliatory gestures in her direction since she uttered the words, "I don't want no comforting from you just now. Go on and leave me alone."

But when visitors started showing up at Johnnie Mae's, it was Daddy who whispered to me, "Go sit by your momma, she needs you. You don't need to say nothing. Just be close by."

Among the visiting relatives was a big-bosomed woman cousin dressed in a bright floral blouse, faded denim overalls, and high-top boots like Daddy's work-boots. Daddy called her Ginny and pulled her into a hug when she offered him her hand. Nobody seemed to take any notice that she was dressed like a man, but though her fashion didn't draw any attention, her conversation did.

"So Gene, when you plan to go out to look at your poppa's place?"

Johnnie Mae and Frank and the three other grown-ups in the room inhaled their conversations and turned to look at Daddy, who stared at Ginny with an expression that seemed to be a combination of disbelief and mild interest. When he didn't answer, she went on.

"I went over not that long ago just to see. The drive going up from the main road is a little overgrown, but I didn't have no trouble getting up to the house. The house looks pretty good considering it's been sitting empty for so long. Wouldn't take much to get it ready for your family. You know the county's run electric lines pretty close by the house now. They had run a gas main cross y'all's land before Poppa Sugar Pie died. All you'd need to do to make it modern livable would be to pipe the well and get proper running water inside. That won't cost you much. I know someone does that kind of work real cheap."

She'd flung the words out rapidly like she was afraid of being interrupted. The whole time her words were pouring in Daddy's direction, she kept her gaze fixed on his face.

"Ginny," Johnnie Mae warned in the sudden silence.

"I recognize your warning tone Johnnie Mae, but I ain't saying nothing offensive. We all know it's a shame that place going to waste out there like it is. We all talk about it enough. You know I was bound to bring it up, since I know for a fact wasn't none of y'all chicken littles going to. Anyways, I wasn't talking to nobody but Eugene. This ain't nobody else's business. So all y'all go on back to y'all own conversations."

"This ain't hardly the time," Johnnie Mae said.

"Like I said, this ain't none of your business. Maybe Gene and

I need to talk private-like someplace other than here, maybe the front porch."

My mother had been watching this scene quietly. Daddy's eyes met hers, and what I saw pass between them was beyond my reach. My father turned toward the front door, and he and Ginny disappeared onto the porch and closed the door behind them.

CHAPTER TWENTY-TWO

"YOUR MOMMA AIN'T UP to it, so you coming with me," Daddy said the next morning, pulling me out of a game of pick-up-sticks under the pecan tree with Johnnie Mae's daughters.

"We gon' visit my family land," was all he said.

The truck cab was again filled with silence as we sailed along the smooth stretch of blacktop headed away from the direction I imagined Blossom to be. Daddy drove with the same tense focus he'd had driving to Johnnie Mae's, jaw clenched, face immobile. We turned off the main road onto a wide, lumpy dirt road that looked like orange clay gone yellow in the sun.

"Look out the window," Daddy said after we had bumped along for a while with dust flying up around the truck. "From now on, everything you see along here belonged to my pop."

What I saw were wide open fields overgrown with shrubs and wildflowers. Off in the distance the land was forested.

"In them woods is every kind of tree you can think of, willows and sycamore and cedar and sassafras and magnolias and sweet gum trees, but mostly good old Mississippi pines of every kind, that and oak. My poppa use to say, a man could make a good life for himself off the timber from them. Now, if I had a nickel for every time Poppa said something like that to me I'd be a rich man."

I didn't see the pride I expected when I looked at Daddy. In fact, his face was pinched in a way that looked angry. He kept silent for a while, staring straight ahead.

"Know what a sharecropper is?" he ventured after a while.

"My teacher, Miss Washington, had us study about the Negro workers in Mississippi from the time of slavery days to now," I said. "We studied about sharecropping."

"My granddaddy and my daddy was sharecroppers. They worked the land in growing season and worked at the timber mill when the harvesting was done. Somehow or other, Poppa managed to buy this eighty acres of Mississippi countryside after moving from place to place sharecropping his whole boyhood and most of his manhood. He finally got to farm for himself just when things were starting to change and folks was getting less willing to work farms for a living. Poppa could only get one or two workers to help him for a while. I was the only son he had to work the land with him. My brother Harold wasn't never gon' be any help. Poppa made the farm work for a while. Then I went overseas. When I come home, everything was different."

This was more than Daddy had ever said to me about his family. I kept still, pretending to be absorbed by the landscape out the window, afraid that any movement or comment or question might close Daddy down around his past.

"I should've been able to help him when I got back. But I couldn't."

He turned to me. "Sorry, Little Bit. Being out here is stirring up my mind."

I wanted to say stirring was good. That maybe if he kept talking I would learn something that might help me understand the year we had all just had. Why hadn't he brought us here to stay with his family? Surely Johnnie Mae would have helped us when

Momma went to the hospital with Baby Ida Bea. But his gaze had already turned inward again and silence descended around us.

Daddy maneuvered the truck into a left turn over a small dirt levy, and we started up a slight hill on a road that was no more than a wide dirt path with tire tracks. Weeds were growing everywhere in the path but they were pressed flat in the center of the little trail like somebody else had driven through recently. On the sides of the path, the branches of wild shrubbery were taller than the truck. Thorny milk thistle with purple-pink blossoms smiling in the sunlight grew in pale green thickets among the shrubbery, scraping the sides of the truck.

We rode slowly with Daddy concentrating as if he were feeling with the tires for the exact path etched somewhere in his memory. A few hundred yards more and there in front of us the path opened out into a clearing of sorts. Someone had recently hacked away at some of the overgrowth. In the center of the clearing the graying façade of a house was visible through a chaotic curtain of chopped and unchopped overgrown weed stalks. Some of the stalks were the lush greens of the current June, others the straw-colored remnants of past springs and summers. Along one side of the clearing stood several majestic trees. I recognized the elongated heart shape of mulberry leaves on a couple of them, and my heart did a little flip-flop in my chest.

Daddy brought the truck to a stop at the side of the house near the base of the first tree. He opened his door, stepped onto the running board, jumped to the ground, and stood for a moment as if listening for something. From the back of the truck, he retrieved a small double-bladed axe that he must have borrowed from Frank. He set off toward the house swinging the axe from side to side in front of him, toppling more of the parched stalks in a crackling symphony as he headed toward the house porch.

I got out of the truck and followed him to stand in front of the old house that was larger than anything that we had ever lived in together. Sunlight glinted off of the few window panes that were still intact and visible from this side of the house.

"Home sweet home," Daddy said, so low that I could barely hear him. "Let's see how she's held up."

He went gingerly up the six front steps to the porch. I followed. The steps were surprisingly sturdy under my feet, and the floor boards creaked a little under Daddy's weight as he walked toward the front door. Rusting swatches of screen fell to the floor and splattered into tiny burnt-orange flakes when he opened the screen door. Tiny butterflies flittered in my stomach when his hand griped the blackened doorknob. Maybe someone would be on the other side. Maybe Uncle Harold who they said died before I was born. Maybe my brother Samuel who hadn't died after all but had been left here to grow up with Uncle Harold.

What greeted us when Daddy swung open the door was a cavernous room, empty of life except for the bold yellow sunshine slanting through two tall windows to the left. The first room opened out into another empty room. And through an open doorway on the other side of that room I could see a strip of dusty gray linoleum floor. Disappointment yawned in me.

"You wait," Daddy said, and he went on through the rooms, pausing to glance around and look up at the ceiling every few paces. He disappeared through the doorway of the back room and I was alone on the porch of my daddy's boyhood home.

Daddy materialized in the back doorway again. "You can come on through now."

I stepped inside the still air of the house. The walls in the front room were smoky yellow with lighter rectangles and ovals where pictures must have hung at one time. In the middle room

I could see the faded patterns of pale pink flowers in the stained and peeling wallpaper. The room at the back of the house was a kitchen. A big wood-burning kitchen stove, gray cast iron with inlays of cracked porcelain, still stood in one corner. In front of a tall, bright window with wavy glass was a big metal sink with an attached counter. Built into the counter was a rusted water pump, its crooked arm lifted toward the ceiling. On the other side of the room was a half-opened door leading to a smaller room. Beside that door were stairs going to another floor. Daddy had already gone up. His heavy footsteps echoed above my head. I headed for the stairs. Through the partially open door near the stairs I saw cans on some shelves and realized it was a pantry. I pushed the door open farther and stepped into the dusty, little room filled with cobwebs. Several unopened cans were scattered on shelves. Rust from the metal of the cans had eaten through the labels, making them unreadable. The cans bulged with little rust-speckled domes, and I thought about the fact that just a few months earlier my brothers and I would probably have gladly eaten what these bulging cans contained. On a low shelf some broken canning jars sat in puddles of dry, black, lumpy debris that had probably once been fruit. A cracked and faded cardboard calendar displaying the image of a brown-skinned Jesus with a benign smile, fierce black eyes, and wavy, black, shoulder-length hair was nailed above a narrow counter on the wall opposite the shelves. The calendar's edges had dried and curled, obscuring everything except OCTOBER 1950 in hard block lettering and the picture of Jesus.

My heart pulsed in my throat, marking rhythm with the slow in and out of my breath. There was a sudden rustling in the weeds on the other side of the thin glass panes in the pantry window. It sounded like a child crying softly, and I jumped when Daddy laid his hand on my shoulder.

"Penny for them thoughts," he said.

I shrugged. The sight of those rusted cans, the spoiled pre-serves, the brown-skin Jesus calendar, the sense that the last per-son to leave this room had intended to come back pierced me with sadness.

"The sleeping rooms is upstairs," Daddy said. "Go have a look."

At the top of the stairs was a small landing that opened out into a narrow hallway. At the end of the hallway was a large win-dow. I walked to it and looked out onto the front yard. I could see the tops of the mulberry trees and Mr. Gamet's truck off to one side. Straight ahead was the overgrown path we had driven to get to the house, and beyond that path was the dirt road that led up from the blacktop road. In the distance, a pale-blue pickup was moving along the otherwise empty highway. Beyond the overgrown shrubs in the other direction were large open pastures scattered with brown cows and on the other side of the pastures, woods and rolling green hills. It looked like something out of a story book. Why had Daddy moved so far away from here to the life we had back in Blossom? Why hadn't he brought us back here to live instead of that awful place we were now living in?

I went back into the hall and peeked into the rooms. On one side of the hallway was a large room with more of that faded rosy wallpaper from downstairs. On the other side were two smaller rooms with walls so dingy it was impossible to tell if they had ever carried any color other than that of bare wood. All of the rooms had the same yawning emptiness as the rooms below. Dust and spiderwebs were their only occupants. I closed the door on the last of the rooms with that same pang of sadness I'd felt looking at the rusted cans and fierce eyes of Jesus in the pantry. I tried to imagine my daddy as a little boy in one of these rooms but could only conjure up his adult face and body. What I could imagine was Roy Anthony, Earl, and June Bug tumbling around in these rooms, stomping up and down the stairs.

When I got to the bottom of the stairs, Daddy had propped open the back door and was sitting in the sunshine on the top of the back steps. He was staring out at the chaos of weeds in the yard. I looked at the Jesus calendar in the pantry again and wondered at the significance of October 1950. Did Grandma Inez, Daddy's mother that I never met, can those jars of preserves? Whoever canned them had set them in the pantry for someone to eat. As I looked at the crusted remains of fruit that had been waiting there perhaps since 1950, I thought about my grandpa buying the land this house was on. He bought the land. Grandma fixed the food. They had been preparing for some sort of future. What had happened?

"You are the future," Miss Washington had said to me and my classmates more than once during the school year that had just closed. "You must learn about your past in order to have a good future," she had also said, setting us the task of looking back at slavery times and what happened afterward, right up to the details of the Civil Rights March on Washington, D.C., that she told us she had attended just before school started.

Had Daddy's parents envisioned a future that might contain me? Was Daddy imagining some sort of future as he sat out there on the back steps of this house where he'd grown up? I went out and sat down beside Daddy on the steps. He glanced at me. "Ah," he said, as if he had been wondering where I was. But then he went back to staring into the yard. Something had shifted in him since our arrival at Johnnie Mae's, and I wondered how far that shift went. I looked at the side of his face now and carefully weighed the questions I had been carrying around. I looked out at the weeds and thought about the possible consequences of asking them.

"Daddy, what happened to Samuel?" I pushed my hands beneath me on the steps to keep them from trembling.

"What? Who told you—"

I could feel his eyes on the side of my face, but I kept my focus on the haphazard growth in the yard.

"I ain't a baby no more."

"Did one of your cousins say something to you?"

"I been knowing for a while, Daddy. Samuel is my brother who died."

"Your cousins been saying things?"

I shook my head. I wondered which cousins he meant and what they knew. I stole a glance at Daddy. He was looking straight ahead again. Then I felt him look at me, and this time I turned to meet his gaze. "I ain't a baby no more, Daddy," I answered.

"You had to grow up a lot this year. I ain't too proud about that."

"It just don't feel right for you to keep treating me like I'm June Bug or Earl 'cause I don't feel like I'm a child no more."

"You still a child."

"I don't feel like one."

"You got a lot more years of being a child."

"Why can't I know about Samuel? I get to know about Ida Bea."

I was pushing it, and I could see Daddy's emotion in the way he kept clenching his jaw and releasing it without even opening his mouth.

"My teacher told us we got to know about the past to have a good future," I persisted. "Ain't what happened to you and Momma my past?"

Daddy turned his gaze to me again. This time he let his breath out through his nose with a soft noise as if he were admitting a new truth.

"Some things is better left buried."

"But which things, Daddy?"

"Things that might hurt people all over again."

"Would I be hurt?"

"There ain't nothing good about this story, Maddy. Everybody gets hurt by it in some amount."

I didn't know the nature of the hurt he was talking about. I only knew that I wanted to know what had happened. That it seemed important for me to know. That I wanted to hear it from him. That in the past few days our world, mine and his, was turning toward a different light. I wanted that light to bring us all something good. Maybe he needed to tell the story out loud.

"I know more things than you think, Daddy," I ventured and looked at him out of the corners of my eyes. I knew more than I thought I wanted to know about way too many things.

"If it wasn't for me, you would have a sixteen-year-old brother," Daddy began. "I've played that day over in my mind so many times, and it always comes out the same. It's my fault he died."

Daddy looked down at his lap. His elbows were on his knees, and he was absentmindedly rubbing his hands together, making fists and releasing them, entwining and then unwrapping his fingers, the swirl of his emotions playing out in the shadow shapes his hands were forming and unforming on the ground below.

"Samuel buried in the same graveyard where we gon' put your baby sister. Your momma ain't been back here since that burial. Didn't even come to bury my momma or pop when it was time. But she wanted to put Baby Ida Bea here. With family."

"You know I fought in the Great War?"

He looked at me and I nodded. "You are a VFW." I remembered that from the Christmas party.

"Veteran of a foreign war," he said gravely. "Me and most of my friends from around here were dressed up in uniforms and sent to help the Allies in the war. Most every one of the ones that went over there from here never made it back. I came damn near to never getting back myself. Somehow I made it home. Me and Jimmy the only ones. Jimmy came by Johnnie Mae's last night. Nobody around here but him got no idea what that feels like. To have seen what we seen. Done what we done. Then get sent home to live like normal folks again."

I had asked to hear this story, but now knots of emotion were tightening in my stomach. I pressed my stomach in toward my spine to sooth my fears.

"We were visiting my folks right here. Momma and Pop was still alive then. It was May 12, 1949. I still see it in my mind like it was yesterday. Certain things are like that in my head. They just keep getting turned over fresh with every sunrise. The day Sam died is one of those days. It was a lot like this one, a easy feeling day. I set out with Sam, down these same back steps. Momma called behind me, 'Be careful with that baby.' Course I was going to be careful. I was just going out cross that pasture yonder and over the backside of that hill."

He pointed toward the weeds through whose curtain I could see neither pasture nor hill. But I remembered my view from the upstairs window.

"I was taking *my son* over to Jimmy's. Me and Jimmy went way back to grade school days. He was Air Force. I was Army. He went in before me. Came out before me. When I got out, he was by then married with a couple of kids of his own. You met him at Johnnie Mae's last night."

Daddy was repeating himself, but I just nodded and pictured the dark anxious face of the man whose eyes never stayed still. Whether he was talking or someone else was, his eyes kept dart-ing around like he was continually counting all the objects and the people in Johnnie Mae's living room.

"You ever heard buckshot in the woods?" Daddy asked, like he had forgotten who he was talking to. "A lot like rifle fire in a wooded battlefield in Germany. There's woods on the other side of the hill on Jimmy's family place."

Daddy looked at me, but I saw by the glazed terror in his eyes that he wasn't seeing me. He was seeing his memories.

"When you in the woods it's hard to know where the shooting is coming from," he said, his voice like gravel. "So many things for the sound to bounce off. Sometimes you can't tell if the enemy is behind you or in front of you till you see a bullet hole. You can tell by seeing which way the bullet went in. But when you being shot at, you don't have time to look for no bullet holes."

Daddy's hands were clasped in a fisted prayer between his knees now, and his long fingers were frantically kneading the backs of his hands.

"That's the way it was in Jimmy's woods that day. I couldn't tell where the shots were coming from. First one, then another, and another. Shots seems to be coming from everywhere. I was going to run with Sam to Jimmy's house. But I couldn't get my bearings. I was in hell all over again with my unit in Germany. Couldn't remember if we were running away from the firing or towards it. George Kayland was right next to me. He got hit by some kind of fire that took away half his body. One minute he was there. Next minute, nothing to recognize him by. Death was snatching men all around me. They were just going to pieces. I was running and firing. Stumbling over men on the ground. Them that wasn't dead was hollering and moaning. Didn't know where I was going, where the enemy was. Just kept on running till something exploded inside my head. Thought death had took me too. At times I still think it would've been better if it had."

Daddy's chin dropped forward onto his chest and his shoulders began to shake. As he wept, I leaned my face against his shoulder and wrapped my arm as far around his back as I could. His body shook, but there was no sound. I held on, feeling the great rivers of grown-up sadness flowing through him, and for the first time in a long time I found myself feeling sorry for him. Something beyond his control had a hold of him and wasn't letting go easy.

"God," he said suddenly, cradling his head in his hands. "Remembering sets my head on fire."

"The first time I went through it, I woke up in a Army hospital. They told me I had shell shock. That was before I ever met your momma. She didn't know nothing about that. I never told her. I realized later I should've told her. Should've let her know what she was getting herself in for. But I thought I was done with it."

"When I come to my senses that second time, they had just fished Sam's body from the creek about a hundred yards from Jimmy's front door. While I was running from the enemy in my head that day, Sam had gone off in the woods by hisself and fell in the creek. The same creek that me and Jimmy and them use to play in as kids. It was my job to protect him. That was all I had to do that day. Protect my little boy. But I couldn't keep my head when death came."

Daddy was staring straight ahead again, wringing his hands between his knees. In the sunlight, sweat and tears glistened like tiny jewels on his face and neck.

"They say it was rabbit hunters shooting in the woods. They the ones that found me. They went looking for Sam when they heard I'd had him with me.

"Your momma had let me come here with the boy. Her grand-mother, her last living relative, was dying. She'd been trying to tend her and Sam. I was supposed to be helping by bringing Sam here. My mama was going to look after him for awhile. She blamed herself when he drowned. Said she'd had a bad feeling when I set out to go see Jimmy.

"Your momma thought Samuel's drowning was her fault. Some kind of judgment from God because she had given over his care to somebody else. Said Samuel would still be alive if she'd just been strong enough to keep looking after him and her sick grand-mother. But it wasn't nobody's fault but mine.

"I couldn't even comfort Dot. I wasn't fit for nothing. Me and her stayed on here with my folks for awhile. But the war kept exploding in my head. I'd find myself back in the fire, and I'd do crazy things. They had to put me back in the asylum. I was up there for nearly a year. After a while I wasn't fighting the war in my head every day no more, so they let me come home. When I got back, Dot found it somewhere in her heart to give me another chance and start again, though it took her a long time."

Daddy put his elbows on his knees and opened his hands in front of him, palms facing skyward. "Your momma's a good woman. Better than I deserve. I made some promises then. Didn't know how hard it would be to keep them. I'm never really *out* of the war. It keeps coming back to me. Drink helps me through it. Sometimes your momma helps, but—"

He looked at me suddenly. "I know drink's bad medicine. I ain't been drinking as much. I'm working on fixing it. Just couldn't make myself change at first. You seen the worst of me. That fills me with shame. Don't know if I can ever be the man you and your momma and your brothers deserve."

Beyond a feeling of anguish, and beyond the haze of trying to sort through the details of Daddy's story, I felt sorry for Momma. Now I understood why she had gone away from the rest of us to try to keep Ida Bea alive. She had been trying to make up for Samuel's death—for not being there to take care of him. I understood too why she had made me promise to take care of my brothers. She was afraid Daddy's mind might come apart again, and she believed in me. It was sad to think that I was really all she had.

"How old are you?" Daddy asked.

"Twelve."

"A twelve-year-old girl had to do a man's job. What kind of man does that make me? It was you your momma trusted to take your brothers. She should've been able to trust me to do it. It's always going to weigh on me, like Sam's dying."

Daddy was acknowledging something, or maybe promising something. I turned to meet his stare. His eyes were clear for a change, no spidery lines clogging the corners. I hadn't smelled whiskey on his breath since Momma came home.

"I can see by your eyes that you older than you got any business being," he said. "'Old before your time' my momma use to say about children with too much grown-up knowledge. She said that about my sister Ida Bea. My failings done made you old before your time. I wished I could take back some things that happened. But time don't flow in that direction."

Daddy wiped his face with his hands. "I've got to ask you not to tell your momma about some things that went on while she was away. I won't name them, but you smart enough to know what kind of things I mean. Things that would just make your momma feel hurt."

I nodded slowly. I did know what kinds of things, which included just about everything that had happened in the past eight and a half months.

I had nothing more to say. No more questions to ask. No accusations to fling. No promises to exact. Daddy seemed to have run out of words as well. So we sat in silence, turned inward on our private feelings. I poured back over the details of Daddy's story about Samuel. I felt relieved to know that Daddy hadn't done anything to Samuel to cause him to die. He had just failed to protect him, like he failed to protect me and Roy Anthony and Earl and June Bug in Momma's absence. Momma had been right all along. I was big enough to keep us all alive. That realization made me feel good, about myself, about Momma, even about Daddy.

When the sun had lowered itself from directly overhead and the shadows in the yard had shifted, Daddy stood, lifted his arms, extended his fingers high above his head, and stretched himself into a slow and deliberate yawn.

"We better be heading back," he said. "I didn't expect this to be part of the trip. But it was time, I suppose, for you to know the whole story. Better you heard it from me. Family secrets have a way of coming out, 'specially among country folk. But some things you got to keep close to your vest for as long as you can. The sooner you learn that, the better chance you gon' have in life."

He put his palm on the top of my head and gave a little shake. "You've got a head full of secrets now, don't you, Baby Girl? Come on."

By the time I was on my feet, I had already begun to forgive him.

He stepped aside and motioned for me to go on back through the house ahead of him. I drifted obediently, glancing around again at Daddy's boyhood home, my sympathy expanding and extending itself for the damaged man that he was.

When I stepped onto the front porch, I saw that the hood of the truck was up. The driver's side door was open too, and a man's legs were visible beneath the truck as if the man were squatting or leaning across the driver's side seat doing something beneath the steering wheel. Daddy stepped onto the porch behind me. Without a word, he grabbed my arm and pulled me back behind him.

A white stranger walked around the front of the truck. His shoulders shot up quickly and his chest went concave making the bib of his worn denim overalls look momentarily empty when he saw us.

"Shit," he spat out. "Hey J.D., we got company."

The legs sticking out of the truck moved and the other man, J.D., unfolded himself and headed around the truck. He leaned something against the truck bumper and wiped his hands on the legs of his gray work pants. He seemed to be deliberately stalling as he carefully pushed the sleeves of his plaid shirt up around his elbows. He retrieved the thing he had leaned against the truck, and the two men stood looking in our direction. With the sun shining directly into their pale faces against the backdrop of Mr. Gamet's red pickup, the gnarled trunks of the mulberry trees, and the hilly pastures in the background, they looked like the bad guys in a western just before a showdown.

For a moment I thought, or more likely hoped, they would turn and walk back down the drive. But when J.D. took a step, it was toward the house. The other man fell in behind him and walked in single file. The thing that J.D. had leaned against the truck turned out to be a rifle, a full-sized version of the toy one that Miss Glenda's oldest boy had. J.D. swung the rifle stiffly at his side as he walked along the path that Daddy had hacked for us to reach the house. The little axe he had used to clear the path was lying on the edge of the porch.

"We was wondering if we might borrow your truck for a bit," J.D. said when the two stopped a few yards away from the house. "Ours stopped back a ways on the road." He gestured vaguely toward the drive with his rifle hand. My eyes followed the direction of his gesture and made out the shape of a light blue truck cab above the brush at the end of the crook in the drive.

"Probably just needs a little gasoline," his companion said.

"We can go to the nearest filling station and get some and come on back with your truck," J.D. said.

For a moment there was silence as Daddy faced off with the two men. I could feel the heat radiating off Daddy's back. A tremor was shaking one of his legs.

"Did you hear me, Mister? We need to borrow your truck."

"Don't think so," Daddy answered. "Ain't mine to loan."

"We'd bring it back," J.D said.

"Can't agree to that."

"You got any idea who we are?"

"Nope. Can't say I do." Daddy's hands hung casually at his sides, but I could see that his leg was still shaking.

"I'm J.D. Morrisey, and this is my brother Bo. Names ring any bells?"

"Can't say so."

"Well, you could talk to some of the other folks hereabouts and they could tell you some things about us. Namely that we borrow from our neighbors from time to time, and we ain't the most patient men in the county. In fact, we tend to be downright hotheaded if you take my meaning."

Daddy and J.D. stared at each other like blank walls.

"I'm asking you nicely. Can we borrow your truck?"

Bo shifted his weight uneasily.

"Nope." Daddy was resolute, like Roy Anthony answering a dare.

"We could bring the girl along as a kind of guarantee that we'll return the truck." J.D. grinned, swung the rifle up in front of himself, then fingered it with both hands. He cocked it and swung it skyward. He leaned back and a shot rang out, knocking him a little off balance before he leveled it again.

I flinched as the sound of the shot rang inside my head and echoed across the countryside.

"Sometimes this thing just goes off by accident. I wouldn't want it to be pointed at you or your little girl when that happens. So why don't you just give me the keys to the truck 'fore something accidental happens."

Daddy turned quickly and shoved me so hard that I fell backward through the open door and landed on the floor in the house. He yelled in a voice more animal than human. There was the sound of flesh hitting flesh and a tumultuous grunt from bodies slamming to the ground. I rolled onto my stomach and lifted my head enough to see that Daddy had leapt off the porch and landed on J.D. They were scrambling around on the ground, pulling, pushing, punching each other. Each seemed to have a hand on the rifle. Bo moved around the fighting men, kicking at the gnarled figures and grabbing at the cold metal barrel of the rifle when it appeared to be pointed randomly with no indication of whose finger was nearest the trigger.

I took in the grunts and groans and shifting figures in the shivering weeds at the edge of the porch. I whispered, "Oh God, oh God, oh God . . ." into the floorboards. The tussling chaos in the yard seemed to go on a long time. Suddenly the painful cracking sound of wood striking bone rose on the air followed by a deep guttural groan. Daddy and J.D. fell away from each other, and Daddy was the only one with his hands on the rifle. He shifted to his knees and staggered to his feet. J.D. rolled over from his back onto all fours, then pushed himself up to kneeling. Bo backed up behind him. Daddy cocked the rifle again and leveled it at J.D.'s chest.

"I was in the army, goddamn you. In the goddamn war," Daddy said, gasping for air. He heaved a few breaths and backed away from J.D., who held his outstretched arms in front of his body with his palms facing the barrel of the rifle as if he believed he might be able to ward off a bullet. Blood was flowing from his nose and his mouth. One side of his face looked like raw meat.

"I killed men that look like you. You got no idea what that was like," Daddy growled, his voice deep in the back of his throat. "Colored man taking orders from a white man who had trained him to kill other white men. The enemy. Kill the enemy, they said. I did. Killed the enemy. Till they shipped me back. Shell shocked, they said. Shell shocked. Lost my mind. More than fifteen years, still ain't really found it again. Was just getting to okay. Then you come along. Makes me think of killing the enemy again. Are you the enemy?"

"Look, we didn't mean for nobody to get hurt." Bo was talking now. He was holding his hands out too, but with palms skyward and closer to his body. "We just aimed to have a little fun. A little road racing in two trucks. That's all. We would've brought your truck back, honest. See. We ain't never shot nobody. Don't shoot my brother."

"What am I suppose to do?" Daddy said. "How is a man suppose to keep his head straight when everywhere he turns ain't nothing but troubles?"

"We won't ever bother you again."

"Is that suppose to fix everything?"

"No sir, I don't imagine it will. But it looks like you got a family to consider. That girl in there. Maybe some others. You know it'll go real bad with you if you shoot a white man."

J.D. had dropped his hands and was looking at the ground. Daddy kept the gun aimed at him as his brother continued to talk.

"Our daddy was in the war and it kind of made a mess of him too. But he ain't never hurt nobody behind it. He just keeps to himself mostly. I promise you, we'll leave you alone and you can keep to yourself too. Just don't shoot my brother."

Daddy's back was to me so I couldn't see what emotions were playing out on his face. But I thought it just possible that he would pull the trigger.

Suddenly a shot rang out and Daddy stumbled backward and let the rifle drop to his side. J.D. fell forward.

"Get on away from here," Daddy yelled. "I don't ever want to see y'all again."

J. D. pushed himself onto his knees as Daddy's words registered. My breath returned when I realized that both of the men were still alive.

"Go!" Daddy yelled again. "God help me, and the devil can take me. I'll shoot you if I ever see either of y'all again."

Bo moved forward and helped J.D. to his feet.

"No more trouble from us, mister. No more trouble at all."

J.D. nodded too and let Bo lead him back down the cleared path toward the drive. After a few steps they stopped and turned back toward Daddy, I thought to ask for their rifle. But whatever was visible on Daddy's face was enough to turn them toward their own truck again without a word. They stumbled on until they were out of sight. Daddy stared after them until long after the sound of their truck engine accelerating along the road had vanished.

At last he turned back toward the house and looked at me still crouched on the floor. There was more pride in the angle of his jaw and the brightness of his eyes than I had ever seen him carry.

"Tell me, baby—Maddy?" he said grinning at me suddenly. "How'd you and your brothers do living in a place like this?" He swept his arm in an arc that took in the surrounding fields and the house.

My imagination soared on the wings of possibility. "Fine I think, Daddy. Just fine."

CHAPTER TWENTY-THREE

DADDY'S FAMILY CHURCH, Mt. Hebron Baptist, was a simple white-washed wooden building with wide steps that led up to a small hooded porch and wide oak doors. A boy, not much older than me, stood on the tiny porch. In spite of the rising heat, he looked cool and efficient in his black suit, starched white shirt, red tie, and black cotton gloves. His face was a mask of solemn deference when he nodded and said, "Sir," in response to my father's greeting.

"This is all the family I've brought today," Daddy said, steadying his hand on Momma's elbow and nodding toward me beside her.

"Everybody's inside," the boy whispered as he opened the doors. Momma stepped into the vestibule and Daddy followed. When I stepped inside behind Daddy, I saw that Momma was already being led down the center aisle by two women clad in white. Daddy paused for a few seconds and then headed after them, his head bowed like a little boy.

I was alone in the vestibule, held in place by a colorful austerity in my surroundings. Several rows of pews near the front of the church were filled with people in their Sunday finery—women in bright summer dresses, the tops of their summer hats facing me like the sun-hungry faces of flowers. The men's backs were straight in their dark suits. A sprinkling of girls and boys around my age sat among the grown-ups. I tried to pick out Cousin

Johnnie Mae, her girls, her husband Frank, but they had melted into the gathering of relatives and family friends.

The light poured in through arched windows of plain glass on each side of the building. Another arched window of red glass with a translucent gold cross in its center took up most of the back wall behind the pulpit.

Daddy and Momma and the two church ladies were walking right into the rich yellow sunlight streaming through the huge glass cross. Their bodies blurred around the edges, and they were no longer human figures, just dark centers with yellow and red light splaying out around them in spiky lines. My stomach clenched and then released when they turned into the front pew—one white-clad church lady, then Momma, then another white-clad church lady, then Daddy.

Straight ahead of me was the tiny white casket, its lid open like a yawning mouth at the foot of the cross.

I tilted backward, but there was a white-clad lady beside me. "Come on, sugar," she said and took my hand. I walked beside her, rigid with fear as the yellow cross grew bigger and more yellow in front of me. The red light around it pressed in, urging me toward the center of the cross and the coffin surrounded by a small army of waxy white calla lilies. But before I could be completely swallowed up by the red, the yellow, the white, I was whisked into the pew behind my mother and father.

I stared at the backs of my parents' heads, both equally foreign and strange to me. How could I belong to these two people?

A woman dressed in a satiny yellow choir robe with a red stole moved to the center of the sanctuary. A fluid, rippling a cappella hymn that was simultaneously soothing and agitating to me flowed through her and out into the room. I was glad when she stopped singing. My mind wandered to the yellow cross when the preacher stood in the pulpit to read from the Bible, then began a sermon about the sadness of losing a child and the joy of a child in paradise. The window was too much, I thought, too big, too bright.

"God loves the little children," the preacher proclaimed, staring in my mother's direction. "He welcomes all the innocents into heaven."

I glanced toward my sister up there in her white casket. How would she be in heaven? Would she be taken out of her casket and taught to walk and play? Would she grow up, or would she be forever small?

My mother began to sway back and forth in the pew in front of me. A low underwater sound accompanying the movement. I thought perhaps she was humming a song. Then she leaned into the shoulder of one of the church ladies and mumbled, "My baby, my baby." The lady put her arm around Momma and fanned her with a paper fan.

The people in Momma's pew stood up, and I was urged to my feet by the church lady beside me who cupped her hand under my elbow. *Good*, I thought, *we can leave now. I can turn my back to that too bright, too much cross and that little casket.* But to my horror I realized that when Momma and Daddy left their pew, they headed *to* the cross and the casket, not away. My mother was moaning, a painful ruffled noise I'd never heard her make. It spread out around the room, and when it rose to a low wail, other women in their pews started dabbing at their eyes with handkerchiefs. Despite Momma's cries and her wobbling knees, she was going forward with the church ladies who were holding onto her on each side. I was confused by the contradiction between her wailing and her steady movement toward the source of her anguish.

When she was in front of the coffin she yelled, "Oh God, my

baby, my baby! Why did my baby have to die? Why did you take my baby away from me?" She rocked back on her heels and the church ladies moved with her like a wave. "Why have you taken another one from me? Haven't I suffered enough?"

As I watched the commotion at Ida Bea's coffin and listened to Momma's continuous singsong plea, "Why did my baby have to die?" reverberating off the red and yellow glass, a little thought grew in me—what about me and Roy Anthony and June Bug and Earl? We lived.

Then the ladies turned Momma away from the little coffin and led her back down the aisle, past my pew. I saw a look of grief so complete and full on her face that I was overcome with shame. I wanted to tell her I was sorry, but I was being moved past her and led to the casket by my church lady who was crushing my fingers inside her wide, flat palm. I closed my eyes. When we stopped moving I knew I had to open them, see death, maybe understand death, understand my mother's grief, and understand why she had abandoned me and my brothers for this baby.

I looked down on a tiny dark face resting on a cushion of pleated white satin. An ethereal white blanket was tucked in around her so that only her neck and head were visible. Her body was a swaddled lump. It was clear that my sister was not asleep. The stillness was too complete. Her skin was too smooth, tight and shiny like the waxy plastic face of a doll. Her lips were deep purple. One of her eyes was slightly open, and something that looked like dried glue, honey colored and thick, was visible on the lower eyelid. Beneath the half open lid was the dull whiteness of the side of an eyeball.

I couldn't connect that face to the squirming, mewling baby sister who lay, months ago, with a thin red line of blood at the base of her umbilical cord while Momma and Ma Parker looked at her in quiet fear before Momma dressed her and took her back to the hospital. But I could see the finality of death. I understood why Momma had been trying to keep death away from my sister. I didn't understand why she didn't succeed.

The church lady's hands were on my shoulders, her fingers pressed into my flesh. I thought there was something I needed to do or say before I turned away. Perhaps a kiss on the forehead as Momma had done before the church ladies led her away. But I could go no further than thinking about it. My body would not bend in the direction of my dead sister.

I let the church lady turn me around, put my back to Baby Ida Bea, and lead me back up the aisle and out into the bright, living air outside the church.

Momma was sitting with one of her church ladies and Johnnie Mae in the backseat of someone's car, a dusty white Chevrolet parked at the bottom of the steps, and I expected to be ushered down and into the car beside them. But the lady who was holding my hand stopped near the bottom of the steps, and we became the beginning of a line. More people came out of the church and lined up beside us, or on the other side of the steps, facing us. These were Daddy's people—cousins, uncles, aunts, old friends.

Daddy and Cousin Frank appeared in the doorway at the top of the stairs holding Ida Bea's tiny closed casket between them. Someone had backed Mr. Gamet's truck up near the white Chevrolet and opened the tailgate, and I could see a piece of green carpet laid in the back. Daddy and Cousin Frank walked solemnly down the steps. Daddy's cheeks were wet and his eyes sparkled in the sunlight as he stared straight ahead. My church lady pressed a lacy white handkerchief into his free hand as he passed us. He took it without slowing, or even glancing our way. He simply clenched his jaw and squeezed the handkerchief in his fist.

They eased the tiny coffin into the middle of the truck bed, closed the tailgate, and got into the cab. The church lady tightened her hand around mine as the truck pulled out of the churchyard and into the road. The car carrying Momma followed, and a station wagon filled with other women from inside the church pulled out behind it. More cars pulled into the road behind them. The few of us remaining watched plumes of dust fly up behind the truck and the cars. We kept watching until the last car disappeared around a curve in the road.

Everyone sighed at the same time, a great exhalation that felt like a sloughing off of grief. We fell away from the formal lines we had formed on the church steps. My church lady bent and wiped my face with another lacy handkerchief. While her face was still level with mine, she looked into my eyes and smiled. It was the first time I had been so carefully regarded that whole day.

"You a strong child," she said. "But they're going to the burial ground where your Daddy's people be. I didn't figure you needed to go see your little sister going in the ground. You seen enough for today, sugar."

She straightened up and took my hand again with weathered motherly authority. Her strong leathery hand anchored me, kept me from floating off into despair, yearning after my mother who had disappeared with Ida Bea again.

"Come on back here to the kitchen with me," she said. "We got to finish getting the food ready so everybody can eat when your mama and daddy gets back from burying their dead."

In the church kitchen, a small wooden building off to one side of the church, she wrapped her body in an apron and blended in with the other women who were already there when we arrived. They were all busy with the preparation of food. I perched on a stool out of the way and turned my attention to the sound of the children playing outside.

I thought about my brothers, and I imagined them playing outdoor games with Miss Glenda's kids. It occurred to me that they were old enough to handle a funeral, had experienced enough horrifying things in our past eight months with Daddy to know how to close down around certain feelings, though it probably was better for them not to see Momma crying in the way that she had. Certainly June Bug would not have managed that well. I longed to be where my brothers were now, somewhere in the midst of play, still oblivious to the tight hold that grief can have, but for the moment I was glad to sit in a corner of this kitchen warm with the scent of food and with these women practiced at taking care of others.

CHAPTER TWENTY-FOUR

"MAMA, WE BACK FROM the burying."

The boy who had ushered us into the church earlier stood in the kitchen doorway. He was still wearing his suit, but the gloves were gone. My church lady turned to him.

"Where Eugene and Dot?"

"They ain't ready to eat yet. Mrs. Dot still pretty shook up, so Sister Miller and Sister Stallworth took her back in the church to rest. Mr. Eugene, I don't know where he went."

"I reckon we can go ahead and start feeding the children."

The women busied themselves piling food onto paper plates.

"Darren, why don't you take this girl on out and set with her while she eat," my church lady said to the boy still standing in the doorway. "What's your name, sugar?" she asked turning to me.

"Madeleine."

"Surely family don't call you Mad-e-leine."

"No ma'am." I blushed. "They call me Maddy."

"That's better. Darren, take Maddy out to eat."

She handed us plates that sagged under the weight of mashed potatoes, chicken and gravy, biscuits, and something that looked like green beans. I followed Darren out the side door of the kitchen toward a collection of picnic tables and benches set up in a grove of scraggly pines. I cupped my plate with both hands and kept my eyes down to keep from stumbling on the uneven ground as I picked my way over the tree roots poking up through gray soil and the rusty pines needles crunching quietly under my feet. I was surprised to look up and see that we had passed through the pine grove with the picnic tables and were heading into the woods. "It ain't far," Darren called back over his shoulder.

The gurgling sound of a creek rose in the distance. As we walked on I wondered if I should be worried about something, anything, because now we were in the woods, out of sight of the church and kitchen. Except for the knot of confusion in my stomach about my mother's sorrow, my emotions were placid. Instinct told me I was safe. And anyway, my experiences with that man at Loralee's and the Dorsey Street boys made me think I could fend for myself with this boy who walked resolutely ahead. So I continued following as if I was used to following tall skinny boys into the woods. We meandered, even passing under the canopy of a small grove of mulberry trees. As I glanced up, a little joy spread through me at the sight of the big heart-shaped leaves and bright red berries on their way to ripeness.

Finally Darren called, "Tah dah."

I looked up to see him standing beneath a tree whose branches were like feathery green switches of hair sweeping the ground in some places. The tree stood on the edge of a creek that was gushing clear water over jagged rocks, fallen branches, and grayish-brown dirt.

The image of the boy in his black suit, holding his plate aloft in the soft green shade, and the glistening dragonflies hovering over the creek behind him eased the tightness collected inside me. Some distant part of me sighed and my knees almost collapsed as waves of relief washed through me. I wasn't sure what I was responding to, but for the first time that day I felt my lips widen with joy.

"This here is my favorite tree," Darren announced. "I like to come here, 'specially after a funeral. This here is a weeping willow. We weeps together."

He set his plate near the base of the tree and took off his jacket. He hung it on a small branch that seemed cleared of leaves just for that purpose. "Come, sit a spell, rest them weary bones." He grinned and made a sweeping gesture that began with his hands praying in front of his chest then opened out to include the world before him. His smile, the first I had seen on him, made his thin dark face look familiar.

He sat on the ground, facing the creek, extended his legs straight out in front of him, leaned his back against the tree's trunk, and picked up his plate. I found a spot beside him, but several feet away. I lowered myself to the ground, heedless of the stiff crinoline slip, my yellow dress, and the sound of my mother's voice in my head issuing complaint about dirt stains. Darren pulled two plastic forks from his shirt pocket.

We ate in silence. I wasn't as hungry as I thought I would be, but Darren's mother, my church lady, had been involved in the making of this food. She had looked into my eyes, directly into my feelings, when even my own parents were too caught up in themselves to notice me. There was something important about taking in this gift she had offered me. So I ate slowly, methodically sampling even the overly salted gravy and the mushy green beans.

I watched Darren out of the corners of my eyes. He held his plate flat on the palm of one extended hand. His other hand carefully forked food into his mouth. Even the cautious, resigned way that he chewed his food seemed familiar. I tried to place it, tried to place him. An occasional breeze moved the branches of the willow, and each time Darren would lift his eyes skyward as if waiting for something. In those moments his face showed yearning, a soft mysterious desire.

I recognized in it my own desire for a return to the way things had been before Momma went away with Ida Bea. In the days since Ida Bea's death and my mother's return, this yearning would rise in me like a sudden dust storm—at the sight of a blade of sunshine slanting across the barren dirt of our yard in early evening; at the sight of a butterfly wavering over a flower; at the sound of June Bug whining in his peculiar way. The feeling would come quick and pointed and pierce my senses like a tiny arrow and then would be gone. Each time it was like a tiny lesson in grief and I was left with a little less sadness. Maybe that is what I saw on my mother's face when they led her away from Ida Bea's coffin, a collection of little lessons in grief that had come together in the face of her dead child and crowded out everything else in the world—including me. Perhaps now she would be a little less sad.

The noises of the flowing water intruded slowly into my thoughts. I found myself collecting words to describe the sound—bubbling, soft, easy, clear, kind, relaxed. Soon I was no longer thinking about my mother and her grief.

"You got a baby sister in heaven now." Darren interrupted my silence. "I bet she sitting up there smiling, maybe even laughing at us right now."

I looked at him to see if he was mocking me. But his face was without guile, his eyes startling with the sharp contrast between their black centers and milky white edges.

"You and your little sister the only babies your mama got?" he asked.

"I got three baby brothers at home. Well, they ain't babies really, but they too little to be at a funeral."

He watched my face for a moment, then turned away suddenly, raising his chin to stare up into the branches of his willow.

"Your mama sure was tore up," he offered after a while. "You know something I don't understand?" He met my gaze with a steady friendly stare. "The way people act when somebody dies, 'specially when children die. Reverend Beasley says everybody who ain't twelve years old automatically goes into heaven when they die. Heaven is a whole lot better than here. So people ought to be glad when children go there 'cause from what I been seeing, grown-ups are all waiting to go to heaven. Most of them probably won't make it. 'Cause they don't seem able to keep away from things that'll keep them out of heaven. Little children that die, they get to skip the whole mess. They don't have to try to be good to go to heaven. You know what I mean?"

Bound by his stare and the good sense of his words I nodded.

"It's already too late for me to get into heaven easy," he added, looking startled and burdened by this knowledge. "I turn fifteen in July. But I'm being as good as I can. I have to be anyway. I've been marked by God to be a preacher, and if I'm not good, God will strike me dead. Reverend Beasley says God don't allow no slacking in the ones he marks."

Marked by God, echoed in my head. *Marked by God*. What was it to be marked by God? How did such a thing happen? I studied Darren's face. There was that earnest yearning everywhere in his face. The knowing contentment of a child like June Bug who seems to understand a mystery the rest of us don't get.

"How did you get marked by God?"

Now it was his turn to study my face for signs of mocking. After a long moment he looked down at the ground where he had set his plate.

"When I was twelve, I had a dream about God and a bunch of people out in a big empty field. They were just walking around and around all confused, bumping into each other and asking each other, 'Where he at?' So I went out in the field too to see what was going on. When I got out in the middle I saw a lot of children just lying on the ground and the grown-ups was just stepping on them. They didn't even seem to see the children. They just kept walking around and asking, 'Where he at?' to each other. I ran in the middle and started trying to get the children out of there. But I kept getting knocked down and stepped on too. Then this voice said to me, 'You need your God.' And I said, 'Where is my God?' All of a sudden, everybody got quiet and the grown-ups stopped walking and the children all stood up and looked at me, so I walked out of the field and they followed me. Then I looked back and saw that even the grown-ups were following me, and they were quiet and letting the children go first. So I led everybody into the woods and we came and sat down together by this very tree.

"I didn't understand what the dream meant, but I was very shook up by it, the crazy grown-ups, the bloody children. So I told it to Mama and she just started saying, 'Praise the Lord.' Then the next Sunday she brought me around to Reverend Beasley after church and told him, 'I think God is calling my boy to preach.'

"Reverend Beasley said he thought so too when I told him my dream. 'Boy, you been marked by God. You bound for glory.' That's what he said. So then I started studying with him, and now he says I'm about to be ready to do some of God's work from the pulpit. He's going to let me preach during the revival meetings this year in August. Later on I'll have to go to some kind of preaching school, but I've got to finish regular school first."

He was staring out over the creek as he spoke. When he stopped, I kept watching his profile, waiting because there seemed to be something more he intended to say. I could feel it shimmering in the air between us. As I waited, I thought about how it seemed that his whole life was laid out before him in a neat, tidy way and was guarded on all sides by grown-ups who knew how to take charge. Knew how to lead little boys through the nightmares dreamed up in their beds, how to lead confused little girls away from tiny coffins and gravesites and too much thinking about death. I wondered if anything so tremendous as being marked by God could happen to me. Maybe it already had. Darren had rescued the children in his dream—kept them from being trampled. I had kept my brothers from harm during my mother's absence.

"I think there's something else I'm supposed to tell you," he said, drawing my attention back to the soft green air under the tree. "I think it's right that I tell you. But first you've got to promise that you won't ever tell nobody else. You've got to promise with a cross over your heart that you will keep this between us. Can you promise?"

I could, and my promises were binding. I was full of stories and secrets now that had blossomed in the midst of my own life, and they would have to be managed somehow.

The boy was waiting for my answer. I could imagine him in the pulpit with the glare of that yellow cross behind him and the rapt attention and respect of the people in front of him. No pain would come his way and everyone would want to please him. Yes, I wanted to be part of that. Perhaps it would wrap around me, pull me back into a safer, easier world.

I nodded.

He pulled his knees up near his chest and turned to face me. "I know this is telling secrets, but sometimes holding secrets too tight feels all wrong. So. You're my sister," he said.

The words dropped onto the ground in front of his knees.

I thought about Sister Miller and Sister Stallworth, and even his mama was probably Sister Somebody. But he kept looking at me, his chin raised so that he regarded me from behind half-closed eyelids, waiting.

"I don't go to your church," I stammered.

"Not that kind of sister. Your daddy is my daddy. You're my blood half sister."

There was no trace of humor in his face, and there was no misunderstanding his words. But my older brother died, a stubborn little voice said inside my head, and at first that thought would not let me move away from the impossibility of an older brother. Then I thought about Daddy and Loralee and understood how he could be my brother.

"How did you get to be my brother?" I blurted. He just looked at me, his eyelids half lowered again. He reminded me of June Bug. "Does my momma know?" I wasn't sure why I asked that question, but it seemed like the most important one.

Darren shook his head. "Your daddy don't even know. Me and my mama is the only living people that know."

"But how can't my daddy know? He ought to know when he done made a baby." I was back to the impossibility of it.

"How old are you anyway?" he asked.

When I told him, he nodded knowingly. "Some things you ain't old enough to know yet."

"I know where babies come from."

"Well, good. So I'll just tell you the part about me being your brother. When my grandma was fixing to die, me and my Mama came back here from Jackson so my mama could take care of her 'cause Mama's a nurse. I heard her and Grandma talking one time when they thought I was sleeping. Grandma was telling Mama that she had to tell me the truth about my daddy and mama. That was a long time ago, I was nine or ten then. It took me some time, but I finally asked Mama about it after I had my preacher dream and she was acting different to me. Turns out she ain't my real mother. I didn't come out of her body. My real mother was a lady she met when she use to work at a hospital somewhere away from here. This lady was a patient in that hospital. Something bad had happened to her. Your daddy was in that hospital too, but he got well and left before I was born. He never even knew that I was going to be born. But Mama knew all about it because the lady had told her. Anyway, something went wrong when I was getting born and my real mother died. 'She left the world so you could come into it,' Mama said when she was telling me the story.

"So then Mama took me and left the hospital and decided to raise me like I was her own. She says she couldn't love me any more even if I had come from her body. All I know about my real mother is her first name, Loralee. Mama said she didn't know anything else about her, except she didn't have no other family. She did look for my real daddy though and found out that he was married so she said she figured it was better to leave well enough alone."

During the telling of this Darren held my gaze. Now he turned his face upward and looked out through the branches of his willow toward the thin splotches of blue we could see beyond. "And," he added, "Mama said there's something weak in him anyway and he probably wouldn't be a good daddy to me even if he knew I was his."

He paused again as if studying the fluctuating greenness of the willow's shade. "I've seen him a few times now, knowing he's my daddy. I see she's right. She is right, isn't she? He has some sort of weakness?"

I nodded slowly, the heavy weight of my father's stories sitting in the pit of my stomach. I thought about Daddy and Loralee in bed at her whiskey house that night and wondered if she was the same lady from the hospital. Daddy had told me he was in a hospital because of his mind after Samuel drowned. Maybe it was the same hospital and the same Loralee. But it couldn't be. Darren's mama had told him that lady from the hospital died. I couldn't imagine my church lady telling a lie, and I couldn't imagine the Loralee I met being somebody's mother—though I could imagine her giving away a child if she had one. Should I say something about any of this to this boy who was marked by God? How would his life change if he thought his real mother was still alive? No, I decided. I would not mention having met a woman named Loralee who was a friend of Daddy's. Some secrets I would hold. But I was unwilling or unable to completely shield the man who was our father, because it was suddenly clear to me that this was my brother; there was no mistaking it. I could see the outline of my father clearly there in him, the shape of his body, his hands, his eyes, his teeth.

I was not bothered by the fact of having yet another brother, but I was stunned in the way that a child who finally knows too much is stunned, with a tiny pool of silence separating each disturbing detail, each new and strange piece of information that has to be accepted because it is truth. I had another brother. I had him all along.

How would Momma feel? It seemed to me that my father's unknown son was some kind of betrayal. I thought of Daddy's grief pouring from him as he told me about his time in the war and Samuel's drowning, and then his relief and fresh pride after the triumph over the rifle-wielding brothers. In those minutes I'd had a glimpse of the core of the man my mother chose to marry and make babies with. There was something good deep down in

Daddy that Momma had recognized, and I had seen a little bit of it too. And yes, there was weakness mixed in there as well. I didn't try to explain any of this to Darren.

Under that willow tree in the Mississippi woods I stared at this boy who was my new-found older brother. I looked at him with the same kind of awe I had for Esther, knowing her story—a hateful mother, a rape, a grandmother capable of both brutality and healing. But unlike Esther, Darren was still doggedly pure, held high above the grime and chaos of ordinary life in spite of not having his real mother and having a father he was better off not knowing. The fact that there was a blood connection between him and me made me think that maybe I could have a life that did not have to sink under the wreckage of other people's weaknesses.

"None of it don't bother you?" I wanted to know.

He shrugged, then turned an easy smile in my direction. "Seems to me there wouldn't be much point in being bothered 'bout it all. It's the way God made it. It's the way it is."

In one fluid movement he was on his feet, stretching. "What you think of me?" he asked in the silence he had created.

"What you mean?"

"Just that. What do *you* think of *me*?"

"If I've got to have a big brother, of all the big boys I know, I guess I would pick you." I stared out at the creek. My boldness in making that statement did not extend to allowing me to make eye contact with this boy, this new brother of mine.

"See, so I ain't doing too bad. You just met me today and already something makes you think I'm good enough to be your brother."

I did look up at him then and saw that he was grinning down

at me. "I don't know what your life been like with our daddy, but I saw you in the church," he said. "You cried for your momma, and you wasn't scared of death. I reckon you going to be alright too. Don't you think?"

From my gut came a hopeful flash of agreement, but it seemed to me like it belonged to someone else. I nodded and tried to follow the connections he had made.

"Hey, can you climb a tree?" he demanded.

"Course I can. Like a monkey," I answered, repeating something my father had once said about me.

"This is a good climbing tree." His face was tilted skyward into the branches of his willow. "Come on."

He unbuttoned the cuffs of his sleeves and rolled them up, then bent and took off his shoes. I looked at the folds and gathered skirt of my dress and felt the scratchiness of my crinoline under-slip. "How can I climb a tree in this?"

"Come on," he said again. "Get ready."

"Don't look while I do," I said to him with a sudden familiarity, as if he were Roy Anthony or Earl. I went to the other side of the tree, lifted my dress and pulled down the crinoline half-slip and stepped out of it. With a little fussing, I figured out how to tie the front and back sides of my hem into a serviceable knot between my knees. Dirt was one thing, but Mama would have a fit if I tore this dress, even though it was a charity item found by Mrs. Keyes on one of our Salvation Army forays. I took off my shoes and socks. I folded my slip and placed it neatly on top of my shoes and put my socks on top of that. I walked back around to the other side of the tree, expecting at least a snicker from Darren. Roy Anthony would have howled and laughed and carried on.

"See, you're going to be alright. I wouldn't have thought of that," he said, pointing to my knotted-up dress. "Why don't you follow me up so I can show you the best places to put your hands and feet. I like to go way up to the top, but you can stop any time you want to, if you get scared or something."

I have a big brother, I thought, as I watched the black fabric of his pants legs disappear up into his willow tree.

"Come on!" he hollered down.

I started my slow ascent up into the world of my big brother's willow tree. It could have been my mulberry back in the Quarters, its bark rough and decisive against the palms of my hands and the soles of my feet, the leaves whispering their stories into my ears, caressing my skin when they had the chance.

As I got farther and farther away from the ground, the world began to shift, change itself into a place where there were no dead sisters, abandoning mothers, hungry little brothers. I rested and looked around me, sturdy brown limbs reaching outward and upward, yellow light streaking through swaying green, and splotches of turquoise sky peeking in at me. The devouring life of the grown-up world was down there on the ground somewhere, mingling with the white dots that Darren's and my paper plates had become, flat and lifeless, no bigger than buttons. *That's right,* I thought, *that down there is not my world. This up here is mine.*

ACKNOWLEDGMENTS

My gratitude goes to Carolina Wren Press, which casts a net wide enough to catch authors like me, and to the judges who selected this novel for the inaugural Lee Smith Novel Prize. To Lee Smith for being a talented and prolific writer who warranted the honor of having a prize offered in her name. To my editor, Robin Miura, who has been a great champion and astute guide in helping to bring this novel into the world.

I will be forever grateful to the friends and writing colleagues who read drafts of this novel along the way and offered invaluable feedback—Lenore R. Harris, Betsy Miller, Margaret Wingrove, Cheryl Lawrence, Martha Engber, Marty Kendall, Byddi Lee, Doug Stillinger, Cathy Thrush, and Alan Tracy. And to Shelley Marlow, who has been a stand-up friend with a no-nonsense, positive attitude toward all things creative and artistic.

Thank you to the Community of Writers at Squaw Valley for accepting me into their workshops, giving parts of this novel an audience, and showing me what it meant to be part of the larger writing community. To *Voices* literary journal for publishing a chapter of this novel under the title, "The Centerpiece," and to *Equinox: Writing for a New Culture*, for publishing a short story of mine titled "Mulberries," which became the impetus for this novel.

My deepest, heartfelt gratitude to my family, especially my mother, Bobbie, and my daughter, Kristin, who have been unwavering in their faith and support of me as a writer and in their belief in the strength of the stories I tell in this book. They have each understood the necessity of writing for me and propped me up and encouraged me to keep working on finding a publishing home for this novel, even when my efforts felt futile. Thanks to their loving support and our collective stubbornness, you are now holding this book in your hands.